EVAN & THE LAND OF LETIN
∞ A Heart Afire ∞

JARED T.L.C.

always,
DIG
DEEPER

always,
LET
LOVE
IN

Jared T.L.C.

Copyright © 2015 Jared T.L.C.

Layout design by Ryan Evans

ISBN: 978-0692447475

Printed in the United States of America

Evan & the Land of Letin

for my brother, Chris—who introduced me to Kvothe,
& my sister, Tori—who helped me befriend Oscar.
for without them, you'd never have the chance to know Evan.

A NOTE TO THE READER

Before what you hold in your hands could be called a book, its contents were merely notes collected throughout the most significant of my journeys. I jotted them down faithfully as I witnessed them, unsure where this story was headed, but certain from its origins that there'd be a tale worth telling. What eventually came to be was far more important than even I had imagined.

As the years passed, however, I felt a growing need to turn these notes into a novel. What will be considered fiction in your land will be viewed as an insider's view at history in mine—history that needed clarification.

For the people of Earth, I complete the story of a New Jersey teen gone missing in 2009. His friends and family deserve to know what became of their beloved boy.

For the people of my land, I look not to alter the minds of either sect that label him a hero or villain. Instead, I look only to tell the untold truth of one of our history's most important figures. Without further explanation, I begin to tell the beginning tale of Evan Transce.

OVERTURE

"Tell me one of your fairy tales, Grams," the young boy said, lying beside his grandmother.

His mind was slowly slipping toward sleep. He could imagine no better sendoff than one of her stories.

However, quiet voices in the back of his head were getting louder, telling him he was growing too old for these tales.

But her stories were different than most. The colorful language she used brought foreign worlds to life in his mind. She'd sprinkle the text with unfamiliar words that allowed his imagination to reign free. Listening to her narration as his eyelids became heavier, her ideas became palpable. He knew that on the other side of his eyelids, if only he had the might to open them, he'd see all of her words come true.

Tomorrow, the boy would celebrate his tenth birthday. Perhaps tomorrow his innocence would come crashing down, lost in scattered debris. Surely then he'd no longer yearn for fantastical stories. But for now, on this September night, snuggled against the curve of his grandmother's shoulder, his purity remained intact. A fairy tale was all he wanted.

"Please, Grams? One more story."

"Oh, I don't know, sweetie. Maybe another time."

Last time she read to him, his parents arrived. His mother didn't mind a bit. She was ready to tuck herself beside her son and listen to the tales she'd heard since birth. His father, on the other hand, wanted no part of it. His son was too old for fantasy. It was time for the young man to learn about reality.

Evan & the Land of Letin

"Pleeease, Grams."

His dark eyes looked up at her. The unique speck in his eye shimmered against the glint of the gooseneck lamp. This little speck of grace was hard to resist.

Grams looked around the living room. The boy's older sister was already asleep upstairs, and his big brother lounged on a couch across the room. On his lap he held a book with a bespectacled boy fixed in flight atop a broomstick printed on the cover. His brother had already accepted his grandmother's tales as fiction, so onward he secretly traveled through the genre's endless wonders.

A chance to share her stories with a young one who still had a fraction of their heart open to believing in her words was rare. Her writings weren't actually meant for children, but now it had become a family tradition. She peered through the wide windows that looked out upon the dark and quiet street, assuring no early arrivals.

"Okay," she said, with a whisper and a smirk. "Let me find a good one."

She stood and walked toward her bedroom. The faintest sound of a violin escaped through the doorway. She smiled, for but a moment, her ears deceived her into imagining that beyond the door's threshold, a complete orchestra led by Gustav Holst performed *The Planets*—one of her favorites. Upon entering, of course, the room was empty. The seven-movement suite circulated the room as the old black record spun on the phonograph. No sign of her husband there to receive the sound.

Where is he now? She closed her eyes and sent a prayer his way. Wherever he was, whatever he was doing, he silently risked it all becoming a hero nobody would ever see.

In their bedroom, the entire right wall consisted of shelves filled with the family's favorite music on vinyl. On the opposite wall, a packed bookshelf lined with spines of all colors, sizes, and scents. There were brand new hardbacks not yet read, only cracked open to smell their fresh-pressed words and ponder their possibilities. Below were her prized relics—faded first editions from before her birth that ran the risk of losing pages if not skillfully handled. And atop, filling the highest shelf, an entire row devoted to leather-bound journals.

These notebooks were her personal pride and joy. To the few outsiders who had seen them, they were her lovely, but sadly, unpublished stories. To her they were so much more. These were the sole testaments on this Earth to her life's work.

"Grams!" the boy called from the other room. "How about the one with the Lamp? And the Eight?...you know, the beginning...with those brothers?"

Aha. One of her favorites. She plucked it from the top panel. Among the many accounts hand-scratched and legible only to her blue eyes, she knew precisely where each story hid.

She returned to her grandson on the couch and cozied in close to him. Stamped atop the leather journal, a lemniscate—a symbol the boy quickly learned held endless wonders. He closed his eyes with a satisfied smile on his face, as his grandmother opened the book and began.

∞

Deep within the infinite nothing, the Lamp began to blaze.

This glowing speck in space was entirely alone, surrounded only by unlimited possibilities. Enlightened by the endless power, the Lamp itself became the ultimate power.

Life burned and yearned for further creation, so with a flicker, eight hearts blossomed and began to beat within the belly of the flame.

Growing swiftly in might, beauty, and intelligence, the fiery womb sought to send its little angels out into the world with the intent that they'd create it. With a slight push, the eight beings erupted from each side of the fire, shooting through the blackness at speeds unmatched by any other being that would soon be in existence. In human terms (terms that wouldn't be set until a much later time), it took mere seconds for the Lamp to send the Eight to opposite ends of oblivion.

Soaring far and wide, high and low, flames dripped from their ever-changing bodies. Upon the free space where the sparkling residue settled, the starry sky, as we know it, illuminated. Once the Eight grazed the far outskirts of infinity, all the while igniting life as far as the eye would ever see, they simultaneously turned and began their descent home.

The return took much longer than their departure, for this time, the Eight moved composedly, singing and dancing, playing and creating, all as one. Though amazed by the countless stars abound, they hoped for similar minds to gaze at their wonders.

Upon select stars, they'd suppress the flames, and atop them, assemble earth complete with mountains they'd mold and oceans they'd engineer. They knew only time would enable earthlings to evolve, but together, weaving in and out of each other's paths, skillfully crafting and connecting every bit of blazing life, they perfected the possibilities of further miracles to manifest.

The sounds they sang while splashing in the water and the wind that whirled when they danced in the fields lingered through the air forever after the beings leapt to the next star they'd inearth.

They repeated this process an untold number of times, not once letting their majestic minds wander or burn out. Rather, they remained brightly ever-present, growing increasingly inspired as they drew closer to home. Thus, each molded spark of life was unique, yet no better nor worse than the last.

The Eight wished for their worlds to be perfect all while painting the universe. For perfection was a concept embedded deep within them. However, being the wise ones they were, they knew perfection was impossible. For even they, the very creations of Perfection, were imperfect. Nonetheless, they'd spiritedly strive for the impossible until they finally reached their haven. And when they did, they froze in midair as one...

Following a timeless amount of tireless creating, the beings were completely taken aback by Perfection. They knew that all their work was inspired and made possible by the Lamp, yet without realizing, they had somehow forgotten how truly stunning it was. From where they floated they could see their art in full, yet next to the Lamp, it was all nothing.

Without speaking a word, the Eight agreed that the Lamp deserved limitless praise. They deemed to shower the Lamp with unending gifts, fully aware that no amount of offerings they gave could possibly equal the gift given from the Lamp. The greatest gift of all–the gift of life.

Nonetheless, they'd spiritedly strive for the impossible. They'd joyfully work to justifiably thank the Lamp.

Evan & the Land of Letin

To do so, they encompassed the Lamp in a garden abundant with all the wonders and treasures of the worlds. Everything incredible and magical they'd made before was recreated to be even greater, and this was done so naturally, for all that received beams from the Lamp instantly dazzled too. Every pebble glistened and could heal, every droplet glowed and could invigorate. Each sprinkling of life reflected the exuberant power of the Lamp back to it.

This land was the greatest masterpiece of all, literally steps away from Perfection. There couldn't have been a more superior place in the universe to reside, but as the Eight saw it, they couldn't live here. This land was made strictly for the Lamp.

So they closed it off, surrounding it only with nothing. Around the sprawling garden they left mere blackness to remind themselves of what once was and would never be again...

Atop the darkness they built one last beauty. A place not so different from the others they'd created, except this was to be their home. It was to be a place of peace, one where they'd settle for all-time, moving only if the Lamp called them back.

For many days, times were as times should be— peaceful and sprightly, with nothing foreseeable distorting the harmony. But as they soon learned, even the best of moments can go astray.

From where they rest, with their inexplicable abilities, the Eight could see every happening across the universe that they chose to. Some happenings, however, they wished they had not seen.

On distant earths, they saw things that disturbed them. Things divergent from the natural cycle they thought they'd set forth. Things that could only be described as evil.

Fear and regret consumed the Eight. These were feelings they'd yet to experience, so it shook every ounce of their being. They'd set this world in order, how could things have gone so off course? Was it their responsibility to stop the disasters? If so, could they? Trillions of thoughts rushed through their heads and clouded their minds. While this uneasiness was alien to them, it strangely excited them. These distant occurrences assured them that there was more to life than even they could know. It provoked the brilliant beings and got their minds musing.

Being as prudent as they were, they felt it would be unwise to revisit the foreign orbs and intercede. As they thought, what they did was done, and they should not, and possibly could not, undo the unpleasant proceedings. They had hoped for similar minds to gaze at their wonders. That desire was fulfilled. But as they now learned, there was a painful price to pay. It was a phenomenon even they couldn't comprehend. Nonetheless, it was now part of life.

This land they called their home was hardly different from the others, so it was likely for kindred life forms to flourish here as well. In fact, small trickles of life had already kindled and began to creep about the surface. If the Eight wished, they could have easily razed each and every earthling. But they never would. It was against their nature. Instead, the Eight decided to do what they did best—create.

It was their intention to spend the remainder of their existence in peace. To ensure this wish come true, they looked to produce a being that would serve as a guide and protector to all things living across their land. All that was magnificent about the Eight they hoped to place within this new being.

Physically, they chose to model their new creation in part after the creatures far in the distance that had began to walk upright and think independently. Vices aside, they were truly marvelous creatures. These were beings they'd accidentally crafted, so the Eight grew inspired

Evan & the Land of Letin

at the notion of what could be designed intently. This new creation, they believed, could be rid of all flaws, allowing for their planet to be rid of all evil, and thus, run its course without further intervention.

They sculpted the creature's brain to make it innately genius and carved its heart to make it intuitively full of love. Every detail of its fashioned flesh radiated pure beauty.

Before they breathed life into the body, each of the Eight took the chance to individually cradle their creation, admiring what they had collectively accomplished.

As the First of the Eight held the youngling in its arms, it could not have been more proud. If the First had ever grown attached to an invention, it was this one. The First couldn't imagine, or rather didn't want to imagine, what their land would be like without this new creature. Without intent, the First wished that their little being outlived the Eight, so they'd never witness a moment without their protector. The First then passed its favorite creation to the Second.

As the Second held this being that was to be the great guide to their land, while it was unquestionably gorgeous, it seemed rather fragile in its mighty arms. This land they called their home was full of wonders made possible only through the seasons, and with these seasons came various harsh conditions. If this being were to do all that they hoped, it must be able to withstand any condition across the globe. Without intent, the Second wished that their little creature be able to withstand the elements and weather any storm sent its way. The Second then hopefully laid the creation in the lap of the Third.

As the Third stared into the sleeping face, it envisioned the baby one day growing into a hero. The Third saw their creation wielding the water, exerting the earth, administering the air, and forcing the fire any way it wished in defense of their land. The Third knew that its vision was no simple daydream. It knew it would one day become reality. With a smile on its face, but without intent, the Third wished that their creature could master all the natural elements of the world. The Third then confidently handed the creation over to the Fourth.

As the Fourth cradled the child, its attention was drawn to the tot's rounded eyes and pointed ears. These characteristics were slightly larger than one would expect for a creature its size, yet still, their measure allowed for the artistry of its parts to be showcased. The Fourth imagined that the beauty of the creature's eyes and ears be matched only by the power of them. If this one were to properly guide and protect their homeland, it must be aware of the happenings across the map, regardless of where it stood. Without intent, the Fourth wished that their little creature's eyes could see an ant climbing its mountain from miles away and its ears could hear the faintest purr of a cat on the opposite pole of the earth. The Fourth then gently handed the creation over to the Fifth.

As the Fifth held the baby, an uncomfortable foreboding filled its head. *What are we doing leaving the hopes of our home in the hands of this thing?* The Fifth knew this *thing* was tremendous, but still felt as though their expectations may be too great. Fear engulfed the Fifth.

The Fifth foresaw flames. More flames than the Eight had fixed on one earth. But the Fifth's vision soon became full of smoke.

The Fifth knew not what to think, so without intent, the Fifth wished that their little creation possess the foresight to see whatever the future holds. Whatever the future may set afire. The Fifth then wearily passed their creation to the Sixth.

The Sixth sensed unease from the Fifth but became carefree once the baby lay atop its heart. The Sixth lifted the baby in the air, inspecting and admiring its beautiful

Evan & the Land of Letin

form. Though small, the Sixth could already sense the incredible strength of the creature. The tasks the Eight were depending on the child to uphold would require not only great might, but surely great speed and quickness. This creature already possessed an ideal figure, now it needed to properly utilize it. Without intent, the Sixth wished that their little creation be the master of its body. The Sixth then swiftly passed the creature over to the Seventh.

The Seventh was in awe of this marvelous creation, but the Seventh also admired all of their work—even the accidents. The Seventh knew that this one would have to hold dominion over the others, and in order to do so, he must be able to properly communicate with all the beings of the world. This creature must be able to hear the songs of the sea and sky as one. So, without intent, the Seventh wished their little creature be able to understand and speak every language of their world. Finally, the Seventh handed the little one over to the Eighth.

The Eighth's smile shone as brightly and lovingly as the beams of the Lamp below. The Eighth wanted to bless this creature with a gift that had been given to them and had allowed for this very moment. A gift the Eighth saw as the greatest good of them all. One that allowed for the possibility of limitless power. The Eighth wished that their little creature be a masterful creator.

At last, the Eight cradled the baby as one. In their individual minds, they reviewed the secret hopes they held for the child. In their individual minds, they all secretly knew each other's hopes. The Eight beings still worked from one power, evident by this precious child in their hands.

After deep admiration and irrepressible excitement, the Eight kissed the forehead and heart of the child as a final best wish for a true mind and a just spirit. On contact of the second kiss, its heart began to beat.

∞

Within moments of the creature's first sunrise, it not only spoke its first words, but also personally addressed each of the Eight, praising them for their work, questioning details of his mission, and even advising them on worldly improvements. By midday, not only did it take its first step, but began circling the globe, familiarizing himself with his new domain. By midnight, he not only completed his trek around the world, but held council with all the peoples across the map, proposing a plan for peace.

All the creatures across the nation, from those who flew across the sky, to those who swam in the sea, and even the ones who lingered in-between, graciously accepted the proposal and instantly put the plan into motion.

For many days, times were as times should be— peaceful and sprightly, with nothing foreseeable distorting the harmony.

∞

The great creation who helped ensure peace was nearly content, and while he wasn't quite envious, he did see the many creatures of the land experiencing a happiness that he simply did not share. He observed the people and wondered what it was that brought them joy.

Atop the land's highest mountain he sat pensively and let his thoughts fly. It seemed a lifetime until his mind was set.

He called upon the Eight, and in an instant, they were there.

"Child, why have you called us?" the Eight asked, some full of excitement at the sight of their son, others worrisome as to what could be wrong.

"My parents," the creature said, his smile spread

Evan & the Land of Letin

across them. "You've provided so much for me…a life rich with beauty and the tools to experience so many wonders…" The Eight knew there was a "but" coming. (Seldom does one need foresight to sense the inevitably approaching *"but."*) "But I'm afraid you've forgotten one thing."

"Only one thing?" one said with a chuckle. "Then we should be proud!" Several of the Eight laughed, but still stood before their child, growing curious.

"What is it, boy? What is it that wearies your mind?"

The son drew a deep breath. Never before had he requested something from the Eight.

"Since your very first breath, you've always had each other. Always had like minds to be by your side…never have you known what it's like to be alone."

"Neither have you," one of the Eight interrupted. "You've always had, and will always have, us. And the many creatures of this world."

"And I fully understand that…and I'm very grateful, but there's no one to spend the days with."

A loud silence swept across the conversation.

At this, one approached the child, who felt more like a child in this moment than ever before. The parent spoke the child's name in their original tongue, a name that would come to mean so much and never sounded more beautiful than when spoken by the Eight with elegance and love. "Duendelyn, there can only be one of you."

He smiled, knowing how much the Eight loved and cherished him, but he also grinned knowing they knew his true intentions, and for some unspoken reason, were avoiding his forthcoming request.

"I know…but perhaps, someone *like* me…" he emphasized, continuing cautiously. "Perhaps…a brother?"

Several smiled and some laughed while others sighed at the request. Few stood sternly, unamused and unmoved by his wish. After the Eight's initial reaction, one finally spoke.

"Perhaps, no."

Another, troubled by the notion continued, "Son, your job is to keep the peace and—"

"And I have." Little could be said to dispute this. "And I will. But in these times of peace, what about me? What about the freedom peace provides? Can I not have someone to share it with?"

The child's request and argument seemed fair, but the Eight took a moment to discuss what action they'd take. They discussed for what seemed to be an eternity, as their son waited nearby. All the while, peace endured.

At the end of their debate, only four agreed that their child deserved a brother, but the four in opposition did not forbid it. Instead, they simply chose not to collaborate in the creation of another, so off they went in separate ways to settle peacefully in solitude.

The four who remained could not deny their child, their favorite creation. So they granted his wish and created another—a brother.

∞

The baby boy shed no tears upon his birth, rather he knowingly smiled at his elder. There were no unintelligible coos, only words that could be considered wise. There was no crawling, the little brother went straight to walking.

And so, the elder took his new companion around the globe, showing him all the miracles of the land, sea, and sky. Upon each incredible sight he shared, the younger brother pointed out something equally or more so amazing that was never noticed before.

Their contentment together grew into happiness. Their brotherhood was true and full of love. The elder was grateful that the Eight (or rather *four* of the Eight) granted his wish. In return, the older brother continued his peacekeeping journeys. More often than not, the younger accompanied, learning and helping along the way.

Between their quests, the brothers had vast freedom. To pass time, they composed art, crafted tools, and of course, played. And in the process, the brothers discovered competition.

The two would often make up games as they went along, each match more intense than the last. As always when brothers compete, pride reigned and tempers flared. While this was unavoidable, even among these special brothers, both were intelligent enough to leave such emotions behind once the games were complete. But amid intense competitions, even for the greatest of men, it becomes difficult to control such passions.

One fateful contest, matters quickly went awry. As the elder dominated every aspect of their match, the younger grew dejected, jealous, and angry. With his feelings smoldering and smoking his mind, the younger brought forth an attack on his brother unlike the two had ever seen.

With a newly constructed tool, the younger slashed violently at his brother's head, and down he fell to the ground. He clasped his face, covering his eye from which red fluid poured.

Never before had either of them shed a drop of blood.

Never before had either of them shed a tear, but now the younger could not contain his.

"Do not weep," the older said calmly. But the younger couldn't stop. The more his brother bled, the more the younger cried. "I am alive," the older insisted with a smile.

For the first time, the younger apologized to his brother.

"Do not apologize. It is all part of the game. It is all

part of life!" the older laughed and continued, "It was an accident."

With that, the younger felt yet a new feeling—guilt. For it was no accident. The younger knew precisely what he was doing. Amid his rage, he meant to hurt his brother. And he did.

On the grass next to where the elder lay was his left eye. No longer was his eye perfectly round nor the beautiful color of the sky. Now it was sliced and covered in blood. Upon the elder's once immaculate face there was now a void, a black hole from which bits of his insides seeped through.

Unable to bare the sight of his brother in pain, he cut out his own eye. This gorgeous green orb trembled in his hands, dripping red through his fingers.

At that moment, the younger murmured words never before muttered, words he hadn't known he knew. His words not only requested, but begged for help. His mutterings were that which only the most desperate of beings would dare to utter. Who or what he called to, he wasn't sure. The Eight? Perhaps a higher power? He implored that this eye he held dripping in his hands, his eye, be given to his brother. Sacrificed.

When the elder removed his hands, no further blood flowed. Instead, intact was an eye. A green eye. His brother's eye.

Neither of them could truly comprehend what happened that day. The older, though thankful for his brothers' sacrifice, now was the one feeling guilt as he saw the gash upon his brother's face.

The younger brother became repulsed by his reflection. That is, until he realized that along with his sacrifice, some mysterious things were now happening...

The offering he made also put him in favor with the Eight. They viewed his sacrifice as brave and heroic. As reward, they offered the younger brother a single wish.

His request? A lover.

22   *Evan & the Land of Letin*

∞

Soon, a new race had risen. A race of people like the brothers. The chosen ruler of the people? Rightfully and understandably, the elder. The younger brother grew more resentful than ever.

But he now, accidentally, had something special. Something he considered a craft which he worked on diligently in secret.

He was certain that this craft he had now mastered would give him more power than any other.

Even his brother.

∞

"Evan…" the old woman whispered.

"He fell asleep around the creation of Duendelyn. You probably didn't notice his brother go up to bed either. Probably trying to avoid nightmares. That whole slicing of the eyes isn't quite appropriate for the children."

"I'm well aware, but you know it's not really meant for them. It's our tradition. It's meant for me," she paused. "And you. To remember…

"Sometimes I have to read it all the way through, just to remind myself. The impossible distance and fluctuation in time can do the unthinkable to your mind."

"Of course, I'm also well aware…I think the time is coming for me to take refuge."

"Very soon," she responded, nodding her head.

"I've meditated on this for some time, and as much as it pains me to say…I believe he may be the one they speak of in the Royal City."

"I know that he is," she said, wiping the tear rising from her eyelid.

"I'm sorry, Rita. You know I wish none of this had to

happen. We all wish. But in the end, good will come from it...at least, I hope. I've chosen to avoid looking ahead."

"If only we all had such control," her tears could no longer be repressed. "He's only a child."

"Now...now he is, but when the time comes, he won't be. He'll be a man courageous enough to seek justice surrounded by those beautiful lies. And on that day when he finds the truth, he'll be worthy of the blessings he's due."

"It sounds as though you've already decided."

Her ocean blue eyes honed in on mine.

"I can't decide. And even if I could, I wouldn't. Despite any holy text or prophetic discussions," I said, "He alone will decide his destiny."

Evan & the Land of Letin

MOVEMENT 1
Evan & Earth

1

As a passerby glancing at the house numbered 428 in the middle of Lantern Lane, you'd never expect anything extraordinary to happen behind its red front door. And why would you? The house numbered 428 was a typical middle-class American house, more or less like the one you've just pictured there in your mind. It was a bi-level with four bedrooms, a kitchen, dining room, family room, and a living room featuring a wide window looking out at all that passed by on the street.

The same simplicity could be said for the rest of the houses lined up on either side of the long lane. It was quite clear that the original neighborhood developers used a single blueprint to build all the houses upon Lantern. Sure, over the years each resident took measures to differentiate their house from the next, and the new owners always took it a step further by building an addition here or there. Whatever was added (and there was always something added), the houses still showed hints of being related to those next door. They were all recognizably built from the same model.

Few changes were made to the house numbered 428. After all, this was a house like few on Lantern Lane, for it had the same owners from day one. And from day one, 428 looked nearly the same. Every few years its inhabitants would paint another coat of cornflower blue and scrub off any scuffs from their red front door, but that was it.

Upon this red door was a brass knocker, which scarcely saw use, for there was hardly a need for it. The red door was always unlocked and accessible to those who wished entry.

Among those coming and going were the owners' eight children, and later, their twenty-three grandchildren. With each entrance and exit through the door, each guest noted themselves slightly, or sometimes drastically, changed. Of course it wasn't the house that changed the people. It was the residents. It was the owners who made this house a home to all who entered. And while the people changed and the people changed, the red door remained as fresh as the day it was first painted.

On this day, as we start our story, the red door opened and closed as many times as it ever had. For before the door, visitors came bearing flowers or fruit baskets and always a visibly broken heart. For the painters of that door, the original and only owners of 428, Rita and Liam Powers, had passed away.

Saying, "passed away" certainly implies a peaceful occurrence, like Rita and Liam simply let themselves slip from this world to whatever comfort they may have believed lay next. And while we wish that was the case, it wasn't at all. In fact, quite the opposite was true.

Seldom does the death of an 85-year-old human come as a surprise. Even when it's a pair of 85-year-olds who've been married for 66 years who dies together. There's always talk saying they couldn't live a day without each other, so they passed on as one. But such fantastical talk wasn't murmured. Instead only suspicious and scared words were whispered. Words from folks who couldn't comprehend what occurred in the middle of the night several days prior at 428.

The neighbors' angst and confusion over the situation was understandable, considering Danny Penny, the local fire chief (and a dear Powers family friend), said very little on the matter...at least publically. But behind closed doors, he said in his South Jersey accent, "In all my years, I've never seen nothin' like this." And that was the truth. But not only had Chief Penny never seen anything like it, neither had any of his fellow firefighters.

Neither had anyone else on this particular earth.

Sure, too many people have had the dreadful displeasure of death by way of fire, but the flames that took Rita and Liam Powers weren't the typical house fire one hears about on their local news.

"It's like the fire came from inside them." Penny said quietly to his men at Engine 22. Fair assessment considering the scene, but not entirely accurate. "Not only did it start with them, it stopped after them too."

Not a piece of furniture in flame. Not one wall charred. The only things that burned were their bodies.

Calling it a horrific scene would be putting it mildly, but since spontaneous combustion wasn't a viable explanation, Penny filed the source of the fire as a nightstand candle.

"Musta forgotten to put it out. It musta tipped over while they were sleepin'.""

He knew this wasn't the truth, but being as there was no plausible explanation, he refused to let his mind wander.

Now, let there be no confusion, Daniel Penny the Third was a sincere and good-hearted man, but this particular incident was far beyond his understanding. He knew no matter how many questions were asked, the hardest ones would be unanswerable. And surely there'd be questions directed at his childhood friend, Grace, and her family.

He knew these were good people, so as he saw it, he saved them lots of further trouble and misery.

But when Danny Penny looked into the dark, pain-filled eyes of Grace's youngest son on the night of fire, the boy's eyes flickered with truth. He knew that young man saw something strange that night, just as he did.

Possibly something stranger…

2

The news of Rita and Liam's deaths came as a shock to the many that regularly saw them around Cherry Hill together. If there were an award for "Loveliest Old Couple" they would have had trophies from each year of the eligibility lined up above their fireplace. They were without a doubt lovely, and as many folks noticed, exceptionally lively for their age.

Until the very end, Rita lived for discussions with anyone and everyone, from former students to the mailman. She'd keep conversations stirring long after one would expect their attention to hold. She'd consume guests with their talks, not with her stories, but rather she'd draw forth deep memories and suppressed emotions out of her guests. She'd have them telling things they'd never share with anyone else. But with her light blue eyes engaged in the speaker's, and her head nodding assuredly, her guests always felt as if whatever was spoken was completely worth sharing.

Rita's other-half, Liam, could be seen cycling around town looking sixty years younger than his birth certificate stated, seemingly partially prepared for a triathlon. However, he wasn't one for such competitions. Once he retired from the Air Force and became the father of eight children, reading in his tired old dad throne, maintaining his backyard garden, and watching his beloved Phillies, accumulated for all the excitement he needed.

Or so it seemed to those who saw him.

And even those who lived with him.

But for those who knew what really enlivened the couple, for those who knew who how they really spent their time, this situation, this pair of deaths, was no surprise at all.

It was simply a matter of time before the flames caught them.

Evan & the Land of Letin

3

Evan's eyes scanned the aisles of strangers, and in the front by the altar, he saw guest he viewed as uninvited. A guest he felt was responsible for the two caskets in front and the rows of black in pain. Evan stared deeply into the flickering head of the candle, feeling an anger so fierce, it was as if the flame was his mortal enemy. And now it was.

Fire took my grandparents. Of course Evan knew it was silly to blame and hate the flame for this, but he did. He didn't care if it didn't make sense. To him, this whole situation didn't make sense.

If there was anyone who had reason for such crazed thoughts, it was Evan. For it was he who awoke in the middle of that night to the smell of burning. Before the alarm could sound, Evan was in the hallway. He could hear the flames snapping from the other side of his grandparents' bedroom door. The boy, even in his frenzied state, knew if there were a fire on the other side, it'd be unwise to open it. But leaving it shut wasn't an option either. Not with his grandparents there.

Once he shoved the door open, banging it against the wall, Evan could do nothing.

The top of his spine down to his toes clenched as he was frozen still, his eyes fixed on his grandparents embraced and engulfed in flame.

Before Evan could take his next breath, the fire, as if finished its work or caught amid a bad deed, seared and stopped, disappearing into the night, leaving only two signs of ever being there—the bodies of the old lovers, sizzling and blackened beyond recognition.

Since the fire, the typically amiable and attentive Evan became grey and distant. No one could blame him for this, for they knew what he saw. Or rather, they thought they did. The fire department labeled the cause of the fire as a toppled candlestick, a far easier explanation than a vanishing fire.

Flames don't just disappear, he told himself. *Maybe they're right.* He didn't dare tell anyone the details of what he witnessed. *They'd just think I was crazy.* But a part of Evan wanted it so badly to be a toppled candlestick.

These thoughts plus more clouded Evan's mind every moment, so when the pastor delivered his moving sermon, the best he could do was half-listen. However, he did tune in for his cue to approach the lectern for a reading. In his grandparents' funeral plans, they requested a recitation of their favorite prayer.

"I'll now ask Evan, one of Rita and Liam's many grandchildren, to come up and recite the couple's favorite prayer—The Prayer of Saint Francis."

Evan stood and exited the row. His buffered black oxfords clicked down the center aisle. He could feel the congregation's stares and imagined the few that averted their glances, feeling too badly for the sad boy. He tried to erase everyone from his mind when he reached the microphone, but now he could hear his rapid breaths echoing through the speaker-system.

Relax, Evan. Relax.

You got this.

Evan wasn't much for prayers, but even he had to admit, *I do love this one.*

He inhaled and began to speak.

"Lord, make me an instrument of your peace.
Where there is hatred, let me sow love.
Where there is injury, pardon.
Where there is doubt, faith.
Where there is despair, hope.
Where there is darkness, light.
Where there is sadness, joy.
O Divine Master,
Grant that I may not so much seek to be consoled, as to console;
To be understood, as to understand;

Evan & the Land of Letin

To be loved, as to love.
For it is in giving that we receive.
It is in pardoning that we are pardoned,
And it is in dying that we are born to Eternal Life."

Evan looked up and the church responded, *"Amen."*

4

Following the mass was the burial, and following the burial were refreshments at his grandparents' home. Funeral festivities carried on late into the evening. The Powers family ate, drank, and spoke of childhood stories.

Laughs floated from the kitchen and into the upstairs bathroom where Evan stood, staring in the mirror.

The boy removed himself early to prepare for bed, for tomorrow, he was heading back to school. Looking in the mirror, his fingers combing his wet hair, Evan pondered the prayer.

He knew that in the simplest of ways, his grandparents were great instruments, constantly providing hope, joy, and understanding. *What greater calling could there be than to make oneself an instrument of peace?* Whatever it meant to be an instrument of peace, Evan deemed it something worth striving for.

It is in dying that we are born to Eternal Life... Evan wasn't so sure about this, but he figured whatever became of his grandparents now, even if it was an everlasting nothing, it would be better than their final burning moments. Yet, he contemplated the statement from a different approach. *Perhaps now they live on through us.*

He thought about his sister, home from college for the funeral. Even during this tragedy complete with its unbearable proceedings, Clementyne kept her big eyes intent and her head nodding sincerely at any storyteller sharing their memories of times spent with Rita or Liam. She'd occasionally share her wide smile or her own keen words if the story permitted. For a student in the middle of her first year at grad school, forced to rush home for the funeral of her grandparents, she remained impressively calm and levelheaded. Bits of her grandmother's sincerity—and a great strength most knew nothing of—shined through her.

Evan considered his brother, Caden. While within the confines of his home, his brother could be considered generally dark and distant regardless of whether any deaths had occurred. The majority of Caden's time, Evan thought, was spent alone. But thinking more, in many ways, so was their grandfather's. Subtly, Evan realized, they were incredibly similar. While Grammpa was spreading seeds in the backyard garden, Caden was often planting new flowers in his own plot of land. Caden's garden was quite different being as it consisted primarily of plants that shot peas from their floral-mouths at oncoming zombies, and that the only physical contact he had with it was digital, as he swiped his finger across the screen of his phone. And while this strange similarity brought upon a smile as the thought passed, this alone wasn't what connected the two.

More importantly, Evan noticed, was their constant thirst for knowledge made evident by the books they were always reading. As the images arose in his mind, he noted how similarly they sat. He envisioned his brother sitting in the corner of his room, and his grandfather settled in his ancient armchair. Both sat with their backs straightened and their chests uplifted, each with a foot neatly settled upon the across knee, and one hand conforming to the book's spine. While their eyes looked down, scanning the pages, their heads stayed straight as if about to deliver something critical to the masses.

And often after reading, both had the habit of sharing their new findings with no one who cared. Their books were always something that awakened an excitement within them that, when they shared, scarcely had the same effect on the listener. For Grammpa, Grams always had the perfect balance of wit and candor to tell her husband she wasn't interested. Caden, on the other hand, was a sensitive explosive that no one quite had the tools to handle except for Evan. As youngsters, Evan viewed his older brother as a hero, fondly capturing every word he shared. As the years went by however, his interest diminished.

But still, it was Evan that his older brother would divulge details to of his beloved fantasy fables. For it was solely Evan that knew about his brother's passion for elves and dragons. Something about Caden's Hobbit-loving self wasn't coinciding well with the devilishly smooth, lady-killing demeanor that he so perfectly put on and executed in the outside world.

It was through Caden's rants that Evan had perfected the art of locked-in eye contact while his mind was miles away. A simple, yet highly effective tool for maneuvering through seemingly unbearable conversations. A tool Claudio, their father, had adopted as a lifestyle. For Claudio (*Claude*, as his two oldest children had begun to call him), though a constant operator of the locked-in eyes, still hadn't mastered the part in which it wasn't abundantly clear that his thoughts were far, far away. For Claudio, his dark brown eyes took on a slick glaze, that even though your irises met, it was obvious that his presence wasn't there. Where was it? Who knows? Lost in his thoughts, perhaps. Anywhere but here.

For poor Claudio, it seemed his prewritten destiny to live such a life given a family name like Transce. Claudio and his siblings, though they no longer spoke, all shared that last name and all passed through their lives as if they were indeed entranced.

Whether Claudio had always lived this way was impossible to say, but for Evan, this was the father he always knew. Except for the few times that he'd seen him on stage.

Claudio and his band served as the in-house entertainment nightly at a local bar, The Mud-Turtle. Their music was a great draw to the younger crowd, back when the unnamed house band was young themselves. As the years passed, and the band's shaggy hair became streaked with grey, the clientele didn't attempt to recapture their youth at a hipper bar, instead they remained loyal to The Mud-Turtle. With Claudio on guitar and grizzly lead vocals, they'd skillfully rearrange pop and folk classics, everything from Diana Ross and the Supremes to Simon and Garfunkel, into modern rock and roll covers. On very special nights, when both the crowd and band had their share of spirits from the bar, Claudio would test out one of his originals. It was always on these nights that a newcomer would approach the band after their set and suggest the talented Claudio take a shot beyond comfortable confines of The Mud-Turtle and strive for the stars. It was on these nights that Claudio retreated into the back-office and stayed long after hours.

Playing, drinking, playing, and drinking at The Mud-Turtle had been Claudio's life for his entirety, so once it closed several years back, he was understandably lost in the world.

Claude took on employment from his Uncle Gio who headed the family pest control business. It didn't take long to see that Claudio the Exterminator wasn't going to work out. He loathed the job, citing it as the source for the onslaught of health problems that followed. Claudio didn't acknowledge a lifetime of poor nutrition or his lack of exercise habits, nor was it his personal love for the bottles beneath The Mud-Turtle's bar. It was all the sprays and fumes he unavoidably inhaled while ridding the town's houses of insects and rodents. It was singularly the bug sprays that led to Claudio's open-heart surgery.

Standing next to Claudio, one might suggest he drop-off the watch he'd been wearing at the local repair shop, given its excessive volume. But no, that particular watch he'd been wearing was digital. The nonstop *tick-tick-tick* was the sound of the replacement valve in the middle of Claudio's heart. *Tick-tick-tick*, the very sound of it made Evan nearly as queasy as the rare sight his father shirtless. It wasn't just his hairy chest that rounded and bordered on becoming breasts that made him nauseous, it was that thick straight scar down the middle of him that hovered right atop his heart. When Evan let his mind attach to the conceived image of his father's open-heart surgery (surgeons slicing through his chest, sawing through his bones, and meticulously dissecting his heart), it made him squeamish, unconsciously placing his hands over his chest in protection.

Since the Transce family moved into 428, Claudio's single job became serving as a faithful son-in-law. This was no task that Rita and Liam required, rather, it was one that Claudio willingly took once stepping through the red door. He wanted to go above and beyond for his parents-in-law. Making dinner every night, doing their laundry, taking interest in Liam's garden. Whatever was needed, without needing to be asked, Claudio did it.

Throughout the process however, Evan noticed that his father seemed to be becoming more and more physically comparable to his parents-in-law. His back began to hunch, his gait took on a slight hobble. A life fully within that blue box seemed to age him a decade or two. If it weren't for Rita's snow white hair and Liam's pearly bald head (which was almost always covered with his favorite ball cap), you may have thought Claudio was just as old as they were. In many ways, the old couple behaved as if they were dozens of years younger, as if their ages didn't even exist.

And while it seemed that Claudio was content in his new role at 428, his wife was anything but. For Grace, back beneath the same roof she was raised under, so much had changed since she was a child, yet nothing had changed at all. Both of Evan's parents used their own methods to escape from the here and now.

Grace's path to freedom was slightly different from her husband's, as hers came as she walked into her kindergarten classroom five times a week. Grace, like her mother, gave only her birthed children more attention and affection than her classroom ones. In Mrs. Transce's classroom, she was queen. This wasn't because she was the type of ruler who demanded respect via a strict set of rules or a series of intimidating expressions. Instead, she was respected, worshipped even, because a piece of herself became one with the children. In that classroom, a piece of Grace went back to being six years old, adopting that wide-eyed amazement of life's simplest things.

Mrs. Transce, like her mother, was that rare teacher who gave her life to the kids, so when that summer sun came around, luring the little ones out to vacation, so much of herself left with them. What was left for Grace was her real life, one she saw as being stranded in a house with her soul-mate she viewed more as a cellmate. The last couple of summers at 428, the only thing that kept Grace sane were the long afternoon talks with her mother in the garden, as they both sipped cocktails. Now, for his mother's sake, Evan was dreading the summer. He couldn't imagine his mother without her mother.

For the first several days, Grace took her parents' sudden deaths as well as anyone could. But Evan was certain the initial shock had yet to settle in. She'd been engrossed in the tedious details of funeral preparations and all the while, she had each of her seven siblings by her side. The mournful circumstances for all eight of the Powers children to be in assemblance were anything but ideal, but still, when the eight gathered around that same dining-room table they sat at as children, smiles and laughs were inevitable.

They shared stories of the summers in Wildwood, when they'd all squeeze tight into the VW Transporter. They recalled the makeshift meals their mom would concoct, none better than her famous bean-heavy chili. They spoke of their birthdays, on which their parents would take only the "birthday-child" out for some time with just mom and dad. On these days, the oldest was left to chaperone, which of course, led to some special stories themselves, like the time little Alec disappeared and the time they all disappeared on little Alec.

The oldest children, Rita the Second and Liam Junior, told of how their dad used to take them out flying. Back then, the pilot in Liam was still fresh, only a few years removed from the Second World War. During wartime, Liam's job was as a flight instructor to the allied French pilots. After the war, he had dreams of teaching his eventual children to fly as well. Liam Jr. explained how they'd take off from the open field behind St. Peter's Church before they built the school and turned the space into parking lots and playgrounds. Then a third child came along, then a fourth, and a fifth, and so on. Liam sold the old plane and his flying days were over.

As Junior told the stories, Evan pictured himself in that old plane. Piloting the plane, he saw the back of his grandfather's head. He wasn't wearing the proper protective helmet, only his red ball cap. In the seat beside him was the silvery cloudlike hair of his grandmother. From behind her, he looked up at them.

This image felt like a memory to Evan. Like an actual moment in time, which if it weren't for the passing of time, needed only a breath or two to come alive. It felt real, almost tangible beyond the passing streaks of clouds. Evan shook his head, knowing it must have come from a dream.

Or did it?

In that room with the eight children of Rita and Liam Powers, each of them grieving inwardly in their own way, outwardly they rejoiced at the remarkable lives of their parents, considering themselves blessed to be born from them. In that room, with the eight children, Evan felt the presence of Rita and Liam Powers as if they'd never left.

His brother, his sister, his father, his aunts and uncles, and everyone's connection to his grandparents, proof, perhaps, that they did live on.

These thoughts plus a hundred more collected in Evan's head as he stood in the bathroom looking into the mirror. Though his eyes stared into his own, his mind was in more places than he could track.

Those eyes he stared into, his eyes, were one of a kind. They were the darkest of browns which bordered on black, nearly blending in with his pupil. They were the hard eyes of an animal within the soft face of a young man. At the top of his left eye, a quarter of his brown eyes weren't brown at all, but rather, this slightest bit was purple.

There was no explanation for why this portion was purple. From what he could see, and what others told him, there was nobody in his family with violet eyes. As for the fact that it was only a fraction, his freshman year biology teacher told him it was called *sectoral heterochromia* among other things far too scientific for Evan to remember.

Above his eyes sat a thick set of eyebrows, and while they were thick, they were by no means bushy. Rather they were sleek, as if painted on with a large-headed brush. However, whoever painted them could have allowed for a bit more space between his eyelids and the brows, for as they were, it looked as if poor Evan was constantly scowling, which for the most part, was not the case.

As his skinny fingers swiped a drip from his forehead, he acknowledged how much better he looked and felt with a fresh shape up. His hair, like that of many

Evan & the Land of Letin

males his age, was typically untidy. But his mother insisted he look respectable for the ceremonies. She aimed for a polished fade but Evan decided to meet her halfway, taking a couple inches off his all-natural look. With a soft, shaved face, and the very short curls atop his head, Evan looked beautiful.

Now, if you were to say that to Evan, he may agree with you. But he'd never see it as a compliment. All he ever noticed was how small and slender he was. His facial features, aside from his animal eyes and scowling brows, were almost elegant. He viewed his body as fragile and girlish. And while his features weren't textbook manly man, like the models in the magazines with Spartan abs, he certainly was handsome in his own way. And while he may not want to view himself as being beautiful, he undeniably was.

Yet none of these things were what Evan concentrated on at this moment. Looking at himself, thinking about his family and how much of his grandparents he saw in them, he searched for his grandparents in himself.

He stared and he stared.

He thought and he thought.

After looking at himself too long, sadly, nothing came to him.

But for a brief second he became startled. For but a moment, he forgot that the person he was looking at was him. Evan felt like an alien in his own skin.

Perhaps this was one of the many woes of life before a mirror that his grandmother had spoken of.

"Nothing but vanity and false visions of our identities can come from looking into a mirror," he remembered she said, but never fully understood.

In the entire house numbered 428, despite there once being ten family members living within, Rita and Liam were conscious to have but one mirror—this exact octagonal framed looking glass that Evan now stood before.

He stopped trying to ponder the many matters that fogged his head. It was time to sleep. He opened the cabinet to retrieve his toothbrush, placing his left hand on the hot water lever, and then turning it.

At the bottom of the sink, near the drain, Evan saw a single ant crawling. He pushed back the lever to stop the flow, but it was too late.

The water gushed down upon the ant, sending it swirling several times around the sink then down the drain into blackness.

Evan paused, his heart thumping.

He stood confused, tears forming beneath his dark eyes, forcing even more confusion.

Evan cried, but clenched his hand over his mouth to suppress the sound, not wanting anyone to hear. He looked again into the mirror, his eyes puffing and his face red. He was disgusted with himself.

What am I doing? he thought. *Crying over an ant? I'm pathetic.*

Yes, he was crying over an ant. An ant that he'd seemingly killed. But he was surely crying for so much more. More than he cared to admit. He put his toothbrush away without brushing. It was for certain that Evan was in need of rest. He flicked the light off and sleepily exited the bathroom.

This night, as he entered his room, his bed looked exceptionally inviting. In his sleep-deprived state the most obvious reason for his desire to hop aboard was the prospect of several hours of deep retreat. But even more appealing was the soothing light cast over his whole bed. Where his bed lay, beneath a pair of windows, the nearly full moon let forth the most tranquil glow upon his sheets.

He walked toward the window to get the best view of the moon. It seemed to hang directly over his head, high above the tall backyard tree. One glance at this floating rock in space seemed to put him at ease. He couldn't tell you whether it was waxing or waning, but he could say that it felt as if a bit of his being was reborn every night as he looked up at the moon. *So beautiful*, Evan felt it wrong to shut it out. He decided to leave the blinds up, letting the moon share this night with him.

The boy slid into bed, and then docked his phone on the stereo speaker that stood by his head. This had become a nightly ritual for some time now. It seemed to be the only way he could fall asleep.

The music allowed for his thoughts to fly away, bringing Evan along with. Within his digital music library there were a select few playlists designed strictly for his almost sleeping mind to imagine different lives more desirable than the current state of Evan Transce. Some nights he played the part of Jean Valjean before a packed theatre, suddenly blessed with the voice of Colm Wilkinson. Other nights he was a fourth Fugee, the integral member that kept the group together.

Tonight though, as he tapped the play symbol on the phone's screen, he was but a listener.

*

Ahead and behind, nothing but darkness.

Possible missteps hold promise of downfall with probability of death.

Deep awareness of this? No.

But deep awareness of now? Yes.

And instinct saying onward, against the pull. Drudge.

Through the drips of water, through the mossy surface, and through the circular deception.

The ground becomes wall. Wall becomes ceiling. Ceiling becomes ground.

Spiracles sealed, the nearly weightless creature becomes airless, each tiny creep heavier than the last.

But hope—or something like it.

Above, a ring of dim light. Each step closer, closer, closer, the ring grows.

Finally, unmoved and unshaken by its life nearly gone, beyond the ring and up. Across the silver threshold.

From out of nothing but darkness, the ant prevailed.

5

The sunlight seeped through the leaves before making its way through the window, warming Evan's sleeping face. Through the leaves, the beams cast a faint lavender glow over the entire bedroom. At first glance, lavender may seem a strange color for leaves from a New Jersey tree to be, but it wasn't strange at all.

Evan's grandfather told anyone conscious enough to notice the tree's peculiarities that it was a normal *fagus sylvatica*. He claimed there was one just like it in his backyard as a child. Had he told this to anyone equally knowledgeable as he in botany, they'd know that this was no *fagus sylvatica*.

The trunk of the tree looked like several thin trunks fused as one, spiraling toward the sky. Its branches, though visibly sturdy, swayed to and fro with the passing wind, moving individually and gracefully, like the fingers of a ballerina lifted in air.

Liam planted it in the heart of his backyard, at the center of where his eventual garden would be. Directly around the tree, Liam dug and filled a small pond comparable to a moat. More impressive than the physical labor involved in the pond's creation was the old man's skillful navigation across the internet, researching the proper way to pull off such a task without damaging the tree's roots. But, with lots of tarp and a high-grade pump, he did so successfully. And now, if you were to stand in that backyard, your eyes might buy into the illusion that the tree had risen from the water.

Evan was not among the few who noticed the strangeness of the tree, nor was he among the even fewer who questioned its stunning growth. In the event that Liam had planted the tree the first day he moved into 428 (or the next day, as he claimed), just over 60 years had passed. A tree of its size would have had to been planted around the time of Liam's birth if circumstances were normal. However, circumstances, like this tree, were not normal.

But Evan saw nothing abnormal about the tree. To him, it was simply the tree in the backyard. In fact, it wasn't even that. To the boy, it was just a tree.

"Evan," a firm hand rocked his sleeping body. "Wake up, Ev."

Startled, he opened his eyes.

It was his father. *Thankfully.*

"Slept through your alarm again. Better get moving, champ."

Claudio exited the room as Evan's eyes scanned his surroundings, trying to remember where he was. Presumably triggered by the sunshine upon his face, Evan was having a variation of his least favorite reoccurring dream. The nightmare was never precisely the same, but every few months his dreaming mind traveled to a war ravaged plain where he was the lone survivor.

Sometimes there were remnants of toppled buildings, in others, he walked endlessly on a desolate wasteland.

The only constant was fire.

There were nights when he flew high above the blaze, a pilot like his Grammpa, amid the war to end all wars, as the flames snapped beneath him. Other times, he stood on a sandy mountaintop, looking down at the shore. Where there once was water now danced an ocean of fire.

Evan couldn't pinpoint when he started having these dreams, but he had a few fair guesses. It was long before the fiery death of his grandparents, but now, the nightmares took on new meaning and felt scarier than ever.

He pressed a hand against his warm cheek, reassuring himself that he was here, real, and not on fire. After a few groans and cracked joints, his feet slapped down upon the wooden floor.

Staggering across the wood-planks, Evan inched closer to the one thing that restored life into his body at this early hour—his shower. It wasn't that he was obsessed with cleanliness, though he enjoyed being clean as much as the next. Rather his reasons for multiple showers were unclear even to him. But parts of Evan so desperately craved the fall of water upon his head. Above all else, even his bed beneath the moon and the music, the shower was his sanctuary.

While many claim to get their best ideas while showering, the opposite was true for Evan. No, he didn't get his worst ideas. Instead, here, he had no ideas. Here, it seemed as though Evan ceased to think. As the droplets pattered on his head, slipping down his body, his thoughts fell silent. There was stillness within which he couldn't explain, even if he had a thought to explain it.

Evan stepped out refreshed and ready to start the day anew. But this feeling was fleeting as he opened the door, for standing at the top of the steps was his Uncle Alec.

He'd forgotten that until tomorrow, Alec and his family were still staying at 428. Evan had almost forgotten why.

Today the attorney was set to come read and distribute the contents of Rita and Liam's Last Will and Testament. Evan was relieved to be going back to school on this day. Divvying up his grandparents' belongings seemed a peculiar ritual that he preferred not to be around for.

As he looked at Uncle Alec, he could see his smirk on the verge of laughing at the terrible joke he was prone to deliver.

"Grace, a skeleton just stepped out of your bathroom."

Evan heard his dad laughing at the foot of the stairs.

Complete failure. Can that even be classified as a joke? Evan shook his head and swiftly walked into his bedroom. The situation nearly got infinitely worse as he almost stumbled over the cat sprawled out across the door's threshold.

Who are you? The boy also forgot that there was now a cat living in their house. His sister brought it with her when she returned home from school. She said she'd heard the poor thing, collarless and filthy from head to toe, purring in a pile of wet leaves right after receiving the call about her grandparents.

"There was no choice but to take him in," she said. *"I think it was a sign."*

This was a very un-Clementyne-esque thing of her to say. With Clementyne, Logic and Reason came first with Unnecessary Emotions a few notches down, and then deep down on the list in miniscule print were Chance and Miraculous Happenings. She was one of the last people you'd expect to use a "sign" as an explanation. Evan wanted to tell her he was fairly sure his grandparents, first thing upon dying, did not take the shared form of a feline nor send it there to comfort them. Evan knew there was no connection between his grandparents and this cat, but for some strange reason, Clementyne felt otherwise. There was no doubt she was feeling vulnerable after the bad news.

Despite what Evan thought, the nameless cat was a gorgeous creature. Its Bengal-spotted fur was grey with a silver sparkle in certain lighting. Though Evan just missed stepping on it, the cat hardly flinched. Instead, it shot its cold eyes up at the boy as if deciding whether to spare his life. But as cats do, it rolled its head back on the ground, ignoring the simple human.

You little monster, Evan thought. *I should kick you.* Of course, he did not. Rather he stepped over the cat and slammed the door, forcing it to scram.

Evan slipped on his favorite pair of dark jeans. They fit his slim legs snugly, but since the short boy could never find anything exactly his size, they were a tad too long. He folded the ends up an inch to his ankles.

Opening a drawer, he reviewed the three stacks of shirts. Atop the first, a plain white t-shirt. *Too light,* he thought. Not the message he wanted to be sending the first day back after his grandparents' deaths. On top of the middle pile, a plain black t-shirt. *Too dark. Way too dark.* Also not the right message. He didn't want to seem like he was still in mourning everywhere he went. Whether he was or not wasn't the point, he didn't want to *seem* like it. Topping the final stack, a grey t-shirt. He picked up the grey shirt featuring a small pocket on the left breast. The shirt fell unfolded as he held it outstretched as if analyzing something genuinely perplexing. After a moment or two, he decided. *Just right.*

Down to the sock drawer, to his dismay, only one lonesome clean pair rolled forth; a set of grey salt and peppered wool socks fit for winter. He glanced at the small pile of white tube socks until one too many curious tan stains averted his eyes. He slipped on the thick socks, instantly feeling his tightly-packed toes perspire.

Bottoming off his outfit were his red high-top PF Flyers. His PF's were a daily essential. He owned other shoes, of course; running shoes for running, baseball cleats for baseball, black dress shoes for funerals, but for every other occasion, every other day, it was those red PF Flyers.

Evan & the Land of Letin

Evan credited the shoes as being the sole reason for his ability to run faster and jump higher than most. For someone of his stature he had commendable leaping ability, and as for his speed, Evan was one of the fastest people who'd ever dash across your eyes. The shoes being responsible for his skill set was nonsense that even Evan didn't truly believe. The shoes possessed no super power, but he had become as attached to them as a young Benny the Jet circa 1962.

Evan picked up his phone, glancing at the time. *7:42. Where did the time go?* He hurried over to the door and before he could exit, he noticed the backpack leaning against the wall. *Almost forgot.*

He slipped it over his shoulders and pulled the straps, tightening the heavy pack to his back. Drawing a deep breath, for a moment he felt like a traveler setting off on a long journey. On second thought, it seemed more like a parachute-pack, and he was a soldier about to jump in air and out into battle.

This time through he caught himself upon the doorframe, avoiding a stumble upon Rocky. The old dog looked up at him unmoved.

Rocky was his grandparents' dog that they'd rescued from a shelter several years back. The folks there told them he was a boxer, born and bred to become a star in the fighting ring. But after quickly failing with neither much bark nor bite, he became the bait dog and now had dozens of slashes and scars to show for it.

Evan had never really warmed up to Rocky, but now, since his grandparents' death, the dog had a newfound interest in the boy. It appeared the dog now deemed Evan his new master, following him around the house and even sleeping outside his bedroom door. This opened up a spot in Evan's heart for Rocky, as he could only imagine how lonely the dog felt.

As the dog sat on his hind legs, spine sturdy and straight, Evan thought that it was Rocky that now looked like a soldier. This one, keeping a keen guard in case an attack was brought upon by any intruder in the form of an unwelcomed cat. Evan smiled at the dog.

"Thanks big guy," he whispered. "I'm not very fond of that monster either."

He gave the dog a pat on his head, to which Rocky barely reacted. The dog remained statuesque, not inching from his post, only acknowledging Evan's existence with stiff eye contact.

Something about the pet's eyes in this moment uprooted bumps on the back of Evan's neck that slipped their way down his spine. These weren't the black, blank eyes of an animal at all. While they were dark, they had a depth to them that looked like they'd seen it all and had something to say about it. They were not human, but oddly close.

As a child, Evan had imagined miniature Martians living within pets, monitoring human behavior as they properly planned their takeover. A part of Evan backtracked to his childhood fantasies, but time for reminiscing and wondering was limited. He scampered down the stairs, chatter from the kitchen growing louder and louder with each step.

Reaching the foot of the stairwell, he glanced into the kitchen. The buzz ceased.

Sitting around the table and leaning against counters were the eight Powers children, each with a cup of coffee in hand, and each with a set of eyes staring straight at Evan. The silence lasted a mere second but was unquestionably noticed by all.

"Good morning, sunshine!" shouted Uncle Alec, oozing with sarcasm.

"What's up, Evan?" asked Uncle Ayden, as each of the others followed with a similar textbook greeting. He scanned their faces, each one, Evan sensed, with grins too wide to be authentic. This unscheduled uncomfortable start to his day couldn't end soon enough.

Evan & the Land of Letin

Evan laughed nervously.

"Well, I've gotta get going. So, hello, good morning, and goodbye," Evan said, giving the group a collective wave.

Sitting at the far head of the table, Grace gave her son a warm smile, this one very real. Her eyes met her sons as she displayed that unmistakable maternal look that essentially reads, '*I Adore Everything About You.*'

"Have fun," she said.

Evan thought this all-too-typical phrase to say before the start of a school day was rarely applicable, and today was not among the few exceptions.

"I'll try. I think I'll have just about as much fun as you guys."

The eight let out subdued laughs, Evan's point was well taken. Nothing would be fun about the reading of the will.

Aunt Rita dispensed a sullen sigh, "We'll try."

Evan gave a final wave as he stepped down the final few stairs leading to the front door.

"Son," his mother's soft voice called from the top of the steps. Evan could tell by the look on her face that she was on the emotional fringes. He, however, didn't wish to feel a thing at this moment. The false bravado he was building up for his return to the outside world deflated a bit as she began to step down.

His mother's face carried heavy bags under her eyes that Evan figured were filled with tears on the verge of overflowing. The lines on her forehead were rigid, suggesting a determination to not shed a single drop. As Grace reached the bottom, she opened her arms to hold her son. Evan returned the best hug his skinny body could muster.

Signifying its end, he gave her a gentle pat on the back. And then another pat, and another, but she wasn't ready to let go.

She gently tilted his head downward and kissed her

child on the forehead.

"Are you sure you can handle this?" she asked. Evan felt as if the question was truly directed at another part of herself, but answered not with the same question, but an honest answer.

"I gotta go back eventually," Evan paused and smiled, "Right?"

Grace laughed quietly which made a part of Evan inwardly rejoice at seeing the life left within her. "At least it's Friday."

She smiled as her son opened the door, crossing over into the early April morning. He was never one to monitor the weather's behavior, so he was pleasantly surprised that it was actually starting to feel like Spring outside. The tiny hairs on the back of his upper arm stayed in place, confirming that the temperature was to his liking. He pulled shut the red door, the knocker falling with a gentle clink.

6

Through Evan's dark eyes, the short drive down Chapel Avenue was the same as it was every other day. His thoughts rummaged through the loads of assignments he had to catch up on, fluctuating between high stress and low nonchalance. As his mind raced much faster than his car clogged in the traffic, he somehow failed to see that the rows of cherry blossoms which lined both sides of the street had begun to fulfill their earthly destiny by blossoming. For the school-goers that did see the pink explosion floating above their heads, it sparked hope of better weather, which in time meant the end of the school year, which in time meant a brighter future. For the few thousand who saw the cherry blossoms, for a moment, life was beautiful, and if not beautiful, than it was at least bearable, which was more than was typically provided on the road to school.

Evan & the Land of Letin

It was a shame Evan didn't notice, for their beauty would have provided just the boost he could have used on his first day back. The cherry blossoms only stayed at full strength for a week or two before fluttering upon the street. During this special time, Chapel Avenue resembled a road in a magical land that led to a city full of promise. After that, it was just as it was before–the traffic-infested road that led to Cherry Hill High School North. No worries, though. Surely Evan would notice the blossoms on his drive back home.

The nearly empty hallways told Evan he was late for homeroom. He shifted his pace from snail to tortoise. As he finally approached homeroom, an unfamiliar voice echoed into the hallway. Evan paused, leaning against a wall, just beyond the view of the open door. *It's still not too late to turn back*. He quickly weighed the pros and cons of taking the nearest exit, listening to the substitute teacher call roll. The name calling went smoothly, with the repetitive, *"here, here, here,"* until she neared the bottom of the list.

"Loring…" she read aloud. Evan heard the scattered laughs sprout throughout the classroom. Just as Katie Dawson began to explain in her know-it-all fashion, the reason for Loring's absence, he entered.

"Evan," he said. A swarm of subjective eyes shot his way. He scanned his classmates. Judging from their wide-eyes and sagging jaws, one may have thought it was Evan who died in the fire. "I actually go by Evan."

The sub also sent a confused look compiled of squinted brows atop her bulgy brown eyes.

To clarify, he told her, "Evan's my middle name. I find it easier to live with."

"Understandably so," she said with a snicker, which in turn led to more giggles in the back of the room. Evan had to relive the humiliation of his horrible first name every time there was a new teacher that didn't know he detested the thing. It was a family name, he was told, given to him in honor of a great-great uncle or something. He didn't really know, nor did he really care, but thanks to that extremely great uncle, whoever he was and for whatever he did, the boy now had what he and many others considered to be a hideous name.

"Well, Mr. Transce? Is it?" She leaned her creased forehead toward him. "It may help to know that homeroom begins at 8 o'clock."

This woman was an unneeded reminder for why he hadn't terribly missed this place. There were thoughts in Evan's head suggesting sneering remarks to snap back, but he thought better of it, and he forced a smile. "Thank you, ma'am."

Evan settled in the back row. Upon the desk was the latest edition of *The Dragon's Pen,* the school's weekly newspaper. Evan, like the majority of the student body, scarcely opened *The Dragon's Pen*, but this week something interested him. From the corner of the page, there seemed to be an extra paper slipped in. He pulled it out.

Atop the sheet, in bold red letters, it read, "**MISSING**". Beneath the headline, Evan read the name, also in large print: **Antwon Peeples**. Evan reviewed the picture and quickly decided he'd never seen the boy before, but it was hard to decipher. The picture chosen for the flyer was of poor quality, and though it wasn't printed in black and white, it may as well have been. The boy wore a black turtleneck that nearly merged with his skin. He stood in front of what seemed to be a black curtain. He bore no smile, only two wide eyes that looked lost themselves. His whole face looked expressionless except for those eyes. Desperate searching eyes. Eyes that appeared to look for the boy to which they belonged, who was already fading away into the darkness.

Evan read the blurb beneath the picture. The missing boy was a freshman there at North. He felt

Evan & the Land of Letin

terrible that he hadn't heard about it sooner, but when he looked at the date the boy went missing, the day after his grandparents' death, he understood why he hadn't heard. *I've been pretty preoccupied myself.*

Evan stared. Beneath the face of Antwon, a black-ink reflection of Transce stared back.

Dingg, Dingg, Dingg.

As always, the three electronic chimes signified the end of a period and the beginning of four minutes of pure ruckus in the hallways before the next class began. Several students raced the corridors with underclassmen held on their back where a bag should be. Countless couples pecked, licked, and nearly gnawed at each other's faces–some as if alone in their own world, others with eyes roaming to assure they received their due attention. Students walking while reading textbooks collided with other students walking and sending text-messages. "Watch where I'm going!" a device baring crasher barks.

Though their treks between classes seem ill-mapped, packed with unnecessary detours to friends' lockers, somehow, beyond the understanding of any outsider looking in, students reach their destinations. For Evan, his first stop was Miss Popolo's Trigonometry class.

Miss Popolo's hands scrambled across her desk, searching for the day's lesson plan, or as Evan had seen time and time again, stalling a few extra seconds as she mentally prepared to create the day's lesson on the fly. Hobbling to the electronic whiteboard, Miss Popolo tapped against the screen, forming a perfect circle upon it.

Nice, so far I'm following. But the next scribbles she scratched turned this familiar friend into an unrecognizable foe. The class let out a collective groan.

"Wake up!" Miss Popolo squawked, "You guys really need to know this."

Lies, Evan thought. Miss Popolo glanced his way as though his thoughts were visible upon his forehead.

With her eyes still on him, she continued. "...For the next exam."

A pair of distant giggles trickled through the hall, forcing Evan to wake up. Every morning his sleep deprived self forgot she was coming, so each time the excitement rekindled. Now, after being absent so long, his excitement was at its peak.

Before splitting from her friends and finally entering the classroom, her laughter permeated the air one last time, tickling the cilia in Evan's ears and turning his whole flesh goosey. Evan perceived it as the sound of an angel, beat only by the sight of her.

"Sorry I'm late," her voice squeaked. Her long-lashes flicked, leaving her eyes glittering. Anyone could plainly see she wasn't sorry in the slightest. She was purposely late, day after day, which made her daily apology increasingly offensive. But if she wasn't late, she was just like everyone else, and as Evan could plainly see, she was not everyone else—she was Jayla Hayes.

She was the only girl to this point in the brief history of Evan Transce that could literally draw forth the strange emoticon formation of a heart into his head. <3 In fact, she actually drew forth a whole slew of mental images that no other creature could. Through Evan's eyes, Jayla was superiorly spectacular to any other in her species walking the Earth. To a certain extent, she was pretty amazing. Anyone or anything that could make Trigonometry class manageable for the mathematically inept Evan deserved a fair amount of praise.

No, Jayla wasn't exactly Evan's friend, unless of course you counted Facebook friendship, of which he was merely one of 1,421. So, no...they didn't really talk in class. In all honesty, she didn't even really look at him either, but Evan did enough looking for the both of them. As Miss Popolo screeched on about trigonometric functions, Jayla's darkly lined eyes scanned across the phone terribly hidden upon her lap. Evan's eyes, oblivious to what was being taught, scanned Jayla Hayes.

Her hair, a feature Evan scarcely noticed on other girls, was smooth, straight, and strawberry blonde. It fell neatly at the middle of her shoulder blades, swaying weightlessly with each turn of her neck. She could style it endlessly, but today, she wore it down. Her bangs delicately draped across her blemish-free forehead like a curtain pulled aside revealing the most stunning of shows.

The many text messages that would cause Jayla's face to beam her glowing smile would cause Evan's face to do the same, with his smile being a little less lustrous. As the two shared smiles that only the one knew were shared, his mind imagined it were he whom she messaged, inciting that smile.

Today, however, he wished he hadn't been looking at her, and certainly not smiling, because today, for perhaps the first time in history, Jayla Hayes looked at Evan Transce.

She didn't look *through* Evan, as most girls tended to do. She didn't simply glance at him with a passing eye that searched for something more pleasing. She full-on-looked at Evan. Direct-hit into his dark brown, purple-specked eyes.

His heart froze mid-beat and his eyes shot directly down to his textbook, which was now several pages behind. *That didn't happen*, he thought. *Don't look up. Don't look up. Just don't look up.*

Evan looked up. And there she was, seemingly waiting for him to look back up, right into her eyes. Evan wasn't sure what was happening…

Jayla smiled, a sort of slick side smile that lifted her left cheek. A smile that seemed to say, *"I caught you."* He could feel his cheeks burning, rising up his face, producing beads of sweat at his hairline.

Dingg, Dingg, Dingg.

Students stood, breaking their eye contact. The old phrase, "saved by the bell" was now a blessed mantra to Evan. Though it lasted only a few seconds, the eye contact with Jayla felt like forever to him. He wasn't sure whether it was heaven or hell, or whether he'd want it to happen again, or perhaps, if things got adventurous, he'd even talk to her... *Whoa.*

Evan zipped back to reality and felt sillier than ever. *At least Trig is over.* As he gathered up his books and shoved them lopsided into his backpack, he paused, and from the corner of his eye, tried to get a final glimpse. His last Jayla fix of the day. She carefully slipped her paisley bag over her shoulder with one arm, as the other flicked her hair in slow motion time. She knew Evan was still watching. She walked out of the room in impeccable popular-girl-form, and as she exited, Evan realized his jaw had sunk wide open. Saliva had already begun to dampen the corner of his lips.

He discretely wiped his mouth as his eyes slowly rolled to his right. He shifted his head, ever so slightly, to see if any of the remaining bodies saw him salivate.

Whew. They hadn't, plus even if they had, in Evan's book, they were even nerdier nerds than he was. He'd seen them drool over their textbooks. *Oh look, there's Chester Slobberman at it now!*

Chester was indeed *slightly* drooling as he reviewed the class's notes, but barely. And his last name was Sabberman. Evan's thoughts betrayed him, as they were being particularly unfriendly. But right then, they got what they deserved.

Evan froze once more as he realized he'd forgotten to peer to the other side. The left side of his face felt as if it were singeing, as skin tends to feel when its wearer is being uncomfortably stared upon. Evan swiveled his neck the other way, hoping no eyes would be there to

Evan & the Land of Letin

greet his.

Several feet above the sitting Evan, his sideways eyes engaged in the most awkward contact with a pair of sagging, severely fatigued eyes that belonged to Miss Popolo.

"Hopefully you'll put some of that focus into your trigonometric functions next week," she said with an arched eyebrow.

The blood rush returned to Evan's face. He wasn't as embarrassed as he was ashamed. He felt pathetic, and understandably so. His gawking toward Miss Hayes was one of the less admirable things Evan did, but hey, he was human. More specifically, a *male* human.

He tittered and out came an inaudible mumble back to his teacher. As the sounds escaped, he realized they hadn't quite made words, so he nodded in support of her suggestion. At this, her tired face un-creased, turning from judgmental to sympathetic. Evan slipped his bag on, the corners of the books jabbing at his back, and swiftly stepped toward the door at record pace.

"Have a nice day, Evan." Her voice carried an apologetic undertone.

He turned, wanting to look Miss Popolo in the eye, but he was unable to do so. "Thanks. You too."

Onward he shuffled behind wall to wall congestion in the intersections of corridors E and F. Throw a layer of greyish-green face paint on these students, add a few Hollywood scabs and scars, and here at slow moving traffic at the intersection of E and F, you'd have the perfect cast for any zombie film. But this day, across the hallway, the bright face of one particular girl emanated joy and consciousness among the shuffling undead.

She wore a wild-flower patterned dress with a leather knit belt that matched the brown braid of hair that crowned her head and the high boots that quietly declared a rebel lived within. Though the boots gave her a boost, the girl was tiny. Yet among the half-awake students, her presence was as recognizable as a single lily rising from asphalt.

From down the hall, Evan's eyes met hers, and without control, out escaped a cheek-lifting smile. He tightened his lips, not wanting his teeth to escape too, for he didn't want to seem overexcited upon seeing her. At his smile, her eyes brightened, nose crinkled, and her smile beamed toward him. Her smile was all teeth, completely aware of the slight gap between her top incisors and completely aware of its insignificance.

A slim pathway opened between the creeping students and she ran through. Her floral dress fluttered against the backpacks of the passersby as her boots scampered louder. Without hesitation, she slung her arms around him. Though petite herself, the momentum of the thrown hug sent the equally small Evan stumbling backward. Her twiggy arms squeezed him tight with the might of a hundred hugs saved up for this one. The hug he returned, once his arms slid from under her unyielding embrace, though not as strong, was equally as sincere. As they released she moved her hand over his, clasping it, as it fell to his side. The other, for a brief moment, touched his cheek, as if in a wise, nurturing gesture to monitor his health and safety.

"How are you?" she asked, unhanding him.

"I—"

"Stupid question," she cut him off. "I'm sorry I asked. You're terrible. But you're here, and safe, so I couldn't be happier."

This was far more truth than he would have given. The scripted and cryptic *'I'm fine'* would have been his quick-reaction answer, but she was entirely right. This encounter was already brightening his day.

"I've got something for you." She pulled her bag open, looking through it as it hung over her shoulder. "Ah, here it is."

She pulled out a small, flat, fire-engine-red, tin pin.

Evan & the Land of Letin

She pulled the breast pocked of his grey t-shirt and plucked it there. Evan pulled at the bottom of his shirt so he could get a better look at it.

"What's this?"

"This," she gave the pin a flick and widened her eyes as if she were speaking to a child, "would be a heart. Or rather the *symbol* of a heart. An actual depiction wouldn't have looked anywhere near as aesthetically pleasing, so this red," she turned her head to look at it from another angle, "ass-shaped thing will have to do."

This early morning encounter was pretty much Heart Lee Goodwin perfectly personified—beautiful, caring, and brilliantly witty. People called her Heart Lee, like it was one name, *Heartly*. When Evan met her parents a few years back, with a child named Heart, he wasn't surprised in the slightest to see that they were clearly flower-loving folk back in their day.

"Thank you, Heart Lee. Very much," Evan held back a laugh. "But what's this for?"

"Well, Evan Transce," she said, ready to disperse matter-of-facts upon him. "As you may or may not know, even after you graduate and leave off for Iowa or Ohio, or wherever it is you're going, this place will still be here. So, school will continue on in full, still with all the sports, clubs, and of course, student government, which I intend to be president of."

"Really?" He didn't mean to sound so shocked.

"Don't be surprised. I'll have a lot to juggle, no doubt. But don't you fret–The Peace-Seeking Dragons will continue to be my top passion, and I'll need to learn how to majorly multitask before I take to the Capitol in a few short years."

"No, no. I mean, I know you can do it. Jeez, there'd be no Peace-Seeking Dragons if it weren't for you."

Evan was feeling bold and honest, perhaps a side-effect of being around one who exuded such traits.

She blushed. A Heart Lee rarity. "Evan, I

appreciate that. But it's untrue. You are the ultimate Peace-Seeking Dragon."

Evan laughed. *Maybe once upon a time. But not anymore.*

That once upon a time was probably his first week at North when there was a brawl in the cafeteria. This fight scared freshman Evan senseless. There'd never been a real, fist-jabbing-leg-stomping-security-guard-intervening fight at Saint Peter's...there wasn't even a security guard at Saint Peter's. Even the slightest verbal dispute over a kickball game was dealt with by a team of highly trained peer mediators. Later that same day Evan was shocked to find out there were no such mediations at North, just a summoning to E-33, Vice Principal's Office where punishment was heavily laid down. Evan thought it'd be nice to have an alternative approach here. Peer mediations, perhaps more. Perhaps there could be a group that could do more than just mediate dispute, but could perhaps prevent them. Perhaps there could be a group that promoted peace in the school, in the community, beyond...

Undoubtedly idealistic and maybe even naive, Evan scheduled an appointment with the principal, and as they say, the rest is history. If the North yearbooks are to be considered history. The principal even helped create the mascot-oriented name, which Evan pretended to be thrilled about. The group's first year of existence was mostly just Evan's few friends who graduated with him from Saint Pete's, who reluctantly attended a meeting or two accompanied by a half-dozen escapees from the Island of Misfits. They counterproductively debated the definition of "peace" with tempers flaring every meeting. It wasn't until his sophomore year when a freshman named Heart Lee Goodwin joined the club and actually started to help Evan lead the group in the direction he'd originally intended.

They were doing peer mediations, assemblies, volunteering their time at shelters in the city, plus more.

Now, the Peace-Seeking Dragons boasted 67 members with no signs of dwindling after Evan's departure. After Heart Lee's, well, that would be a different scenario.

"I wasn't surprised that you're running, but I mean, April just started. Elections aren't for at least another month."

"May 16th. Forty days, to be exact. But, Evan Transce, you should know by now that I'm a person who knows what I want…" she paused, and at this, Heart Lee looked steadily into his dark eyes. There couldn't have been a clearer sign of Heart's affection toward Evan, but he was clueless. Maybe it was that purple spot in his eye that blinded him. "And I go after it immediately. Some may call it early, some may even call it late, but I know it exactly as it is, which is right on time."

Dingg, Dingg, Dingg.

Evan was frazzled by the bell. Heart Lee barely seemed to notice it. Or if she did, it certainly didn't faze her. He didn't want to be late to Mr. Wright's history class, one of the few classes and teachers he was fond of. But he also didn't want these four minutes to end, for every moment with Heart seemed to somehow set his mind right. She sensed his angst, so with a shove, sent him speed-walking down the hallway.

"I almost forgot!" she called out.

Evan turned back to see Heart Lee in no rush, for she stood in the same exact spot. Alone in the hallway, without an apparent care in the world, the girl looked angelic.

"Not that you'd need an invite, but there's a soiree of sorts at my home tonight."

"A party?" Evan asked. *I'm not so sure I'm ready for that kind of work just yet.*

"Sure. *A party*," she scoffed.

Evan smiled, letting his eyes gently roll. "We'll see," he said with a hefty sigh.

Heart Lee's nose scrunched and her smile spread

once more, revealing the small black gap between her teeth like a source of pride. From across the hall she could read Evan perfectly, and knew his *'we'll see'* would transform to a *'yes'* well before he did. He took another step, trying to save a few seconds of history class, but froze once more as Heart's send-off took him by surprise.

"Bye, Crazy Love."

She hadn't called him that in years. He couldn't help but smile and return her old sobriquet.

"See ya, Sweet Thing."

Evan waved as he turned the corner.

"Oh! And you've got to wear your heart-pin tonight to get in," she added. "Show your Heart pride."

Evan nodded as he passed from her view. He wasn't sure if she were serious about wearing this pin all day and into the night. But this was Heart. She was probably serious.

7

Evan slipped into the darkly lit classroom, settling into the nearest seat. Mr. Wright reviewed the roll book and didn't notice his arrival. For the third time in Evan's high school career his class was watching *Glory*. He must have missed a lot, for he wasn't precisely sure how they'd returned to studying the Civil War. *Fine movie*, he thought, especially the first year they watched it and missed three consecutive periods of actual work. The second time wasn't as good since the viewing came paired with a worksheet. Based upon his fellow classmates haphazard scribbling of seemingly random notes, this watch would be the worst, for now there'd surely be an accompanying essay.

Fighting the urge to fall asleep through Morgan and Denzel's campfire conversation was a success, but as Evan walked into Physics and saw the projector set up, it seemed the battle against his heavy eyelids would commence once more.

Mr. Foster was showing a documentary on what he enthusiastically called, "Einstein-Rosen bridges," and what humans less excited about the Sciences called *wormholes*. As Mr. Foster flicked the lights, pressing play, before Evan spared two thoughts pondering the possibility of instant inter-universe travel, his eyelids heaved down, briskly and briefly sending him into darkness.

Dingg, Dingg, Dingg.

Lunch period came next, well before Evan's appetite for lunch food. As he did every other day, Evan settled on a poppy-seed bagel with strawberry cream cheese. On pointed-toes, he scoured the lunchroom for his friends. With no sight of them, he exited through the bulletproof door that led to the courtyard. As it slammed behind him, he saw them.

They stood under a tree, each with an arm around the other's neck, posing for a picture, as they were so exceptionally fond of doing. They wore their daily snapback hats, striped V-neck shirts, and skinny jeans, with spotless sneakers on their feet. Don't be confused though, both looked extremely different, at least in their minds. While one wore a Boston hat, the other's was a New York. While one bore red stripes, the other had blue.

This was Trey and Zane, Evan's best friends dating back to Mrs. Gene's kindergarten class. Thankfully for Evan, they didn't continue on the private school route come high school like most of their Saint Pete's classmates. This assured Evan at least two friends at this big, scary school. Four years later, his friend-count remained about the same.

"My man!" Zane yelled.

"E.T.!" added Trey.

From across the courtyard they ran toward him, forcing a group hug that quickly escalated into a jumping carousel around Evan, complete with yelled honks and hoots from the two. Knowing them, they likely planned for this celebration. This was the first time seeing them since the funeral, to which they appeared in matching tailored suits. Following that, they definitely wanted this meeting to be as upbeat as possible. Plus, Trey and Zane were never two to shy away from attention getting behavior. Every eye in the courtyard was now on them.

The student photographer reviewed the picture of Trey and Zane. Either satisfied with the results or lacking patience for the boys' theatrics, she turned to walk away.

"What were the pictures all about?" Evan asked.

"Oh, snap!" Zane shouted. "You wanna get in?"

The photographer hadn't quite walked off, so she turned back, a hand on her hip, the other serving up the camera, "I can retake it if you want."

"What's it for?"

"We got voted as 'Most Likely to Star in our Own Reality Show' for the yearbook." Trey responded. "Boom!"

The duo shared their not-so-secret handshake, complete with a chest-bump, twirl, double-slap, and ending with an exploding fist-bump, leaving two slow-motion shimmering hands falling from the sky. Evan released the faintest of laughs, in part at their old routine and mostly at the fact that they were still doing it after so many years.

"I can see it." Evan said. "I mean, not that I'd watch it. But I could definitely see it."

"See it?" asked Trey. "No, no. You'd co-star on this hit show, bro!"

Evan forced a laugh. He could *not* see that. "Thanks, but no thanks."

With a shrug, the camera girl was off, and the boys went strangely silent.

This made for Evan's second unplanned and

uncomfortable silence of the day. The lack of sound rang louder than any of the boys' yelling could have. It went on, each moment increasingly more noticeable, like the growing space between Evan and the two. Like the growing space between Evan and Earth.

In a strange way, the silence seemed to suit the boy. But before he could fully settle in, Trey interrupted.

"Ah! I want one," he said, tapping the tin heart pin, leaving a ringing dink.

"What? A pin, or a heart?" Evan laughed and continued, "or a Heart Lee?"

"All the above," answered Trey. "Dude would have to be blind not to want a Heart Lee, or blind not to see she wants an E.T. Yeah, boy!"

The two bombarded the smaller Evan with noogies on his head and tickling fingers on his stomach, but he wouldn't crack a smile. Evan never encouraged their daily Heart Lee jokes. Zane realized his lack of enthusiasm and strayed away from the fun-poking.

"I take it you're goin' to Heart Lee's tonight?"

"Uh, I mean, I was thinking about it," Evan replied.

"You're goooo-," held Trey for two, three seconds, "-ingggg."

Evan stared at Trey with a perplexed, tilted head, as he did when his friends said or did such strange things.

"You. Are. Going," Trey stagnantly finished.

"Are you guys going?"

"Are we going? HA! Trey, would you look at this guy," Zane said, backhanding Trey's chest. "Are *we* going? Of course we're goin', Ev. We're gonna debut our new single at the party!"

Back at the formation of their rap-duo, Trey and Zane tried desperately to make it a trio by way of Evan. But he couldn't quite picture the "Chilluminati", as they called themselves, to be his outlet. So he respectfully declined, time and time again.

"Yo, but for real," Zane took on a wide-eyed,

raised-brow, sullen face that he adopted when speaking of serious matters, "It'd be good for you, bro. To get out. Escape." He paused, keeping his brows raised, which Evan thought was pretty funny. Evan laughed. Zane continued, "But for real, though."

Evan shook his head, and Trey added his own take.

"Yeah, man. Let your hair down. Let it be, bro. Let it happen." Trey began to laugh and the nonsense that was spewing from his mouth. "Let the party in. Let it in to your soul! Let it in, brother!"

The three laughed at the two's buffoonery. Though not diagnosed, his best friends were definitely insane. But that was half of what made them so special to Evan, and half the reason he knew his own insanity was perfectly normal. Although the boys phrased it in such a ridiculous way, they really did have an excellent point that he fully understood.

"Alright. It might be nice to go. To uh," Evan smiled, in disbelief of what he was saying, "*Let it in.*"

"Man," Zane said, swinging an arm over Evan's shoulder. He spoke slowly to emphasize the importance of his words, "we don't have to know what is we're letting in, we just gotta let it. Just let tonight bring us whatever magic it wants to bring us!"

"Like that…" Trey said, his face fixated on something behind his friends' backs.

Evan turned, and strutting across the courtyard, sunglasses down, pretending to be in her own world, passed Jayla Hayes. Evan felt his blood pump faster at the sight of her, then remembering the awful eye-exchange from earlier, he quickly turned around, not wanting to be caught again. He looked at Trey and Zane, both begging to be caught with their fully-peeled eyes and swiveling necks.

8

Evan arrived a minute or so early for Mr. Strunk's class, but early, late, present, or absent didn't really seem to matter. As soon as the bell rang, Mr. Strunk passed out a reading quiz without acknowledging the existence of students in the room. Evan was not aware that they'd begun a new study. He read the top of the quiz: *A Midsummer Night's Dream.*

Yep, I'm failing this one.

Whether he knew of the quiz or not wasn't going to effect his grade, for in this, his final year of high-school, fully struck with senioritis, the best studying he did was last minute web-searching on his phone prior to class. This last minute "reading" often resulted in scores hovering just above or below the failing line. On this quiz they had to read quotes and decide which character said them.

> *"Over hill, over dale*
> *Thorough bush, thorough brier,*
> *Over park, over pale,*
> *Thorough flood, thorough fire,*
> *I do wander everywhere."*

Evan wanted to answer Puck or Bottom like he did for every other blank space, because they were the only character names he knew. But he also recalled there being fairies in this story so that seemed a fine guess, too. *Fairy #2*, he wrote.

After reviewing his work, he estimated the best he could have gotten was a 40%. *Not my finest work.* Before passing the quiz in, Evan realized he'd forgotten to pencil his name atop the page. For a second, he contemplated leaving it empty, *pretend I was absent one more day.* But instead, in microscopic print, he scratched *Evan*

Transce, assuring that he got at least one thing right.

Following the quiz was a class discussion on the play, for which Evan gained no points for participation. When English class was thankfully over, next came Señora Romero's Spanish class. Today, like every other 'viernes', the class performed short skits speaking only Spanish on the week's topic. This week the students shared speeches on their favorite family member. Since Evan had missed the whole week, Señora Romero said he was exempt, for which he was grateful, for most speeches were about 'abuelos y abeulas'. This was Evan's fourth year learning the foreign language, yet all he seemed to retain were the basic greetings and colors. He'd become content with the fact that he'd never fully speak another language in his life.

Understanding very little of the speeches, Evan let his mind wander. He wondered how the distribution of the will was going. He looked at the clock, *Should be over by now.*

Maybe they left me something, he thought.

Silly, stupid, selfish, another thought interjected.

...But maybe they did...

Maybe they did. *But what would they leave?* He mentally rummaged through their menial belongings and felt extremely displeased with himself for doing so. Nothing spectacular, but the more he thought about it, anything from them would be special.

Maybe one of Gram's wine glasses would be cool, just to put high on a shelf like a special artifact. His very own Holy Grail. Thoughts flew from random item to item, not particularly desiring any, just reminiscing about the special memories associated with each. Deep in his mind, Evan recalled an item he actually did want, strictly for the laugh factor attached to it.

Months back, Evan stumbled upon Grammpa hard at work in the cellar on what could best be described as a tin-scarecrow. The old man worked feverishly on the thing, using all sorts of bolts and bits of scrap-metal, unaware that Evan was watching. Finally the boy couldn't contain his curiosity, and asked with a laugh, *"What's the tin-scarecrow for?"*

Grammpa's face went red as he wrinkled it, embarrassed and angered that his grandson had seen what was obviously supposed to be a private piece of work.

"My garden! What else would it be for?" Liam snapped back.

This short-tempered reaction was unlike him, which at the time made it seem rather funny. Now, this memory spurred a mixture of emotions for Evan. It almost scared him, remembering his grandfather in this defensive and riled state, which he rarely was in. *Something was wrong.* Then a slice of Evan felt sad and guilty, for his Grammpa never did end up using it in the garden.

I must've made him feel bad. He probably threw it away. He knew if he had the tin-scarecrow today, he'd find the perfect spot for it in the garden. A spot it deserved. Somewhere where he could look out his window every morning, see those hunks of metal configured into a little man and smile.

Consumed in the recollection, Evan lost track of time. It was one of the best Spanish classes in recent memory, for the 44 minutes zipped by without Evan having to utter a single word.

9

Evan had missed the organized ruckus that was gym class, so he walked swiftly to the locker room to retrieve the shorts and shirt still waiting, wrinkled, and unwashed from their last use. Before pulling open the huge, linebacker friendly door into the locker-room, a very familiar, very grizzly voice spoke from behind him.

"Don't bother changin'."

Evan turned to see Coach Foxx with his typical grimace on the verge of a growl hardened upon his face.

The coach's black cap was tightened upon his head with the green 'N" woven between a roaring dragon on the front panel. Its brim was bent precisely to match the curve of his thick, blonde Fu Manchu. Along with being Evan's gym teacher what seemed like every other semester, Coach Foxx was also the varsity baseball coach. So, after Evan serving three years on the JV, for the first year, Coach Foxx was now his coach.

Coach looked eternally angry, but today, Evan thought, he looked even more so. *Could he seriously be mad I missed practice considering…*

"Nice to see you back, Transce," he said, unfolding and shoving two wads of Dubble Bubble into his mouth.

Seriously? he thought. *I didn't even know he knew my name.* He was partially right, for Coach Foxx didn't know he went by Evan. Coach had seen the kid's first name a few times on his roster, but it was far too strange for him to say aloud. He only remembered "TRANSCE" because it was printed in-caps atop the back of his number eleven jersey.

"Henry pulled something in his shoulder yesterday on an embarrassingly awful throw, and Reilly's in a slump with no signs of climbing out, so uh…" he paused, perhaps stunned for what he was about to say, "…you're gonna get the start. At Short tomorrow…against South."

What!? After missing days of practice and an implausible injury on an apparent errant throw from their best player, Evan would now be getting his first varsity start. Not in Left Field, where Coach would throw him in during late inning blowouts, *No*, this was at Shortstop, the position Evan felt he was born to play. This wasn't against a scrub team either, where a player like Evan would be the star. This was against the Cherry Hill South Griffins, a team stacked just like North's.

Evan & the Land of Letin

If North had to go 1-21 on the season, *which would never happen*, it wouldn't matter as long as that single victory came against the Southside Griffins. Evan didn't care that Coach had obviously considered starting the star freshman Alex Reilly over him; he'd selected Evan. And now, he didn't even know what to say.

"Wow...thanks a lot, Coach."

"Oh, don't thank me. You, uh...earned it."

Through Foxx's permanently snarling face, Evan could still see the man was plainly lying. If it weren't for a school-wide rule requiring all seniors who'd played at least a previous year on JV to automatically become Varsity, he was fairly certain Foxx would still have him down with the underclassmen. Foxx, being the big, bulky man that he was, preferred the trollish students with the propensity to hit the ball out of the park over the swift, elflike Evans of the world that played small-ball. The boy knew that he could have earned the spot given the opportunity, but in truth, he had done nothing to actually do so. This was a fortunate product of other unfortunate circumstances, but now, he was going to earn it, plus more. Evan was certain he'd shine so bright tomorrow, Coach would have to find a permanent spot for him in the lineup.

"I don't want you dressing for gym today. With my luck, you'd get injured playing Ultimate Frisbee. Howboutchya head down to the, uh, library and catch up on, uh, homework or somethin'."

Based on Coach's hesitation to say the words, it seemed the library was a far-off land with homework a relic of a forgotten past. Evan could understand that fully, for they remained foreign to him on this day. As logical as Coach's idea was, he didn't execute it. In addition to being far too excited about the news to be able to get anything done, he wasn't into the idea of being productive on what was supposed to be his gym period. Instead, he sat on the hill behind the school, completely content at looking out on the giant field where his classmates flicked a Frisbee.

The red saucer moved effortlessly through the air, far further than Evan knew was possible. Such a simple and useless invention, but one that Evan awed at as it defied gravity. He didn't know how his classmates did it, sending it flying, dozens upon dozens of yards with the slightest flick of their wrists. Every time he tried, the thing went wobbly, dinking against the ground. He was glad that today he could simply be a watcher of the Frisbee's graceful flight.

As relaxing as it was, he began to feel a bit anxious over his inactivity. There was so much to catch up on.

I shouldn't just be sitting here. He considered going to speak to his guidance counselor, Mrs. Stratus, to inform her that he still hadn't decided where he'd be enrolling next September. She'd been sending him notes for weeks, requesting that he'd swing by her office. After last meeting, Evan was in no rush for her gloomy guidance.

"Peace Studies? That's a major?" she robotically giggled, *"Have you put a lot of thought into what you'd be* doing *with that?"*

Doing? Does she mean, what will my job be? he thought. He honestly hadn't considered it a whole lot, but he didn't want to at seventeen. She tried to convince him that the two schools he was heavily considering also had fine Political Science departments, and that was *"close enough."*

"You can do that!" she decided with a smile.

I can do that? I could do that. But I sure as hell don't want to. A peaceful politician? 'Til Heart Lee proves otherwise, it seems like a paradox.

He replayed the conversation with Mrs. Stratus in his head, complete with commentary by his distressed thoughts. He decided there wasn't much worth in wasting either of their time by heading into her office, because no decision was made and he certainly wasn't in

Evan & the Land of Letin

the mood to be pressured into one either.

Below, Evan was brought back from his thoughts, as a classmate made a diving, belly-flopping catch against the hard field to win the game. After the initial yells of wonder and worry, the class fell silent, for the boy remained motionless. Coach Foxx trotted over, but before he could reach the boy, he sprang up with a wide smile sprawled across his face and grass stains streaked across his shirt. His teammates swarmed him as he thrust the red Frisbee midair in celebration.

They lifted him, cheering loudly, carrying him into the locker room, like their meaningless victory was a World Series clinching game.

Evan laughed, alone on the hill.

10

With gym over, it was time for the eighth and final period of the day. Typically, Evan was late for Mr. Herman's Psychology class, but without the extra step of changing from his stench-woven gym clothes, he arrived early.

From inside the classroom, the gentle sound of a guitar strumming floated from the speakers and into the hallway. Prior to every class, Mr. Herman played a song or two, welcoming and waking up his students. Some days it was Mozart, others it was Kanye. He always aimed to expose his students to a wide variety of music in hopes of invigorating *something* within. As Evan crossed through the doorframe, he felt relaxed, as he assumed was the key reason for today's selection. But it wasn't the soft melody alone that provided the sense of solace. Mr. Herman's room was unlike most at the school, for it was actually decorated, actually designed to inspire the students it served.

Where there would typically be blank white walls, Mr. Herman had framed photos of great thinkers, great doers, and great peacemakers. From the ceiling hung potted plants with low-hanging leaves, while in the back, a small fountain flowed. A mini-bust of Dr. King stood on his desk, next to a statue of Siddhartha mid-meditation, which neighbored a realistic mold of the human brain. Sitting behind the desk in his rolling office chair was Mr. Herman, eyes closed.

The shut-eyes upon the teacher's face weren't like those one was accustomed to seeing during the school day. His head wasn't slumped against the desk, nor did he require an arm or two to support his head. He sat, back straightened, head held high, hands intertwined. Evan wasn't sure he had seen clearly through his teacher's thick salt and peppered beard, but it even appeared Mr. Herman was smiling.

Evan wanted to turn back, wait until a few more students entered the room. He felt awkward witnessing this private moment. But there was no chance to exit. Mr. Herman's eyes opened, and the smile, which was indeed a smile, grew wider.

"Evan. You're here."

"I'm sorry, I…"

"Don't be sorry. Here is the only place you could be."

Mr. Herman's voice was calm, almost monotone, while his smile was still spread full.

"I'm deeply sorry for your losses. I refuse to comfort you with beliefs that I don't know are certain, nor will I lie and say I've been there, or I understand, for I don't."

But something about his teacher's eyes contradicted his words. His eyes, dark like Evan's, had a depth to them. Like a pair of ancient wells wetter than ever with the waters of knowledge and understanding.

"Only you know, Evan. And anyone who tries to tell you otherwise deludes your vision of what you know to be true."

A picture of vanishing flames flickered in Evan's

head. He couldn't muster a word.

"Hopefully you already know this, but if you need anything, that's what I am here for."

"Thank you, Mr. Herman."

The bell rang as the rest of the students settled in. The teacher clicked a few buttons on his laptop and on the front board emerged a pyramid with lots of print.

"Today we will be discussing Maslow's Hierarchy of Needs."

Evan felt compelled to take notes for the first time all day.

"On this pyramid, you'll see Abraham Maslow's motivation theory, which was that humans must fulfill certain needs in order to reach their full potential."

Evan began copying the pyramid into his notebook, scratching notes of what Mr. Herman said as he went along.

"At the bottom, we've got 'Physiological Needs', which are the most basic instinctual needs for survival. Here, there's breathing, eating food, drinking water, and sleeping. Without meeting these needs, Maslow believed, one cannot advance up the Hierarchy, to the next level, 'Safety.'

"These needs are relatively basic as well. Here there's protection, let's say, 'a roof over your head', as well as order, laws, limits. Whether you've got a home and plenty to eat, it'll all mean nothing without laws assuring no one can just walk in and claim your home and food as their own.

"Without meeting these 'Safety Needs', according to Maslow, one can't move on to the third level, which is 'Love & Belonging."

Evan wasn't sure whether he agreed with Maslow, but then again, he hadn't spent his life studying psychology. He was interested in this hierarchy, which was more than could be said for the majority of the class, who gazed from board to clock to phone and back again.

"At this level, is the need to be a working cog in a family, whether that be a traditional family, or part of a team, club, organization, or even a gang. The yearning to be an accepted member of a group is a natural desire, but once again, if one doesn't meet the needs in the prior stages, one can't properly participate in a group or hold a healthy, steady relationship."

Seems to make sense.

"Up here are 'Esteem Needs', which are tricky, for there's really two parts to this one. While we all want and deserve to be respected, for some, often those with low self-esteem, there's a deep urge for attention, status, and fame. In truth, their egos run their lives. For those who seek these things, whether they get them or not, their progress on the Hierarchy ceases, for those external factors aren't what spurs intrinsic growth. But for the other part, those who seek self-respect, self-confidence, and independence, they often see similar traits in others, and it's those rare few who advance to the top of Maslow's Hierarchy, to 'Self Actualization.' According to Maslow, reaching 'Self-Actualization' is realizing one's full potential.

"Some say it's 'being fully-human.' Here, people embrace the truth. They embrace and accept their flaws as well as the flaws of others. They see life as it is, where all are equals, regardless of society's status or cultural differences. Here, people are less concerned with petty stresses, like 'which color should our new sheets be,' or 'what if the Phillies don't win the division', for if they've completed the hierarchy, there should be few stresses, and one should be more concerned with meaningful, universal issues."

Evan reviewed his notes, looking at the pyramid long and hard, trying to assess where he stood in his life. He was unsure.

He looked up at Mr. Herman, who had his eyes closed. Not in the serene state of earlier, but deep in thought, as if trying to recall something he may have missed.

"In recent years, some psychologists have altered Maslow's theory by adding a few steps. There's one particular version that has eight stages, and at its pinnacle, beyond 'Self-Actualization' lays *'Transcendence.'*"

Something about the way the word came out of his mouth seemed to humor Mr. Herman. He laughed in a way that Evan wasn't sure whether his teacher thought the idea of "transcendence" was ludicrous, or those who didn't believe were the loony ones.

"There's plenty of theories and beliefs on what 'transcendence' is. By definition it's simply means, 'going beyond'. So, does it mean going beyond one's self? Going beyond being human?" he seemed to ask himself. Eager to move on, he asked, "Does anyone have any questions?"

Evan did. *What's your philosophy on transcendence? How can a human transcend? Can a human transcend?* He wasn't sure where his interest was coming from. But when no other student raised their hands, he didn't want to be the sole student asking what were sure to be labeled strange questions by his peers.

"Huh? No questions? Fantastic! Before we're dismissed, I've got a short story for you about one of my brothers from college. We'll call him, hmmm…*Kay*. As I've told you before, I went to school over in Philadelphia, and loved it so much, and that's why I eventually made it my permanent home. But for my fraternity brother, Kay, he was born and raised in the city of New York. And boy, was he a New Yorker through and through. We'd go to an Eagles game together, but to him, it was nothing next to the Jets. We'd go to a pizza place, and it wasn't worthy of touching his pristine New York mouth. I promise you, we went to South Street for a cheesesteak and he swore there was a better place up North.

"One day, he had finally landed a date with his biggest crush on campus. He told her he knew the perfect place he was going to take her, he really talked it up. He failed to mention that this special little place was all the way up in the city...New York City. They spent the majority of their date stuck in traffic on I-95. And while the place was fine, he made me visit during a summer break, there's dozens of similar Italian places right there in Philly. Needless to say, there was no second date for Kay and his dream girl."

Evan's gaze slid across the room. Almost every student seemed to be zoning out, either on their phone or with their heads pillowed against their forearms.

"For me, this simple story is more than just a warning not to go on a first date two hours out of the way. What I'm trying to say is *be* where you are. *Here*.

"Don't let your mind wander far off, living some separate life that you're not a part of. Going back to what we learned today, being present, in the here and now, is the most important need Maslow skipped right over. There's no denying you'll find yourself in places you don't want to be, seeing things you wish you weren't seeing, but resistance to *now* is resistance to the very life you're living."

Wow. Mr. Herman's words hit Evan hard, permeating to his very core. Yet he wasn't sure why. They seemed to awaken a glimpse of Evan, deep behind his thoughts which realized those thoughts, in fact, were far-off.

I'm not here.
But where am I?
Dingg, Dingg, Dingg

The bell rang for the last time that day, that week. For the last time, Evan left the classroom without properly saying goodbye to Mr. Herman. The teacher took no offense, for the lesson and story appeared to have had the hoped for effect on Evan. The student searched his thoughts which had re-seized control over his head. As he exited Cherry Hill North, walking across the parking lot, he tried to monitor each faint whisper within, finding a thought that would hint at where he was mentally located.

The more he thought about his thoughts, it became clear that not only were they not here, but they weren't in one place at all. Rather they were scattered about like the fallen cherry blossoms that would be covering Chapel Avenue in a week or so.

A fraction of his thoughts were on his grandparents, no doubt. He didn't want to think about them, but it was impossible not to. Everything he saw, every word he heard, could relate back to a time spent with them. Moments, that at the time seemed so insignificant, were now more important than anything else.

He realized the seemingly clichéd things he'd always heard about life being so precious were so entirely true. *So fleeting, so fragile*, he thought. One moment in full bloom, the next gone forever, leaving only cloudy memories, barely enough to prove you were even here.

Strangely, this made him think about the ant. The ant he killed. *Never again...*

A piece of Evan considered something else he had always heard, about people always dying in threes. He considered the three Cherry Hill kids a couple years back that decided it was their time within the same short week.

Evan wondered who the third would be now. Hazily, he failed to realize that deaths don't come in threes, rather much closer to three-thousands, that is if we wanted to quantify them at all. According to this flawed theory, the number three to Evan's grandparents' one and two had already died within seconds of the fire. Still, Evan's mind raced.

Would that ant count?
Maybe the third is me.

Ugh, shut up Evan.

His mind then came across that boy. That missing boy who was fading into the picture. *What was his name? Antwan? Antwon?* Maybe he was the third.

Evan was shocked at how terribly strange it was, that after seeing the initial report in *The Dragon's Pen,* he heard no mentioning of the missing boy all day. It was as if a single week had passed and everyone had given up, moved on and forgotten about him. *Awful.*

On the topic of awful, a thought backtracked to the eye contact with Jayla. He wished it hadn't happened. *How embarrassing. Ugh. And she smiled like I was a joke. Then Miss Popolo, too.* Evan felt nauseous replaying it in his head.

Another piece of his mind went back to his exchange with Heart Lee. Something about those brief moments somehow settled him. Sure, they made him feel happy, but it was more than that. As he drove, he looked down at his pin. He'd forgotten he'd been wearing it all day.

He remembered that he had to go to that party tonight. *Sorry, the soiree of sorts.* Zero part of Evan was up for that, regardless of how much he knew it'd be good for him. Even when family hadn't died he wasn't one for the party scene. *But I'll do it for Heart. And Trey and Zane.* He certainly wasn't doing it for himself.

Come to think of it, I really shouldn't go. What he should be doing, he thought, was grab his glove, some balls, a bat, and his brother, and go out to the diamond to field some grounders. He had missed a full week of practice, and tomorrow...*Wow, I'm starting tomorrow.* Regardless of how distressed he was, this fact made him smile. This fact provided something he could genuinely look forward to. He couldn't wait to tell everyone. *Grammpa would be so proud.*

Part of Evan was already on that field, geared up his is green North Dragons uniform, excited beyond belief.

Another part of Evan, a part deep inside that he was hardly conscious of, was much further away. Out of Cherry Hill, out of New Jersey. Passed Iowa or Ohio, and the little liberal arts colleges there awaiting his word. Little thought was put into either of those places and a whole slew of thoughts barraged him for not thinking about that more. He had almost subconsciously decided that he wasn't going to either. He sure wasn't going to stay here though, no way. *But where?* This part of Evan was already far away, beyond the approaching full moon and the impending rain.

Sadly, Evan made a right turn off of Chapel Avenue and onto Lantern Lane. Again, he missed his chance to view the cherry blossoms. This time around was particularly sad, for this time would be the last time he'd have the opportunity to see their allusive pink majesty on this green Earth.

11

As Evan entered through the red door, its lock clinking behind him, the house numbered 428 was eerily silent.

The sounds he was prepared to hear were not there. No longer would there be spinning records resonating from his grandmother's room, nor the AM radio mumbling from the cellar as Grammpa worked. But some sounds should've remained, like the voice of a TV judge courting over the family room. Claudio should've been sprawled out on the couch on the cusp of sleep. Evan peered over the couch. His father wasn't there.

Normally his mom wouldn't be home from work yet; she'd still be wrapping things up in her classroom. Clementyne would be several states away at school, and Caden would be starting his shift at work. But today they were home, or at least they should have been. Everyone stayed home today except Evan. *I thought I saw mom's car out there...*

His heart pumped heavily, sending his circulatory system into hyper-drive.

"Hello?" he called out. The full veins on both sides of his forehead protruded as he looked around nervously. Again he yelled, this time his anxiety came through, "Hello!?"

Being home alone wasn't typically a problem for Evan. The problem was that he knew everyone should be here. *Everyone should be here.*

He sprinted the steps, glancing at the empty kitchen on the midlevel, and continuing all the way up. He frantically knocked and pulled open each of the bedroom doors except for his and his grandparents.

You could hardly blame him for his excessive paranoia.

Thoughts thrust forth images of the fire.

The vanishing fire.

The scorched bodies fusing together as one.

Perhaps, he thought, the flames had come again. He shook his head, dissatisfied. *Crazy thoughts. Crazy.*

In the middle of the hallway he stood, consciously attempting to inhale and exhale in an effort to compose himself. Evan slowly walked back down the stairs, one hand stopping and sliding down the iron railing with each step. As he arrived at the landing, he felt slightly better as he saw an inkling of life.

It wasn't the life he had hoped to see, but it was encouraging to know he wasn't alone. Sitting before the glass backdoor, was the cat. *Monster.*

Its tail was raised, tantalizingly twirling and twitching like a viper charmed by its owner's tune. For the cat, its preferred melody was the gentle chirps from a flock of birds that bounced beyond the glass door, pecking at a patch of soil.

In an instant, the birds flew off together, and either instinctively or enviously, the grey cat sprang on its hind legs, pawing against the glass. To Evan, it was unclear whether he yearned to catch them or to join them.

Evan approached the door, and as he got closer, his remaining worry subsided. Around the table set up in the backyard sat the Transce family. Grace and Claudio seemed to be pleasantly chatting while Clementyne and Caden shared a laugh. At their feet laid Rocky, his nose tapping on a budding petunia.

While his paranoia had passed, a new feeling arose. It was calming not only to see his family alive, but to see them all together, all so happy. Yet in the same breath, it was faintly haunting, for the family almost appeared picture perfect without Evan. He noticed this, and perhaps strangest of all, wasn't particularly perturbed by it.

He contemplated letting them be, but his sister spotted him. Evan opened the doors and eight eyes turned to greet him.

"What's up, little one?" his sister asked.

"Not much." He was pretty excited to share his news about starting tomorrow, but first, "How'd everything go today?"

"Fine, I suppose," his mom said. "As far as these things could go. For starters, we've still got a roof over our heads for a few more years…"

Hadn't even crossed my mind. Evan failed to realize that this home wasn't their house. He'd become attached to it over the past years that it felt more like home than any place he could imagine. The idea of leaving in a few years already seemed awful. Before his worrisome thoughts could run wild, his mother spoke again.

"They left you something."

"They left me something?" he returned the question, though he'd heard perfectly well. "What is it?"

"Go see for yourself."

"It's in your room," his dad added.

Without another word, Evan headed back through the glass door with Rocky slowly trotting behind him. He ran up the steps, leaping over two, three at a time. Evan paused before the white door leading into his room, his mind just as blank as to what was on the other side. Whatever it was, Evan was already certain it was the greatest gift he'd ever been given. He turned the knob, pushing open the door.

At the center of his bed, atop the black sheets, the bright color of the gift shone like a beacon of light amid a dark sea of nothing.

Grammpa's hat.

He slowly walked over, eyeing the old baseball cap along the way. Gently picking it up, Evan carefully held it like a fragile artifact. He ran the backside of his fingers over the red-dyed wool. It was fairly old, older than Evan for sure. Aside from Sundays at church, or the unfortunate post-shower sightings, Evan had never seen his grandfather uncapped.

While the "P" insignia upon the hat represented Philadelphia's baseball team, its dated font differed from that which the team now wore on the field. Its once vibrant red was now partially darkened by years of dirt and sweat, while another patch atop its crown was faded from seasons of beatings by the sun.

As Evan stared at the cursive "P", it now represented much more than a city or his favorite team. He envisioned his grandfather sitting at the dining room table, grinning cheek to cheek, all lips, not letting the white of his dentures through. Evan smiled similarly.

Powers, he thought. He envisioned all members of the Powers family around that dining room table. Sure, Evan was a Transce, but the blood of the Powers ran healthily through his veins. He thought about his mom with all of her siblings. The mental image of this made him happy. He felt content.

Peace, he thought. That was the perfect word to describe those moments when the entire family was gathered around. Those rare moments only came during holidays, and during these times, it were as though no time had passed and the present would last forever.

For a moment, Evan considered trying the hat on. But this would be strange, he thought. Almost sacrilegious.

I can't…

Then why'd he give it to you? another thought snapped back.

Perhaps to encase it in a glass box with a little blurb etched on a commemorative plaque explaining its significance at the Museum of Liam Powers?

Of course he left it for me to wear. Of course.

But something still felt unsettling. Evan looked at the open doorframe where Rocky's eyes stared on. He walked over, shutting the door. This felt better.

Evan took a deep breath and nodded, affirming what he'd do next. He slowly placed the hat on his head, pulling the brim forward. Just above his thick brows, just the way he liked it.

It fit perfectly.

Evan smiled. He wasn't sure why, but wearing this hat felt right. He ran his hands over the red wool, precisely adjusting it, and while he did this, Evan felt something. Something hard, small, and lodged under the left side of the cap.

Evan took off the hat. Green under-brim, black under-crown, everything looked normal, except from under the left side of the flap that ran the circumference of the hat, the slightest bit of white paper poked up. Evan slipped it out. It was heavier than a folded piece of paper should be. Something was wrapped within.

Evan unfolded the small package carefully. Whoever placed this inside the hat wrapped its contents purposefully. He unfurled the left flap, then the right; the top and the bottom, until it was fully opened. Laying atop the paper was a small metal charm.

Staring at the medallion, Evan sat down on his bed,

placing the paper beside him. He brought the tiny object closer to his eye to examine its intricacy, holding the slight thing with the tips of his fingers. The metal appeared to be silver, worn over the years, which gave it a dull grey color. *What is it?* he thought.

At first glance, it resembled a miniature key, but that wasn't it. The shaft part of the key-that-wasn't looked like two thinner shafts twisted together as one, spiraling toward its head before splitting off and forming two long-fingered hands. These miniscule hands mirrored one another, meeting only at their fingertips, clasping what appeared to be a tiny grey marble. At the bottom of the charm, the curved scooping blade-shaped form of the object gave this mystery a name. *A shovel?*

A shovel. A pendant shaped like a shovel hardly large enough to dig an ant hole and far too ornamental to shove in the ground. Evan smiled, his heart puttering.

In his excitement, he almost failed to notice the small slashes and swirlings of print on the inside of the paper. Evan picked it up. There was no signature, but after living at 428, seeing his grandmother's To-Do lists posted about the house, lists that made buying milk and bread seem elegant, there was no question. Her cursive was unmistakable and infallible, like an ancient work of art from a time when beautiful handwriting was cherished. As he read, he heard her voice within.

Dig Deeper.

He read it again, *Dig Deeper.*

This shovel would be doing no digging.

Obviously it's symbolic, genius.

But was this meant for me? Should I ask mom?

No, no, no.

This was clearly hidden. This was carefully folded and placed in the hat. This was a secret. *But why?*

He reviewed the charm again. Twirling it in his fingers once more. From one angle it looked as though the hands cradled the marble gently. From another, it

Evan & the Land of Letin

was as though the two hands pulled, claiming the little orb as their own.

Looks like something out of fantasy movie, he thought. He considered showing it to his closet-nerd brother. All those fantasy novels he read and loved, surely he'd have a literary allusion he could attach it to, possibly stringing together a solid theory on this thing.

From his desk, Evan pulled out the drawer he used primarily to lose track of junk he had no use for. He pushed aside dozens of used ticket stubs, loose change, and the pocket-knife his dad gave him at thirteen which he never touched except from the times he pushed it aside to find other useless items. Surprisingly, in this little drawer stuffed with garbage, he found what he was looking for—a spool of thin twine. He wasn't sure why he had this, or how he had this, but he knew he wanted to use it now.

Measuring with his eye, he unwound two feet of twine, then snipped it using a pair of rusty scissors also found in the junk drawer. Evan threaded the twine through the top of the charm, for there was the slightest gap between the marble and the two mid-fingers meeting at their tips.

Here, the charm hung. To avoid it sliding about, Evan looped the string around, accidentally forming something resembling a loop-knot. He brought the ends of the cut twine together, double knotting them to assure no fails.

He briefly removed his new favorite cap then slipped his new favorite necklace over his head. The small shovel hung right above his heart. Evan picked up the peculiar pendant to look once more, smiled, then drew it to his lips with a kiss.

12

Evan opened the door only to find Rocky standing

on patrol. The dog peered at the boy and rapidly sniffed the air. The boy lifted his arm, wafting the air beneath his pits toward his nose. No peculiar scent. Then, as it dangled, he realized that not only was he wearing the shovel shaped charm, but atop his head was a hat that had become very familiar to the dog. Rocky stood on his hinds to get a better whiff.

"Down boy."

Down the dog went, all fours to the floor, ears tucked back and head toward the ground. Still, Rocky kept a keen eye attached to Evan, the boy who wasn't the man the dog foolishly hoped for. Evan looked back into the dog's dark eyes, which earlier seemed so un-doglike, triggering chills. Now they took on their natural animal glaze, with a glint of sadness.

Grammpa would take the dog for a walk twice daily. That obviously hadn't happened in quite some time now. *I've never taken a dog for a walk before...*

"Let's go for a walk, big guy."

The dog's long nails clacked against the floor, as his back paws alternately tapped excitedly. His nub of a tail rapidly ticked and tocked to and fro.

"Whoa, relax, Rock. Had I known it meant so much I woulda taken ya sooner."

He patted the dog's boxy head that bobbed up and down. Before grabbing the leash and heading out, Evan ran upstairs to fetch his earbuds.

Downstairs, he clicked the chain-link leash onto Rocky's camouflage patterned collar, wrapping the excess chain around his hand, and opened the front door.

The afternoon sun sat at its peak while a soft breeze slid across his face. Evan tapped the phone's main button, then with a few finger flicks, he fired up the device's music feature. He scrolled through his playlists named after band's abandoned names: *Johnny & the Moondogs, Mookie Blaylock, 2nd Nature...*

Evan & the Land of Letin

As Rocky panted and patiently waited by his side, Evan decided upon none of them and chose the ultimate choice for the indecisive music listener. He tapped on the intertwined arrows signifying "shuffle" and set down toward the sidewalk.

A gentle voice counted to three in his left ear soon followed by plucks on an acoustic guitar. The simple chords repeated thrice before drums came rolling down his right-side canal. The instruments continued their ascending melody until they met somewhere amid Evan's mind, sounding just right.

A product of the 1990's developing his consciousness into the new millennium, Evan wasn't exactly sure what it meant to be "feelin' groovy." That said, as he progressed down the sidewalk on Lantern Lane, the simple music was so satisfying it seemed to suit his mood completely. As Evan passed a nearby oak, he gave several of its low-hanging leaves a high-five.

The boy looked down at the dog. Rocky didn't pull on the chain like he imagined all dogs did. He wasn't dragging Evan down the street, though looking at the dog's back muscles shifting with each step, he knew he easily could. Instead, they walked down the cement pavement side by side, like equals. Like perfect partners, much like the pair he imagined to be sitting on miniature stools in his opposite ears harmonizing as one.

The duo shared layers of '*ba-da-da-da-da-da-da's* that faded as the song concluded. Just minutes into this walk and Evan was sure that he accidentally shuffled upon the ideal soundtrack, that he wasn't willing to let pass. Before the song's tracking bar reached 0:00, he quickly scrolled through his albums. Passed *The Miseducation*, *Narrow Stairs*, and *Off the Wall*, straight to P*arsley, Sage, Rosemary & Thyme*. He hadn't spent lots of listening time with the album. It was among those added to his collection under a strong endorsement from his father. Though his dad was seldom right on most things, he was seldom wrong on musical recommendations. Unfamiliar with the tracks on the album, as "Feelin' Groovy" faded out, Evan again tapped "shuffle" as he turned the corner.

A chime dinged on his right, followed by twin melodies on opposing guitars. The song drifted like the stratus sheets in air, just as Evan approached the neighborhood "Pit."

This was a strange name for the place, for it was really multiple pits inverted, or as they're generally called, *hills*. Despite not having any cherries on the hills, these hills at The Pit were undoubtedly the most prominent in Cherry Hill.

Beneath the greenery, these mighty hills were converted landfills; mounds of trash that town children gathered to play atop on daily and older children fiddled around on nightly. As a stranger unknowing of the unseen dump, the large patch of rolling green amid the indistinguishable houses was a refreshing sight to behold.

At the center of The Pit was its highest hill. At the top of its highest hill, the silver skyline of the close-by City of Brotherly Love could be seen in the distance across the Delaware River. Long ago, Evan pretended these hills were mountains, the only ones he'd ever conquer. He hadn't been to the top in years. He looked down at the old dog and the old dog looked back with a strong stare that Evan imagined to say, *"What are we waiting for?"*

Evan started up the path as Rocky galloped ahead. As they climbed up the man-made hill, Evan envisioned pure ridges, deep in the distance. The duo in his ears shuffled on to their next song.

As Evan reached the top of the hill, it wasn't as he had expected. He anticipated the place as he'd remembered it—scattered with folks picnicking, tossing balls, staring off into the distance. Here, now, he stood alone. Only Evan. And Rocky, of course.

The well kept trail leading to the top deceived Evan

into believing the peak would be the same. Here, the green grass ceased to be green, taking on a sun-beaten yellow hue. Here, the grass ceased to be mowed. It grew at lengths reaching Evan's knees and Rocky's chin, giving the dog the appearance of swimming in a sea of weeds.

They walked passed a makeshift firepit surrounded by crushed PBR cans and empty cartons of cheap cigars. Bags and boxes of sweets and fast foods decorated this utmost layer. It was as though the top of this converted hill revolted, yearning to return to its days as a dump.

As Evan looked out west, the unfamiliarity continued. Maybe it was the grey sky blending in with the greyer skyscrapers, but it was hard to distinguish where the buildings stopped and the sky started. Evan thought these massive towers looked out of place, like they weren't meant to be. Like an assortment of silverware from different sets strangely stabbed into the soil.

He reminisced about his adolescent love for that city which he scarcely visited, and remembered wanting to work or live there one day. He was certain that over there existed a better life.

Now, he no longer related to any of those feelings. They didn't fit into the puzzling framework of what he wanted from his life.

He stared at the enlarged knives and facedown forks, now wondering what it was in particular that he wanted from his life. Looking out into the distance, he thought, if this were a cartoon fairy-tale, this would be the part where he'd exclaim to the world all his dreams, all his loftiest yearnings, and there'd be no doubt in the audience that one day he'd do it all.

But now, there'd be no such song.

Evan had no idea what he wanted.

Does it matter? he thought.

The boy sighed and mentally accosted himself for

being jaded at 17.

But he wanted something more. He wanted to want something…something to strive for.

But there was nothing.

He looked down at Rocky, as the dog looked off pensively himself.

"Let's go, boy."

During the trek home, Evan decided against the earbuds. The sky grew darker, its clouds teeming to unload their storm. Evan and the dog picked up their pace as the pines that lined the sidewalk rattled and swayed with the wind. Moving to the left, dipping to the right, it was though they danced to a music Evan couldn't hear.

In fact, there was a plethora of sounds Evan wasn't aware of. From the birds in full chirp about the severity of the impending storm, to the animalcule workers moving rapidly right beneath Evan's down-coming foot.

Or perhaps, he did hear something below, for just before his red PF's crushed down, Evan's eyes caught a glimpse of what appeared to be a puddle of oil or another slick black substance. Upon second glance, he realized that the black slime was ever so slightly moving. He crouched down to get a better look at the dark glob.

Crawling atop each other in every direction were hundreds, thousands of ants.

Evan gasped in equal parts disgust and wonder. He assumed there must have been bits of food or spilt drink that gathered them in this spot. Crouching still, Evan couldn't take his eyes off the little creatures. Each second he grew more amazed as he realized how many there were. *Incredible.*

For the first time on the walk, Rocky pulled ahead, either ready to go or ready to show him something else.

Evan walked onward, four square pavements forward when he saw a similar black spot. This one smaller, but still as he looked closer, more ants creeping and crawling abound. Evan looked back from where he stood and could still see the other ants in full. He wondered if these two colonies were actually part of the same group. Or if they even knew each other existed.

Four pavements to an ant could seem like four solar systems.

After a moment, he doubted they'd care or even think about such things, assuming of course that they could care or think about anything at all. Evan decided his thoughts on this subject were wasted. He mentally tossed them aside and moved on.

Four pavements ahead, he stopped again.

Crawling to the left, then in an instant to the right, indecisive, inebriated, or lost, walked a single ant.

At this sight, Evan felt a slight sadness within.

Four grand pavements away from any other ants, to this lonesome renegade, this was worlds away.

This ant, Evan was certain, was lost forever.

13

Evan turned on the TV.

"Aside from the numerous natural deaths caused by this severe drought," the news reporter said, standing against a desert landscape, somewhere on the opposite side of the Earth, "there have now been several killings at the clean water access point. Officials here are saying—"

Evan turned off the TV.

Rain pattered against the window. Through the light of the moon, Evan could see with clarity any of the single drops that poured down. His first thought went to his morning baseball game.

I hope it clears out in time. Either way the field will be disastrous. Errors await. He tried to toss the negativity aside as he set downstairs for dinner. He still hadn't had the opportunity to tell them he'd be starting tomorrow.

In the kitchen, the table was fully set, tortellini alfredo

on the table, Transces tucked into their seats, yet it still felt empty.

Each night, the family could count on a semantic debate between Caden and Grams that Evan always cringed through. Now, with only the sound of his own food gnawing in his ear and forks clanking against the plate, Evan missed the conversation. Amid the third or fourth delay in discussion, he thought it ripe to announce his big news.

"Sooo," Clementyne's big eyes turned to Evan intently. His mom looked up. The gentlemen continued scarfing their final bits.

"I'm starting tomorrow," Evan said.

The room responded with silence.

"Starting what?" his brother asked, face still toward the plate.

"I'm starting at shortstop…for the North Dragons."

The men looked up. Their eyes wide and faces blank.

"Against South."

Caden dropped his fork, sending it rattling against the ceramic plate.

"You're serious?!"

Though there was no debate Caden was the superior ballplayer in his high-school days, the opportunity to start at North never fell into place.

"Ev, that's great!" Clementyne said, eyebrows arched with a bulging smile.

Evan turned toward his mom who looked back at him emptily, like she hadn't heard the good news. With a shake of her head, she snapped out of it, sending her soft smile his way.

Evan turned to his dad. Surely he'd be thrilled. Instead his face looked frozen still. Stuck, stern, and serious, clearly unaffected by his son's news.

Tick-tick-tick.

Claudio's face remained statuesque, but words muttered out.

His voice was deadly.

"Perfect reason for you to be home by twelve."

"What?" Evan asked, bewildered.

Claudio looked at his son, rubbing his palms over his temple in what looked like an attempt to return life to his face. Again he spoke, this time in his normal, much-preferred lighthearted tone.

"It's just more reason for you to be home by midnight, that's all."

Evan's brow furrowed, further enhancing his look of confusion on the edge of anger. He shook his head, utterly lost.

Where to begin?

"First off, who said I was going out?"

"Look at yourself. You're all dolled up. All red everything," Caden chuckled, trying to steer the conversation toward joviality.

"Dolled up?" Evan harshly responded. "All red? I'm wearing two red things, thank you very much. What the hell are you even talking about?"

"Whoa, relax!" said Caden. "Brother, it's just that normally you'd be in your PJs by now."

Evan saw no humor in this, but his sister did. She softly laughed, and at this, there was no mistaking Evan's scowl.

Clementyne spoke, "What, Ev? He's got a point."

"What do you know?!" Evan shot back. "You don't even live here." He redirected his fury at his father. "And why? Why be home by midnight? I'd normally be home by then and you know it. Or you should know it anyway. Now all the sudden it's an issue? Where is this coming from? And why is this suddenly a concern?"

It was true. His parents were never those for strict guidelines and curfews, for truly there was very little need, especially with Evan. He stayed out of trouble and they knew all of his closest friends. It seemed this was coming straight from Evan's former position in Left

Field.

Evan could feel his bottom lip quiver and his cheeks flatten in preparation for the forthcoming tears. But the angriest part of Evan disgustedly shot those emotions away.

He looked back at his mom in hopes of gaining a clearer perspective on the situation. Completely uncharacteristic of Grace, she was unable to look her son in the eye. Her face looked on the verge of dropping tears, or rather after a week or so stuck in that position, it had permanently adopted its new shape.

"Mom, what's this all about? I don't get it."

Despite her battle to withhold her tears, she shed them once more. Her drooping eyes scanned Evan, searching for the right words to say.

"We just want you safe. That's all!"

She delivered the line more dramatically than Evan thought she could muster. Fitting with the theatrics, she stood at her seat, slamming in the chair and storming out of the kitchen in tears.

What the...? Evan's face was fully scrunched with his shoulders lifted and hands upturned. He mentally searched for reasons and explanations for all of this.

"I mean, it's raining pretty bad?"

Those remaining at the table had no words to say. They stared at their dishes blankly, Clementyne unable to force down another bite, the men wishing for more food to appear and distract them from whatever was going on.

"I'll drive safely?"

Still no words or eyes on him.

It was like he'd suddenly vanished.

Searching for a reaction, Evan made his stance public.

"At the end of the day, regardless of new, nonsensical rules, I'm gonna do what I want."

Their shocked eyes all shot at Evan.

Evan & the Land of Letin

He was still there.

14

Evan weighed the pros and cons of attending Heart Lee's. If he didn't go, he'd already be home, thus avoiding the possibility of being late. But he knew getting out of this house would be best for all parties.

Reluctantly, Evan strapped on his stretchy band Timex over his right wrist. It was a gift from his dad a few birthdays back. He'd only worn it a time or two, typically uninterested in the hour.

Every man must own a watch, his father told him. *Time is king.*

Evan trotted down the stairs, toward the exit, off without a formal goodbye, only a loud and sarcastic "See ya's!" before slamming the red door.

He drove out of Kingston and into Barclay, one of the finer neighborhoods in the township of Cherry Hill. Barclay was built amid what once was a forest full of tributaries. The neighborhood developers artfully designed it to give the homeowners the illusion of having miniature forests complete with little rivers unto themselves.

Though Evan had been to the Goodwin household a handful of times, he still had to keep his eyes peeled. The house hid in an unmarked cul-de-sac where a large pine blocked the court's solitary street light. Once in the circle, the log-sided house was nearly invisible among the forestation. Finally spotting it, Evan parked in the cul-de-sac's sole unoccupied spot.

With a light jog and his hood up, Evan approached the front door. With each step and its following splash, the music from indoors grew louder. Playing was Lil' Wayne's latest, a song that none of the kids inside rapping aloud to could realistically relate to, but Evan was sure they were indeed rapping aloud.

Evan reached the porch, where the roof's overhang

sufficiently protected him from the rain. He pulled down his hood and stretched his sleeve over his palm, rubbing the beads of water from the heart pin until he could see his own red reflection.

The wooden entrance door was wide open, but the secondary glass door was sealed. Evan scanned the faces of those already inside as they drank from red plastic cups. Each party attendee seemed dressed up in comparison to their daytime selves. The guys wore long-sleeved button-ups as the ladies bore dresses that they could only wear now, for these sheer tops and high-cut skirts were sure to break school dress code. Though Evan knew nearly everyone indoors by name, they were by no means his friends and certainly weren't folks he believed he had the proper stuff to small talk with all night.

Uggggh, Katie Dawson. Whhhhy?

Glenn Glover, star quarterback and daily d-bag.

Nikki Parson, constant peace-sign toter and continuous basher of all those below her on the popularity totem pole. Something about that Nikki and her peace signs really riled Evan up every time he saw her. *How can you badmouth everyone as you wear that? Do you even know what that's a symbol for?* Evan really let it disturb his inner-peace. *Ugh, she's wearing one now!* Evan glared as he saw the small peace-pieces dangling from her necklace. As she talked among a small group of girls, she pointed across the room. With a lean forward and a whisper, the girls giggled. Evan could almost feel the alfredo rising up his esophagus.

Before the glass door, Evan felt as though he were behind a window with a mirror on the opposite side. He imagined he were watching an entirely different species on the other side of the glass. He was at a futuristic zoo where the new ruling people studied the strange social habits of awkward teens. The more he watched, the less he wanted to walk through the glass door. One of his red shoes turned, as he'd decided he'd seen enough, but before the other foot could step back fully reversing him, there she was.

The urge to run away passed.

She smiled and her nose scrunched. While everyone else was dressed in their sharpest or skimpiest, she wore a loose-fitting white t-shirt with green block letterings with the word "WAKE" stacked upon the word "UP!" On her legs, faded black jeans, and on her feet, nothing. Her pink toes with their unpainted nails intermingled with the high-heels and fresh-out-the-box Air-Max's freely as she drew nearer to the door. The girl's single embellishment was a flower tucked behind her right ear. Against the dark, bark color of her hair, its purple petals looked like a firework frozen in time. Reaching the other side of the glass, Evan noticed dabs of black and yellow springing from the center of the flower. Without his grandfather's fervor for flora, Evan had no idea the flower was simply a poppy. But to his untrained eyes, it looked magical. Or perhaps that was just her.

She pushed forth the door and Evan slipped in. Heart's bare feet slapped against the soggy welcome mat as she slung her arms around Evan, squeezing.

"I'm so happy you're here," she said, still holding him. "Not that I'm surprised. I knew you'd come."

As she hugged him, Evan could feel the wetness of his hoodie seeping through to his skin. Surely she felt this too, but she didn't care. They un-embraced and Heart's eyes were immediately caught by the shining pin. Her eyes widened in delight as her mouth formed a circle, as faces tend to do upon seeing the most precious of things.

"I did not however, know that you'd actually wear this," Heart Lee said, as she cupped his face with both hands. Her brown eyes dug into his. "You're a special one."

She giggled. Heart Lee grabbed Evan's hand and guided him into her house. As he looked around it became abundantly clear he wasn't supposed to be wearing this pin. No one else was.

What an idiot, a thought assaulted him. He tried to ignore his belligerent thoughts, refusing to beat himself up over it. Heart Lee wouldn't allow it. Anyone else would have laughed at such a naive misunderstanding, but she did not. As she held his hand and led him through the party, he suddenly felt like the guest of honor.

She looked back as they walked, "Can I get you anything to—"

"E.T.!" a voice yelled from the packed dining room.

A pair of bulky bodies engulfed Evan, almost sending him to the ground. Trey and Zane picked up their carousel routine just where they left it in the courtyard. As the duo finally composed themselves, Evan anxiously asked if they'd performed yet.

"Nah, man." Trey said. "Not tonight."

"Yeah, you know. Technical difficulties." Zane added.

In the Chilluminati's year and a half of existence as the self-proclaimed Next Outkast, Evan had never seen them perform live. Come to think of it, he wasn't sure if he'd even heard a song yet.

"Oh, well. I was really looking forward to it."

"Next time, brother," Zane said, patting Evan on the back.

"They'll be no next time," Trey said, stone faced with a robotic voice. He froze before zipping his head toward Evan with a *dtzzz* sound he added as his neck turned. His unblinking eyes engaged in Evan's, like those of a droid. Finally, Trey cracked his blank face and broke into hysterical laughter.

Evan's mind's eye rolled. *Just Trey and Zane being Trey and Zane.* More times than not, Evan seriously doubted whether there was a method for their evident madness.

From behind the boys, up walked a bearded young man Evan didn't recognize. *He seems a tad too old for a high-school party.* As he neared, it seemed that the white of his

Evan & the Land of Letin

eyes had been dyed blood red. He threw his hands on the shoulders of Trey and Zane gently pushing their faces closer to his. With a smirk, he whispered as his eyes quickly rolled back and forth between the two. Evan couldn't hear a word over the loud music, but by the time the bearded man was done, Trey and Zane seemed to have adopted a similar sideways smirk. The man patted the boys on the back before turning to exit. Trey and Zane turned to do the same without acknowledging Evan. Well into their stride out of the room, the two simultaneously turned back excitedly.

"You want in, bro?" Trey asked.

"Yeah man, there's plenty." Zane added.

If the fiery eyes of the bearded young man was any indicator of possible side-effects that could come from whatever the boys were partaking, Evan was fairly certain he wanted no part of it.

"I'm good. Thanks though."

Suddenly alone in an empty room, Evan saw no choice but to venture into the kitchen where the party was at its peak. There, the only thing louder than the stereo's bass was the boys' yells as they'd sink a cup playing pong. Wall-to-wall was occupied with North's social elite. Evan exchanged pleasantries with classmates that he only knew through shared classes or stares at new profile pics. Upon the beer drenched and barley-stenched kitchen table laid a soiled list of upcoming opponents. Trey and Zane scratched their names in not once, twice, but three times, Evan counted.

Even if Evan had a partner, he wasn't going to waste a single iota of competitive energy on a pong game. Between the potted plants that sat on the window's ledge was a slither of space where only one of the petite cheerleaders could have sat.

Or Evan.

He hopped up. His feet dangled a foot above the ground as he took in the party's sights.

On the wall to his left, the boys lined up, red cups in hand, half of them cracking jokes while the others stood with brick faces determined to look tough. On the opposite wall, ladies giggled as they took group selfies and instantly uploaded them. Occasionally, following nudges from the boys and whispers from the girls, two of the opposite sex would meet mid-room entirely incidentally. Evan couldn't hear what was said over the music, but based upon the flaming cheeks and awkward giggles, he was positive there were some terrible pick-up lines being dispensed. Several of the "unplanned" meetings resulted in the newly formed couples exiting the kitchen to hoots and roars from the wall of forced manliness. Though only a foot off ground, Evan felt as if he had a bird's eye view of this roundabout dance between his peers. Here, as he watched, he felt he had no place in this choreography.

"Evan."

A faint voice called from behind him.

"Evan," he heard again.

He looked toward where the sound appeared to come.

At his back was the black night accompanied by a rain that forcefully beat down, showing no signs of stopping. Evan looked up at the sky. The moon hung high, but in its full form, it looked as if he could reach through the window and grasp it.

"Evan."

He thought that in its mighty splendor, perhaps the moon was able to speak. He stared at its craters and imagined rolling right down them. *Yes*, that's what he wanted to do, grab that moon, pull it down, and roll in its deepest crater. Sure, he knew this was an impossible thought, but that didn't make it any less appealing. Continuing to stare at the perfect grey marble in space that lit up the sky without a single flame, Evan smiled.

The boy stared so long, his eyes began to play tricks

Evan & the Land of Letin

on him. Ever so slightly, it seemed the moon's light would gently fade back and forth, right along with his breath. Like the moon had a heartbeat of its own.

"Evan!" the voice was soft no longer.

He turned, looking to his right. Behind a group of giggling girls was an archway leading into a dark room from which the voice came. Evan slid down from his ledge reluctantly.

He crept over to the doorway and looked into the darkness. No one, only music.

Very softly, he heard the *'la-la-la-la's'* of a song he recognized fading, and after a moment of silence, the strums on a guitar from a song he loved rose through the black room. Just as his heart anticipated, the light taps on the cymbal joined in. Then finally, a voice. A voice so perfect, it sounded as though it was siphoned straight from a block of Irish bluestone.

"Your favorite album," Heart Lee said.

That it was. *Moondance.* The reason she called him "Crazy Love", track number three. Their shared love and appreciation for the great Van Morrison was what originally bonded the pair and led to their friendship. They discussed their favorites over crowded lunch tables despite the handful of judgmental glances and remarks. She preferred *Astral Weeks*, so he timidly called her "Sweet Thing", track number three.

Deep in the corner of the room, Heart sat alone in an oversized chair. Next to her, a dimly lit standing lamp illuminated her face. Evan crossed the room, carefully avoiding the table on which the record spun.

"Have a seat," she said, patting her hand atop the leaf-patterned cushion. She was curled up in her chair, cradling her knees against her chin with one arm as the other held a wineglass with sparkling purple liquid within. She gently sipped as Evan sat down.

"Why are you hiding here?" he asked.

"You call it hiding, I call it saving my sanity. I'm

surprised you're not doing the same."

"Well, I would have been, but then you disappeared."

"You were having a blast with your buds."

"Yeah," he said sarcastically. "*A real blast.* They disappeared too."

"Aw, poor Evan. All alone. I honestly can't feel sorry for you. Abandoned in a room is preferable to mingling with this bunch."

He laughed. Evan couldn't disagree.

"Why did you even have this party?"

"This what?"

"This par—"

"Oh, this soiree, you mean?" she said seriously, "It's a necessary evil."

Evan wasn't following, "How's that?"

"This party—," she caught herself speaking lowly of her social gathering and jokingly covered her mouth as her eyes went wide. She scrunched her nose, then continued on the serious route. "This, it's just another part of politics. The part I hate. Where you have to pretend you're someone you're not to make good with your peers. Me, having this party, it's all bullshit. It's all a way for me to pretend I enjoy their company so I can steal their votes. Right now, I guess I'm not doing an exceptionally good job, just sitting here with you, a senior who won't have a vote. But still, just opening the doors of my house to them and their loud noises when I could be cuddled up in my bed with a book. Ugh, it's just a sad, but oh so necessary evil. Something maybe, someday I'll be able to change."

"I hear ya," he didn't have anything to add that Heart hadn't already thoroughly thought upon. "I don't know. *This*," he said, pointing between himself and Heart, then over to the record spinning atop the table, "isn't so bad."

She smiled and shook her head as she stared into

the boy's eyes.

"You're right. *This*," she mirrored his pointing gesture between the two, and over to Van, "is good. Honestly, Evan Transce, if I could have over one guest this evening it may just be you."

"Heart, that's not even true," he typically avoided saying her name in conversation. It felt odd coming out of his mouth. *Heart.* But it was still a lot easier than saying, Sweet Thing.

"Well, you didn't let me finish. After Harriet Tubman, the Lincolns, the Roosevelts, Dr. King, John Lennon, and uhh," she thought, "oh, Tupac Shakur *and* Hillary Rodham, *then* it'd be you."

"Nice, I'm so honored. Right on a list with a bunch of dead people."

"Hillary is not dead, nor will she ever be. And instead of focusing on the fact that they're deceased...*debatably*," she winked, "notice that they're all brilliant, earth-changing people in their own special ways."

"You're right," Evan smiled. "I'm very honored. And completely unworthy."

She looked at his one of a kind, purple-specked eyes and on her face was nothing. Not the slightest note of humor or a trace of forced on seriousness. Pure blankness. She spoke, "You are worthy."

Evan couldn't contain the instant laughter that exploded from his belly. "You're crazy."

Heart Lee returned no such laughter. Evan's eyes glanced over at the glass she was holding. Its purple content caught the light and dazzled. He stared at the tantalizing liquid and his curiosity climbed.

"What is that you're sipping on anyway?"

"Funny, Evan." she said, unamused. "For your information, I don't need any substance to think without limits, see things as they are, or say what it is I want to say. This is a pomegranate cleanse my mom and I concocted this morning. Would you like a sip? Or would you like to jump to any more conclusions?"

Never piss off Heart. "No, thanks."

"Good choice," she gracelessly spit some back into her glass. "It tastes awful."

Evan smiled and Heart Lee followed suit. The tiny gap of black between her two front teeth was a continuation of the space all around them.

A tiny snap and crackle traveled through the speakers as the needle rose and hovered across the vinyl, reaching its grooveless end.

"I think I'll have some water, though," Evan said.

Heart Lee quickly shifted in her seat.

"No, no. I'll get it."

"Okay. We don't have bottles. The sink is filtered and glasses are in the cabinet above the microwave."

Evan rose and walked across the dark room. As he was set to turn the corner, Evan looked back at the girl. The dimly lit lamp showed only her face in the corner of the room. Though unquestionably beautiful on the sunniest of days, she looked even more beautiful now. Yet, deep in the darkness, he thought, she looked distant, haunting. In the black, her wineglass caught a glimmer of the light, looking like a floating purple moon in space.

Through the blackness she spoke. "Evan, you're the crazy one...for not seeing what I see."

As all too often with Heart Lee, he wasn't precisely sure what she was talking about. He let out a lips-only smile before passing through to the kitchen, breaking their eye contact.

Returning to the ruckus, he quickly realized that quietly sitting with Heart was much more to his liking. He'd move as swiftly as possible, but this was much easier thought than done. The kitchen appeared to be the watering hole for the multitude of zoo animals that escaped from their cages. As Evan wiggled through the crowd, he noticed every other girl wore some sort of animal print. There was a zebra, even a giraffe, and about three or four leopard prints. These leopard ladies snuggled against the walls with the bulky guys wearing skin-tight tees adorned with intricately bedazzled snarling snakes. Among the grizzly guys was a teammate he would be starting alongside tomorrow at Third Base. Evan gave him a nod, which the boy purposely ignored. *Whoops, must not have seen me.* Evan converted his nod to a bob, trying to play it off with the music.

Finally, reaching the microwave, Evan tipped on his toes to reach the cabinet.

"Can you get me one too?" a voice squeaked from behind.

He reached further, grabbing another, then turned. Her darkly lined eyes looked directly into his as her side smile perked.

"Thanks," she said, lifting her strapless shoulder, grabbing the glass.

Every thought of Evan's fell silent. Over the blaring music, all he could hear was the sound of his blood trucking its way through his veins and the air circulating through his nostrils.

"Anytime," he said. *What a stupid thing to say.*

I know, right?

What else was I supposed to say?

Shut up. Shut. Up.

A moment of silence stirred, but she effortlessly snapped it. She extended her hand to Evan.

"My name is Jayla," her side smile blossomed to a full spread.

I know.

I've loved you forever.

Let's not lie.

You know I know your name.

SHUT UP! Breathe, Evan, breathe.

"I'm Evan. It's really nice to meet you."

He gently took her little hand. Her flesh was warm,

matching her red dress.

"Look!" she said with a giggle, pointing at their outfits. "We match."

Evan tittered, feeling his face joining their shared color.

"Have we met before?" Jayla asked, her sleek eyebrows furrowing convincingly. She glanced down momentarily, and when their eyes engaged, Evan could see through her bluff. The girl's sultry eyes seemed to secretly smirk themselves. Evan was even less convincing.

"Ah, you know, I think we have," he said with an air of fakeness he hoped she hadn't sensed. He put on his best thinking face, "Aren't you in Miss Popolo's class?"

"Oh, that's it!" she said.

"Oh man, isn't she the worst?"

"Oh my god. The worst of the worst," she laughed and leaned closer, apparently content on staying to chat. "Do you even know what's going on in that class? I'm so lost."

The backend of her sentences went up in pitch. Any other person and this would have instantly annoyed Evan. *But this was Jayla Hayes.* Anything she said, however she wanted to say it, was flawless to Evan. He did want to suggest that she stop texting in class and maybe she'd have a better idea of what was going on. But doing that would have totally blown his cover that they both were superbly pretending wasn't already blown.

"I'm honestly clueless, too." Evan said. "Math is not really my sharpest point."

Your sharpest point? What is your sharpest point? What are you talking about? Maybe it would be if you weren't staring at her.

"Samez."

Evan wasn't aware that the word buzzed at the end, but if that what was Jayla-ly acceptable, he'd work on it.

"School isn't really my sharp point at all," she said with a laugh. "But at least it's all behind us. Onto college!"

"What are your plans?" *Well played, sir. Perfect segue.*

"Well, I'm going to Rowan for teaching. El, oh, el. They've got a great program for it. Plus it's where my brother goes and he's the president of his fraternity. I should have no trouble making friends. How about you? Whad'ya got planned?"

"Uhh, *pffew.* Who knows?"

"You better figure it out, boy," she said jokingly. He appropriately nodded with a chuckle but his insides attacked him with truth. *Damn right you do, boy.*

"Wait, didn't you make the...*Peaceloving Dragons?*"

This question really caught him off guard. He didn't think anyone knew that, and even if they did, he didn't think they'd care. Especially Jayla Hayes.

"Yeah...I mean, the Peacekeeping Dragons, but yeah that's me."

"That is totally cool. Really good for you."

"It's not a big deal. It'd be even less of a deal if it weren't for Heart Lee."

Heart Lee. Ugh! I'm keeping her waiting.

Relax, she's fine. What could be more important than this?

"Wait, aren't you..." she paused as her eyes squinted, analyzing Evan. "Oh my God, I'm so sorry."

"What is it? Don't worry. Whatever it is, it's whatever. Say it."

Now he was wildly curious.

"You're the one who...I mean, your grandparents just...uh...passed in that fire?"

If the other question caught him off guard, this one was the equivalent of an entire house dropping on his head. It was so random, so irrelevant. It spurned forth a slew of emotions within, ones he couldn't let out now.

"I'm so sorry I brought that up. Jeez, I'm so stupid."

Evan giggled awkwardly, but her apology seemed to set the calm within. Talking about anything with Jayla Hayes would be fine.

"Can't ignore it forever." Evan said. "Gotta go on and live."

Her eyes narrowed as she shook her head. Once again, she looked as if she were reading the boy like he were a perplexing equation.

"Wow. That's really deep, Ev."

Ooh, I'm 'Ev' now? Nice. But actually it's not really deep. It's just the truth.

Before he could respond, she spoke once more. She seamlessly weaved through the conversation like a professional of social gatherings.

"We should hang sometime."

If his thoughts had jaws, they would have dropped open. *Oh my...*

"Yeah, definitely," said Evan. "That would be really cool."

"Well, what are you doing tomorrow? Actually scratch that, what are *we* doing tomorrow?"

Whoa, very forward. But I think I love it.

"Tomorrow," in his mind, he perused his schedule as if it were jam-packed. He had one thing penciled in, and that was it.

"Well, I've got a game tomorrow, but other than that, nothing."

"Perfect! Maybe I'll even come to the game. But at night, let's hang. What's your number?"

Is this really happening? This can't be real.

She handed over her phone, to which he typed his number. In sheer excitement and nervousness, Evan almost input his brother's number which was only one digit different. *That would have been a disaster.*

"Come on, Jay! We gotta go!"

It was peaceful Nikki Parson. *Of course she would ruin the fun.*

"Ah, I'm coming," Jayla yelled back. "Alright, I guess I gotta go."

She leaned over and gave Evan a close hug. She

held it even longer than Evan could have imagined in his haziest of fantasies. As her head leaned against his bony shoulder, she whispered in his ears, tickling the sensitive cilia, "Tomorrow, you're mine."

Jayla released the hug, giving the boy her effortlessly seductive smile complete with her staring sultry eyes. Their eyes stayed locked as she slowly stepped backward, disappearing among the collective of animal prints.

Evan stood still, frozen in shock. *Did that really just happen? It couldn't have.*

No way.

Yes way, Evan. That was real.

It was entirely real. Evan wanted to shout with glee but didn't want to seem crazy to the remaining guests. The party was by no means winding down, but he decided there was zero chance the night could get any better. Tomorrow, however, between the morning baseball game, and then his apparent date with Jayla Hayes, Evan was slated to have his best day in recent memory. Perhaps things were starting to turn around for Evan Transce.

He glanced at his watch. The tall hand approached its shorter counterpart as the time read 11:44. If he left now, he'd be home before the clock struck twelve after all. He partially wished he wouldn't be home on time, just to spite his parents for their unreasonable and uncharacteristic curfew, but he tossed his animosity aside. He was feeling way too good to let his own self-pride wrinkle this fantastic night.

One last time, he wiggled his way through the zoo of teenagers. While they didn't reek of manure or foul food, their excess of perfumes and body sprays were hardly any better. He held his breath until reaching the empty foyer. With his mind racing ahead of him, Evan rushed out of the house without saying goodbye to a single soul.

Still in her corner, Heart Lee looked out the front

window, seeing her friend exit. The teenaged part of her heart tore as she saw the sole boy she'd ever loved, leave without a proper goodbye. But a deeper, unspoken part of her, that was closer to Heart than any other, knew she'd never see Evan Transce on this plane again.

This same part of Heart wasn't feeling sad or anything truly definitive, rather this Heart knew Evan was about to unknowingly sail out, destined to discover and become all that she knew he already was.

15

The raindrops battered down as the wipers batted back and forth, deflecting them. Evan caught himself leaning over the steering wheel with squinted eyes, trying to get a better view of the road. He decided against turning on the radio while on the highway, but as he safely made a right-hand turn into his neighborhood, he could no longer resist the habit.

He turned it on just in time. The harmonica intro screamed through the speakers and Evan immediately cranked the volume up to full-blast. It was his favorite song by The Boss and his band. The piano keys began to dance, and soon, Bruce was singing for the lonely. If it weren't for the heavy downpour, Evan would have broken into a full one-man concert in the car. When the song suggested rolling down the window and letting the wind blow back his hair, he considered it.

The world beyond Evan's window suddenly blazed, lightning daggering against the earth. With the volume at max, Evan failed to hear the thunder. Without hearing the loud boom, he failed to see the irony in his current scene, or perhaps he chose not to.

Consumed by the song, Evan couldn't withhold his excitement. While he kept one hand on the wheel, the other played the part of Clarence's fingers on the sax.

A chirping noise joined the music that Evan hadn't

recalled being in the song. A rectangle of light flared on the passenger-side seat, and Evan recognized the sound as an incoming text.

He lunged over, grabbing the phone, ever so slightly shifting his vehicle in the process. The message was from an unsaved number.

> Heyyy. its Jayla ☺ I had lots of fun w u 2nite. can't wait to hang again 2morro <3

With his eyes still on his phone, he smiled…yet strangely, despite finally receiving the text he waited his whole high-school life for, something about it felt sour.

It wasn't as he hopefully anticipated. With his left hand on the wheel and the other on his phone contemplating a response, the sleek phone slipped, sliding down below the gas pedal.

Evan considered reaching down to get it. *I've gotta keep my eyes on the road.* The wet, slick road. He glanced over at the time.

It was midnight.

He'd be a few minutes late after all. His mind previewed images of him successfully snatching the phone without a flaw.

I can do it.

No, no, you can wait.

Evan looked out his side mirror, no one behind him. He looked at the rearview to double-check. *Coast clear.*

With a hand still on the wheel, he lowered his other arm below the dashboard, grabbing blindly toward the phone. He groped without success. Finally, without patience, he glanced down for a helping eye. It was an inch away from his grasp. He bent a bit further and felt the weight of the vehicle pull to the left. His heart raced and shifted with the car.

Finally, he snatched it, pulling his body upright, and shoving the phone into his cup holder where it'd be safe. His breathing sped while the E-Streeters powered on at full strength. Evan couldn't hear his thoughts. He turned the music off.

What am I doing?

He inhaled deeply. *I'm lucky.*

He decided a text could wait, he'd be home in a minute anyway. He looked out his side window, no one in sight. Once again, to double-check, he looked in the rearview mirror.

There, two eyes looked back at him.

They were not the nearly-black animal eyes that belonged to Evan.

The eyes that looked at him were blue, cold enough to pierce through him like icepicks.

He gasped, staring back in the eyes, fully captivated, fully horrified.

A loud horn blared before him, shifting his gaze.

Evan swerved to the right, missing the oncoming car by a fraction of a foot. His heart punched against his chest as though it might burst through his sternum, severing his skin.

Though only a block from 428, Evan pulled over. He turned off the car, the incessant drum of rain against the roof. He closed his eyes, leaning his head against the steering wheel.

What the hell was that? With his eyes closed, Evan could still see the piercing blue irises with clarity.

Evan was certain they were real, and even more certain they were not the eyes that belonged to him.

Evan sat with his eyes tightly sealed, unable to shake the feeling of the foreign eyes still watching him. He wanted to look back, but he couldn't.

Thunder filled the sky, shuttering the parked car. Evan opened his eyes in shock. Slowly, he swiveled his eyes back to the mirror where he anticipated the stranger's staring gaze.

Growing swiftly, two round beams of light made Evan wince.

The headlights of a car passed him on his left. No one was looking at him in the mirror. But he couldn't be sure they weren't still there.

He slowly unbuckled his seatbelt, and clenched both fists. Evan drew a deep breath that was a partial prayer to have whatever strength was needed to beat whoever hid in his backseat. He quickly swung his body around, leaning over the midsection with his fists raised. His eyes scanned every square inch of the car's backseat.

There was no one.

Alright, it's official. I've lost it.

His thoughts tried to coax him, assuring him it was all in his imagination. *It was nothing.* The thoughts that knew otherwise fell silent.

For the time being, Evan accepted the fact that it was indeed nothing. *It didn't happen.* It was all in his head. For Evan's sake, it had to be.

After a minute more in silence, he felt composed enough to finish the drive down Lantern Lane to his house.

Evan clicked off the headlights before turning into the driveway. The clock said 12:12. He was late, *but barely*. He was sure his parents wouldn't care.

He tiptoed the walkway toward the door, treading so lightly, he blended with the raindrops. Evan turned the knob on the unlocked red door, passing through the smallest slither that would allow him through. Slowly, the door sealed with only a creak. Evan sighed. He was in. He was safe.

Without a rattle, he lowered his keys to the foyer table then slipped off his Timex, placing it beside them. At the foot of the stairs was Rocky. The dog didn't bark alerting his arrival. Evan was grateful. He patted the dog on his boxy head and began to creep up the stairs, Rocky trotting behind him.

Upstairs, the light from his parents' bedroom escaped into the hallway. There was zero way to step around the fact that he was late. They knew, and apparently waited up for him. All Evan could do was accept his lateness for what it was and hope they did too.

Evan turned into his parents' doorway, only peeking his head through. At the far side of the bed, his dad laid fast asleep, mouth open, and body sprawled out. Across the wide gap in the center of the bed was his mother. She sat up, wrapped in her own comforter, reading a book. Her glasses sat at the tip of her nose so she could glance down to enjoy her novel without bending her neck. As her son appeared in the doorway, she was already peering over the top of her spectacles to meet his glance. She shut the book without a place-marker and set it on her nightstand.

"Hey, Ma. Just wanted to say goodnight."

"Goodnight, Evan."

He pulled out of the doorway swiftly. Nothing more than a goodnight was said. *This is good.* But as he stood outside the door, expecting to hear the click of the lamp switching off and concluding the night, he didn't.

"I know you know you're late," Grace said. Evan winced. He thought he was free. "I hope you didn't think that I didn't notice…or that I don't care."

"Yes, I do know. But I don't know why you do."

Initially, Evan thought that he had simply thought those words, not spoken them aloud. But they skipped passed the initial screening before shooting out of his mouth. Evan surprised himself, noticing how defensive and aggressive he sounded.

"You've got to be home by twelve from now on," his dad's groggy voice matched Evan's in hostility. "It's that simple."

A portion of him wanted to end it right then with a

simple, *"Sorry, it won't happen again,"* but a larger portion of Evan couldn't give in so easily. *Where is this coming from? How is it that simple?*

Speak out! Make your point. Go get 'em!

Evan reentered their room.

"Honestly, no. I don't get this at all. I'm home, I'm safe. I am sober. Nothing else should matter. And then you're saying *'from now on'*, what does that even mean? I'm supposed to be home by twelve every night? If you were awake, you would know that I normally am."

Evan could feel his heart rate picking up and his face turned red as flame. The veins beside his temples pumped full of blood as he clenched his jaw momentarily. Evan was picking up some steam and saw no sense in stopping.

"This one night, I went out. For the first time in a while. And I needed it. And you know what? I had fun. For the first time in a while. I needed that. I would have been home exactly on time but the weather was rough, and…" he paused, he couldn't explain what else caused a delay, nor did he want to. He wanted to forget about those eyes in the mirror as quickly as possible. He saw them again in his mind. The icy blue stare stirred shivers on his flesh. Evan shut his eyes and shook his head, trying to rid himself of the image. *It was so real.*

It wasn't real. Just like the fire.

*It **was** real.*

Just like the fire.

Evan was on the verge of tears but he didn't want to cry. His chin quivered as he tried to resist the urge.

"Sometimes I won't be home by midnight on the dot. But you shouldn't care. I *won't* care. I'm seventeen and it's insane that all the sudden you're gonna start with this curfew. Like I did something wrong in the first place. It's ridiculous, and I can't believe I'm even having this conversation right now. This is the last thing I need. I'm done. I'm going to bed. Goodnight."

A single tear slipped through his facial barricade and Evan flicked it away, disgusted. He exited the bedroom and entered the bathroom to brush his teeth. He scanned the basin for any creeping creatures. It was clear. He turned the valve and lowered his head into the sink, splashing water against his face.

"Evan," his mom said. "Can you *please* come out of there? I need to talk to you."

He rolled his eyes in frustration.

"Mom, I'm over this. Can't it wait 'til tomorrow?"

"No, Evan," she quickly responded. Strangely, he heard a hint of what he detected to be fear in her voice.

Evan looked at the mirror, at his frustrated face with water dripping from his furrowed brows. The beautiful boy's anger had him looking as close to ugly as he could. He yearned for sleep and an end to this day.

He opened the mirror's medicine cabinet to grab his toothbrush. When he shut the cabinet, returning to the mirror, the face...the face that looked back was not his.

The eyes that struck his were not his.

Again...they were icy blue.

Without a thought, Evan clenched his right fist and slung it between the blue eyes.

The mirror shattered, falling before he could make out any definitive detail about the face to which the eyes belonged. The pieces of glass rained down around him, breaking into smaller pieces as they crashed against the water bowl and counter. From outside the door, Rocky let out a howl that bellowed throughout the house, unlike one he had ever heard from the dog before.

"Evan! Evan!"

His mom pushed the door open without a knock, sending it swinging against the wall with a slam. Evan stood frozen, staring at the mess around him.

He felt a cold drip down his fingertips. He looked at his fist. Small shards of the shattered mirror stuck in his skin surrounded by a healthy flow of blood. He didn't feel the sting until he saw his wounds.

Though Evan could hear his mother's cries beside him, she felt distant. He could feel the stares of his family now gathered in the hallway, but they felt faraway.

Analyzing his hand, he saw five jagged fragments sticking from his skin. Two on his knuckles that pierced on contact and three on the top of his hand that most likely fell there when the mirror shattered.

Fragment by fragment, he picked them out. Evan tried to silence his brain that cried out in distress as he removed the shards. Each one hurt more than the last, each one seemed deeper than the last, each one caused more blood to flow, until nearly his entire right hand was covered in blood.

"Stop!" his mother cried.

"Run some cold water over it," his father suggested.

"What's happening?" his sister asked.

"What the hell is going on?" his brother added.

"Everyone shut up!" Evan screamed.

He looked at the faces that all looked back at his in horror. His mom couldn't cease her cries. His dad's face was blank and white, drained of its blood. Caden looked angry and confused while Clementyne's big eyes looked glazed and concerned.

"Just leave me alone," Evan said softly, coldly.

He wanted to cry, feeling one hundredfold the confusion, anger, and fear they were feeling. Evan had to cry, but not here. He had to get away. With blood still dripping, he ran from the bathroom, passed the packed hallway, and down the steps. He heard his father call him back, but he ignored him. Evan walked across the living room toward the glass backdoor. He saw the night continue its rainstorm and he wanted to join in. He opened the door and stepped out, but before he could shut it, he heard his mom yell.

"Evan," he paused and listened. "I love you!"

I love you, he thought, but lacked the power to say the words. He pulled the door shut and began to cry.

Evan stood against the glass door, just beneath the overhang of the roof. The rain pounded down just before his eyes, yet not a drop crossed over to where he stood. The roof created an invisible barrier that appeared to work wonders. Regardless, his face couldn't avoid dampening, for the tears were in full flow. They poured heavily like the rain, but unlike the loud downpour, he remained silent. There, standing next to 428, the only house he ever considered to be a home, his face was set stern and solemn, resisting the fact that he was crying.

A gust of wind broke the invisible wall of Evan's sanctuary. The rain mixed with his tears, the cold gust nearly freezing his wet face. He turned away, back toward the blue house. He lowered the brim of his red hat, just above his brows, and flipped his hood overtop for extra warmth.

With his face toward the house, he realized the backdoor was cracked open.

Weird, he thought, *I swear I closed it.* He pulled it shut, clicking it back in place. It was certainly shut this time.

"Meow."

Evan blinked in an attempt to defog his eyes. He peered passed the cold air cloud caused by his breath and into the misty yard, in the direction in which the sound seemed to come.

"Meow."

He surveyed the yard again, this time more thoroughly. Between the elements and his emotions, life was barely visible.

But in the middle of the very soggy yard floated two small spheres reflecting the light off the full moon back to him. Beneath the dark floating marbles, a black hole gaped open and sounded into the night, *"Meow."*

Damn it. That Monster.

All Evan could see of the grey cat was its fluorescent eyes staring at him, daring Evan to come into the heavy rain and catch him.

No, he thought. *I'm not going out there. That cat means nothing to me.*

The cat was far from being a family member. He'd been there for only a week since his sister brought him home, and in that week did nothing but lay in Evan's way. He'd shoot his cat eyes at Evan disgustedly, like the boy should be honored to be in the feline's presence. Evan wanted to let him go, let him find his way back to his original home. But he couldn't. His sister was convinced this cat was special. A sign from their grandparents. Evan deemed this insane, but even in his anger couldn't leave the cat be.

Smooch, smooch, smooch. His lips kissed the foggy air in the direction of the cat in a sorry attempt to lure him back.

"Come on, Monster," he said in a cutesy voice set aside for speaking to infants. "Come here."

Monster gazed back mockingly, turning his head away, offended.

"What am I doing?" Evan asked aloud.

What cat comes to a smooch? Very few, and Monster certainly wasn't among the exception.

The shovel-shaped necklace shifted across his chest just beneath his grey shirt as Evan exhaled deeply. He was venturing beyond the invisible barrier of safety. He lifted his right foot from the dry pavement and stepped into the soaked grass with a plop. He felt the wet soil slush beneath his foot. Quickly, Evan stepped forth with his left foot and *mush*. His foot sunk into an unseen puddle. The dirty rainwater instantly seeped through his canvas PF Flyers, soaking his sock.

The wet sock instantly demoralized Evan, sinking his spirits, as soggy socks tend to do, especially to an already emotionally muddled teenage boy. Evan tried to gather his messy thoughts. He had to grab this monstrous wet cat and get back inside immediately. He'd sort everything out with his parents as soon as he got in, simply so he could sleep in peace. Of course, he also had to tend to the blood and rain drenched wounds dripping down his fingers.

Evan picked up the pace, slogging through the backyard, subconsciously praying he didn't step in any of Rocky's slop. The cat crouched precisely still, not but a few steps away from the fast-approaching boy, unaffected by him or the rainfall.

Evan bent down to snatch the monster. It scrammed. With three impressive jumps, it launched itself ahead, below the backyard tree, next to the surrounding pond.

Evan's patience was gone. He sprinted ahead to catch the nimble cat, his hood falling back in the process. As he reached the cat, it lunged across the small pond with incredible ease. Evan's eyes widened in surprise.

The cat clawed at his grandfather's precious tree, pulling itself up on all fours and climbing up the smooth bark. Moving so fast, so effortlessly, it scaled the bark as naturally as a squirrel. As the creature ascended, spiraling up the tree, circling the intertwining limps tantalizingly, it almost seemed as if he were taunting the boy. Its grey tail looked like a snake as it twitched and twirled around the trunk. From above, the tail flicked and flaunted its owner's mastery, tempting the timid boy to come to him and surely fail.

Even if Evan could climb the tree as easily, he wouldn't have. If the cat could get up there so simply, he could surely get down just as well. Plus, strangely, beneath the thick purplish foliage, not a single droplet slipped through the cracks. The cat was safe, Evan decided.

Evan looked down at the pond. Unlike the puddles

behind him, it was still and undisturbed. In the pond was his reflection. His thick brows looked angrier than ever, the whites of his eyes matched the red of his new cap as they begged for sleep. The soft skin beneath his eyes wilted in exhaustion. He was beat, too spent for his subconscious to formulate a single thought.

Evan glanced from his body, to the moon. In the watery mirror, he could see it in all its splendor. So bright, it lit up the whole night without help from artificial lights. With the circle centered behind Evan's head, his reflection resembled an oil on canvas of one far holier than he.

Evan's eyes were playing tricks on him again. The radiance from the floating rock was no longer gentle and white, but vibrant and purple. A purple that wasn't quite purple, but his mind could only classify it as such.

He blinked and rubbed his eyes with the back of his hand, clearing his pupils of tears and rain, but the color did not alter. The sphere remained a glowing, invigorating purple. It inspired him, entranced him, he couldn't look away. But a glow underneath the sphere then caught his eye.

In the reflection, where his bony body adorned in black and grey and capped off with red should have been, it wasn't. Instead stood a beautiful woman in white who stared at Evan Transce.

She wore a simple dress that hung elegantly from her slim figure. Where her dress ended and her skin was revealed was indeterminable, for both were a glowing white. The only bit of darkness on the woman was that of her black hair. Her hair was without braids or any design. It hung straight behind her back to where it was no longer visible. Crowning her head were glistening flowers that could have been grown from glass.

Her features, like her dress, were simple yet naturally alluring. Her cheekbones were strong and prominent, supporting her wide eyes.

If it weren't for those eyes, Evan would've said she was the most beautiful human he'd ever seen, but those eyes weren't quite human. They were slightly oversized, perfectly fit to display their beauty. Though her eyes disqualified her from being the most beautiful human, they instead made her the most beautiful being he'd ever seen.

Her face wore a gentle smile that curled her lips.

She looked kind, yet without question, powerful.

Slowly, the lady behind the water began to move. She raised her hand to her hips and gracefully upturned her palm. With her eyes looking into his, and this subtle gesture, she invited Evan to join her.

Without a thought floating through his mind, the boy stood in peace.

Without a thought or bodily effort, he began to lean forward.

Without the desire to resist, Evan fully tipped and fell, splashing into the still water.

MOVEMENT 2
Evan & (What Remains of) the Heartland

♥

Evan sealed his eyes and clenched every miniscule muscle in his body in preparation for the splash then probable crash against the shallow ground. He expected the cold water to flood his clothes and uncomfortably hug his flesh, but oddly (aside from in his already soggy sock), he felt no such sensation. His mouth was shut, packed with a bubble of air in cheek, ready to hold his breath below the surface until his body begged to be pulled upward. At the very least, he thought he should've felt cold as the soil-ridden water slid across his face, but he barely felt a chill.

Evan opened his mouth to inhale, yet no water rushed in. To his surprise, only air.

The air that he took in was heavy, scraping against his airways, instantly causing a violent cough. The subtle taste of smoke circulated his mouth, a horrid taste he readily knew. Evan opened his eyes, terribly confused.

There was only a minimal change in the darkness. It appeared as though he had awakened in the middle of the night. The bit of moonlight that creaked through the blinds revealed only the outline of life.

But there were no blinds, for he wasn't in his bedroom. *I'm outside*, he recalled. The full moon must have been shielded by the grey overcast.

Evan turned to his left, tracing the outlines of thin trees. He squinted, trying to force nocturnal abilities upon his eyes without success. Through his blurred vision, the trees appeared frail and leafless. His eyes scanned his surroundings, searching for light, growing increasingly confused.

I just fell into a pond of water, he thought…*yet there was no splash.* As his thoughts voiced in loud number their many concerns, he realized that he currently laid face-up, upon a hard, solid surface.

Evan nervously placed his hands against the ground to push himself up, and instinctively pulled them back.

The slick ground upon which he was sitting was freezing. *It couldn't be.*

He pressed the backside of his wounded hand against the ground once more. It was what his mind denied.

With the slices on his hand against the ice, the chill soothed the pain. He began to circle the backside of his hand against the frozen water, converting his gashes from stinging to comfortably numb.

His mind raced, trying to make sense of his current insensible situation. The fastest logical explanation he came to was barely logical at all, *but it had to be.* To Evan, there could be no other explanation.

Amid the darkness and his jumbled emotions, he must have failed to realize that the pond had frozen over. *Yes, that's it.* And upon the hard contact, he must have lost consciousness. *Yeah, definitely.*

Of course he didn't remember losing consciousness, but he'd never blacked-out before, so this was probably standard. *Oh, for sure.*

In his sleep, he must have rolled onto his back, and now here he was. He didn't care to figure out why his head and face weren't throbbing from the fall against the ice, but this was what happened. He was certain.

Now he just had to ease himself up, and take a few steps toward the grassy land.

Carefully, he began to stand, nearly slipping back on his bottom. When he was steadily upright, Evan wearily began to shuffle across the black ice. He made an effort not to lift his feet, in fear of stepping too hard and cracking the frost. But there wasn't the slightest fracture. The ice was strong and sturdy.

As he shuffled further, about three slides, an inkling

of worry began to swell in his head. *I should really be on land by now*. He kept shuffling.

And shuffling.

After eight shuffles ahead without reaching his backyard, the inkling of worry was now inflated into full-fledged fear. His grandfather's backyard pond was barely a pond—it was a small moat around his treasured tree. Now it felt as if he was shuffling across the ice on a full-sized pond, perhaps even a lake.

Where am I?

Before Evan's full-fledged fear developed into an uncontrollable panic, the ribbed rubber tip of his wet PF Flyers hit the ground. He stepped on the hard earth and regained a bit of his composure.

Evan looked toward his house, where the backdoor light was typically turned on, but it was off. He thought his mom would have stormed outside to stop her son from getting soaked in the rain. Certainly if she didn't come out instantly, after a while she would have ventured out to look for him. At the very least she would have left the light on to welcome him in when he decided to return.

But she didn't. It was off. It seemed she was more hurt than Evan realized.

His brother would surely still be awake. Even if hours had passed, he'd spend the lightless morning with his room illuminated via video-games or delving into a book before sunrise. He peered to where the light of the TV should be flickering out the window, but it wasn't.

Evan cleared his eyes and blinked vigorously in an attempt at a clearer view, but it was useless. He did not have to be a bat or a wombat to see that there were no windows for the lights to shine through, nor were there walls on which windows could be cut through. He took a step forward to where he thought his home should be, but only dead trees surrounded him, filling the space where the house numbered 428 on Lantern Lane was supposed to be.

Evan wasn't in his backyard.

The blue house with the red front door was gone.

Fear sucked the clean air from him, leaving Evan breathless. His spine sank on the verge of dropping to his knees until a moderately comforting thought plummeted forth with a plausible explanation.

This is just a dream, he thought. *It has to be.*

Pop! A sizzling bang exploded behind Evan. He hunched, shielding his head from the loud sound.

Evan equated the sound with the pops Trey and Zane caused by squeezing their Dorito bags in the lunchroom. But this pop was far louder, like the sound from a bag large enough to fit a small hill.

Evan turned in the direction of the sound, still covering his head in protection. *Pop! Pop!* Two more bursts sounded, followed by dozens more descending in volume. Evan's pointer-fingers plugged his ears until the sound subsided.

As he listened, he heard a soft crackling among a constant sizzling that filled the air. Though Evan couldn't see, he accurately assumed it was coming from the ice he'd just walked across. It sounded as though the surface was breaking apart all at once.

The boy bent down and stroked his hand toward the melting ice. His hand, unexpectedly, was met with warm water. He circled his hand in the water searching for remnants of ice. There were none.

The solid ice had cracked and melted in a matter of seconds. There wasn't a drastic change in the temperature, and even if there were, ice didn't melt in an instant. This confirmed Evan's suspicions—*this is a dream.*

He didn't know how to interpret this dream he was having, but he'd concern himself with that once he awoke. Evan remembered learning about this type of dream in Mr. Herman's class. These were called 'lucid dreams', in which everything felt completely real and the dreamer could control their actions.

Still, there remained a handful of questions. Before Evan could attempt to answer any of them, a startling light blazed in the darkness.

A flash of orange filled his surroundings for a mere second, but in that moment, enough light was provided to confirm Evan was standing in a decaying forest. Though it was only a moment, it was enough to see these trees weren't typical. They didn't stand upright, thrusting toward the sky, rather they twirled and bent in every direction, some swirling, some jagged, all in their own unorthodox pose.

Now was not the time for Evan to ponder the oddities of the trees, for whatever or whomever that light came from left painful results. Nearby in the woods, an agonized yell that bordered on a lion-like roar echoed through the lonely forest.

With his eyes fixed on the source of the light and the scream, Evan couldn't be certain in the dark, but it seemed a very large bird was rising to the sky.

From a distance, the bird appeared larger than an eagle or even a vulture. Evan peered hopelessly, praying for his eyes to adapt. Through the shades of dark greys, he could see the bird begin to shift direction, heading toward him.

Though Evan could barely see, the bristling of the thin trees and the increasingly loud sound of flapping wings assured him it was coming his way.

Evan turned, and as mindfully as he could, blindly began to run. He kept one arm fully extended, serving as a bumper between the trees, as the other arm was bent, shielding his face from swooping branches. Unaware of the terrain, he moved considerably slower than his full swift speed.

The flapping grew louder, and louder, until it sounded to be just above his head. Evan could feel the wind from the wings propelling down upon him.

He couldn't outrun it. It was useless. But this was a dream. If the great bird were dangerous, it would force his body to wake up. Evan folded upon the ground and curled up in fetal position, clenching his body from what the beast may do. His thoughts begged and pleaded, *Wake up, wake up, wake up!*

Evan did not wake up, but the beastly bird continued passed him, thrashing its colossal wings far ahead and high above the treetops. Somehow, it neither saw the boy, or if it had, it didn't care about him. The massive, winged-creature was gone.

With his eyes closed and his body burrowed, Evan slowly tried to gather his thoughts. He could barely hear them over the resounding thump-thump-thumping of blood-flow through his temples.

There was no doubting this was a dream, but it still left a bounty of questions swirling across his brain.

There was the simple, *Where am I?*

What was that flash?

Who roared in pain? What roared in pain?

What kind of bird was that?

Why couldn't I wake up? Why can't I wake up?

In his memory, Evan recalled often waking himself up from nightmares before things went too downhill. He wondered why he couldn't force himself awake as the beastly bird flew above him. *Maybe I can*, he thought. *Maybe I just need a little more focus.*

With his eyes shut, Evan tried to visualize his last waking memory, but strangely, it felt blurred and distant, as though it happened ages ago. He couldn't remember, perhaps just a side-effect of the dream.

Wake up, he thought. *Wake up!*

He opened his eyes, but nothing changed. He was still asleep, deep within this dreadful dreamland he deemed he unconsciously created.

Evan yawned, rubbing his eyes with a clenched fist. *Why am I still so tired?* This was certainly a new sensation. He had never heard of anyone being tired while dreaming.

I'm asleep, in a world of imagination. I should have unlimited energy. I should be able to do anything...

But he couldn't do anything. He barely had the power to lift himself from the ground. Lying there, Evan felt as if he could fall asleep.

Fall asleep in a dream, that's a strange concept. Maybe, he thought, *if I fall asleep in this dream, I awake in real-life?*

He was fairly aware that this thought was a product of his lack of sleep and was mildly out-there, but now as he lay in this unknown dark forest, maybe it wasn't so crazy. There on the rocky, branch riddled ground, Evan began to doze off...

An injured wail echoed through the woods, vibrating the frail trees.

The howl sounded from the direction of the previous roar. Uncomfortably close.

Evan didn't feel safe. He pulled himself up, resting his hand against a nearby tree for support.

He decided he was going to get as far away from the beast as possible, maybe even out of the forest, preferably somewhere with lights. Hopefully, he'd awake before he reached his undetermined destination. Either way, Evan felt it wisest to move.

The white soles of his red shoes crunched against fallen twigs as he began to walk. After nudging into several trees, Evan snatched a branch to serve as a walking-stick. Blindly, he felt around, attempting to determine a match for his size. Evan tossed away the first appropriately sized stick, for its top felt like a wooden hand frozen in place. He soon settled upon a thin branch that reached his stomach and was curved at the top, resembling a carved cane. He held it pointed in front of

Evan & the Land of Letin

him, hovering back and forth across the ground, clacking as it made contact with its wooden brethren.

Evan coughed a hefty, wheezing cough that circulated around the trees and across the forest. The air around him felt thick and dirty, almost painful to breathe in, leaving an acute sting as he exhaled. If there were a choice in such matters, he'd prefer not to inhale it.

Drudging on, with each sluggish step, the boy grew more tired. He couldn't recall losing consciousness, but there was a faint image evasively floating around in his mind from before the fall that he felt may provide some answers.

Evan had no idea how far he'd walked, but his legs were already cramping up. *Coach would be ashamed*, he thought.

His next thought couldn't remember coach's name. Or what he was the coach of…

With his legs getting heavier, and his airways revolting against the smoky air flowing through them, Evan halted. He figured he was now far enough away from the wailing beast, so he leaned against a nearby tree.

Here, in the darkness, he heard the most terrifying sound…

Nothing.

Across this forest that should be overwhelmed with sounds of creatures calling and critters scampering, there was nothing. The breeze should be heard and magnified by the accompaniment of ruffling leaves, but there were no leaves. The trees were leafless. *This place is lifeless.*

Evan believed that such profound silence could only be caused by one of two things—the first being the absence of life to begin with, but the uncountable amount of dead trees instantly destroyed that theory. If anything, they served the second theory.

Evan thought, *Something very sad happened here.*
Something very bad.

The silence consumed him, raising the hairs aback his neck with a passing shiver.

Evan coughed again, this time more violently, this time with more pain. Whatever he was breathing in, he was certain had a play in whatever happened to the life that should be around him.

Evan decided it was pointless to imagine the apocalyptic situation around him, for this world wasn't a real one. *Right? This is all make-believe.*

He turned and glanced over his shoulder. Evan couldn't see or hear anything. The absence of light and sound made him increasingly uneasy. Nothing about this quiet place felt calming. He needed to get out of this forest. Onward he continued to walk.

Evan trekked up short hills, his legs throbbing, then down them, his legs numb and weightless. Tapping oncoming trees, the walking-stick led the way with as much clarity on the direction and progression as Evan.

No streams ceaselessly flowing were heard, nor the late night caws of the nocturnal. Only the patter of Evan's steps against the ground, intermixed with the occasional crunch upon a crusted leaf.

Step after step, he soon lost track of time. Evan felt he'd walked miles in a matter of minutes. Or perhaps it was the contrary. Maybe he'd walked a few feet and it'd been hours. In the darkness that verged on becoming blackness, the concepts of time and distance seemed distant and untraceable.

Evan squinted. Ahead appeared to be the faintest of lights, if it could be called that at all. Rather, it appeared to be a place where the black setting turned into a dark, dark grey one. He slowly approached until he reached a place where his eyes could process the images before him.

Evan stood atop a hill. Below him, amid the forest, sat a wide circular clearing. From here, he could see the vastness of the woods. Across the clearing, as well as all

Evan & the Land of Letin

around him, the dead woods continued for acres beyond what the boy could calculate with a clear mind on a sunny day.

In the center of the defoliated area stood a tower. From the top of the hill, the tip of this structure peaked at his eye level. The thin tower appeared to be wider at its top and slimmer at its base, like an upturned cola bottle or a flipped bowling pin.

High above the building, Evan saw the source of the dim light.

In the center of the sky floated an enormous white cloud. Evan tried to determine whether this cloud was the sole cloud in the black and starless sky, or was it the only pristine and pure puff in the air surrounded by a sea of black, smog-riddled haze.

Either way, this cloud looked enchanting, powerful. This cloud escaped or survived whatever hellacious things happened below.

Evan's eyes once again scanned the flipped-bottle tower. Cautiously, he stepped down the side of the hill to get a better view. As he moved on, he became more impressed. It was no illusion. The tower did become noticeably larger as it reached the sky. Nothing about it made sense, *it's impossible*. But knowing it was impossible, yet seeing it before him stirred wonder and excitement in Evan, emotions nearly impossible in this bleak and decayed woodland.

Evan stepped ahead, wanting a better look.

"Turn back. Now," a voice whispered.

The voice was so soft Evan almost mistook it for one of his own thoughts. But it wasn't his thought. It spoke in fragments, its tone was much gentler than his, like that of a young boy or a woman.

Softly, as if to match the voice's volume, Evan spoke. "Hello?"

"Do not. Speak," the meek voice answered. "Leave. Now."

The voice sounded sincere and certain of its words. Evan didn't respond, instead he slowly backtracked up the hill. He turned, lowering his stick to the ground for guidance. But with a misstep, he lost his footing.

Evan slipped down the hill, quickly tumbling out of control. With agonized groans and a resounding thump, he reached the bottom with a crack as his walking-stick snapped.

The fallen boy looked up at the tower and his heart froze mid-beat in fear.

From the side of the structure sprang the shadow of a wall-scaling figure. The man, as its outline suggested, peered out at the land, his torso in air with his legs and one arm pressed tightly against the tower.

Unsatisfied with its vantage point, the man sprung up the side of the oddly shaped tower, scaling the sides not like a man at all, rather like a spider-man or spider-monkey. The figure moved weightlessly, running on all fours like a greyhound racing vertically up the wall, showing zero trace of being effected by gravity.

As it reached the tower's wide top, it crawled quickly with its arms to the ground in support. Reaching the tower's center, it stood. With its spine straight, it was as tall as any man, maybe taller. Though its features were black and its eyes undetectable, Evan knew it stared in his direction.

"Do not. Move," the soft voice said.

Evan's eyes looked back at the figure, hoping its unseen eyes didn't catch his. Suddenly, flipping from behind the outline, a shadowed tail twirled into sight. Its ears stood upraised at the top of its head, like a wolf's on alert. From behind the shadowed beast came crawling another amalgamated animal, then another, and another, matching the first's look of search set on slay.

The four mysterious figures stood tall and terrifying, not ceasing their shaded stares in his direction. Evan laid perfectly still and silent, cognizant not to raise his chest in breathing.

Their dusky faces examined the darkness where Evan hid.

The seconds felt like an eternity to the boy. Finally, one crawled away, then two in the opposite side, until only the first remained, still staring, still sure that he'd heard something in the dark. At last, he too resistantly resigned, back peddling into the night until his outline faded.

"Wait," the voice said.

Evan did not dare to question the voice, aloud or even in his mind. He was already certain that it had better knowledge of his current situation than he did. Evan laid scared and silent for what he mentally labeled several minutes. The shadowy figures did not reappear.

"Crawl away. Now."

Without a thought spared, Evan obeyed. He turned onto his belly then snaked across the hard surface, using his forearms to drag his weight. As he reached the hill, he stood and began to run up the slope, a lot less gracefully than the beast on the tower.

Reaching the peak, Evan ran behind the nearest tree, squatting down in exhaustion and relief. He rested his back against the parched bark, craving water himself, but thankful to be from the view of the tower.

"What were those?" Evan asked. He was unsure whether he'd get a response, yet felt sane speaking to the darkness.

Without delay, the gentle voice dutifully answered, "Her creatures. Her creations."

Evan wasn't fond of this answer, for it incited a handful of other questions in his head.

"Who is *she*?" Evan whispered.

"She is. Most powerful. In this land. Or any other."

It spoke softly, slowly, like the concepts behind the words were taxing to the speaker's mind. After a pause, the voice continued, "She is the Witch. Of these Woods.

Of Wardrake."

"The who of what?"

"Who she is," the voice answered. "Does not matter. What she will do. Does."

Evan imagined the worst of what the words could mean.

"She will kill you. As she has. The rest."

The fragmented talk of witches and death muddled Evan's mind. He didn't know where to begin in attempting to make sense of it, so he mentally set it aside.

"Who are you?" Evan asked.

He received no answer. Evan knew the voice hadn't just vanished. He asked again, "Who *are* you?"

"Too big. To answer. Too small."

Unsatisfied with this response, Evan rephrased the question, "What is your name?"

"Can not laugh. If could. Would."

Can't laugh. If I could, I would. The soft voice's strange way of phrasing began to make sense to Evan, yet he still couldn't comprehend what was meant by the words.

"Too big," the voice said, "Too..." it paused, "Philo. Sophical?"

It asked in a way of a young child using a newly learned word for the first time.

Evan wanted to know who, or what, and certainly where this voice was coming from, but then it questioned him.

"Who are *you*?" the voice asked.

"I am Evan," he answered without a second of thought.

"Not your name. Who you are," the gentle voice replied.

This time, Evan knew what was meant, and tried to grasp his thoughts around it.

Who am I? He asked himself. *I...I...* Evan didn't know where to begin.

"Too philosophical." Evan replied.

Evan & the Land of Letin

There was silence.

"I'm hoping if you could laugh, you would?"

"Yes," the voice replied. "Laughing inside."

For the first time in the darkness, Evan smiled. He touched his face, half startled by the strange sensation. He began to like this gentle little voice. Sure, he couldn't see who or what it was coming from, but it was company, preferable over the hundreds already in his head.

It occurred to Evan that this voice also resonated from his head. If it wasn't already inside, it was as if it spoke directly into his ear. The thought brought an uncomfortable tingling sensation through his right ear. He plunged his pointer into his ear, soothing his anxiety.

"You are here," the voice said. It sounded louder, and spoke as if not directly to Evan, but out to the blackened earth and sky. "The time is now."

"The time for what?" Evan asked.

"To…" the voice paused, "Sleep. You must sleep. Ahead. You have a long. Journey."

Something in Evan's mind told him tomorrow was a big day for him, but for what reasons he couldn't pinpoint. Regardless, sleep did sound incredibly appealing.

"Ahead sits a ditch. Twenty steps. Your size. Ideal. For your body. Full of leaves. Watch out. Few carcasses."

"A ditch?" Evan asked, disturbed and disgusted.

"You are not. In Helvendah. Not yet. No sleeping. On air. You are in the," the voice paused to breathe, "Final living. Forest. As you may. Have noticed. It is. Barely breathing. You sleep where. You can."

Evan wasn't going to argue with a voice that sounded so certain. Though quiet, it was also strong and knowing. After all, this voice had already directed him from whatever dangers crawl across that tower. Evan stepped forward. So many questions swirled and swelled in his mind.

"What is Helv...endah?" Evan spoke slowly in an attempt to pronounce this strange new word properly. He missed the accent on the end, nonetheless, Evan's shapeless escort understood.

"It is where. We shall go. It is where. They await you," said the voice. "Look up."

Through the curved and awkwardly bent branches, the only thing Evan saw was the pure white cloud. Through the outline of the twigs, the cloud resembled a severely splintered porcelain platter floating far away in the sky.

"Up there. Atop the sole. Clean cloud. Sits the Kingdom. Of Helvendah. The first. Great city. The final. Great city. Forced to leave. To survive. Now they plot," it paused. "To revive. Our earth."

A kingdom, a city in the sky? Left to survive whatever devastation occurred here? Evan tried to process the relayed information. With each passing moment, it all made less sense.

"This is a crazy dream," Evan said.

"No time. For dreams. Only reality. Now."

The words skimmed the still surface within Evan he barely knew existed. At first, these words soothed him. In the next breath, the words flared panic, sparking at truths he wasn't yet willing to accept.

Evan progressed deeper into the woods, toward the told ditch.

"You never did tell me your name," said Evan.

There was a palpable silence in the dead woods, so vast, it was as though the two exchanging voices were all that existed.

"I am nameless," the voice said. "I am. Only blessed. With this chance. To guide you. On this special," he searched for another word. "Saving mission."

Evan was beginning to feel a bit of pressure. Like he was expected here and expected to do something great—

something he was fairly certain he could not do.

Finally, he reached the ditch, and his inner worry subsided, for at the sight of this leafy bed, he reminded himself it would all be over when he awoke.

"There will. Be plenty. Of time. To discuss. The matters of. The Heartland. On our trek. But for now. Sleep," the voice said, slipping into silence, blending in with the night.

Despite inner-warning against lack of comfort and cleanliness, Evan stepped into the slight furrow. A strange odor of decay engrossed his nostrils, yet sadly, he could say with clarity that it was no worse than the lingering scent of the stinging air all around the woods.

Evan pulled his black hood over his face to best protect from any insects and rodents he imagined might also be taking refuge in this trench. While every thought told him this was disgusting, he tried his hardest to quiet them. All he could whisper within was, *It's just a dream. It's fine.*

As Evan shifted his body over the crackling leaves, he could feel how desperately his body needed sleep. He was devastatingly tired, which was such a strange sensation for one believed to be asleep. Despite his state of sleepiness, Evan couldn't silence a single thought.

What if this is real? a thought whispered to another, as if not to panic the others with its growing suspicion.

Insane, another commandingly shot the notion down.

This is a dream.

I hope…

When you fall asleep, you'll awake. Right at home.

The thought of home confused Evan, as he couldn't quite picture the place in his mind. But the concept remained intact. *A place of comfort and security, with family.*

Evan tried to imagine his family. He obviously knew he had one, yet their faces…their names, seemed blurred and hard to grasp. This scared Evan until more thoughts talked him down.

Surely this is because I'm so tired.

What about all that stuff that little voice said?

Well, if this is a dream—which it is—all that stuff must have come from your mind, I mean, our mind. That being said, I don't know what it was talking about. We can at least give us credit for being creative dreamers.

Why would anyone dream up this hellhole?

At that, a new thought plunged forth from the depths of his mind, a thought that terrified him, a thought that he at once resisted. *Could this be hell?...am I de——?*

No way. Don't get me started. Would you just relax so we can go to bed?

He needed sleep and he needed to silence his thoughts. Something was missing.

Evan reached into his pocket and pulled out his phone. He slid his finger across the screen to unlock it, then with a tap opened up the music on the device. He glanced at the upper right corner to gauge the remaining battery life.

3%. Enough to play a single song, if that.

He ignored the whispers wondering why he had a dying phone in his dream, at this point, he couldn't ponder that. There was no time to scroll through and select the best song for the situation, each moment wasted was a second less of music the phone would be able to muster out. He tapped the intertwining arrows signaling "shuffle."

A soft piano chord resonated through the previously soundless space with ease, as if the miniature speakers were a grand piano live in concert. On the screen appeared the profile of a girl from the nose up. Half the screen was black, shadowing across her face making her features mostly unseeable. What could be seen was one of her eyes, darkly lined, and closed, with her brown bangs lined above them. The piano intro continued, its sounds dark and longing, blending in with the dead woods and its lonesome traveler precisely.

The pace of the chords went faster, yet remained somber. The volume grew and grew, rising to the lifeless twig branches that swayed with the song. If the boy weren't so tired he would have been concerned of waking what could be sleeping in the night, but as it were, with a few heavy taps on the keys, his consciousness was already drifting into the darkness.

The song's lyrics evoked distinct images from the past.

Fogged pictures in the back of Evan's mind became clearer. He saw a bland brick building that reminded him of confinement. He saw a road lined with blooming pink flowers filling the trees and planting seeds of hope in what he called his heart.

The singer's sultry sound sent him closer toward sleep, tempting to steal the memories as quickly as she brought them.

Evan saw his family.

His brother, nose in a book, escaping.

His sister, hard at work, escaping.

He saw his father, staring into space, escaping.

He saw his mother, crying on her bed, unable to escape.

They seemed distant, yet real, just beyond his heavy eyelids. Something in Evan's consciousness told him they'd never be tangible again.

The singer belted, as if pleading and preaching to the vast universe with her pocket-sized vocal chords.

Oddly, however, in Evan's last waking moments, her words became foreign, impossible to understand. Nevertheless, the untouchable notes she cried into the night stunned Evan, prodding him fully asleep.

The insurmountable silence returned, louder and larger than before...

Evan's phone died.

The music was gone.

A tear dripped over his nose from his closed and

sleeping eyes.

✳

Staring at the flame, his face flickered in and out of the darkness.

The first sun would be rising soon and he'd yet to get a wink of sleep. He was beat and dejected, but his mind was still buzzing. He was so close to completing his latest and longest task. It was within his grasp until it smashed and shattered away.

So close, he thought, *but still universes away.*

Ironically, as he stood at the heart of the heart, he felt as though he were being watched. But he also knew this was impossible. This dark, domed room was windowless, deep in his highest tower, sealed with the tightest security measures his bright mind could muster. He was fairly sure no one even knew this room existed, but he supposed, paranoia came with the territory. He'd never let anyone see this room, not a single soul. *They'd never understand.*

But he understood, and in his mind, that's all that mattered.

He'd sacrificed so much, but this world had taken so much more. Even when he reached the land of promise that his parents spoke of long ago, it wouldn't make up for all he'd lost.

He could bear to lose no more.

So he saw no choice but to fight on. Work hard in secret, deep into the night. Flash his smile and choose the right words for his people during the day.

Now, the idea of a forced smile sickened him. Her little smile flashed and dazzled in his mind, stinging every inch of his sad soul. If his eyes hadn't told him otherwise, he'd swear at that moment, his heart broke into uncountable, unrecognizable pieces.

He'd lost all the ones he loved the most. His father

first, and most recently his mother. His brother started this whole mess, and his lover, she'd been gone for a few lifetimes. Still, the one that hurt the most, the one that sliced through the slit in his empty chest daily was his princess.

As the fire danced against his pupils, beneath his icy iris, a pearl of water rose.

He wiped the tear away in disgust.

♥

Evan opened his eyes, and in the pervading blackness, felt like they were still closed. It was overwhelmingly dark, yet he felt totally refreshed, reinvigorated, as if he had a full night's sleep.

Hours had surely passed. It must've been morning, maybe even afternoon with the way he felt. Oddly though, not a single ray escaped through the barrage of leaves held up by the backyard tree. There was no purple cast through the translucent leaves either. In fact, there was no sunshine or sun to shine anywhere.

There was no bed, no bedroom, no backyard tree. There were plenty of trees, twisted and bending in decay toward the ground, but they weren't in his backyard.

A panicked Evan leaned up and a pain jolted through his back. He had spent the night atop a makeshift mattress compiled of crunchy leaves. He threw his arms over the top of the trench and pulled himself up to the ground. As he pulled his legs over the side, his foot hit something, sending a faint *ding* vibrating through the woods.

Evan crouched toward the source of the sound, reaching out to feel. He sat, legs folded, and picked the item up to inspect it. Running his fingers over the curved, hollowed, topless item, Evan didn't need a speck of light to determine that it was a bowl. He thrust his hand inside to feel its content. His fingers ran across cool, fat berries that Evan instantly assumed to be grapes.

They were plumped to perfection; he could already taste their juice in his mouth. His stomach grumbled. Evan wasn't typically a breakfast person, but through the time spent walking and a full night of sleep, he'd worked up quite the appetite.

He threw one of the grapes between his teeth and gnawed down. The juice exploded in his mouth and Evan was startled. They were not grapes. The juice was sweeter and was sprinkled with soft seeds that almost felt like cooked rice on his tongue. Without much thought, Evan chewed and swallowed down.

Wow, he thought. They were better than grapes. They were better than any fruit the boy had ever tasted. Their juice was sugary, yet not overly so, simply natural and hydrating. The seeds Evan likened to rice were savory, with all the flavor of a sautéed steak packed into little bites. Evan reached into the bowl and popped another into his mouth. Then another, and another.

He couldn't stop. He hadn't realized how hungry he was. In addition, they were just so delicious. Even if his belly were stuffed to the brim, he would have probably gorged on them until they were gone.

And that's just what he did.

As Evan finished, he let out a contented belch with the empty bowl resting upon his folded lap. In the silence, he took in his surroundings. With the help of a good night's sleep and a satisfied stomach, Evan was ready to admit some realizations.

"This isn't a dream," he said aloud, fully thinking he'd only thought it in his head.

What it was, he was far from sure, but he knew this wasn't a dream.

Every sensation was too real to be his imagination. There was this unstretchable kink in his back, the pain from which he fully felt. There were these same clothes

Evan & the Land of Letin

as the day before. Evan could feel the hat hugging his scalp and smell the stench stemming from his unwashed, spent-the-night-in-a-dingy-ditch garments.

He wiped his hands against his favorite jeans, trying to remove the berry residue. As his fingers ran atop his front-pockets, he remembered. *I should still have my phone…*

Evan plunged his hand in his pockets. *Empty.* He stood up, reaching in his rear pockets. *Empty.* As quickly as Evan realized an out to this current mess, just as swiftly, it was gone.

The boy panicked.

Jumping back in the ditch, the leaves crunched as he stomped. Blindly swiping his hands, swimming through the pond of dead foliage. He threw the leaves aside, up in the air, beside him, desperately feeling for his phone, his port way to home. Finally, his fingers tapped on something hard, he lunged at it with both hands.

His little glass phone—his rectangular savior. Evan cradled it with both hands, like a great treasure. He tapped on the home-button…but there was no response.

That's okay, that's okay. Musta turned it off.

Evan pressed strongly on the power button.

Upon the screen, no sleek once-bitten apple appeared like he'd hoped. Only a barren battery flashing a portion of red, begging to be charged.

No, he thought. *No.* Evan pressed again, not accepting the result. Then again, until finally not even the dying battery appeared. Only a black and empty screen barely reflecting a glimpse of Evan back to himself, looking as wretched as he felt.

He dropped the phone to his lap and his head to his hands.

This was no dream or nightmare. It was much worse than that.

This was Evan's reality.

He needed to figure out where he was, for phoning

home was no longer an option. Despite the hours of sleep, '*home*' still felt like a shrouded vision from far back in the past.

A vibrant red door opened and closed in his mind, its brass knocker clinking, echoing in his head.

No further images of a house or the family that occupied it came into his mind. Evan was worried, afraid, for despite concentrating upon the thought of his family, he couldn't draw forth their faces or names.

The slightest portion of Evan began to doubt there was a place called home to go back to.

So, instead of going back, he thought, *I must move on...*
Deeper into the black and empty labyrinth.

Evan tried to recall the happenings of the night before. These memories came back with ease. He could hear the injured howl in his head, he could feel the wind from the flapping wings against the back of his neck, he could see the upturned tower and those men that crawled like monkeys. He silently thanked the universe, or the blackness, that he sat here now, safe from the many harms he came so close to. It was then, Evan remembered the voice.

It was gentle and kind, soft and sweet, yet wise and authoritative. But there was no one, not a single person he could detect in the darkness.

"Hello?" Evan quietly called out. "Hello?"

No response. He tried to recall the voice's given name. *What was it?*

"Nameless? Nameless? It's me, Evan, from last night. Are you there?"

Through the shadows, the voice he searched for spoke.

"Here...here," the little voice said, sounding groggy. "If your guide. Could groan. He would."

"Did I wake you?" Evan asked, speaking out into the night that ought to be day.

"Yes. No worries. Your guide. Awoke early.

Gathered. Those mannberries."

Evan snickered. "Mannberries?"

"The essential. Fruit. That lay. In that bowl. You are welcome."

"You got those. How?" Evan wondered how a bodiless voice could have harvested the berries and placed them in a bowl. Perhaps, after all, the voice did come from a body…one that hid and watched him. Both notions bothered him, making his skin crawl, until he relaxed, remembering this voice was helping him. This voice was his friend.

"They were delicious," Evan said.

"They are. Also crucial. For survival. Your guide managed. To grab. Just enough. For the. Whole journey."

Evan could feel the lonely content of his stomach begin to topple and churn.

"Is there something. Wrong?" the voice asked. Through the darkness, the voice managed to detect the blank and worried face upon Evan.

"Enough for the whole journey?" he asked with a gulp.

"Oh Blessed Eight. You ate them all. Didn't you? You ate them all."

Evan's stomach began to shake. With this sensation, Evan realized that stuffing his face probably wasn't the best idea.

"That was supposed. To be enough. For the. Entire trek. Not to mention." *Of course there had to be a 'not to mention.'* "The seeds. Of the. Mannberries. Swell in one's. Stomach. A bite fills. Your guide. For days. For you. They expand. Fill you. For hours."

Now, as his stomach was overly packed, grinding and grumbling, the mannberries wanted out.

Evan quickly stood, just in time to vomit, splashing against a nearby tree.

"Lovely," the voice said.

It wasn't over. Evan could feel his bottom quivering. He clenched to prevent soiling his sole pair of pants.

He sprinted behind the tree covered in the mannberry juices, unbuttoned and slid the jeans down. Bent at the knees, he leaned back against the dry bark of the trees and just let it flow.

"Oh glorious," the voice interjected.

"Can you not watch me, please?" Evan said in pained agitation.

"Sorry sir. Just doing. My job."

Evan continued until comfort returned to his again empty stomach.

"There are. Dry leaves. By your feet. Good for wi—"

"I know what they're good for," Evan cut him off. "Thanks."

The boy walked a safe distance away from his bodily fluids before sitting down and resting against another tree. He wiped under his chin with the backside of his hand where an ounce of his berry-drool remained.

From this spot in the wasted woods, a gap in the twisted branches allowed for the white, heavenly cloud to be seen. He wasn't sure it was reflecting light, for there was no light to reflect, rather it appeared to glow, gently illuminating the bleak picture before his eyes.

The forest seemed to go on forever. He stared into the darkness at the dead trees. To Evan, with the way they twisted and turned, they looked like the scattered bones of slain giants stuck in the ground. A blackened rib jabbing out *there*, fingers bents and grabbing in desperation *there*. The sight, the stinging, and the increasingly heavy smell around Evan made him sick.

"Where are we?" the boy asked.

"Your guide told you. Last night. Specifically. The Woods. Of Wardrake. Broadly. The Heartland. Even broader. The Final Earth."

The voice paused.

"That is. As far as. Your guide's mind. Can go."

"I'm from Earth," Evan said, mentally questioning the statement. "I think…"

"We all are. Not necess. Sarily. The same one."

Evan inwardly began to test different theories. The thought of slipping through a hidden time-warp was mildly exciting, until he realized that this dark and dying land was all that remained. But it was possible, he thought, at this point, anything was possible.

The voice from outside Evan's head directed his way through the desolate forest, avoiding the withering trees and hidden bunkers where he assumed water had once flowed. Though the voice insisted they were taking the fastest exit route, wilting tree, after dying tree, after dead tree, it quickly felt like an eternity.

Each step more trying than the last, each step as useful as two steps backward. Just as Evan felt ready for the forest's curling trees to close over him until he passed in a peaceful surrender, they reached the end of the woods.

No longer were there trees blocking the sight of the perfect cloud or its glow. Though it was no sun, the faint light was still powerful. It felt as though Evan had been locked in a dingy house and had finally been set free unto a dark and dreary day. This little light was still enough to substantially lift the boy's spirits.

Despite now being able to marginally see, there was still not much to look at. The stiff trees lined up beside Evan as far as the cloud's glow allowed him to see.

Before him the view was even less enthralling. There was nothing. No buildings of any sort, and save a few renegade trees that had also met their demise, no vegetation. Only an endless black field of blank space.

In Evan's memory he recalled sprawling fields, but those were green and overflowing with opportunity. He remembered the urge to run full speed across those spaces, letting the wind wail in his ears until he collapsed, out of breath, laughing.

This field induced the opposite sensation. There was no green, only uncountable shades of dark grey that threatened on becoming black. Not only did Evan not want to run through it, he didn't want to walk through it either. The space looked less inviting than the one behind him. Those woods, he realized, *they were dying*. The void ahead, this was long dead. He didn't want to take one step forward, fairly certain that he'd reach the same fate.

Ahead and above, the cloud was the only thing to see. Evan recalled what the voice said about a city in the sky. True or not, something about the oversized cloud sparked hope. It was the only thing still beaming with life surrounded by the dark space. Evan could be that, he thought. *I'll be my own spark.*

This grounded spark tried to see the positives of his situation. Aside from the fact that this cloud and whatever was supposedly atop it was in the air, the path ahead looked clear of obstructions and probably passable. While Evan couldn't see terribly far, and the cloud only provided a minimal light, he wasn't terribly wrong.

"We are on. What once was. One of many. Roads to. Helvendah," the voice said as Evan listened. "Not that it. Matters. Roads are. For people. And their. Supposed structure. No more people. No need. To follow. Roundabout paths.

"Soon we will stray. From the road. It twists and turns. Once showed. The beautiful. Scenery. No more beauty. No more. Scenery.

"We take. The true path. The path of. Nature."

For Evan, the trek felt terribly long and insanely mundane, as you might imagine a straight journey without an ounce of animate life might be. He walked on, unsure whether minutes passed or hours on hours. In Evan's head, minutes and hours blended into one and the same, a new concept to the boy which was strangely both comforting and unsettling.

Between sporadic conversations with the guiding voice, all Evan had to entertain himself and remain sane were his thoughts, which he wasn't sure were really keeping him sane. As thoughts do, they wandered and wondered and worked together trying to figure out an explanation for their current whereabouts. Evan tried not to intervene, perhaps too tired or just curious, and simply listened.

That's Heaven, a thought said with conviction, as Evan looked up at the impeccable nebulous.

Making this hell?

No, no silly. This is purgatory.

That's preposterous, said a thought full of reason.

It's possible, said another, more open to alternate explanations.

His thoughts swirled and swooped as the boy just listened.

The concept of purgatory was absent in Evan's mind for quite a long while, yet he couldn't decipher why it was a notion that he'd managed to hold on to while others slipped from his brain's grasps. Perhaps the idea of purgatory frightened Evan back in his early school days at Saint...*Saint*...he couldn't remember the name of his old school.

As he walked across the dark and lonely field, a blurred and sepia toned image of a teacher popped into his head. He faintly saw life from a smaller Evan's perspective, sitting at his desk. He recalled the teacher facilitating a conversation and debate about the existence of purgatory to a class full of what Evan calculated to be fourth graders.

"You mean, if I'm a saint, I still need to wait to get into Heaven?" questioned another student's annoyed voice, hiding far back in his memory.

Younger Evan could sense the unease and fear flooding the room until in penetrated him as well. But then he decided it couldn't be that bad.

The boy envisioned a massive white waiting room, full of comfortable seats. No, they weren't quite seats, rather they were La-Z-Boy thrones. White leather ones, of course. There were rows of flat screens upon the wall, one for every deceased waiting on their judgment. But these were no ordinary televisions, they showed whatever the viewer desired, interspersed with personalized encouraging messages from God.

A silver-bearded giant clad in white robes spoke with a smile, *"Hang in there, Ev. Remember, the fruit of the spirit is love, joy, peace, patience, and a few other things—but patience! Be patient and eternal light is yours. See ya soon!"*

"Now, back to your previously desired program," an angelic voice said.

"No, Luke," the deep voice of the man masked in black said, *"I am your father."*

"Noooooooo!" wailed the young man clinging to the metal pole.

After the long wait, probably just enough the make it through the original trilogy (and maybe the prequels if things got desperate), he'd have his long awaited one-on-one sit down with the Big Guy. Impossibly, he'd look even better than he did on the TV.

Together they'd watch a low-light reel on Evan's most sinful moments. He'd explain how he was sorry he occasionally cursed, fought with his brother, and sometimes explored his own body when that "Genie in a Bottle" music video came on. *I didn't know what was going on down there.*

And of course, his Holy Father would understand. Then, with a pat on the back, they'd watch the highlight film of all his greatest moments, like when he shared his snack with the snackless at recess, and once told that unfortunate looking girl in class he liked her new glasses even when he didn't mean it.

God would then punch a hole in a magically

appearing golden ticket, and off he'd go, escorted by angels and saints down the white carpet atop the clouds, through the pearly gates to everlasting peace and riches.

Evan could handle purgatory in exchange for the Promised Land above.

A part of Evan was semi-starting to buy into that maybe, *just maybe*, this was purgatory. Sure, it wasn't as he'd imagined, but his hopes were from the mind of a pure-hearted optimist. He grew up, life changed, and now he had to accept that this barren dark land was bleak reality.

The rest of Evan still wasn't believing it.

This side repeated the intricate point, that in order to wait in purgatory, *if there was such a place*, they were quick to emphasize, *you would have to be dead. You are not dead…yet.*

This was a very valid point, Evan thought. He couldn't remember dying, so he was fairly sure that he was still alive and relatively well. He didn't think often about the afterlife, but now as he got older, he didn't believe if there were an afterlife it would occur in this same bloody body. He also didn't think he'd awake suddenly with magically working wings either.

He hardly knew what to think or believe, but being as he could still feel his heart beating on time, still hear the onslaught of incessant thoughts in his head, he knew he was still alive. This hellish place was no afterlife.

I'm not dead, he thought as his empty stomach weighed him down and his skinny legs felt heavier and heavier with each step. *But I will be soon.*

Shut up. You can't think like that.

Oh, you know I'm right. At this rate I won't make it to see my, he tried to trace which year was next…*18ᵗʰ birthday?*

Evan couldn't remember whether the next was his eighteenth or whether he was already eighteen. He didn't know whether this was another forgotten piece of his past, a side-effect of being in this dark land, or whether this was just a product of him not caring. He'd failed to keep track of his birthday for years now. He hardly considered it a birthday at all.

Evan greyly envisioned the last time he woke up on his birthday brimming with hope, excitement, and wonder. He couldn't recall how old he'd turned that day, or what year it was, and now eerily, he couldn't even remember the exact date. But he did, however, remember the moment his birthday no longer was just his birthday. Rather, it was more significantly, the day he learned how sad and twisted our worlds could be. The day his innocence went up in smoke and he began to question all goodness and godness in existence.

He saw his teacher flick on the TV. Half of his classmate's jaws dropped while the others covered their mouths his shock and horror. A plane daggered into the side of the tall silver building as its brother flamed and billowed smoke. People jumped and fell from the tall towers until finally the building did the same, tumbling and crumbling upon themselves. Clouds of debris rose, swelling across the cityscape until finally, his teacher thought it prudent to turn off the TV.

The screen went blank but none of the children's minds did. A powerless television couldn't reverse what was seen or what had happened. Nothing could. And like so many others, nothing could uncloud Evan's mind from the monstrosities he'd seen and now had to comprehend. Nothing could recapture the purity Evan awoke to on that sunny September morning.

With each step, the boy's body ached more than he previously thought possible. His skin tightened against his ribs, his stomach completely barren. His heart slushed instead of rapidly pumping, while his throat instinctively swallowed the bit of spit that remained. The toxic air that entered his nose felt like it directly penetrated his brain, making his entire head feel on the cusp of caving in.

Without a word of consent from the guiding voice, Evan plopped his body on the ground. The surface was harsh, covered with crushed rocks. In normal circumstances this would have been one of the least comfortable places to park one's body, but since circumstances were far from normal, the rocky ground felt as pleasant as a feather-stuffed mattress to a fatigued Evan.

"What are. You doing?" the voice returned. "No time to rest."

"No choice but to rest," Evan said in winded spurts. "My body is done."

"You are what. My people. Would call," the voice paused, "Lazy. We work and walk. Until our backs. Break. We work until. We are done. We work for. Each other."

"Unlike you," Evan responded. "I'm not looking to die. I'm looking for some shelter. Some food. And some sleep. It doesn't look like I'm getting all three right now, but I can do my best to get the latter."

"So be it. Much is. To be learned. About you. Perhaps. Hope in you. Has been misplaced. See you. In the morning. For a more. Productive day."

Hope in me misplaced? I'd say. What hope are you talking about? Hope for what? All of these things Evan wanted to sling back, but the majority of his being wasn't up for a yelling match with a bodiless voice in the darkness. With its character assessment on Evan complete, the voice was again gone, vanishing into the silence.

"Hello?" said Evan, whispering into the blurred night. "Hello?"

Nothing.

A sudden breeze brushed against the dead bark of a nearby tree. A screeching creak echoed through the endless night.

The boy looked at the tree, alone and as starved of hope as he.

As tired as Evan was, he couldn't fall asleep so easily. He needed the nightly distraction from his restless mind. He reached for his phone, sadly remembering this device could no longer miraculously make phone calls and play music on demand.

He shut his eyes, fluctuation in the darkness was minimal. His thoughts fired nonstop, filling his brain. Evan opened his eyes as his mind began to get the best of him.

Lurking in the murky shades of grey were the spider-monkey-men, creeping on all fours directly toward the curled up boy. Swooping just above his head was the giant-winged bird—this time it wouldn't miss him. This time it'd plunge upon him, pecking and gnawing until all that remained were eyes attached to a drooping brain so he could still process and feel it all.

Like a child who'd just watched his older brother's favorite scary movie right before bed, Evan yearned for a night light to set his mind to rest.

The wind pushed beneath the brim of his cap, chilling his skin. The hoodie and t-shirt were hardly enough to protect him from the slightest of winds. Evan closed his eyes and consciously dreamed of the perfect remedy in his cold state—*a fire.*

It would provide just the right amount of light to lead him safe through the night and keep him warm in sleep. Of course, Evan hadn't the slightest notion how to create a small fire.

Strangely, something in the back of his mind felt foul, disgusted, and irreverent for wanting a fire. He didn't know why, *fire*, he thought, seemed a natural longing considering his circumstance. But Evan's thoughts

Evan & the Land of Letin

whispered uneasily about the prospect of flames.

Despite these confusing feelings, Evan thought (or so he thought to have thought, but actually said aloud softly...)

"I wish for a fire."

With eyes sealed, aiming toward sleep, Evan began to envision a fire. A faint orange glow came to the center of his mind's eye. It was soft and feeble, but as it gently flickered, it naturally soothed the boy. As it gently flickered, the back of his eyelids slowly fluctuated between dark and glow, like the flame was actually on the other side of his closed eyes. Oddly, as Evan inhaled, his nostrils flared, detecting smoke in the air.

I can almost feel the heat. The warmth traveled through his arms, legs, around his entire body, until he became alarmed, opening his eyes.

Before Evan, a small ball of flames twisted and turned in air, floating a foot or so above the ground, burning and churning against itself.

Startled, the boy pushed his body back, away from the flame.

Evan stared at the fire and felt as if the fire stared back.

It was steady, serene, and seductive, as if every precise movement of its flares was choreographed. It was tame and vigil, like its sole duty was to comfort and protect the boy at this present moment. Despite logic and reason in the face of something unexplainable, Evan felt safe. The parts in his mind that had shunned the idea of fire fell silent, perhaps already deep asleep or scared into submission.

Evan wanted to join his sleeping thoughts. As the flame watched him, he watched back, amazed and grateful for its presence until finally, his eyelids grew too heavy.

Evan was off to sleep, out of the darkness, and into a land of dreams that he wouldn't remember in the morning.

♥

The boy awoke to a darker morning than the night he slept through. His friend the fire was gone.

"Blessed morning. Searched for mannberries. Zero in sight. We must aim. To reach. The Water Rise. Of Helvendah. Today."

"Water Rise?" asked Evan.

"Yes. You will see. Soon enough."

Evan stood, already fighting against his body intent on lying down. With a groan, he stretched, his knees clicking into place. Evan hoped this would be the last day of walking through the dark land.

In his head, visions of last night flashed in fragments like a vintage film reel. He couldn't be certain if it was true, but the same could be said for everything around him. He saw it, felt it, and smelled it so clearly.

"The strangest thing happened last night," Evan said. "Or, at least, I think it did."

"Yes..." the voice said.

Evan tried to think of the most convincing way to tell his story, but he knew every recanting would sound unbelievable.

"As I was trying to sleep, I couldn't get comfortable. I thought I was seeing things in the dark, the wind had picked up and I was getting pretty cold...I asked myself, what would be the best thing to ease my current troubles?...except of course getting me out of here, which may have worked in hindsight, but anyway..."

"Yes," the voice said, its interruption indicating to Evan that he should get to the point of this story.

"So," he said, taking a deep breath, doubting his own tale, "I wished for fire."

"No," the voice said, quickly.

"No? Yes. I did. And you'd never believe it...but it

appeared. This small fire ball appeared, floating and dancing in midair."

"No," the voice repeated. Evan waited, worried, for the voice to continue. "This is bad."

The boy shook his head as he walked, confused. "Why?"

"They know. Where you are. It knows," said the voice. "You invited. The fire."

"Invited the fire? I don't know what that means. I didn't invite, I mean, I did, I guess, technically, but I didn't know, I don't know what the problem is. Or if it really even happened."

"It did happen. You are lucky. Far worse did not."

A silence swelled full of unsettling thoughts.

"You must see," said the voice.

"See what?"

"The problem. It is. The only way. To understand. Bare right. We must detour."

Despite Evan's best wishes to go directly to their destination, he followed the voice's instructions off the straightened path. Evan didn't think it wise to argue with the voice, considering whatever he unknowingly did with the fire put him on his guide's foul side.

As he glanced up at the sky, oddly, after only a few short steps, the cloud looked further and more unreachable than ever. It was as though a few missteps negated the days worth of travel.

"Prepare your mind," the voice said.

Looking at the cloud, it looked like a shrinking white splotch fading away into a blanket of blackness. Evan wanted to turn and forget whatever the voice insisted he see. Each blind step, Evan inched closer to the brink of a breakdown. He was nervous, impatient.

"Prepare your mind."

"For what?" Evan sneered. "Where are we going? And Why? We're so far off the path."

The voice responded with an answer that made the

boy clench his jaw and grind his teeth.

"Prepare your mind."

Along the horizon, Evan noticed a strip of orange light blinking above a barricade of tall hills. The guide instructed Evan upward, toward the light.

Though the terrain was manageable, in Evan's exhaustion, it felt mountainous.

"Why are we doing this?" he asked, determined to slump over.

The voice remained silent.

Evan heard a series of snaps circulate the air, like a thousand whips lashing out at once. Evan stepped onward, their sound growing louder.

He coughed, clutching at his chest and covering his airways with an elbow. The land's deathly scent was more powerful here than anywhere else. Evan felt as though one good inhale might knock him out permanently.

He looked ahead, certain that he was inching closer to the summit. The orange strip in the distance was now an overpowering glow, flashing violent shades of red.

The temperature was noticeably hotter here. Beads of sweat soaked the lining of his cap. The more steps taken, the more the steps felt like climbs. The more he climbed, the more he dripped. Evan's shirt stuck to his sweat-seeping back, as he unzipped his hoodie and tied it to his waist.

He paused, closing his eyes, letting his breath catch up to him. When he opened his eyes, he could see a bright outline of the summit. He was so close. A few more careful steps and he was there. He stepped and climbed, almost stumbling beneath his jelly-like legs. Before finally reaching the top, the voice spoke.

"Evan. Prepare your mind. For what you are. About to see. Nothing like this. Happened on. Your earth. Or you. Would not be here."

Evan wasn't sure what it could be, but its glow was

glorious and promising. It whispered to him, *there is life here.*

"Go now." The voice said.

Evan reached over the top and peered at the source of the light. Instinctively he pulled his arm over his eyes, partially to shield from the harsh glow and partially to shield from the equally harsh sight.

Again he peered his wincing wet eyes over his arm. His heart beat angrily, thumping excessively, feeling set on escaping from his chest. His breath tried to take in clean air but coughed in rebellion of the blackened sky. Evan shook his head, deeply and simultaneously confused, scared, sad, and angry. His thoughts fell silent, forfeiting any possible explanation for the vast fire before his eyes.

The fire spread wide before him, fully claiming the horizon as its own. Its massive flames splashed like waves, snapping and sizzling like a fiery symphony through the air.

A vivid image of himself standing on the shore and staring at a mighty ocean came to his mind. Immediately the image became scorched to ash, blowing like sand in the wind, overtaken by the unbelievable fire before his eyes.

Hell's Ocean, he thought.

"It looks like an ocean of flames," Evan said.

"It is. An ocean of flames," the voice responded.

"How?" Evan asked. "How did this happen?"

"Perhaps. Our world's greatest. Mystery. Some say. Acts of terror. By the goblyns. Others say. Proud work. Of the witch. Either way. It is power. Full. Uncontrol. Able. Seemingly. Irreverse. Able. It has wiped out. Every landmass. And their people. It has destroyed. The sea. And its people. It has spread. Viciously. Consciously.

Evan & the Land of Letin

Like it. Possesses. Intentions. Of its own. Few dispute. That it does.

"When you request. The fire. It hears. It comes. It watches. And waits to strike.

"The Heartland. Is all. That remains. Of the. Final Earth. As you can see. Not much remains. Of the Heartland. The kings and queens. Of Helvendah. They wish to stop. The fire. And they will. They will. Revive it all."

"And this is what I'm here for? I'm supposed to help with this?"

"According to. The last whispers. Of the land. Yes."

From the top of the hill, Evan gazed at the mighty fire, unable to shake the strange feeling that it gazed back at him.

Evan was angry and pained. *An entire ocean, an entire land—gone. Dead.*

Sure, a part of him felt silly for despising the flame like it possessed a soul of its own, but another part of Evan didn't feel silly at all. This part knew there must be dark and deluded beings behind those bursting, dancing flames.

In the center of Evan's mind, black and white images floated across a lonely space in his head before erupting in a blaze.

The fire twirled and taunted as it burned the crusting bodies curled beneath it.

This flame was from a time deep in the past, Evan thought, yet it was this same flame now before his eyes.

No! his thoughts screamed. *Shut up*! *Shut up!*

"Shut up!" he yelled aloud, as his hands grasped his head, turning away from the fire.

"Your humble guide. Is sorry. For showing you. This. It had to. Be done. We must go."

Evan couldn't disagree. He wanted to turn away from the fire and forget that he'd ever seen it. Pretend he'd never have to see it again. But instead, he looked back at it, certain of his suspicions and determined to do the impossible and nonsensical.

I'm going to defeat that fire...

♥

The voice led Evan down the hillside. The fire raged behind him, its red flames licked the darkest corners of his mind, igniting an array of restless thoughts and feelings. Evan was hostile, dazed, and growing more hopeless, until a gentle glow in the distance below him caught his eye.

Unlike the unattainable light above, or the overwhelming one behind, this bit was slight and soothing. As Evan looked at the soft purple orb, so close and promising, he thought this should be his new target. Walking down the slope, the light was at eye level. With a little more vigor in his step, he progressed to the foot of the hill. Now, looking up at the purple light, it appeared to be emanating from a sphere hovering midair.

Increasingly curious, Evan walked faster, and much to his pleasure, the light stayed settled in its space. As he was but a few steps below the purple light, Evan froze as the glow revealed more of the sight before his eyes. It was unlike anything he'd ever seen.

The purple came from a large glass structure. Though circular, it was no sphere; it was a many-faceted polygon with too many angles and corners to count.

A room, Evan thought. While at first glance, this glass room appeared to float, it did not. Somehow the glass room sat atop the point of the cone-shaped building, about the size of a hill. The siding of the structure was sleek and black, like solid obsidian.

"Evan. This building is. Foreign to me. My people have. Never spoke of. This. It would be wise. To turn around."

Evan wasn't up for a debate. Aside from the

pinnacle's purple glow, nothing about this building looked welcoming, *but what other options do I have?*

Nothing about his whereabouts was welcoming. Evan was starved, tired, and inching closer to his body collapsing on him. If he were the picture of perfect health in possession of a clear mind, Evan would have turned away from the black pyramid to ran for safety.

Back home, he might have labeled the building an Unidentified Grounded Object and with great conviction he'd work up the courage to tell the authorities despite being labeled insane.

But here, now, no such thoughts crossed his faded mind. Evan knew this place looked like a beacon of insanity, but he couldn't help but wonder how much worse it could possibly be than his present situation. Evan stepped forward, closer to the glossy black tower.

Inside there might be food, water, and a place to rest. Maybe there'd be people who could help him make sense of this world. Despite its alien appearance, something about that glowing purple peak drew him in. Any light amid the darkness would've been appealing, but this felt different. As if the light longed for him. As if the magnetism was mutual.

Images of himself curled up in a comfortable bed circulated his mind. The idea felt both like a forgotten memory and preview of things to come. These things lay ahead, in that purple-lit room atop that black tower. Evan knew it.

The light reflected off of the glistening siding. He looked for another source of light on the building, perhaps a window, but there was nothing. It was entirely blank, without any sign of an entrance. With its cone shape, it looked like a dark and deadly Christmas tree, with that spectacular purple prism as its only ornament.

I need to get up there, the boy thought. He wasn't sure why, but he craved it, he *needed* it. A part of Evan thought it strange to think this, as though the thought didn't even belong to him.

"Do not go," said the familiar voice.

"There's no choice!" he snapped.

The words shocked Evan as they spilled from his mouth. He knew there was a choice, but now the words he spoke felt like they weren't his at all.

"I just need some sleep," Evan said. "And food...and water."

This much he knew was true. His stomach felt as if it had become cannibalistic and suicidal, simmering against its own fleshy walls, chewing itself. His dry esophagus felt lined with the bark of a dead tree. The act of breathing was scathing, as the air scratched against his parched mouth, desperate for a droplet.

"Does this look. Like a safe place. To rest?" asked the voice.

Evan's deadly lack of bodily necessities disallowed him from formulating a helpful response.

"Does any of this look like a place to rest?" he asked, raising his hands to the land around him. "I don't know anymore. This is all hell."

The voice fell silent.

"Hell?" the voice asked. Evan thought that if the voice had the ability to convey sadness, it did so subtly in this moment.

"No. Evan. Not yet." The voice fell into the blackness once more before giving some final advice. "Do as you please."

As I please? Evan inwardly scoffed. The very idea anything pleasurable seemed luxurious and dream-worthy. Right now, he could only comprehend what was needed, and right now, he wasn't even getting that.

Evan approached the base of the black cyclical tower. Each step closer, the more haunting the structure that hung over his head looked.

Dying thoughts whispered, *Don't go.* But it was far too late, far beyond reason to turn back now.

Evan & the Land of Letin

Evan walked around the curving side, searching for an entrance. Making his way to the opposite side, he looked up. Halfway up the tower, a deck of some sort jutted out. He took a few steps back to get a better view. From the deck, a series of steps led all the way up to the shining room. Surely at the top of those steps was an entrance to Evan's hoped-for destination, but here at ground level, there was no way in.

Evan touched its siding. Cold, slick, yet strangely soft—like wet skin. As he walked around the building, he kept a hand on its exterior, hoping to feel a possible door. The wall's texture was uniform all around, allowing for Evan's hand to slide across it smoothly.

Disgusting. He could feel a sticky film forming at the tip of his gliding fingers. Quickly, he returned back to his perceived starting point without a single sign of an entrance.

Evan bent over, hands atop his knees, contemplating his next step. He looked up at the pyramid and considered climbing its walls until he reached the platform. *It'd be difficult*, he thought, borderline impossible with his lack of energy and climbing experience. Regardless, the few remaining optimistic voices within his head shouted words of encouragement.

As Evan raised his foot against the side, before his eyes appeared the slightest of holes in the black wall. The hole was small, perfectly circular and white, like a featureless eyeball. Evan leaned closer to get a better look, and as he did, the small hole grew from the size of an eye to that of a mouth.

Against the black, the white was blinding. Evan shielded his eyes. The circle expanded rapidly to the size of a head, until finally it ceased growing, as it was large enough for the body of a small human to step through.

The boy peaked inside. Unlike the outside, the interior was completely white, powerful enough to hurt

Evan's eyes. Inside, the ground and walls looked pristine and polished, yet it was difficult to determine where the ground stopped and the walls began. In the white room, there was nothing. Nothing to look at, nothing to touch or sit upon, completely empty. If Evan didn't know better, he may have thought the white room extended on for miles.

There was nothing inviting about the room, except for the fact that it offered an out from this black and scorched hell. The room was an inversed picture of this empty and forgotten land.

But still, its inhabitants welcomed me.

The peculiar idea came to Evan that this place was not a place at all, but rather a living, breathing, sticky-skinned being. Despite this strange notion, and a chorus of others warning against entering, he stepped through the white hole in the black wall.

Evan looked at the ground and suddenly remembered the color red. And his favorite shoes, though they hardly looked the same. Their canvas exterior was irreversibly stained while dried chunks of dirt crusted on the rubber ribbed-toe.

He upturned his hands and raised them, looking at them anew, like a pair of forgotten miracles. His fingers were drenched in dark shades of earth.

Looking around, Evan examined the dirt path he created upon the white marble floor. As he lifted his head, the hole in the wall rapidly receded until it was gone, leaving no sign of being there and no view of the terrible world on the other side.

As Evan scanned the empty room without doors, windows, or even walls, a terrible suspicion crept into his mind. *Maybe I'm worse off than before. What if this is some sort of trap?*

Relax, relax, whispered a collected thought. Evan exhaled and then began to walk across the room. *There wasn't an entrance on the outside, yet here I am. There's got to be a way out of here,* he thought. *There's got to be a way to that purple room.*

Walking across the marble floor, Evan felt like he was going nowhere. He extended his hands, trying to feel for a wall and only grasping air, until, before his hands, the oddest thing appeared in the air against the white.

Evan walked closer and strange marks floated down toward him. He paused to take a good look at the streak descending his way.

Dirt smudges. Evan noticed diamond prints pressed into them as well as several letters. At first read, the letters seemed foreign, then with a blink, he made out their meaning. Printed in the tracks it read, **PF FLYERS**.

Shoe prints, he realized. His eyes followed the tracks, curving through the white sky, leading all the way back to where he stood.

A circular room, he thought. *A revolving room.* Beyond his best reasoning, he was stuck in a small sphere-shaped room, trapped in a hollowed pearl.

Evan bent to feel the surface. Slick and slimy, just as the exterior. Suspecting a way out, he ran his hand against the smooth ground.

It worked. Before him appeared a small but expanding hole, just like the one that had let him in. He walked toward it, partially expecting the room to turn, as it seemed to have done steps ago, but it did not. The opening remained just above his short self. Evan reached up and managed to grasp his hands around the bottom curve of the hole. With his legs crawling against the sloping wall, he climbed and pulled himself up and through the hole.

Evan fell, sliding down the side of the wall, landing on a level floor. Again, an all-white room, entirely empty, except for a circular black carpet that laid in the center of the room. He examined his surrounding, and behind him, his only exit and entrance, silently shrunk and sealed.

Aside from Evan's heavy breathing, the room was mute. Surprisingly, as were his thoughts.

Every tiny hair on his body went erect and his muscles tensed as the black carpet began to rise from the ground. Each thought and unspoken instinct yelled to flee, but there was nowhere to go as he backed himself against the curved white wall.

As the little carpet rose, it appeared more like a long black veil. It twisted and folded in air, taking shape. Twirling, expanding, and contracting in flight, as if breathing life into itself. While the nearly sheer blanket fluctuated and searched for form, Evan sat against the wall equally afraid and fascinated. Finally, the black figure's shape began to make sense to Evan, resembling something, or someone, his mind recognized.

Though void of definite details, the veil was now a hovering woman. Though plain, her form was perfect. Evan stared at the woman's emotionless face. The jet-black lady with onyx eyes and ebony hair appeared empty of any life. Until she smiled.

This was not the wicked smile Evan expected from the shadowy figure. Instead it was sweet and calming. She raised her arm gently with an upturned hand, welcoming Evan. This smile and gesture evoked a pale image of a similar woman in the boy's mind.

The opaque figure began to glide toward Evan. Her beauty was almost as frightening as her very existence. As she reached him, she extended her hand to his face, touching it. Her touch was soft, cold, and empty.

Without a word, she lowered, twirling her sheets around him. Leaving her cloth hand to his skin, she spun until her black and pure face settled an inch before his. Evan's dark brown oculars paled in comparison to her black ones. Her silky-touch caressed its way from Evan's face, to his neck, and then his chest before he nudged away.

Evan & the Land of Letin

The lady of black barely seemed to realize, persisting in her attempt to seduce the young man, running one hand through his hair as the other continued down his torso. Evan looked at her black eyes and could nearly see beyond her. Specks of the white room escaped through her sheer fabric skin. Evan couldn't decide whether she was real or a piece of his imagination.

Is it alive? Is she *alive?* Evan tried to speak to her. "Can you help me?"

The woman's eyes went wide in shock. The subtle curves above her eyes lowered, her neck slightly tilting. It seemed as though the simple question dumbfounded her. Or even scared her, for she turned around, floating back to the center of the room.

She turned her cloth body, flowing above the ground, and upturned her hand once more.

"Follow me," she said.

Her voice baffled and bothered Evan, for it did not fit with her delicate body. It was husky and heaving, like it belonged to a wounded and dying warrior expending too much energy to speak.

Ahead, a smaller circular door opened. Through it, the black and beautiful figure floated. Ignoring his impulses, Evan followed, seeing no other option.

In this room, the woman and the veil from which she came vanished into the surrounding light. Evan's thoughts bothered by her sudden disappearance dissipated as his mouth began to salivate and his stomach began to rejoice.

On a grand white table sat a feast Evan imagined to be prepared for a king and his entire court. Yet, alone at the table, was only one seat and one polished place setting. Evan scrambled to the table and plopped himself upon the throne-sized marble chair, elaborately designed featuring beasts of all sorts. He failed to notice a single detail of the chair except how exceptionally plush the padding felt on his bottom. His focus remained on the food that filled the wide table. His eyes scanned from piece to piece, inwardly exulting in the banquet placed before him.

The wide spread evoked images of similar foods hidden in his memory, but slight details of each dish were different than he recalled. There was a bowl overflowing with oysters that weren't oysters, for their shells were made of glittering glass; plates of sizzling sliced meats, each a shade of dark red, each rattling a part of Evan ready to viciously pounce upon the table; kaleidoscope-colored cauliflower, purple green-beans sprinkled with nuts, steaming carrots that swirled like cornucopias. There were more cheeses than he knew existed and more bread than he could eat in a lifetime.

Before Evan could snatch a bite, his insides begged for something to drink. To his left hand stood a glass column as tall as his forearm brimming with glistening water. He clenched the glass with both hands and began to gulp. The water went down in one inhaling chug, reviving his spirit as it slid.

That's the best water I ever tasted. He hadn't remembered water being so magnificent. Without intending to, Evan drank the entire glass in an attempt to make up for his body's drought. He could already feel his body returning to proper function, and in turn, his disposition began to perk up. He placed the glass column atop the table and astoundingly, it refilled, rising from the bottom right before his eyes.

Evan looked under the table but only his muddy red shoes were there. He looked back at the glass, and still he thought, *it looks so good.* Again he snatched up the glass and drank it all. *Time to feast.*

Without looking for a utensil, Evan ripped a slab of dripping steak off of a plate. With the food spread all across the table, he quickly decided there was no time to sit. Evan stood, circling the buffet, picking at everything that pleased his eye. He happily guzzled down liberal portions of each vegetable, he took hearty bites of each of the meats, and even slurped down a few oysters, which he had never even done back on Earth.

Every new food that he chomped on and sloshed through his mouth tasted not quite as he remembered, but far better. Oddly, though, Evan had the strangest feeling as the food made its way down his throat. He paused as he tried to comprehend what he was feeling. It was as though halfway down his esophagus, the food vanished. Evaporating before it could actually reach his stomach. Despite all that he gorged on, his stomach still throbbed, pleading for more.

A terrible paranoia flashed before his mind's eye in a single word—*poison*.

Suddenly, Evan bent over as he tried to mentally force the food back up his throat. He coughed, his dry heaves echoing the room. Again he tried, and tried, until he felt something rising, forming in his mouth until he spit it out.

It was all water, slightly cloudier than before, but clearly void of any of the food he thought he ate.

Again, he felt something rising from his stomach. It swelled and stabbed at his chest as it rose, until it reached the top of his throat. The substance clogged his mouth, causing a violent, whooping cough.

From his mouth came a powdery cloud of white dust that dispersed across the remaining food on the table. The strange particles left an acidic taste in Evan's mouth. He spit the remnants of the dust next to the puddle of water on the previously pristine floor.

When Evan looked up from the mess he'd made, another hole in the wall had formed.

The feast left him feeling emptier than before. In this nightmare land of death with only thoughts of bleakness, bones and muscles that'd lost the power to serve, and hopes for something hope-worthy, torn and tattered long ago, Evan didn't care anymore.

Real nothingness, he thought, *an unconscious nothingness would be glorious*. In his current state, this was the most beautiful thought he could conceive.

Like a lab-rat yearning only for an end, he walked through the hole. He didn't do this believing in something better beyond the wall, but because he had to. Like a prisoner prodded into his cell with a loaded barrel against his back, Evan proceeded.

In stacks around him were sparkling gems, uncountable treasures that scraped the curved ceiling. Gold statues of behemoth beasts he didn't recognize instantly caught his gaze. Standing to his right, a gleaming sculpture of a horse-like creature featuring an elongated speared-nose and a spiked-bone spine, while to his left, a toppled cast of a tiger with enlarged, sprawled-back ears that Evan thought strangely resembled wings. If Evan hadn't known better, he might have thought the fantastical animals were actually frozen in place with their intricate details so convincingly carved.

Littered on the ground between each object were oodles of jewels in all colors. *Rubies, emeralds,* he reviewed the obvious ones in his head. There were sapphires, garnets, amethysts, and all sorts of colored crystals he never dreamed of seeing in his most fruitful lifetime.

When the precious glasses weren't scattered on the ground or piled against walls, they were settled neatly in air. Blue spheres floated above, emanating a powerful light that revealed the room in its entirety. Evan walked deeper into the trove, finding no clear path to avoid stepping on valuables. He felt the crunch and heard the crack, but didn't bother to look down and assess the damage. In his normal state of mind, these wonders may have excited him. But now, surrounded by riches without a crumb in his stomach, lost in a treacherous labyrinth, it was all worthless.

He walked passed piles of endless prizes and mounds of foreign objects his mind couldn't identify. Among the many that Evan pondered were glass containers with colored bubbles rapidly rippling and a chain of triangle shaped links inset with thousands of diamonds, simply curled up and tossed aside, and a small bright green tile that every second or so shivered, letting out an electric zap. Quickly, the newness of each object overwhelmed him until a consoling thought interjected.

Don't worry, it said. *It's all an illusion. None of this is real.*
But it is real. I can see it, I could touch it.
I wouldn't do that.

Amid the pile, Evan caught a glimpse of an object he did recognize. At first glance, its familiarity comforted him, yet at the same time, it confused him even more. It was a common artifact that should have no place here.

Its long metal base could have been made of gold, its shade exquisitely crafted of stain glass, but still, *It's only a lamp*, Evan thought. *A lamp?* He wondered if his eyes were deceiving him. He walked closer, and there it was, a regular standing lamp, just like others he'd seen before, laying in this pile of great treasures.

Why? he thought. What was this insignificant and easily attainable object doing with these dazzling, mysterious items.

Behind the lamp, Evan noticed a well-lit, purple-carpeted path. He walked around the hill of hoards, to the clearing. Hanging above the path were more objects he could identify. *Chandeliers.*

While he'd seen a few long ago, none were like these. Together there were four leading down the corridor. The first hung with gilded branches that twisted and twirled like the trees in the dark forest. Instead of hanging still, this one slowly rotated, showing off its design. Its subtle light didn't come from candles or bulbs like one might expect, but rather from glowing orbs bobbing up and down.

Evan progressed down the hallway. On either side of the purple carpet stood great display cases. He peaked over to one, but there was nothing to see except a lonely pile of ashes. He scanned in the one opposite, and in this one, only bones.

The remains looked like that of a dinosaur or another huge beast. Evan could understand why rare bones might be enclosed in glass, yet he thought it odd there wasn't a corresponding plaque next to the case, presenting facts about the remains. Strangely, the bones looked thrown in haphazardly, without any care.

Approaching the next display, the boy passed a large flowerpot holding only dry soil and then walked beneath another peculiar chandelier. This fixture slowly rose and fell, as if its existence was meant to be an annoying obstacle. As it dropped, Evan examined its many moldings featuring the faces of men deep in sleep...*or are they dead?*

Evan scampered beneath the chilling light as it ascended. The neighboring case held even more massive bones, ones appearing to have once belonged to a large cat. The feline had a long neck and fierce teeth, sharp and long as scimitars. Examining the glass, high above his head, Evan noticed deep scratches and several cracks splintering the glass.

At the end of the hallway, he reached the final display case, which served as a tank to murky green water. As he glanced into the dirty water, a violet glimmer caught his eye.

The glimmer in the water seemed to pulsate. Evan approached the ovate shape, beating like a heart, and noticed many dark lines slashed across the light resembling veins.

Evan's nose grazed the glass, trying to get a better view at the glowing wonder. The light appeared larger, larger, moving toward him. Through the grey water, the light pressed forward, revealing its source.

Meeting Evan's dark eyes were darker ones, larger than his. Unlike his round eyes, the beast had black horizontal slits. The boy stumbled back in awe. He was certain he'd seen a creature similar to this before. Its eight tentacles, Evan counted, drifted through its scum-riddled habitat. The light that swam through the water came from inside the creature's head. Like a dozen light bulbs, the brain of the octopus shone brightly in the dark.

"Save yourself, boy," a deep voice echoed from behind the glass.

But the boy didn't respond. Though Evan couldn't see the creature's mouth, or understand how the octopus spoke his language, he knew the words were coming from the radiant beast.

"The warlock who tricks you in this manor of mazes is but a mutilated imp in this final war for the worlds."

Evan thought as though its words flowed straight from its glowing mind to his.

"While his work was wicked, it is done. His acts are trivial next to that of the Great Fire...yet still, the Great Fire is but a droplet in a squalid tank compared to the battles that will be waged."

Before Evan could question the puzzling words, the octopus raised its arms, sticking its uncountable suction cups against the glass.

"Save yourself, now."

Evan thought the great octopus looked like a prisoner pleading. The human placed his hand against the glass, tracing the outline of the tentacle. On the wall beside the tank, a circular door opened. Evan looked at it, and glancing back at the octopus, he felt as trapped as this breathtaking creature.

At the base of the entrance were rising spiral steps, basked in a lavender glow.

The top of the tower, Evan thought. It was the reason he stepped foot in this trap.

He had to continue, but now this creature's words worried him. What was above, and what would it do with him? He wanted to run as far away from this place as possible, back across the blackness, back through the woods, and back through the frozen pond that sent him here. But he couldn't, and he knew it.

Instead, Evan's legs began to march forward without his assent, his fingers dragging against the glass, searching for a grip. Evan glanced back at the octopus in fear, but before he could meet its mirroring expression, his face thrust forward, as if his body were commanded by a mind that wasn't his.

Something beyond the circle pulled Evan through, leading him up the spiral staircase, toward the top of the tower. He didn't want to go, he urged his legs to stop, but they couldn't.

Stop, Evan! Stop!
Wake up! Wake up!
It was pointless.
Upward Evan stepped, reaching the landing.

Light slithered through the many-faceted cupola, casting a fractured violet glow on the dark room. Evan could see that the round room was mostly empty. The only items occupying the space stood on the perimeter, resembling broad tablets. Evan counted them...*six, seven, eight.* The tablets appeared to be plain black, free of any marks or etchings. Their presence prodded and stung, attempting to reveal repressed memories.

A thought whispered to another. Evan caught but a single word...*coffins.* He pretended not to hear it.

His left leg shot forward. He inwardly pled, picturing his body turning and running right through the purple glass. He envisioned, in that moment, he'd suddenly be blessed with the gift of flight, or a heavenly wind would gently gust him to safety. Or, at the very worst, he'd fall to the ground, snapping his spine. Any which way, Evan wanted out of here. But his body said otherwise, stepping closer to the center of the room.

There, upon a platform taller than the short young man, sat a throne carved from black marble. Without ample light, the chair looked empty.

"Ignite," said a heavy voice, cutting through the darkness.

Around Evan, the coffins went up in flames. All except one. The front stone of the unlit coffin slid aside, revealing an empty space. The fire illuminated the room, shedding light upon the throne. Evan realized he wasn't alone in this space. The throne was occupied.

The man that sat there could hardly be called a man, rather, more like the remains of one. Despite his battered and tattered parts, this devastated being lived on. His one lidless eye stared hungrily at Evan. Starting with the hole where a nose once was, half of his face was gone, skin, muscle, skull, and all. Bulging from the top of his head was a dripping and unprotected brain. His lipless mouth showed his teeth down to their gums. His skinless neck was only bones wrapped in veins. His grey clavicles down to his ribs were all exposed. The man was but a deconstructed skeleton. Through the ooze dripping down his bones, Evan could see no stomach, no liver, just dark and empty space. Yet behind the cage of blood-stained ribs, a heart beat on.

Evan briefly glanced across the rest of the dwindling body. No legs and only one skinless arm on which only two bony fingers remained, his thumb and his pointer. He slowly raised his hand and extended its pointer toward Evan, matching the intensity of his eye.

"Rise," said the man.

Evan's body rose to the air. The man of bone twirled his finger and the boy slowly turned midair, as if being inspected. Evan tried to move his arms and legs, but the pain was excruciating, as if his muscles were being pushed into place with powerful force. He couldn't budge an inch, but his mouth let out an agonized scream.

Suspended, his body turned back toward the half-man. With a curl of the skeleton's finger, Evan moved closer to the man, up to his face. Evan coughed, nearly gagging, repulsed by the skeleton's putrid scent.

While the being looked all but dead, his stinging green iris beamed with life, craving more. His eye examined Evan closely, as he heavily breathed between the spaces in his clenched teeth.

"I sense its power is closer than ever," the man sneered. "Where is it, scum?"

"I-I...," Evan struggled to speak, "I don't know what you're—"

"Shut your beastly mouth! Don't attempt to deceive me. A creature of your foul intelligence has no chance. Where is it?"

"I don't even know what *it* is," Evan said, his voice shaking.

The man turned his half-face away, placing his fingers against his skull. His taxed breathing picked up in frustration.

"I know you have it. I've searched the many lands and seas of this universe and felt its power many times, but never closer than in this moment," he raised his finger to Evan's forehead, pressing his bone against the boy's temple.

"If I were as simple as your people, I might think *you were* the power," he snickered, the rancid stench slipping from his mouth. "But that could never be. Yet somehow, you have it...perhaps you've consumed it."

The man pinched, scraped, and pulled from Evan's forehead. He screamed in torment as the bony fingers plucked a piece of flesh straight from his face. The boned-man lowered the bleeding chunk toward his mouth and chomped. Blood gushed between the gaps in his teeth.

"Ugh!" he spat the masticated flesh back in Evan's face. The boy tried to turn away but his neck wouldn't move. Blood splattered against his sealed eyelids. "They'll be no deceit from you, scum. Where is the Lamp?"

Evan opened his eyes, confused. "The Lamp?"

The sound of a thousand glasses shattering at once filled the air. Evan glanced up, seeing the dome above them collapsing, millions of crystal splinters daggering toward his head. He clenched as he prepared for the slices to sail through him, forcing his demise.

Evan waited for the pain, but instead heard only the violent wails of the man of bones beside him. Evan fell, thumping against the floor.

The pain from the fall was nothing compared to what he expected from the glass. He thought, perhaps, he'd already been so badly severed that his body instantly went numb in defense. A whirl of wind circled through his ear. Slowly, Evan opened his eyes to see what was left of his body.

The purple dome was gone. Above him, only sky. The shimmering stars appeared to be hanging directly overhead. If he reached out his hand, Evan swore he could touch them. Then, focusing clearly on them, he realized the stars were actually the uncountable purple shards from the shattered dome, floating harmlessly in place.

Astonished and grateful, Evan stared at the glass pieces until they suddenly dispersed in opposite directions.

The man cried on in agony.

"You will all falter!"

Evan looked up at the throne. The skeleton, covered in glass, struggled with his sole arm to remove several slivers sticking from his brain.

A light laugh rolled from the darkness.

"Was that a threat? Or a curse? I hoped by now you

would have learned that your curses only come back to haunt you."

The voice was strong, yet genial. Evan turned to see the speaker.

On the edge of the platform stood eight white-hooded figures, uniform in stature. Their leather cloaks flapped gracefully in the passing wind. Against the black horizon, the eight stood like beacons of pure hope. The final figure, standing on the right end, broke from the line and began to walk toward Evan. He stepped upon the glass without care to avoid it. Unbelievably, the glass he walked upon did not break further.

"Be at peace," a familiar voice whispered in his ear. It was that of his recently absent guide. "You are safe now."

The hooded figure stepped before Evan and extended his arm. From the end of the sleeve came the figure's hand, almost as white as the cape, offering an open palm to lift Evan from the ground.

Peering up, he tried to see the details on the figure's shaded face. Beyond the bottom of his perfectly curved chin, Evan couldn't see a thing. Looking at the pale hand, his fingers looked so slender, yet so strong, like the branches of a birch tree.

Palm open, steady and waiting…

Wind slithered through the space between them…

Finally, Evan grasped it.

From the hand, a warmth emanated that instantly traveled through Evan and comforted him. He hadn't realized how cold he was. With ease, the hooded figure pulled the boy to his feet as though he were weightless.

Evan silently stared at the stranger.

"How could I be so insensitive? Do forgive me."

The white figure pulled the hood from his face.

His skin appeared to gleam as if beneath its white, silvery exterior was a layer of pure light. Though Evan correctly guessed he was male, with his firm cheek bones, precisely lined jaw, and chiseled chin, the man also possessed all the natural beauty of every stunning being, man or woman, that Evan had ever recalled seeing. In the boy's mind, the man's blue eyes incited images of clear skies and warm water, instantly feeling the comfort of both.

"I am Kaven," the man said with a calm smile.

Kaven brought two fingers from his right hand over the front of his right eye, as if slowly swiping, then he kissed his these forefingers and extended them upward toward Evan.

Evan raised his hand and scratched the back of his neck, with no intention of recreating his new acquaintance's foreign greeting.

Kaven's smile widened and he laughed. He brought his hand upon the boy's shoulder and nodded.

"We will work on that," Kaven said. "What is your name, new friend?"

The boy became startled, as he found himself having to think about the answer. He closed his eyes, in hopes of retrieving the answer, until thankfully, it came to him.

"Evan…" the name rolled slowly from his mouth like a newfound revelation. "…My name is Evan."

The man looked back at him with curious eyes, waiting for more. Evan knew there may have been a second, even a third part of his name, but they weren't coming to him.

The man bobbed his head and smiled.

"Well, just Evan, is it then? It is my sincere honor to meet you. Let's hope you're as singular as your name suggests."

The boy returned a smile, enjoying what he thought Kaven intended as humor.

"Now, fine sir, if you would follow me," Kaven said. "I'll introduce you to everyone once we're aboard our vessel and out of here. This place reeks of wicked deeds," he looked back at the decrepit man of bones still moaning in pain. "This world has its way of naturally punishing those deserving penance. Evan, believe me when I tell you his anguish is nothing next to the pain he's administered."

He didn't need to be convinced. That was a man who just picked off his skin, chewed it, and then spit it back in his face. Evan hoped the dying man fully deteriorated.

"Well, my friend," Kaven spoke as he led the boy across a path less scattered in glass toward the end of the floor. "Let's take you home and get you cleaned up."

"Home?" Evan asked. He was confused by the notion but his excitement shone through.

"Oh, I'm so sorry, Evan," Kaven said sincerely. "Let me clarify. *My* home," he said touching his chest, then gesturing toward the seven hooded figures.

"Our home—The Kingdom of Helvendah."

MOVEMENT 3
Evan & the Kingdom of Helvendah

Evan followed seven of the eight from the platform while Kaven led the rear. Walking through the archway, the boy crunched upon fallen glass as they exited. Stepping out, he impulsively pulled back, looking down at the walkway. The circular stone steps sat in the air, supported by empty space or unseen beams. Despite no evident foundation, the steps held firm as those ahead walked down. Evan exhaled and followed along, stepping on the floating stones. To his relief and astonishment, the steps held steady as rocks lodged in the ground.

The hovering trail spiraled toward another large platform, the one Evan saw from outside. This large terrace was also invisibly supported. Upon it sat a strange vessel Evan was certain wasn't there before.

With its sleek white body, it reminded him of an enlarged and elongated pearl. There were no visible seams on the structure, which led Evan to believe, much to his amazement, that this ship was created organically or magically. Though he couldn't remember what a NASA shuttle or a Knarr longship looked like, this polished vessel looked like a cross between the two.

The white ship possessed a curved underbelly and a thin body suggesting it was set to sail, but seeing as it was up on this terrace with no water in sight, Evan decided it must be meant for the sky. *But how?* he wondered. The airship had no wings, no propeller nor sails, no possible place for an engine or an apparent way to move.

Approaching closer, Evan noticed the deck of the ship was lined with marble statues, blending with the white siding. The sculptures were large herculean men, rippling with muscles, fixed in a uniform pose with their strong arms tugged on white chains linked to the ship. The peculiar statues were not modeled after just man, but also bird. From the hip-down, their thighs were those of massive birds, large enough to match the man's upper half. From these thunderbird thighs came thick-boned legs with ravenous claws. At the center of their stoned faces, where a human nose would be, was a subtle beak that mixed naturally with the men's features. At the rear of the sculptures, tucked at their sides, were regal wings; silky and mighty like those of an angel.

As the first of the white-hooded figures reached the ship's rear, Evan believed he saw one among them twirl their fingers in air. At this gesture, the curled stern of the vessel unfurled to the ground, creating a ramp. Up they walked, as Evan followed in amazement.

Aboard the deck were eight large white seats that could have been chiseled from the ship itself. As the figures filed in, they all instinctively found their seats. Sitting, they faced each other as though there were a dining table between them, except the seat at the bow, which faced outward. Before what appeared to be the captain's seat stood a podium.

"Here, sit in mine," Kaven said, directing Evan to the final unfilled seat. If there were a table, this unoccupied spot would have been at the head of it, opposite the podium. The boy felt unsure, and seemingly Kaven noticed. "I insist."

Evan sat, and at last, they all unveiled their hoods.

He gasped.

Like Kaven, their skin was effervescent, glowing against the black sky.

Enamored by their beauty, Evan couldn't settle his glance upon any particular one. At first, it was difficult to decipher which were men and which were women, for they were all equally gorgeous.

The man *(or is he a woman?)* before the podium

raised his hands as if saying, *'Rise'*. Upon this, the wings of the marble-men extended, wider than any Earthly wingspan. Each barb on every feather was etched in exact detail. Evan instantly wanted to meet the artist behind the incredible work.

The man *(I'm starting to think he's a woman)* at the front began to gently wave his hands up and down. The wings mirrored, flapping upward, rising to the sky, their chains unwinding and straightening as the statues got higher, until with a tug, the ship began to ascend. With precise hand gestures, the captain moved the statues and thus the ship, as if conducting an orchestra.

"Amazing," Evan said aloud.

"Thank you," Kaven responded. "Now that we are airborne, I think introductions are in order."

Kaven approached the captain at the podium, posing as something between a conductor and a pilot.

"This is Valanang," Kaven said, his hand draped across the flight director's shoulders. "As you can see, she's quite busy at the moment."

Despite being the only one amid the eight with short hair (a sleek cut dramatically styled with a pointed-angle leaning toward the right), "he" indeed was a she.

Progressing behind the chairs, Kaven made his way to the passenger at Evan's left. Before Kaven could speak, the boy knew this one was a woman, and an exceptionally beautiful one. To differentiate between the people, Evan focused on their hair, for that seemed varied enough. The woman's locks, which were twisted in a tight beehive aback her head, were especially spectacular. Each strand appeared to glisten a subtle but separate shade of red that fluctuated to a warm violet from various angles as she turned her face.

"This is Marantyne," the woman smiled. Her full lips matched the dark crimson of her hair. "She is our undeniable wisdom."

Evan thought it odd that this woman of wisdom

Evan & the Land of Letin

looked no older than anyone else aboard. In fact, he noticed they all looked relatively young, the oldest no more than a few years elder to himself.

Kaven continued toward the next. This man sat with a glorious smile across his face, his shoulder length brown hair, free and flowing with the wind. He glanced at Evan, his eyes a grassy green, as if grown directly from the earth.

"I am Tellus," he spoke. His voice matched his outer vibrance. "I am sure I can speak for all of us when I tell you, I truly look forward to knowing you."

"Thank you," Evan mumbled, slightly embarrassed by the man's excitement.

Next to Tellus sat another man. His eyes were closed and his head raised high as if in meditation. Across from him sat a woman matching his pose. Whispering, Kaven spoke.

"This is Garvin," pointing toward the man, "and this, Jazamas," gesturing to the woman. "Right now, they are deep at work. We mustn't disturb them, but you'll have plenty of time to acquaint yourself."

Evan couldn't help but think these folks had the most peculiar names and curious practices. He certainly wasn't against meditation, but he did think it quite odd to be doing amid company, aboard…*whatever this thing is*. They seemed like lovely people, however, as Kaven stepped toward the next man, the energy surrounding this stranger nearly sunk all the ship's positivity.

Without a word, the boy could sense his anger and bitterness. The man sat, face toward the ground, as his sharp nails scratched against his clenched fist. His cold demeanor matched his long, intricately braided silver hair. Kaven whispered to the man and the man whispered back, a tangible harshness in his tone. His words sounded like a snarl. Walking passed the fierce man, he moved on.

"That is Cyphur. He will come around…"

Kaven gestured to his final friend to introduce. Evan failed to realize that this acquaintance had yet to lower their hood. Evan peered, leaning to get a view beneath the cowl. Evan detected a dazzle more noticeable than that of the other's.

"This is Glazzaliah. She has a special way with words."

"I see you do as well," she said, turning to look straight at the boy.

Her eyes made Evan's nervously avert, then instantly reconnect with hers. Her irises were red, which seemed unnoticeable next to her face. Encrusted upon her skin were countless crushed diamonds. At first it seemed like a mask, for there was no sign of a mouth from which her soft voice came, but the way the diamonds so closely lined her eyes, appearing even upon her eyelids when she blinked, Evan had a feeling this dazzling pattern was permanently stitched upon her.

"What was that?" Kaven said with a laugh, speaking to the rest of the group. "Here she goes again."

Glazzaliah lowered her hood. Her hairless head was entirely covered in crystals. She brought her hand to her face, rubbing her thumb against her forefinger. Her hand glistened too, seemingly composed of glass or gloved in diamond. She looked to the sky, her red irises slowly scanning the black.

As difficult as it was to glance from Glazzaliah, it got no easier, for from out of the black sky a large bird flew downward. Evan ducked in fear, but the creature quickly settled upon Glazzaliah's shoulder. The word *owl* came to Evan's mind, but that wasn't it. Next was *snake*, but that certainly wasn't right either. This strange animal was a cross between the two, complete with its round bird head and black marble eyes. But there were no feathers, instead, diamond-linked scales and a slithering tale that wrapped down Glazzaliah's arm. It was a creature crafted from nightmares, one Evan wouldn't touch even if he were covered in full-armor.

Its spinning head cocked toward the boy, as he nervously turned away from the animal and back to his new acquaintances. Evan tried to remember their names, but that would be a challenge for another day. Each had unique features, yet at the same time, they seemed similar. *They're people...but are they human?* There was something that set them apart, aside from their sparkling skin.

"And as you know, I am Kaven," he grinned and turned. His smile left a bright imprint on the lightless sky. Kaven took the center of the gathered seats. At the back of his hair, Evan noticed hundreds of pins with little diamonds fixed on their ends.

"Officially, we are the kings and queens of Helvendah," he turned back, his smile sparkling more by the second. At the peak of his black hair, braids lined his forehead, resembling a crown. "Unofficially, we are simply doing our duty. And you, Evan, have the most important duty of all." He paused, looking at the boy with a gently nodding head. "You are going to help us. You are going to help us return this world to its former glory."

All eight now looked at Evan, even the cold Cyphur. Shivers circulated the shoulder where the chilling glance landed. A silence grew between the eight and Evan as they awaited his words.

"I, uh...I appreciate the rescue. More than anything. I was dead...and you all saved me. For whatever reason." He paused again, trying to clearly compile his thoughts. "I appreciate the high hopes, but I don't understand. I mean, I have so many questions. Why? Why am I here? And how? How am I supposed to help you?"

Tellus' exuberant smile weakened. Cyphur's sudden smirk appeared.

"I...I don't want to confuse you," Evan stammered.

"I will do all that I can do, anything to help, I'll just need some help myself."

"All of your questions will answer themselves in time," Kaven said. "We don't have all the answers. Even we do not know. But together, you and I, and all of us will figure this out."

The king smiled, the rest of his fellow royalty followed, nodding their heads in agreement.

"Tomorrow we will begin. You will spend a portion of the day with each one of us, learning and understanding the ways of our people."

Kaven's eyes widened as he spoke, and Evan finally spotted the peculiarity about the people he couldn't previously pinpoint. Their eyes were slightly larger than a typical man or woman's would be, as were their ears. Their enlargement was not drastic enough to cause alarm or to be deemed unpleasant, in fact, it was the opposite. It was though their size only showcased their beauty further. Their eyes seemed like precious gems and their ears like the delicately pointed leaves of a lily.

"What people would that be?" Evan asked.

Kaven spoke without pause, his voice smooth and confident, his words like water flowing across unbreakable rock.

"Our people are scarcely different from yours, Evan." He laughed, almost as in disbelief of what he were about to say, "We are elphs."

To the boy, the word was known but its once familiar meaning was long lost.

"Legends of our people have passed on to others, from world to world, varying from culture to culture, but forget what you've heard." *That shouldn't be a problem.* "You will learn the truth from your experience. You will become an honorary elph."

"We are approaching the Water Rise, sir," said the captain.

"Valanang, if you would raise the ward, please,"

Evan & the Land of Letin

Kaven directed.

She pulled her hands upward, bringing them together above her head. A clear bubble began to form from the rim on the deck, sealing at the top, the statues flying just above the sphere.

"Thankfully for you, we're arriving in the thick of the Day of Moons.*" The Day of Moons?* "You won't instantly get absorbed in the constant stir and spectacle of the kingdom. You can take in its beauty in peace. I am sure you're in need of food and sleep yourself, so for you, those will come first."

"A bed sounds heavenly," Evan admitted.

Kaven turned to his fellow kings and queens, "If no one objects, he'll be staying in one of my rooms."

"Of course not!" Tellus said.

"Certainly," added Glazzaliah.

Cyphur let out a growl.

Kaven chuckled, "I guess we're all in agreement."

Evan could see the sole white cloud amid the endless black, larger and closer than ever. He'd journeyed so far, *so agonizingly far,* for this moment. He peeked at the cloud, and from its bottom, appeared to be pouring an incessant rain, its flow comparable to a river. It seemed to be a waterfall from the clouds. Evan was certain it was, until the moment before plunging into its depths, he realized the water wasn't falling at all, but it was rising. *Aha…a Water Rise.*

The vessel splashed into the side of the stream, the bubble-like shield sealed the water from converging on the crew and drowning Evan. The boy's initial notion of the ship proved to be true, for it served as both a flying machine and now a submarine. The water flushed by, white bubbles gushing around him. Evan couldn't contain his awe-induced smile. The ship surged toward the glittering surface above.

The glow grew bigger, Evan thought, more inviting, more exciting, until finally the ship emerged to the surface with a splash. The flying statues retreated, their links shortening, until they returned to their original pose; their glorious wings tucked back, steady and still like they'd never moved an inch. The unique ship now floated atop the water, comfortably serving as a boat, as though this was its only duty.

Valanang pointed forward and they moved across the vast circular pool. At the water's end, Evan could see the comforting color of green. Surrounding the lake were trees, real living trees amid an actual growing forest, something Evan could only scarcely remember from his life before.

As the boat progressed toward land, the moon's reflection danced atop the water. Evan rubbed his eyes in an attempt to clear them, for he was seeing not double or triple, not even quadruple, but octuple. Eight silvery circles glimmered and slithered with the passing waves. Evan looked toward the sky and saw that his eyes were not deceiving him. The reflection was true.

Amid a sea of stars, lined in a straight row were eight lustrous moons, each identical in size and their full shape. It was as though a higher being placed the perfect spheres on an invisible ledge to comfort and celebrate the people of this kingdom. Evan's mouth gaped, mirroring their shape.

The boy's affinity for the moon was reborn, but now, one moon would never be enough.

The longboat's curled end unfurled as they reached shore. This time, Kaven and Evan led the way, walking off the ramp as the rest of the elphs followed. Approaching the green tree line, the boy could feel coolness, a gentle breeze flowing through the trees.

They took one of many stone paths through the woods. Glancing around, Evan could see flora he knew he hadn't seen before. Some flowers had shining blades that reflected the boy's curious face back to him, others glowed in the dark like the moons above. Tall vined plants, bristled with tiny flowers swayed side by side, moving synchronically, as if practicing a well-choreographed dance to a song only they could hear. Then, strangely, Evan heard it...

Softly, a voice sang, traveling through the branches and leaves. He couldn't be certain it wasn't actually coming from the branches and leaves. If it wasn't the voice of Mother Nature herself, it was that of a knowing girl with comparable power. Evan could hear her song, delicate like the flowers abound, yet impossibly mighty like the trees above him. The voice became ever so slightly louder with each step closer to the city.

As they reached the edge of the forest, the song in Evan's ear stopped abruptly. His senses were overtaken by the light before him. He was frozen, glitter-eyed, and speechless. The elphs lined up beside him. Kaven looked at the human and laughed.

"Welcome to Helvendah!"

Standing before him, each pristine and monumental structure shined like their inhabitants.

Without counting, Evan accurately guessed there were eight. The great white towers looked to be carved and melded from a collection of the entire universe's ivory. Though they all shared the same blinding color, each had unique designs, all too much for Evan to take in at one moment. Each tower seemed to stand separately, complete with countless smaller towers rising from their main structures, but in fact, every building was connected through a series of bridges. Some were visible from ground level while others connected in the sky, wrapping around and through the structures, forming the small city into one colossal castle.

Hovering high above the rooftops and bridges were dozens, maybe hundreds, of glass balls. Resembling floating, empty fishbowls or bubbles frozen in space, they reflected and multiplied the light from the moonshine above.

Onward, Evan and the elphs walked upon a spotless white pavement. One by one, each king and queen trailed off to what Evan assumed were their respective towers. As they passed all but two of the skyscrapers, all that remained were Evan, Kaven, and Cyphur. The stern elph said nothing as he swiftly departed toward his personal abode, which stood alongside Kaven's.

Looking at the building, the boy wasn't sure he should enter, for he wasn't certain how it was standing. Instead of being uniform in width, the tower was largest at its peak. The structure's base was just large enough for a set of double-doors. Of course, these were double-doors sized for a king, perfect to push through with both arms, certain to leave the doors swinging behind for a marvelous entrance.

With a wave of Kaven's hands, the double-doors receded aside, sliding into the wall—an even better entrance than Evan had imagined. Above the doorway, he noticed etchings. The text appeared to be in a foreign script, but oddly, with a rub of his sleepy-eyes, the letters became recognizable. They read, HOUSE OF DUENDELYN.

Evan had never read or said the name before, but he knew he'd heard it before.

"Who is Duendelyn?"

Kaven smirked. "He," pointing to the center of the white room, "is Duendelyn."

At the middle of the circular lobby was a clear towering statue of a man, or more presumably, an elph. In one arm, the likeness held a shield lowered to his side. The other was extended with an upturned hand, welcoming his guests. From the doorway, the clear statue looked to have possibly been made from ice or even crystal, but as Evan drew closer, he saw that the surface of the stone was moving. The sculpture stood atop a fountain, and from the flowing water, Duendelyn was formed. Beyond Evan's reasoning, the statue was

Evan & the Land of Letin

composed of moving water.

He paused, marveling at the most wondrous art he'd ever seen. "Who was he?"

"The truest elph that ever was," Kaven said with a nod.

The boy waited for more, but it seemed this was the only answer Kaven was giving at the moment.

"You will learn plenty more tomorrow," Kaven said, "about him," looking at the statue, "and what it really means to be an elph. But now, some rest is in order."

Behind the fountain was an elphen version of an elevator; a round carriage carried by two of the marble winged-men. They stepped aboard and Kaven flicked his hand. In an instant, out fluttered their mighty wings and up they flew through a shaft, passing dozens of floors in a blur before reaching the top.

"Many live in this house," said Kaven, "but all the way up here is my home. It's actually the highest point in all of Helvendah, and I guess being among the clouds makes this the highest point in all the world. For the time being, I can think of nowhere else better suited for you, Evan. For now, and until you desire otherwise, this is your home, too."

After slogging across the miserable dark land, unsure of whether he was on the verge of death or already there, in this moment, in Helvendah with Kaven, he felt blessed. *My home, too.*

His memories and concept of home were dust particles in this pristine city—nearly undetectable. Whatever home was before could never live up to this.

Through white corridors, passed closed entryways, they reached what Kaven introduced as Evan's room. With a wave, the door slid aside. Evan hoped he'd learn how to do that.

Across from the entry were wide glass doors, slightly cracked open. A breeze rolled through the room, gently rippling the walls. It appeared the walls and its canopy ceiling were composed of soft linen. In one curved corner stood a mirror, in the other, a plush chair that Evan was certain was comfortable, but sure hoped he didn't have to sleep on…

There was no bed, but there were two white night tables spaced apart where a bed should be.

"Tomorrow we'll get you fitted in traditional garb, it's quite the ordeal so I hope one more night in your native clothes will do just fine."

"Oh, of course. These are just fine," Evan said, removing his red cap and placing it on an end table. Filth from the hat sprinkled onto the clean top. He remembered the cap being considerably brighter. Now it was dark, irreversibly stained.

Evan patted his pockets and felt something unexpected. He pulled it out and looked at it unknowingly. The small white rectangle with a black face reflected a darker version of himself back to him. Finally, the word came to him. *Phone…phone.*

"How glorious!" Kaven extended his hand, "May I?"

"Sure?"

Kaven grasped the phone with great care, placing only four delicate fingers on its ends. He lifted it before his eyes, slowly examining it from every angle in awe.

"What powers does it possess?" Kaven asked, staring at the powerless interface. "What kind of mirror is this?"

Evan quietly laughed and shook his head, "This isn't a mirror. It's a phone."

Kaven squinted in confusion and curiosity.

The boy continued, "We use it to call each other," Kaven raised a puzzled eyebrow. Evan thought of a better way to phrase this, "It helps us talk to each other over long distances."

"Who do you *call?*" Kaven asked.

"Uh, family…friends."

"Incredible. And how does it work?"

"Well, you push that little button at the top there and

normally it'd turn right on."

Kaven delicately pressed the top button. "Normally?"

"Right, but it's out of power," Evan said, a hint of defeat in his voice.

"Ah, I see, I see. Did you craft this little masterpiece? Don't sound so dejected. Not all of my projects work to perfection the first go around."

"Oh, I didn't make that," Evan said with a smile, delighting in the conversation, "I'd be a much richer man if I had."

"I certainly doubt that," the king responded. "You are a citizen of Helvendah now. No people across any land are richer. Never doubt that all we have is not entirely yours as well. It most certainly is. That said, I would love to meet the wizard that crafted this magic...what did you call it?"

"A phone."

"Yes, that's it. A phone. As long as we're on the subject of unrecognized items, I have to ask you what this is?" Kaven said, poking his pointer twice against the red tin shape pinned against Evan's chest.

Evan looked down with a cocked neck, analyzing the pin. He had entirely forgotten about its existence. He slightly recalled it having more color and luster. He smudged his thumb diagonally across the pin showing a glimmer of shining red beneath the dirt and darkness.

"This is a, uh..." Evan closed his eyes, remembering the symbol's meaning. "A heart."

Kaven's apparent omni-smile widened and a rich laugh pumped from his thin stomach. "My apologies, I mean no disrespect, but that is *no* heart."

At this, Evan also laughed, for he understood the misunderstanding.

"No, *I* am sorry. This is the *symbol* of a heart. I think it's probably better to use than the ugly organ. I think it's mostly used to represent..." a grand concept reappeared in his mind, a concept he couldn't fully grasp even with all his memories intact. "Love."

"Ah, love. Of course," Kaven said, nodding his head and leaning toward the pin. He admired the thing as if he deemed it perfect. Or nearly perfect. He pulled the tip of his sleeve over his hand, rubbing and removing the pin's remaining muck. The little red heart glistened in its original beauty. Kaven could see a crimson-tinted reflection of himself against the pin. Now it was perfect.

"But it could also represent so many things," Kaven said. "How incredibly appropriate that you wear this now? The one that was sent to restore the heart of the Heartland. I think it's time we all start believing in destiny."

Evan gently raised his eyebrows and shoulders, all while nodding his head. The boy had no idea what to think or say. He hoped one gesture showcasing his wide array of emotions would satisfy Kaven.

"I also think it's time to leave you to your bed. I can only imagine how long overdue a good rest has been. In that bowl there," Kaven pointed atop one of the tables, "is a single mannberry. One of those treats will satisfy you through the night."

Oh, believe me...I know.

As Kaven turned to exit, he flashed his hand in air, extinguishing the glowing orbs above Evan's head. With another hand gesture the door reopened, but before he could exit, the boy interjected.

"Wait," Evan said, looking around the room, "I don't believe I have a bed..." Again he looked over his shoulder confirming the room had no bed.

"How mindless of me," said Kaven as he twirled around. "Here I am, assuming you already know all the ways of Helvendah, like our earths are mirror images."

He twisted his hand reigniting the room's light.

"Here," the elph said guiding Evan between the two end tables, "lay here."

"On the ground?"

"That's right."

"You all sleep on the ground?" Looking at these polished people, Evan found that hard to believe.

Kaven laughed, "You'll see."

Skeptically, Evan bent toward the ground then gradually bent back until his body was sprawled out on the sparkling ivory floor. *At least it's clean*, he thought.

"All right, now don't be alarmed, just relax and enjoy one of the greatest perks of our kingdom. Here we go."

With both hands, Kaven made an elongated motion followed by swift turns of his fingers and raising his palms. Suddenly, Evan felt the hard ground below him become soft and malleable, perfectly forming to the curve of his aching spine and providing ideal pressure to all his sore spots. Evan turned to look at Kaven, suddenly feeling dizzy. *Am I floating?* he asked himself. In an instant it stopped. He no longer felt woozy, but felt settled in place. As he looked down, Evan realized he now lay several feet above the ground without any means of visible support. It appeared Evan's dream bed had risen straight from the ground.

"Sleeping on air," Kaven said with a picturesque smile, "one of my favorite inventions. The air blows right from the floor perfectly adhering to the sleeper's body. The difficult part was silencing all that wind pressure, but after a few prototypes, I got it. You'd be surprised what some simple, classic enchantments will do."

It was remarkable. It was as though Evan lay atop the greatest bed in the universe and it was made exclusively for him. The wildest part, he thought, was that everybody in all of Helvendah was experiencing this same glory.

"Now we can't forget to tuck you in, once you've learned a trick or two you'll no longer need me to do all this." Kaven gestured toward the ceiling and the sheer white cloth began to float down. Without Evan moving a muscle, the cloth wrapped around him like a cocoon, so delicately, so comfortably, its softness against his face almost enough to immediately lull him to sleep.

Once more, Kaven dimmed the lights and finally exited the room, "Lovely Day of Moons, Evan."

Whatever that meant, Evan was sure he loved it.

As the boy closed his eyes, a breeze slid across his swaddle, rustling his sheets. With the wind came sound, and not simply the air's natural whispers, but a voice. A voice that caressed Evan even more than his incredible bed and sheets. Evan knew this was the voice he heard just moments ago, upon arriving in Helvendah.

He opened his eyes and brushed aside a piece of his blanket to glimpse through. Beyond the glass doors, Evan could see the voice's source. Standing atop the neighboring tower was a girl brighter than the eight moons and their accompanying stars.

From the distance, Evan was unable to make out the details of the girl, but he wasn't concerned with her details. They didn't matter. Her voice was enough.

There was a purity in her tone that he adored, but a depth that hinted at darkness. To Evan, her sound fluttered through the night sky like a dozen paradoxical doves. So dazzlingly white, so perfect, that inevitably their unseen side must have been dyed black or not there at all. She sang so soft, yet so mighty, so simple, yet so knowing; Foreign, but familiar; Fantastical, but tangible. Whether it was the boy's mind drifting to sleep or talks of destiny, her voice seemed reason alone to confess his love for her (*whatever that means*) from right where he was across the balcony.

Evan closed his eyes and listened to her words.

The boy stumbles and looks toward the sky
Our stars reflect his inner workings
Our trees project his truth
We wait, we hope, we know what is real
We are, we are, we are

Our stars reflect our inner power
Our trees protect what's pure
We wait, we hope, we know what is real
He is, he is, he is
The wandering child is never lost,
The wandering child is near,
The wandering child is never lost,
The wandering child is here.

A single chill trickled down his horizontal spine, rolling atop its ridges.

Was that about me? whispered a thought incapable of thinking beyond itself.

No, no, no, responded a fleet of sleepier thoughts not lively enough for an introspective debate.

You just need some sleep.

You're right…sleep.

With the help of the girl's intoxicating voice, Evan drifted silently asleep atop nothing but air.

✻

The creature tries not to think of himself yet he can't stop thinking, *I did it. I did my job.* Though his people would deny it, his people would be proud. But now they must hope that the guided one does his part.

Sure, in his eyes, the boy is a giant, but in the universal scheme, he's still hardly bigger than himself.

Is he really supposed to restore this world?

Or is it all lies force-fed to the survivors to comfort them?

Where would the lies come from?

Not here. Here is where the rebirth begins.

I did my job. Can the boy do his?

The rest is up to them. I have faith in them.

He is safe now. I am safe now.

I can probably give up seeing my people again. But who

cares?

I am here. Where they all dream of being.

At last, the animalcule slowly steps from its dark crevice, careful not to disturb the human. Down the canal, he sees the light of the shining city ahead, but he can't leave without a few final words of encouragement.

Before exiting, he whispers in his native tongue, "I believe. In you. Evan. It is time. For you. To do the same."

At that moment, the creature was as close to happiness as he could possibly be.

From out of Evan's ear, the tiny blue ant emerged.

Evan awoke with a tap on his forehead followed by a slight splashing sensation. Standing at the side of his hovering body was Kaven, wiping his hand on an inner-fold of his white robe.

"Sorry about that, Evan," he said. "Oddly, there was a waterant crawling across your face."

"A wha-?" the boy groggily replied.

"A waterant," Kaven said. "Fascinating little specimen, but in actuality, quite dreadful. When the Great Fire spread, these ants somehow developed the ability to store water in every opening in their bodies. Literally, they became walking droplets of water. Valiant buggers, they'd gather in large quantities and march right into the fire. It's sad to say, but it's truly quite useless. All of the waterants could collect and sacrifice themselves to the fire and it wouldn't make a dent. The real problem is that they consume all the water across the land until there's nothing left. Our Rise out there is the only source of clean water left in the Heartland. How this little guy made it all the way up here is beyond me."

The strangest idea crawled into Evan's mind. He stuck his pinky finger in his ear, easing a lingering itch.

Evan & the Land of Letin

He shook his head and tossed the silly thought aside.

"I'm waking you up slightly before the rest of the city. We'll want to get you all cleaned up and familiarized with your surroundings before we introduce you tonight at the Naliah—our nightly feast and celebration of the day's accomplishments. If we can successfully keep your arrival a secret, your introduction will be the greatest of surprises."

The elph soon led Evan to a dining room fit for royalty, featuring a wide window that took up the entire far wall, peering down on the small city. The white gleam that blanketed the unconventionally shaped towers reminded Evan of marvelous lands found only in snow-covered dreams. He smiled. His reality was no longer a nightmare.

At the center of the room was a long table flourishing with more fruit than Evan had ever seen in one place. There was produce that looked like apples, bananas, and clementines, and while these words came into his mind he also knew these were not exactly apples, bananas, or clementines. There were all sorts of melons in every color, complete with bright spots and strange stripes. There were peaches colored a royal blue with fur fuzzier than any peach back home, and single pears with more curves than an entire bushel combined. There was sliced star-fruit which looked quite appealing, complete with the five-pointed symbol he recognized, but its flesh let off a gentle glow that Evan wasn't sure he wanted in his body. Finally, he settled on the strawberries (which Kaven called, "pennberries"), for there was nothing foreign about this fruit. It was still red with its dotted skin and green leaves, except they were much larger than the ones he remembered. His pennberry was about the size of an apple and just one filled him up completely.

Following breakfast Kaven handed Evan a spare hooded-robe so he'd blend in with any early-rising elphs. As he slipped on the crisp white robe, Kaven reminded him that he'd later be fitted for his own attire. Wearing multiple layers, the robe fit snug, Evan imagined that without the shirt and hoodie, it would fit perfectly.

The duo stepped aboard the elevator, and as they reached the lobby, Kaven waved his hand, and onward the carriage flew, out the front doors and into the street. Evan saw a few elphs walking and instantly pulled the hood deep over his alien face. Onward they zipped, back through the forest, before stopping at the Water Rise.

Evan stepped out, looking at the sprawled circular pool. From a distance across the Rise, he saw a few bare-skinned elphs walk straight below the water's surface.

"This is where I bathe?"

"This is where we all bathe," Kaven said with a chuckle. "Do you have a better idea?"

Evan couldn't recall his prior bathing experience but he didn't remember it being so...*so open*. "I, uh...I guess not."

"Believe me, there's no comparable experience in the universe to bathing in the Water Rise."

"So just go in? Like this?"

"Unless you only intend to clean the garments, I suggest removing all of your clothes," Kaven said, seemingly amused with Evan's discomfort. "Relax, my friend. No one is watching you. Plus, we are more or less the same. Listen, I'll go down the way and bathe myself. I'll be back momentarily."

"Oh, and before I forget," Kaven said, reaching in his robes. "Here's this."

Kaven handed the boy what appeared to be a necklace composed of dozens of pearl-sized clear spheres.

"What is it?"

"It's imperative to your survival," Kaven replied. "Be sure to slip it on before stepping into the water."

Kaven was off before Evan could ask more questions. As the elph appeared half the size of himself, he disrobed, and gracefully dove into the water. The boy waited several seconds for Kaven to surface but couldn't spot him. *Musta swam further down.*

Peeking over his shoulders, Evan decided that no one could see him but the trees and their countless leaves. Untroubled by this, off came the white robe, followed by his crimson cap, then finally his mud and blood colored canvas shoes. Evan looked down at his original outfit, now with dirt particles weaved into the fabric, hardened and stiff as if the ghost of a lost life lay within.

Evan pulled the necklace over his head, the crystal balls settling around his shoulders. He looked down at his thin bare body, down to his feet. The soft sand between his toes comforted him. They told him it was safe to walk on. He dipped his foot in the water, testing its temperature. It was warm and welcoming, precisely the conditions he would have chosen if he could control such a thing. Evan stepped down, letting the water rise to his shins.

With another few steps, he walked down the sandy slope until the water was at his waist and his goose bumps retreated. His next step, however, was not as comforting, for the friendly sand beneath his toes was no longer there. Instead, there was an open space—a drop-off.

Rather than tumbling deeper into the water, Evan's body plunged beneath the surface, the Water Rise pulling him.

Evan plummeted quickly, and forcefully. With every muscle he tried to retreat but the water dragged him down violently. Just as all of the boy's brief new life flashed before his eyes signaling the end, the sinking suddenly stopped.

He cracked his eyelids to scope the blurred underwater scenery, but inconceivably, it wasn't blurry at all. His hands weren't fuzzy through water drenched eyes, but they were as clear as he knew them. Around was the purest water, clearer than air, allowing him to see for miles of what seemed to be endless empty water.

Evan looked down, realizing that from his crystal-stringed necklace, a large bubble formed, completely encompassing his head. It reminded him of the shield on the elphen ship. He took a deep breath, then another. In sheer bliss and disbelief that he was breathing underwater, Evan laughed.

He closed his eyes and began to backstroke. He dove, spiraled, and flipped without a care for his surroundings. As the boy swam he felt as enlivened and infinite as the water, almost like his body was part of it. Gradually, he realized he was moving without his dictation, as the water actively washed him. Instead of his absence of control frightening him, it felt calming. While the water twisted and twirled him at its will, the boy's mind went still; silent and serene like a sole bubble ascending to the surface.

The second of peace felt like a well-spent lifetime.

The second of peace lasted longer than it ever had in Evan's lifetime.

A thought afraid of losing its power yelled. This thought was just loud enough for him to hear beneath the silence.

Someone is watching you.

Evan opened his eyes and his heart fell deeper into the depths of the Water Rise. Before Evan's blackened eyes were a pair of huge crystal blue ones, complete with eyelids large enough to crush Evan in a single blink. Below the eyes was a great beakish nose that hung right above a greater lizardy mouth that wasn't quite large enough to house its greatest asset—its sword-like teeth that protruded from its sealed lips. Its elephantine ears flapped with the passing water, resembling wings even too large for the flying men of stone.

With crossed legs, Evan floated in a meditative

Evan & the Land of Letin

posture, and the mighty beast followed, spinning its thick eel-like body into a relaxed form of its own. This took quite some time, for its body seemed to go on as long as the water itself. Only one word swam into Evan's mind to define the monstrous creature, and even the boy with mostly forgotten knowledge thought it was crazy— *Dragon.*

It couldn't be, dragons flew high in the sky. They were friends of fire, they didn't reside in water. They weren't real, and even more importantly, they weren't so...*so calm.*

The gigantic sea-creature stared at Evan, so curiously, so peacefully. Entirely vulnerable, the boy surveyed the dragon's features. Each bone beneath its skin looked jagged and strong, ready to deliver and sustain any blow, yet despite the monster's many fierce details, Evan couldn't detect a fraction of lurking danger.

The dragon matched the human's stillness as if it were the counter image in an illusionary mirror showing its onlooker their true self beneath their skin.

In exultation of the experience before his eyes, Evan let out another bubble-suppressed laugh. The monster's great eyes scrunched, appearing to become a lighter shade of blue, blending with the water. Evan decided that if the creature could smile or laugh, he was doing just that. He looked at its watery eyes and laughed further, its smiling eyes fixed on his.

Evan stared at the black holes at the center of the beast's eyes, when suddenly came a flash.

The dragon's blue eyes instantly turned fiery and widened. Its vast mouth roared open, revealing its uncountable teeth that could do unthinkable damage.

No water could dampen the mighty roar as it sent Evan flinging back through the water, clenching his eyes and shielding his ears.

The tail end of the dragon slithered through the water until it disappeared, seemingly becoming one with the Rise.

A strong arm grasped around Evan's slick body. With a few swift strokes, he was back to the surface.

Here, the boy was no longer alone. The few early risers at the water's edge turned into a few handful, all of whom were now staring at the unfamiliar young man dragged to the shore by Kaven.

He quickly threw a cloak around Evan, pulling the hood over his wet hair.

"Let's go. Up, up, up," said Kaven, pulling the boy to his feet. Evan pulled his green boxers from the ground and slipped them on under his robe. "Just keep walking, don't look at any one."

He didn't care to look. His mind was still down in the Water Rise. Down with…*whatever that thing was.*

"We were supposed to keep you a surprise," Kaven said with a relaxed laugh. "But I think some elphs are on alert after that."

Evan continued on the stone path through the woods, Kaven's arm around him. He had left all his belongings back at the beach: his hat, his shoes, *wasn't there something else?* Soon, he'd probably regret leaving the last of his personal property back there, but now it was barely on his radar. Now he could only care about one thing.

"What was that…that thing?"

"Quite truthfully, I am as confused as you. Legends say such beasts only appear when their masters are nearby and need of protection."

"By such beasts…do you mean *dragons?*"

Kaven laughed. "You see, *such beasts*, or rather '*dragons*', are really only things of myth. Some people of the kingdom have claimed to witness a red dragon formed of metal flying across the sky. I've seen plenty of peculiar beasts, and that one we both witnessed was certainly strange. But a dragon? I don't think so."

Evan walked through the forest that floated in the clouds surrounded by unearthly vegetation guided by an

Evan & the Land of Letin

elph, yet the prospect of a dragon was totally unimaginable to his new friend. Evan thought this was very odd.

"You said the myths say dragons protected their masters?" *Who could possibly be mighty enough to control such a creature?* "Who could be their master?"

"Considering it's unlikely that it was a dragon, there wouldn't *be* any masters…several of my fellow kings and queens will likely have better answers for you, Evan, but I'm sorry. I personally couldn't present such fairy tales to you as if they were truths."

For the first time, Evan saw a hint of sternness in his new friend, a glimpse into the side surely essential to being a successful ruler in any kingdom. Quickly, his outer austerity was gone and his lightheartedness returned.

"Let's get you in our kingdom's finest garb and get this Day of Suns properly started!"

The king and the boy speedily returned to the tower without further unwanted attention. However, as Evan entered for his fitting, countless elphs in every direction lined up to stare at him. He was startled, for with their identical statures and stances, they looked like dozens of clones.

The boy turned his head, and those staring turned theirs in unison. With a sigh of relief, Evan realized the room's walls were constructed of one seamless mirror. The sight of himself too was also a shock, for he hadn't seen himself in a mirror since…well, well before he could remember. But the young men that looked back in the mirror weren't the boy he recalled himself to be.

The white cloak seemed reverent, making his reflections look otherworldly. Whether it was a product of his wardrobe or bathing in the spiritual waters, his skin almost seemed effervescent.

At the bottom half of his face, a dark brown beard has surfaced, *impressively thick*, he thought to himself. His once crisply-cut hair had grown grizzly, puffing and sprouting in all directions.

In the center of the room stood the sophisticated Valanang, surrounded by equally fantastic reflections of herself. From each angle, she looked more and more intimidating. Her hair still stood sharp and slanted like a used tube of lipstick. She wore a tight white sleeveless dress, angularly cut to reveal her flat stomach. At her hip, a knapsack woven from dazzling, diamond-like thread. Most interestingly of all, atop her right shoulder sat a small glass globe filled with water.

On Earth, Evan would have surely thought this attire was strange, but here, he imagined most could only hope to look half as good as Valanang.

She quickly approached Evan, a pearly basin in hand. Her full moon eyes must have caught the boy's intense stare.

"I am Valanang," she said. "We met briefly last night. We are not here to exchange glances. We are here to robe you in the finest threads Helvendah has to offer." Evan averted his eyes, feeling his face flush. "When you leave here, you will not simply blend in with elphen fashion, you will redefine it. First, your face."

She raised the basin to Evan's chin. He interjected, "Oh, no thanks. I just bathed."

"So you are the one out there stirring up all the ruckus? Never mind that, this is another form of facial cleanser. Now lower your head."

Valanang did not seem like the elph to stir ruckus with. Evan lowered his face into the basin. The water let out a sizzle as a light tingly sensation stirred over his face, specifically around his chin. The feeling wasn't uncomfortable, just peculiar. Valanang instructed Evan to raise his head. He did just so.

Evan & the Land of Letin

"Oh, my," she coughed. Now it seemed her face was reddening. "Fantastic. Already looking much better."

Evan turned toward the reflecting walls, and there he was—the Evan he somewhat remembered. The beard was entirely gone, dissolved in the water. Fresh-faced and beautiful. Here, in Helvendah, man or woman, this was a good thing.

"Now take off this robe."

Evan wasn't particularly keen on undressing before the superbly dressed and supremely beautiful Valanang, but slowly, he obliged.

"And this strange undergarment as well," Valanang said with a cocked head and raised brow.

"I'd rather not," returned Evan. *And first I was the one making eyes at her…*

"If you insist. Now, step atop this sheet of fabric and we'll begin."

On the ground was a sheer white cloth. Despite reminding him of the animated black fabric that fondled him at that hellish manor, Evan did as he was instructed. Valanang stepped back, and in her elphen way, began to wave her hands in orchestration. The sheet rose from the ground and began to wrap itself around Evan. With a flick of her hand, one side would drape over his shoulder, with a twisting motion, the fabric tightened around his limbs. She'd snip her fingers as if they were scissors and white cloth would fall to the floor.

From out of her knapsack, Valanang pulled out a spool of glistening red thread, glittering as if it were weaved with rubies. She unfurled this thread and threw it in air, adding it to the flying textiles. The suspended cloth zipped before his eyes, blocking his view of the outfit's progress.

Finally, Valanang took a step back, and with squinted eyes, analyzed her product. She nodded her head, satisfied. Evan looked at the line of his countless reflections and couldn't deny they looked elegant. They looked elph-like, of course, but Evan was content with that.

The outfit's white layers comfortably outlined his slender form, making his boyish body look sleek and stylish. He wore a leather-like tunic, with red-rope accents. His legs were covered in white tights that Evan found surprisingly cozy. At his waist, a crimson belt weaved from the ruby-embedded thread. Around his shoulders hung a hooded white cape that fell just below his midlevel, its inner-lining entirely gleaming red.

To top off the look, Valanang approached Evan's hair. She ran her fingers through his fluffy crown. She attempted to pat it into place, but it puffed back to its natural position. She rummaged through her knapsack for a remedy, but saw none. She decided to pin a handful of ruby-encrusted pins, comparable to Kaven's, behind Evan's right ear.

"Consider this a dedication to your generous host."

Valanang pulled forth a bench, asking the boy to sit. She slipped a pair of tall white boots onto his feet.

"They'll fit to perfection."

Evan wasn't so sure, for he noticed an extreme pointed tip at the top of the toes.

The shoe's material was soft and soothing on his still aching feet, but the pointed center of the boot simply did not fit. Evan assumed the elphs had pointed toes (he'd yet to see one up close and shoeless), as the boots scrunched his toes inward. *Where did I leave my shoes?* He doubted these were going to work, but he had no choice but to try them for now.

Upon leaving the fitting, Kaven and his guest stepped out to the pearly paved walkways of Helvendah and back into the carriage. The movement on the street below and the bridges above was ceaseless. Elphs zipped through the small city in carriages lifted by winged-men, others strapped directly to the winged-men's backs.

Though it was just the start of the day, Evan was already feeling fatigued and ready for another floating rest upon air. He looked up, beyond the glass balls, hovering and decorating the air, to the largest, most exuberant orb of all. Evan closed his eyes, the sun kissing and comforting his sealed eyelids. The warm glow planted a hope within the boy that maybe, he wasn't as far from his curious past as it seemed. He felt as though perhaps, beyond that fiery planet, his previous life lay in complete and undisturbed detail, waiting to become his hopeful present and blissful future once more.

This notion warmed him, until next to the familiar sun came another, slowly rising. Though precisely the same in body and blush, it was foreign. Despite limited memory, the boy knew only one sun.

"You have two suns?"

"Oh, no…we have eight."

"What? Eight?"

"Oh, yes." Kaven replied, "You see, for a productive people like ourselves, we require a long day. Each sun rolls by, and by the time it's ready to descend, the next one rises and we just keep working. By the time the Day of Moons arrives, we celebrate the progress of the Day of Suns and then rest for the next sunrise."

As the carriage glided along, Evan's eyes caught onto a family walking by. Between a small male elph and a slightly smaller female elph, walked the smallest elph, a little toddler, laughing and giggling as he held his parents' hands. Evan couldn't help but smile.

"Do you have any children?" Evan asked.

Kaven nodded. "A daughter."

"A daughter?" the boy was surprised he hadn't met her yet.

"Yes," Kaven responded, "but don't get any ideas. She's a princess." Kaven looked toward Evan sternly. All fathers think their daughters are princesses. This one actually was. Before Evan could nervously respond, the king laughed. "I'm kidding, certainly! I'd be blessed if she ended up with a companion like yourself. Unfortunately for all parties, she's far too old for you."

Too old for me? Kaven looked like he was at most ten years older than Evan. *How old could she be?*

"Here we are. Now you'll get a brief history of Helvendah from our eldest resident, Queen Marantyne."

As they approached the House of Marantyne, she waited outside to greet them. Her smile was as exuberant as the night before. Her red locks (which Evan was starting to think might be purple in this light) were not wrapped in a bunch this time, now they topped her head in uncountable curls, swirling upward like a frozen, colorfully filtered picture of the Water Rise.

She couldn't be a day over thirty, Evan thought. As he got closer, his dark eyes widened upon a better look at hers. Her bright eyes looked to be picked from Evan's breakfast fruit spread, for her irises were the same raspberry color as her hair. Something about them held a secret, and like the foreign fruit from the morning, he wasn't sure whether their inner juice would be the sweetest thing on this Final Earth or poisonous enough to take him off it.

Marantyne and Evan bowed heads at each other as he stepped toward the entrance.

The boy tried to whisper to Kaven, "The eldest?"

His whisper was not loud enough.

"If you don't believe it, you've got much to learn, my boy," Marantyne said with a smirk.

She guided the guests into her towers. While the outside was as white and bright as the rest of the city, inside there was no shine other than that which spilled from a few high windows.

Evan followed her hair through the darkness, which seemed to absorb the slither of sun quite well. In certain shades he was sure her hair was a stately purple, in others, he was certain it was a burning red.

Finally they reached a room full of light. At the room's center roared a tall bonfire.

The flickering fire rose higher than the short trio. Renegade flames snapped off, nearly reaching the ceiling. For obvious reasons, Evan paused, skeptical to how safe this blaze could be indoors. For subtler reasons, like the fact that a Great Fire blanketed the Final Earth, and a trusted voice told him flames were conscious, this room was even less appealing. Even deeper than any of these reasons, for reasons he couldn't quite understand, Evan knew he disdained the fire.

"Aren't you, uh," he searched for the right word, "*intimidated* by the fire?"

"We can't be," Kaven responded. "Fire is an essential fuel to so much we do in the kingdom. While we don't desperately need it, if we show fear, we have forfeited to the Great Fire. It is the fire that should be intimidated by us."

The boy liked this answer. Looking at his gracious host, *a king*, cool and confident, Evan imagined that in the unlikely event that this fire burned out of control, Kaven could suppress it.

"So Evan, while I'd love to avoid this lesson," Marantyne started, as she sat on a plush bench that wrapped around the flames, "if you are who we all believe you to be, you deserve to know the history of our people. How and why we the elphs are here, and of course, how and why *you* are here."

Kaven slid beside her, and Evan next to him, keeping one eye on the storyteller, the other of the bonfire that nearly stroked his face.

"Any proper story begins at the beginning, and any proper beginning can be rooted back to the moment it all began...

"In the universe's first moment, the Lamp awoke. This glorious light was the only power in the universe. Containing all of this power, the Lamp looked to spread its might. So, from the Lamp were born eight fairies…

"The fairies traveled across the universe, painting and creating the many worlds along the way, spreading the unlimited virtues of the Lamp. To properly protect their mother, this unparalleled source of magic, they hid this treasure deep within a world of its own.

"The very Final Earth they created was to be their home, a place where they'd watch over the entire universe for all of eternity. This Final Earth is this sphere that you float above right now.

"To properly protect this planet, the fairies crafted two men, two brothers, that would council all the lands on the planet. These two brothers were the first two elphs this world had ever seen.

"The brothers did so well at keeping the peace of the land that the fairies rewarded them with compatible mates. From there, our people were truly born. I was among the first, and our dear Kaven wasn't too far behind.

"For quite some time, life was peaceful and prosperous. We built the Kingdom of Helvendah and it quickly became the most celebrated treasure on the Final Earth. To properly govern our kingdom, we needed a king. Justly, we crowned the older of the original brothers.

"The younger, sadly, did not take this so well. In his private time he practiced wicked things…dark magic. Magic that we are not proud of…

"His sorcery required that he sacrifice his body, little by little, until that was no longer enough and he sacrificed what was left of his soul.

"He became quite powerful from his new craft, but still he yearned for more. He wanted to reign over not only his brother and Helvendah, but also the entire Final Earth and beyond. To do so, he knew of only one source potent enough to grant him his wishes…"

Sacrifice his body? The image of that mutilated man

with hardly a body left to bare came into his mind, the head from which that thing picked flesh and nauseatingly gnawed.

"That man…" Evan spoke. "That elph…" he turned to Kaven, "was that who I saw?"

"Oblazio," Kaven nodded his head. "You are following quite well."

This was true. As Evan heard the story, it was no revelation. He almost felt as though he had heard this tale dozens of times, long, long ago…

"So, Oblazio searched across the many lands of the many earths. He destroyed nations searching for the Lamp, until he decided that his treasure was back home, back in Helvendah with his brother. This was the only remaining option.

"When he returned to the Final Earth, he brought with him an army. An army of aliens that he'd stolen from their homes, and now using his twisted magic, he controlled them…

"Every step they took was forced by Oblazio. Every elph they slaughtered was by way of Oblazio. Every alien that died in the war was Oblazio's offense. I still remember some of their faces…he could control every slight movement they made. Their steps, their swordsmanship, yet somehow, he couldn't master their faces. All while they rampaged through the land and sliced apart innocents, their eyes…their faces shrieked in terror, pleading for an end."

Marantyne's raspberry eyes darkened as they looked at Evan's.

"Quite honestly, some of them didn't look so different from you, Evan."

"Because they were not so different," Kaven said. "Some of those people were from planets not so far from yours. Your chemical makeup was almost entirely identical…this is why it was an ease for Oblazio to lure you in and control you."

"Though we eventually won the war," Marantyne continued, "the bloodshed seemed to have hexed the land. Not too long after the battles, a new species had risen—goblyns. These nasty creatures believed this land to be theirs, which would eventually lead to more war."

"And you mustn't forget the sorceress—The Witch of Warantyne Woods," Kaven added.

Warantyne Woods? Evan recalled. *The dead forest, the tower with those monkey-men.*

"I believe I saw her tower early in my journey," the boy remembered.

"If that's right," Kaven said, "you're exceptionally lucky to be here now."

"It's believed by many that she's the most powerful being across this earth," said Marantyne. She leaned in, dispersing a whisper, "Some even suggest that she's one of the eight fairies herself...a twisted fairy that has allowed for all of this dark magic."

"Nonsense," Kaven protested. "She is capable, for sure. But a fairy? That's absurd."

"These are not my theories, King Kaven. Simply those of several of your peers," Marantyne said calmly. "I'll hope it's of no surprise that many believe she is at the *heart* of the Great Fire."

The king sat blank-faced, the shadow of the fire flickering across his face, fluctuating its hue from light to dark, dark to light.

"As you may assume," Kaven said to the boy, "at this point, there may be only one power that can overcome the Fire."

Marantyne continued. "Highly trusted words speak of a foreigner to the Final Earth, guiding the elphs to the Lamp. Bringing life to the Heartland and the Final Earth once more."

Kaven's cerulean eyes stared deeply at Evan's dark, almost-animal ones. "My extensive research leads me to believe that the one who will lead us there is you, Evan."

The boy's mind emptied of any useful thoughts.

"I, uh...I don't know what to say." He paused. "Where do these *trusted words* come from?"

"That you will see shortly," Kaven said with a smile. "But please, Evan, do not feel pressured. We'll have faith in those trusted words. You just have faith in yourself. We will all be patient. Be certain that it will work out in the end."

Kaven looked above the fire, as if it weren't there, and straight to the high windows.

"The third sun should be rising about now, we'd better head over to Tellus. He's going to be teaching a class that would be perfect to show Evan."

♡

The duo entered a room comparable to a miniature coliseum, complete with a circular opening at the ceiling. Sitting on stone risers around the room were elphs clad in white, peering toward the floor. On the ground were thin walkways, crisscrossed atop small pools of water.

At separate ends of the planks were four elphs geared in glistening white armor. Evan recognized the dazzling weapon that two of the armored elphs held. They spun their swords at their sides, back and forth as if the weapons were weightless. As their daggers shimmered, Evan swore the blades were crafted from diamonds.

The other two held much smaller armaments that Evan couldn't recall. From a distance, the weapons looked like useless swords without blades leaving only vulnerable hilts. The boy worried what would become of these exposed elphs.

Kaven stared toward the opening in the domed ceiling.

"Last one standing is the winner," he said. "...Tellus has never lost."

Evan looked at Kaven, creasing his brows. *Am I about to see a blood-match?*

The king soothed his worries, "Don't distress. Scarcely does anyone get seriously injured. They're only thrown into the water. Ah, look!" Kaven said, pointing skyward. "Here he comes now."

Descending from the high ceiling was Tellus, his earthy brown hair flapping like a cape on a mighty hero. Evan wondered if this flowing hair was the source of his fearlessness or his super power, for the elph landed flawlessly on his feet at the center of the planks. The small crowd erupted. Evan stood in awe.

The dual sword-wielding elphs rushed toward the defenseless Tellus from opposite sides. Before the fastest elph could raise his sword, he lunged sideways, his soaring body completely horizontal, kicking the elph precisely in the face.

Running behind Tellus came the other sworded elph, aggressively swinging at his blindside. Tellus bunched up as he rolled to his side. Rising, he grabbed the opposition's blade with a bare hand. With all his might, the armored elph tried to lunge the sword into Tellus' chest, but the unarmed elph wouldn't budge. From the back of the room, Evan could see him smile. With an effortless push, he shoved the sword and its holder, plunging far across the air, splashing into the water.

The dropkicked swordsman had risen, and now was running toward Tellus. He pulled the blade high above his head, looking to thrust downward. He stared at the attacker as he gained speed. Tellus didn't move an inch.

What is he doing? Evan thought. *Move! Move!* The elph slashed his sword down upon Tellus. He quickly raised his unprotected forearm. The blade smashed against his arm, shattering.

Splinters of the dazzling blade rained down upon the water. He picked up his opponent with his unmarred

Evan & the Land of Letin

arm and tossed him into the water.

Tellus, standing at the center of the ring, remained still as the two elphs with hilts converged on him. As they got within striking distance, they extended their arms and from their tools blasted barrels of fire. From the back of the room, Evan could feel the heat kiss his nose and beads of sweat immediately form. The flames engulfed Tellus as they relentlessly gushed.

Just as Evan thought he'd witnessed a death, Tellus was standing behind one of the fire-shooters. He extended his foot, and in a swift kick, knocked his miniature flamethrower into the pool. The flames from the opposite elph no longer had a barricade from crashing into his ally. The unarmed elph set afire, shrieking, flailing his arms before wisely jumping into the water.

Now all who stood were the seemingly invincible Tellus and one more yielder of flames. From a pouch of the pyro-elph, he pulled what Evan perceived as sand. The elph quickly threw the sand in air, and there it seemed to stay. Hanging just above the heads of the battlers were sparkling specks of sand. The elph pointed his weapon overhead and let his fire burst.

As the flames hit the floating specks, they instantly caught fire, inexplicably spraying blazing beams at Tellus. These bits of fire-sand were precise, like a hundred hired snipers, each directly hitting the unarmed elph.

The flames didn't effect him, *He really is invincible.* But then, his cloud white and oak green robes went aflame. Tellus staggered back and his enemy rushed him. The opposition retracted his flames and in an instant, the hilt now had a blade—a fiery one that looked to be cut from rubies. The elph pulled back the red sword, promptly and powerfully battering it into the gut of Tellus.

The flaming elph flew through the arena's air,

slowly falling straight into the pool. It was to be this great warrior's first loss.

The emphatic crowd was now entirely silent. Evan peered to see the flames sink below the surface, but to his astonishment, they didn't.

The flames hovered just above the water, unaware of their near demise.

Standing atop the pool, calm as the water beneath his toes, was a flaming Tellus.

How on Earth? Evan thought, and then corrected himself. *How on Final Earth?*

The cool Tellus ripped apart his burning robe and tossed it in the water. Beneath his robes were green pants that looked to be crafted from leaves. Tellus inhaled then began to run, speeding across the water without raising the slightest spatter. Reaching the land he leaped, spear-heading straight toward his bewildered foe.

Tellus crashed into his competitor and together they plummeted across the small arena. They descended toward the water until with a splash, the flame-throwing foe fell beneath the blue and out of Evan's sight.

Inconceivably, landing atop the water, was Tellus.

He stood once more and raised both hands addressing the crowd. It was as though the liquid beneath his bare feet was a steady rock-paved road. The audience erupted in cheers, shaking the ground and forcing Evan to inwardly question his safety.

The boy was amazed, though he felt foolish for feeling so. The fact that the city he was currently standing in floated amid clouds seemed moderately reasonable. *A man landing and running on water though?* He could barely complete a logical thought.

Unbelievable.

Insane.

Unbelievably insane...

Evan & the Land of Letin

♡

"You looked rather concerned back there."

"I was," Evan admitted. "I thought somebody was gonna die."

"Not so easily," the king chuckled. "If there's one thing to know about my people, Evan, is that a true elph never kills. Rather, he extends his heart to all in hope of finding peace."

Kaven and the boy took back to the street where their hovering chariot waited.

"I remember very little from before, it feels like it's been so long but…" *how long has it been?* They stepped aboard the carriage. Kaven looked intently awaiting the boy's word. "I'd like to believe the same of my people."

"I'd like to tell you I knew," Kaven responded, "but I have faith that you'll show me that's true…now, off to the shared House of Garvin and Jazamas, Helvendah's only married royals."

Their dual skyscrapers appeared to be fashioned after wax dinner candles. Connecting their towers were countless crisscrossing bridges resembling the work of a goliath birdeater with enough web spun for a hundred years. Atop Garvin and Jazamas' shared castle, a colossal glass sphere, a crystal ball, much like the smaller ones that floated in the Helvendah air. As Evan approached the twin towers, something about them made him feel uneasy.

Rather than entering the castle, their carriage shuttled up toward the clear dome. Evan closed his eyes, wincing, as they zipped up, quickly rediscovering a fear of heights. Upon reaching the top floor, they landed on a platform.

From here, Evan could see Helvendah in full clarity; all of its strange and wondrous architecture, from the buildings he visited to those he had yet to see. There was a massive coliseum resembling a solidified cloud and more noticeably, a giant boulder.

This odd rock stood out in part because it wasn't so odd at all. From this distance, it looked like he could simply snatch up the little thing. It was just a stone (*in truth, a massive stone*), yet something about it seemed defiant. It took a few seconds for Evan to pinpoint why he thought the rock was rebellious until he recognized it. Its grey sides were consumed mostly by overgrown ivy.

Admiring Helvendah in its full splendor, for the first time, Evan realized the kingdom was nearly colorless. Sure, everything beamed and there were splashes of dazzling tints here and there. On the outskirts was a glorious green forest with endless blue waters, but ultimately, the effervescent white of their clothes and skin dominated the small city. This little moss-covered rock (*which in truth, was a huge rock*), was alien. Evan felt it was calling his name.

The elphen king and his visitor entered through a door on the side of the circular spire.

"Evan!" a female's voice said, "We'd love to lie and say we weren't expecting you."

"So, welcome," the man said, "we weren't expecting you."

"These two," the king said, "are the constant comedians." Kaven walked toward the couple, gesturing the pair, the elphen greeting Evan was becoming quite accustomed to. He crossed his hand over his eye, respectfully kissed it, then he open-handedly lowered it to the duo. The woman had a full smile that looked on the verge of laughter. Her mate was stiff, as if uncomfortable with the present situation.

"Now that we're in their home, I think it's only proper to officially introduce you. Evan, this is Queen Jazamas," he said, pointing toward the lovely woman in a white gown accented with gold trim. The lines around her wide eyes were also gilded, and encrusted between her brows was an aureate pendant.

"And this cavalier is King Garvin." He wore a fitted white frock complete with a silver cape. Lined around the man's nervous eyes were streaks of gleaming silver. Atop the points of his sharp ears were shimmering silver caps.

"These two represent two of the finest qualities of the original elph. They are the last of their kind. If it weren't for Garvin spotting you at Oblazio's, you might just have become a part of his treasure. If it weren't for Jazamas, we wouldn't be so certain about who you are."

The gold adorned Jazamas let out an energetic laugh. "Don't you think you're putting a little too much pressure on this boy?"

"I don't mean to," the king said with a calm smile, turning to Evan. "There's no pressure. I know his destiny will become reality in time."

Once more Jazamas laughed, this one even more spirited. "Oh, I know this. But you mustn't forget Kaven, the future is ever changing based upon the choices we make now. The choices *he* makes now," she turned her golden gaze toward the boy. "Evan's destiny isn't written in the stars nor any hallowed documents. It lays solely in his heart and mind."

Evan looked at her gold-lined eyes and nodded. "I think I like you," he said with a smile.

Jazamas returned the smile, "I am honored."

"My dear. Evan, let's quench those sparks," Kaven said with a light chuckle, "the lady's king is present."

"I am always present, Kaven," Garvin responded bluntly.

Evan noticed that his tone was far heavier than the rest of the group's. Kaven turned toward Garvin, who seemed to have become tense, then he looked away, toward Evan.

Garvin bowed his head and his silver-tipped ears and spoke. "It is truly a great privilege to meet you. Your journey has been trying and I commend you." He lowered his already soft voice to a whisper. "The little glimpse of your future that my wife has shared with me has been nothing short of legendary. I prematurely congratulate you."

Garvin turned, exiting to the platform that wrapped around their high-rise bubble.

"He seems troubled," the king said. "I should join him. Behave yourself around this queen, Evan."

Kaven patted the boy on the shoulder before following Garvin, leaving Evan standing with Jazamas.

"Here, have a seat." The queen motioned upward with her hand and from the polished floor rose two wide chairs, far larger than necessary for either the elph or Evan. When the chairs finished rising, they looked like two precisely sliced egg-halves hovering in the air. Evan imagined invisible chords dangling from the ceiling or more impressively, silent wind at work. He lowered himself onto the comfortable stool.

Evan looked toward Jazamas. She already looked at him with a secretive and serene smile. The weight of her stare made Evan shift in his seat. It was as though the gold medallion between her eyes had the sight of a hundred extra eyes, leaving him feeling a hundred times less relaxed. Evan wanted to know what hid behind her sly smile and golden stare.

"What do you know?" he asked boldly.

Jazamas responded without hesitation, "Too much."

"About me?"

"Yes. Plenty...but I could never tell you," she said with a smirk.

"Why's that?"

"You see, Evan, if I told you, one of many very unfortunate things could happen. One possibility, you'd hear your tentative destiny and it would be come stuck in your mind until it actually became your fate without a single choice of your own.

"Another unfortunate scenario, you'd hear your

outcome and decide you hated it. You'd resist this vision of yourself whole-heartedly, and in the process, direct all of your thoughts and energies upon this destiny, until finally, you unconsciously find yourself living the life you refused to live.

"A final, and oh so, probable possibility, perhaps you hate this vision I have of you, and you incredibly successfully thwart it from becoming reality…but what if I genuinely enjoyed this vision. You see, Evan, what if I love your fate and you loathe it. That would be trouble for the both of us."

"Uh, I mean no disrespect Miss, or uh, Queen Jaz…" the -*amas* wouldn't roll off his tongue smoothly.

The elphen queen's smile widened to reveal her glossy teeth with her buzzing giggle. "Miss Jaz will do just fine."

"Well, Miss Jaz, isn't it my fate to decide whether I like it or not?"

"It is yours to decide, period. And that's the beauty of it." Jazamas paused, slumping in her chair pensively. "Being an oracle is a funny, overwhelming, and unrewarding gift. For you see, Evan, the brightest of all people discover that we are all oracles. We all get to see our individual futures in our minds every day. When we like what we see, we pursue our end aggressively until it is reality. Sadly, for those who don't like their future are often too scared or idle to change their path."

"I guess that's part of my problem," Evan said. He couldn't believe he was having a heart-to-heart with this elph he just met. Something about her felt like he'd known her for ages. Perhaps it was the fact that she knew more about his future than he did his past. "I don't really know what I want. I have no idea, actually. I mean, I don't want anything, really," Evan thought, then shook his head. "I mean, of course I want to help all of you."

"And you will," Jazamas said. "But what about *you*?"

Evan inwardly questioned himself until the only

logical answer became clear.

"I want to go home," as he said it, even this became hazy. "Or, I feel as if that's something I should want...the truth is, I don't remember home." Then his true desire became evident. "I'd like that first. I'd like to remember my past...maybe *feel* something."

"I wish I had all the answers to your toughest questions, Evan. Like, *'Why you?', 'Why here and now?', 'Where are you from?'* and *'How did this all happen?'* All of those are puzzles that deal with the past, which makes as much sense to me as the future does to you."

Jazamas looked over her shoulder, and from the balcony, the men entered. With a flicker of her hand, Jazamas hovered her chair closer to Evan and whispered in his ear.

"Life appears to be beautiful now. Enjoy it. But it will not always be so peaceful and sprightly. Harsher times loom like a lone cloud in the sky. When rain pours droplets of flame, always remain faithful that what you are capable of is much greater than what any sacred prophecy expects."

"Maybe it is your queen that is making the moves on our new friend, Garvin," Kaven said with a laugh.

"I can hardly blame her. He is an exceptionally handsome scu—," Garvin paused. "What is it that your people call themselves?"

Evan thought for a second, until the alien word zipped from his mouth. "Human."

The human and the elph left the royal lovers' towers, pressing on toward the next. As Evan looked up at the beaming sun, he lost track of which number this was. With each passing moment Evan grew sleepier, hungrier, and weaker. He couldn't wait until those eight aligned moons slid to the center of the sky and the city could get to rest.

They flew passed Kaven's towers, *the House of Duendelyn*, to a thin pyramidal structure that resembled an upturned vanilla cone. While all of the architecture was peculiar, Evan thought this one was the strangest. In their own odd ways, they all seemed welcoming, but for some reason this one didn't incite an invitation to Evan. Something about this structure seemed familiar. Its white walls were completely solid, not a single window to let in the light, nor was there a single door to welcome guests. Or so Evan thought.

As they exited the carriage and neared the house, a small hole opened on the side of the structure, expanding until it was large enough to walk through. Evan's jaw lowered, gasping. Carved into the siding above the opening were the words: HOUSE OF OBLAZIO.

Evan's eyes widened while his brow furrowed. The king stepped through the circular doorway, and looked back at a frozen Evan.

"Follow me," Kaven said, lowering his arm in guidance. "It is safe."

Reluctantly, Evan entered the House of Oblazio. Erect in the center of a vast and mostly empty pearl hall was a statue. Evan inched closer, and just like the previous remarkable model, it was composed of moving water. This water, however, was dyed red. Reminding Evan of blood.

"This is the same Oblazio?" Evan asked.

This massive representation was that of a handsome elph, a valiant soldier with his sword held upwardly with both hands, its tip just below his red nose. On the right side of the blade, a wide-open eye. On the other, a strapless eye-patch. Evan found it difficult to imagine this could have been the same wicked boned man that nearly killed him. And if it was, with all the wrong he'd learned this elph had done, *Why is there a monument of him?*

"Yes," Kaven said with a nodding head. "It is hard

to conceive, but believe it or not, before this elph lost his body and soul, he did a great deal of good for this kingdom and Earth. Aside from letting this stand for his descendants, who are perfectly fine elphs, this statue also stays as a reminder that even the mightiest of us can fall...now, where is Cyphur? Of course, he's nowhere to be seen. I'll go find him. Cyphur!" Kaven called as he traveled through another suddenly appearing hole in the wall. "Cyphur!"

Alone, Evan stood before Oblazio. He stared up at the elph's enlarged flowing face. His demeanor was strong and resolute, *Ready for battle*, Evan thought. A battle he eventually waged.

"Incredible, right?" said a girl's voice from behind the other side of the statue.

Evan peered through the red fountain and his heart immediately rattled and froze with a palpable slush.

Standing there was the most beautiful girl he'd ever seen in this life or the little he remembered from the last. Everything about her sparkled, from her straight silver hair that seemed to flow forever, to her emerald eyes, which were likely once the prized jewels of her creator. With her eyes darkly lined, they stuck out like falling stars. Her mouth formed a half-smile that Evan imagined she concealed out of respect for the other women. She made all the others he'd seen, from the ravishing Valanang to the magnificent Miss Jaz, look like wretches.

Evan stood statuesque himself, staring at the beauty, completely forgetting that she had spoken. From her side-smile she giggled. Evan recalled her words.

"Uh, uh, yes," he said. "It really is an incredible piece of work." Evan wasn't sure if he was speaking about the impressive art standing tall before him or the gorgeous girl that his eyes adhered to.

"Don't be ridiculous," the girl said, as she walked around the statue, closer to Evan. "It's incredible that they even let this piece of shit stand."

Evan coughed, not expecting those words from her elphen mouth.

"Well, I guess," he said, "it stands as a reminder that even the mightiest can fall." *You couldn't even come up with your own line?* His thoughts berated him. *Come on, man.*

She looked toward the statue with a squinted eye, then down toward Evan. "I am Delya," she pressed her hands together before her lips then lowered her head in a slight bow. A new greeting Evan had yet to see. He raised his hands, kissing his forefingers, and returning the bow.

"I'm Evan."

"Aha," Delya said, "you are the one that has all of Helvendah chattering? The one they've got me singing silly songs about into the night."

"That was you singing last night?" Evan asked. He decided he loved the voice before he'd even seen its owner. Now that he had, he was sworn to those sentiments. "You were amazing."

"Thank you," said Delya. "But it's nothing special. All of us can do that."

"Oh no, I can't sing at all."

"Well, I guess that makes you the special one," Delya said with a smile that revealed her hidden teeth. His suspicions were correct. Her beauty was unjust.

"That's what they keep trying to tell me," responded Evan.

"They try to tell us a lot of things around here…"

"Delya, away!" a voice growled through a newly formed hole.

Evan looked up. It was Cyphur, the cold elph from his flight to Helvendah. Slowly stepping forward, Cyphur kept his eyes locked on Evan like a silver tiger poised to prance on its prey.

He could feel his heart slither and beat once more, heavily beneath his skin. *I'm in trouble.*

Evan whispered to Delya, "He's your husband?"

"No," she giggled loudly, unfazed by the apparent seriousness of the situation. "He's my father."

Your father? Cyphur hardly looked a day older than Delya. They both looked set in their prime like the statue standing in the foyer. Evan had a feeling he'd turn grey before he'd grasp an understanding on elphen age.

Cyphur inched closer, Delya walked toward him, brazenly brushing her father's arm in passing. His eyes shifted to her, his brows fiercely creased. Ignoring the angry eyes, yet fully aware of their existence, she smiled.

"Hope to see you soon, Evan…*Our Mighty Savior*," Delya said with a laugh. She blinked her darkly lined left eye at Evan as she flashed those perfect pearl teeth.

A wink, Evan thought. Some things were inter-universal.

She appeared to be a pest to these mighty kings and queens of Helvendah and, for reasons he wasn't quite sure, he liked that.

As Delya exited, as did the remainder of Evan's comfort. Cyphur's sage eyes stared at the boy as he encircled him. His glare was icy, angry, as if he were inspecting something truly odious.

Like his daughter's eyes, his too were darkly lined. In fact, all of their features were remarkably similar. If Evan hadn't seen them side-by-side he may have mistaken them for the same person in passing. But the natural warmth that pervaded Delya was entirely extinguished with Cyphur. His high-cheek bones and straight clenched jaw likened him to a ferocious and fiendish feline.

"Kaven wants me to indulge you and introduce you to my craft," Cyphur said. Below his crisp voice, there rolled a purr that verged on a roar. "But I'll have none of that." He stopped circling Evan and stood frozen, a breaths' length away from his face. "You may have these folks fooled but I see straight through your nonsense.

You, Mr. Transce, will be doing no saving. Our people can do much better without you."

Mr. What? "I never—"

"He never asked to be here," Kaven interjected, entering through a fresh opening. *Thank you, Kaven.* "Fortune and fate have brought him here."

"Oh, yes, *fortune and fate*," Cyphur said sarcastically, his voice raised. "I'll allow all of this to play out for the people of Helvendah, for we both know they will love it all. But at day's end, nothing will change and people will still be dying."

"No one else will die on my watch!" the king roared. His typically cool voice was fiery and thunderous, bellowing through the House of Oblazio, shuttering the watery flow of the statue.

Then...silence.

Evan stood still, only hearing the air circulate through his nose and his chest rapidly rising and falling.

Then...laughter.

Cyphur let out a cackle, a sincerely humored sound Evan wasn't sure such a stern man could create.

"What a perverse joke," Cyphur said, settling once more into silence. Speaking to Kaven, the growl that had been lurking was fully heard.

"Get out...now! Or this scuman will make you regret your words."

"It is you that will regret your words, Cyphur," said Kaven, his royal continence returned. "For this boy will surprise you...I shall see you tonight."

Kaven saluted Cyphur with the expected greeting, but Evan noticed something was different. Instead of crossing over his eye, he crossed his chest, then kissed his clenched hand and unfurled it toward Cyphur.

"Let's go, Evan," the king said.

They exited beneath the shadows of the blood-like statue of a once great elph that towered over them.

♡

"I apologize for that Evan," Kaven said. "Though he's a man of unparalleled talent, Cyphur often fails to see beyond his own mind. There's no denying the elphs are a stubborn people, but Cyphur may be the most stubborn of us all."

"It's really no problem," Evan responded.

But there *was* a problem. Or several problems, the biggest of which, Evan couldn't precisely decipher. Ever since Miss Jaz and her cryptic words, Evan felt confused and unsettled about this new society and his hazy role in it. It was as though her words reignited a piece of Evan and urged him to look at Helvendah through different, unclouded eyes.

This was no doubt difficult, for with each passing sun and each new royal elph, Evan grew more tired. But if his counting was correct, this would be the eighth and final dignitary he'd formally meet. If his memory was crisp, *which lately it wasn't*, this would be the diamond-faced elph with the dreadful, scaled owl perched on her shoulder. Evan wasn't so sure he wanted to meet her again.

"Lastly, this is Glazzaliah's home."

It was no surprise to Evan that the odd elph had the strangest house of all. Several of its many towers jutted out and up, tapering toward the suns, adorned with odd shaped rooms striking out from different angles all the way up their planes. Spires curled in dizzying loops, interconnecting with others.

"I'm sure you two will have a rousing conversation."

As they approached the wide-set double-doors, Evan could hear a great chatter, like a large party was taking place inside. Upon reaching the entrance, a woman's voice hissed above the rest.

"Silence," she said. Without hesitation, the crowd

was mute.

The giant doors slid open, becoming part of the walls. Standing in the center was the diamond-faced Glazzaliah, her peculiar owl sitting on her shoulder, its snake tail slithering down her arm. Evan saw no sign of any other guests that could have been making all the noise. He was now certain he didn't want to enter, but as Kaven slipped ahead he saw no other choice.

"Welcome Kaven...Evan," she said with a nod. "If you'll make your way down this hall you can find a seat and get comfortable."

The corridor was formed of ivory, what Evan had come to expect in these elphen homes. But as he reached the sitting room, he was stunned.

Leaves and vines covered the walls as trees stood all about the room. It was more like the outdoors than anywhere else in Helvendah, beside the great garden. There was no floor or plush rug, only grass sprung with flowers. A tiny stream flowed through the vegetation. Her furniture too was crafted from plants, the chairs' bark legs growing from the ground.

Evan was in awe. With a deep inhale, the brisk air circulated his nose, clearing his mind until he exhaled, deciding to take a fresh approach to Glazzaliah and her peculiar ways. *This could be lovely.*

As the trio settled into seats facing each other, Evan felt a tapping on his head. He turned to see, and there, standing tall, was an animal that could only be labeled as a giraffe. Startled, Evan sprung forward, and the animal returned his alarm. The giraffe's long neck swiftly retreated, coiling down to its shoulders until only its black eyes and pointed ears peaked through. *That is no giraffe.*

"Theoluppus, don't be frightened," said Glazzaliah, her words slithering through her diamond-knit mask. "This is Evan. Evan, these are all of my friends."

All of her...oh, my. From behind the trees, appearing

from the thick grass, were dozens, maybe hundreds of different animals. Flying from a tree was a three-headed vulture with a gargantuan wingspan. Crawling from out of the stream was a blackened alligator with at least ten legs, zipping through the grass like a centipede. Perhaps the most fearsome of all, a tiger-like beast that walked on its hind-legs and possessed all the surging muscles of a gorilla.

Evan could feel the hair on his skin stand, trying to pull his body away. He could feel the early morning pennberry trying to make its way up his throat. The boy returned to his original outlook. *I don't want to be here.*

"I can't decide whether I'm the only resident of Helvendah fearless enough to share residence with a growllai," pointing to the threatening creature torn between tiger and gorilla that had already caught his eye, "or the only one that's foolish enough." Evan tittered. "But what can I say? They love me, and I love them more than I can express in my native tongue."

"I see," said Evan, tensely perusing the exotic creatures.

"I'm also aware that you're quite the loved one as well."

"So I hear," he said as he focused on Glazzaliah's red-tinged eyes, the only bit of her being unmasked. Then he turned to Kaven, mentally monitoring his forthcoming response to the words that were forming in his head that he'd suddenly decided to say. "...But I don't know why...I haven't done anything."

Kaven's stately face stood unmoved, not troubled by his words. Glazzaliah chuckled through her sparkled face.

"Don't be silly, boy," she said. "We're having this conversation now. This alone is quite an accomplishment."

Evan was confused.

"I'm not sure I follow."

Kaven interjected with a delighted smile. "You're from a distant land, many planets away. On your land, you were brought up to speak as your people do. Yet, as you sit here now in our city, you speak as if you are one of us."

How could this be? Momentarily Evan had thought it strange yet highly convenient that the elphs had spoken in the same tongue as he, but not for a second did he imagine that he was the one who was speaking their language.

When their words entered his ears they sounded as they always had. When he thought, the voices spoke in the same language they always spoke. But, impossibly, when the words came from Evan's mouth, though they sounded normal to him, they were understandable to the elphs.

"It doesn't stop there," Glazzaliah added. "You can speak with any of my friends here."

The massive growllai raised its right razor-sharp paw in a wave, "Hello, Evan." Its falsetto didn't match the beast's intimidating exterior. He wasn't sure whether to laugh or pass out into a self-induced coma.

Glazzaliah bent over on her stool, speaking only to the boy. "This is a rare and special gift, Evan. A gift only two before you have ever possessed, myself included."

"What was that?" Kaven asked.

Glazzaliah's sanguine eyes squinted as her diamond covered cheeks rose. Evan could tell that beneath her mask she was smiling. She was now speaking in Evan's native tongue. Kaven couldn't understand. Evan followed her lead.

"Who was the first?" he asked. It was as though he'd become hypnotized by the elphen words that he hadn't realized how different they felt rolling off his tongue. Now he could feel the contrast. He was speaking the language he knew deep in his heart and this felt vindicating. It was as though he reclaimed a fraction of his self that went missing.

"The first elph, the one true elph crafted from the hearts and by the hands of all eight of the fairies. It is common fact that the first elph possessed eight mighty qualities passed down from the Eight—everlasting life, the ability to withstand the elements, the ability to wield the elements, the capability to see and hear the happenings across globe, the talent of foresight, the strength to be a master of his body, the capacity to be a masterful creator, and of course, the gift to speak in tongues, understanding and speaking all the languages of the world."

"Care to share any of this with me?" Kaven interjected. Glazzaliah pretended not to hear him.

"As you've seen showcased today, some of our people have inherited these remarkable traits. And we celebrate and admire these people, for they represent parts of the true elph, the greatest being, whose ways we aim to emulate.

"Yet you, somehow, a mere boy, an alien from a distant world, possess this enchanting quality, the most valuable quality the true elph possessed. The one that once allowed him to facilitate long endured peace between all the peoples of the land. Despite what you may dismiss, you're more special than you know."

"All is fair, Glazzaliah," said Kaven, "but back to the elphen, please."

She pressed on, not even glancing at Kaven.

"Perhaps the greatest part of the gift is that it requires no effort. I speak the way I've always spoken and my listener understands. They speak as they know, and as their words enter my ear, they become the familiar sound I recognize.

"With such a powerful gift, a gift we've done nothing to earn, it's what we do with this ability that can define us. So, while you say you're not special, that's understandable. I commend that. What have you done to earn such a label? Nothing. So, you are right, Evan. You're not special. But you're wise for realizing this.

"That said, with this great tool and the true heart and just mind that emanates from your inner-self, you have all the ability to do whatever it takes for you to deem yourself worthy of that title."

Evan's thoughts rattled through his head. *It's what I do with this gift that can define me…what can I do?*

"How you made it all the way here, across the decaying Heartland is quite an accomplishment. I find it impossible to believe you did this without some sort of guidance…perhaps you were speaking in tongues without even knowing?"

Echoing through his mind were the meek words that led him here. The words that sounded from inside his own skull…

"I am nameless. I am. Only blessed. With this chance. To guide you. On this special…saving mission."

He imagined the being to which that voice could have belonged. Evan scratched at his ear canal and the crazy idea that slipped into his mind in the early morning no longer seemed so crazy.

He recalled Kaven wiping the splattered ant on an underfold of his robe. *A waterant.*

"I believe. In you. Evan. It is time. For you. To do the same."

The meek and humdrum voice trailed to silence in his mind and out pounded a proud and strong one…

"If there's one thing to know about my people, Evan, is that a true elph never kills. Rather, he extends his heart to all in hopes of finding peace."

Evan's puzzled gaze turned to Kaven. He blankly stared, his thick brows furrowing.

"Is something wrong?" Kaven asked.

The boy shook his head, shaking his thoughts back to the present, unaware of the scowl aimed at his host. Kaven perceived Evan's shaking head as an answer to his question.

"Good. Well then, we should probably get going, Glaz. The eighth sun approaches and we must be ready for Evan's big presentation at the Naliah," the king turned to Evan with a smile, "I have one last piece of Helvendah I can't wait to show you."

♡

"We're going inside this?" he asked.

"It is my favorite place in the entire city."

The pair stood before the massive ivy-blanketed boulder that Evan had spotted from the top of Jazamas and Garvin's tower.

From an aerial view it was impossible to miss, the single green splotch on Helvendah's clean canvas. From the ground however, though even larger than he had expected, it was not as easy to find. The duo walked off paths and behind Kaven's palace to get here.

"What is it?"

"You'll soon see," said Kaven flashing an excited smile.

As they reached the great stone's green side, there was a small door, just large enough for them to squeak through. There was something odd about this door, that Evan couldn't pinpoint.

Everything about the door was plain, like it had no place in this lavish city...*that's it.* The boy realized this door was exactly as he remembered doors to be in his mind. It seemed to be made of wood, rectangular shaped, featuring a plain iron knob.

Kaven turned the knob and entered the rock. Evan peered inside the rectangle doorframe and saw nothing but black. Not a single light glowing inside or any small windows to let in the eighth sun's light.

"Come, Evan," Kaven's polished, stone voice slipped through the darkness. "Trust me."

Trust me, Evan thought. *Trust me.*

When Kaven reached down to pull Evan from the ground, surrounded by broken glass and covered in his own blood, he wouldn't have thought twice about those words. Now though, he found himself thinking a third time. *Trust me...*

The boy stepped atop the door's threshold, only halfway in the rock. Kaven turned his face back toward Evan. Only his right pointed ear and a single sapphire eye escaped from the shadows.

"All right, are you ready?" Kaven asked. Before Evan could answer, the king spoke. "Ignite."

Dozens of lighted orbs filled the space within the massive rock. Their glow revealed the inside of the stone entirely. Mantling every inch across the towering walls were shelves. Covering the countless shelves were books, more books than Evan had ever seen in one glance. More books than he had ever seen in all of his glances.

Upon the floor, there were standing shelves, leaving only the slightest aisles to navigate through. The boy fully crossed the threshold as his mouth opened in a full gape. The word *library* came to his mind, and while he couldn't remember the specifics of such a place, he knew that word didn't fully define this. *This is...wow.*

"Where do they all come from?"

Kaven tilted his head, perplexed. "What do you mean?"

Evan didn't think this was a difficult question but he redirected it. "Did your people write them all?"

Kaven erupted in laughter, echoing through the grand stone.

"No, my friend," the elph shook his head, still smiling. "The books write themselves. *'Do we write them?'* Ha! What an idea. Only the most foolish of wise men or the wisest of fools would spend a moment of their life writing a book—especially when we've got these. Look around...it's all of them."

Evan's eyebrows creased. Though he couldn't think of any particular title off hand, he knew this wasn't true. Where he came from, all sorts of people wrote books. There were almost as many books as there were people. Evan was fairly certain his host wasn't intentionally lying to him, he just didn't know any better. Evan didn't want to destroy his truth.

"What do you mean '*they write themselves*?'" he asked.

"This is why it's my favorite place. We're standing amid a miracle! One morning as the kingdom awoke, it was just here, overflowing with books. The greatest thing is that there are new ones every day. Here, follow me, there's more rooms, more books I want to show you."

Evan walked through aisles of shelves stacked to the curved ceiling. He looked up until the endless rows dizzied him. Kaven reached another strangely plain door and entered.

Amid the vast room were four lines of ivory statues reading books. These stone men weren't frozen still or formed from flowing water, rather they were more like the great winged men that moved quite naturally.

Excluding a gold clad loincloth, the white statues were nude, simply standing and reading. Their muscles weren't well defined like the angelic statues, rather they were diminutive, slighter like the elphs. Their faces were stuck in a neutral expression, but their scrawny bodies suggested they were unhealthy. Evan couldn't make out what creature the models were supposed to be, and more importantly, why they were memorialized.

Despite his questions, the boy was amazed.

"This is incredible. What are they reading?"

"Their job is vastly important, Evan. They search the texts for predictions. This is how we found you. They read constantly. These sculptures have also been enchanted to search for inaccuracies. Even the Sacred Tomes make mistakes."

Sacred Tomes? "What kind of mistakes?"

"Historical inaccuracies. Sometimes they simply get things…wrong," Kaven said with a shrug.

Evan tried to follow, but the entire concept was completely absurd. *Fully written books appearing out of thin air?* He agreed that if any book appeared out of nowhere without an evident author he might call it sacred too.

"What do you do with the 'bad' books?" Evan asked, then quickly rephrased his question. "The books with the, uh, *inaccuracies*?"

"Burn them," Kaven said.

His wide, blue eyes stared, nearly searing the boy with discomfort.

Evan's face wrinkled in confusion. His heartbeat became heavy, like the world was suddenly slow motion. The boy crossed his arms before his chest. Kaven's left cheek lifted in a subdued smile.

"I am kidding, of course," the elph said with a laugh. "Among the uncountable books, despite the few with flaws, there has never been a bad book."

Obviously we're not from the same place.

"There's value in all of them. What I may view as an inaccuracy, others may view as truth. That's very important to understand," Kaven said. The words didn't flow smoothly like those from his typically rock steady self. As he spoke, the words were swift to escape his mouth, as if they didn't belong there and he wanted them out.

"If my word means anything, I'd say this place is the pride of Helvendah. When I'm not busy at work, this is where you'll find me, reading right next to our ivory researchers. I would love to show you some of my favorite passages, and there will be time for that, but for now, we must get you dressed and ready for your big introduction."

Evan would have liked to have seen some of those passages. Perhaps tomorrow there'd be some time. Maybe it'd be nice to read the words that supposedly referred to him. He'd hope to find some faults in those, maybe resolve this whole thing and get him sent back home. *Aha, you see here, that's not me…that can't be me. I guess that means I can leave now, right?*

Of course, it couldn't be that simple. *Not with all of those books.* He could spend the rest of his life reading and not make a dent in that library. Before he knew it, he'd find himself frozen still, eyes fixed on the page, forgetting to eat, lost in the endless words, failing to realize time slowly shriveling his body. He'd end up like one of those frail, shadowless figures, forever looking for himself in passages that were slowly stealing his life.

Poor creatures, Evan thought…*whatever they're supposed to be.*

Exiting the library, they approached Kaven's home. With the elph leading the way, he too was apparently lost in his own thoughts. Kaven opened his arms, extending them to the sky, embracing the sun's splendid beams.

A universal sign of joy, Evan thought.

And victory…

Kaven chuckled under his breath and turned his straight and sparkling smile back toward the human.

"They're going to love you, Evan. I just know it."

The eighth sun set. Streaks of red and blue flanked the black sky, mirroring the flaming sea below, projected in space and frozen in time.

Returning to Kaven's home, once more they were met by the towering likeness of the house's original owner. As Evan looked up at the towering flowing icon hoisting only a shield and an open arm, it at last occurred to him whom this might be.

"Duendelyn," Evan said, enjoying the way the name rolled off his tongue. "Was he the—?"

Evan & the Land of Letin

Kaven completed his thought. "The first elph?" the boy nodded. "Yes," Kaven said, as he stopped in the hall, admiring the icon. "This is he. The Great One...the One True Elph. The original King of the Elphs."

He circled the statue, viewing Duendelyn with squinted, inspecting eyes, like he hadn't seen him in years.

"He wasn't just *rumored* to possess all eight revered elphen skills, he *did* possess them. He had it all. Beauty, power...yet it was all miniscule compared to the love he exuded."

Evan recalled the bloodlike statue in Cyphur's house, The House of Oblazio. *Cyphur's father...*

"Was he your—?"

"My father?" the boy nodded. "Yes," said Kaven. "The greatest father."

Over the course of the long day, Evan had seen Kaven amiable and enjoyable, royal and stoic. He'd even seen a flash of anger. But for the first time, the king now seemed sorrowful. *Maybe it wasn't a good idea to bring him up. It'd probably be worse idea to ask what happened.*

If Evan had been following his elphen heritage correctly, this latest revelation would make Oblazio and Duendelyn brothers. Evan couldn't help but think that twisted warlock had something to do with the absence of Duendelyn. *The One True Elph.*

The boy still had so many questions. "Since he was King of Helvendah, wouldn't that make you the..." he searched for a proper way to phrase his question, "the *rightful* heir?"

Kaven snickered. "Technically...*yes*," he said in a whisper, "but after my father's perfect reign, I didn't think it right to have another king. No single elph could ever live up to what he did. So, I selected eight elphs, all of whom you met today, all of who possess a skill Duendelyn passed down through the bloodstream. Even with eight of us, we are no equal to him. But we do our best. I know in my heart, he'd be proud."

As Evan returned to his room, standing opposite the entrance was a glass mannequin. To Evan's delight, the figure was adorned in all of the boy's original clothes. The dirty ones he'd traveled through the darkness in. The ones that thinly threaded him back to home.

There was the red wool cap with a foreign symbol of a "P", that took a second for Evan to process. His grey V-neck shirt topped by his black hoodie. There were his mud-stained can't-believe-they-used-to-be-blue jeans, bottomed off by his little red shoes. His beloved red PF Flyers with their ribbed-rubber sole caked in earth. He wanted to run over, rip them off the glass dummy, and wear the comfortable clothes he knew. But Kaven had a different plan.

Before departing, the king instructed Evan to stand upon the white cloth spread across the floor. He removed his clothes and did as he was directed. Without orchestration, up went the robes, twisting tightly around Evan's twig legs and outstretched arms.

As the cloths concluded their wrapping, Evan turned to the mirror. His garb was similar to that which he wore all day, only far more elaborate. Sparkling labyrinthine stitched designs encircled the white fabric adding extra flare. His rope belt was now constructed of thin, gleaming, red-tinted links. His cape with the glittering inseam now sparkled from every angle, as it was now fully red on both sides. This reminded Evan of a hero, *a super-hero...*

He wanted to rip off the cape until he noticed the brooch that held it together, just below the garment's V-neck and right above his beating heart. Appropriately, the brooch's shape was that of a heart, or rather, *the symbol of a heart.*

Wide-eyed, Evan looked down at his new pin in amazement. Unlike the fabric with hints of ruby flashing through, this heart was carved from the real glistening thing. Its many cuts were uncountable, reflecting even more wide-eyed Evans back at himself. Its craftsmanship was supreme, its weight was hefty. In awe, Evan assumed such a thing could only be constructed by the elphs of Helvendah.

He looked in the mirror, suddenly finding himself fighting back the tears forming beneath his bottom eyelids. He wasn't sure whether these tears he refused to let surface were those of sadness or joy. He was dazzling, more beautiful than he'd ever looked. Not only did he appear like royalty, but here and now, in the kingdom of Helvendah, he was. He had it all.

But this isn't me, he thought, staring at his own nearly black animal eyes. *This isn't me at all.* He looked over at the glass mannequin and regardless of its old clothes, felt a connection with its empty core. He had no idea who he was and he wasn't sure whether any forgotten memories would even help find out.

Evan bent over and yanked the tight pointed-toe boots off his feet. He tossed them across the room as the flesh on his feet comfortably expanded with their proper blood-flow. Barefoot, he tip-toed over to the glass that had stolen his clothes. Evan swooped down, reclaiming his canvas shoes. The boy slipped them over his sockless feet and loosely tied the barred-laces.

He returned to the mirror, gathering a deep breath that circulated all the way to the wiggling toes beneath his PF Flyers. He smiled. His shoes matched the ensemble perfectly. Evan wasn't sure that he quite felt like Evan, but this was a step forward.

A loveseat carriage waited outside the House of Duendelyn. In the streets, coaches whizzed beside groups of lavishly dressed elphs on foot. The women wore headdresses with pieces that hovered and bobbed; the men, capes with stitched images that Evan swore moved. As he exited alongside the king, Evan could feel their blue and green eyes shooting in his direction. He felt his face flush, matching the color of his cape.

The bulky mix of man and bird lowered the seat as the duo approached. As they sat, their majestic wings outspread, and swiftly they rose, on route to the Naliah.

Wind gushed across Evan's face as he took in his surroundings. A familiar looking family walked by on the street. Between a small man and a slightly smaller woman, walked the smallest elph, only an inch or so shorter than his mother, laughing and giggling as he wrapped his arms around his parents' shoulders. Evan couldn't help but smile, until he had the oddest idea. The parents looked remarkably similar to those with the toddler that morning...*couldn't be.*

Beyond the castles and their interconnected towers, behind the giant crag of books, sat a monumental coliseum, the cloudlike structure Evan saw from above. As the carriage drew nearer to the cloud coliseum, he admired its cotton-like siding that made the massive building look weightless. As they quickly advanced, Evan uneasily shifted in his seat, for the stone man's wings kept flapping, showing no sign of slowing down and Evan seeing no sign of an opening into the arena.

The boy clenched and winced as the carriage flew straight through its gossamer walls. A cool mist sprinkled his face. Evan wiped his wet eyelids, and when his droplet glazed lashes raised, he gasped.

Within the coliseum, dozens of smaller clouds hovered through the open air. Atop each cloud sat elphs and round tables. Evan peered from the flying carriage to take it all in. Below him, a straight drop into blackness—a reminder that the city sat in the sky. Evan's head whirled at the image as he leaned back in his seat.

With a few wing flaps, they arrived at their dinner table on water vapor. Evan watched as the king stepped on the mist without falling through. The boy reached to touch the white smoke, and despite its appearance, it

254   *Evan & the Land of Letin*

held firm. He stepped across and settled in.

The clouds appeared to move through the open-air coliseum at their own accord. They gently floated, intermingling with the others in no particular order or fashion. Evan gazed at the elphs sitting atop the haze and realized slight peculiarities among the picture perfect people.

They were all smiling, and while this wasn't strange, it was as they smiled that Evan realized how remarkably similar all the elphs looked. Glowing white skin, flashing faultless smiles, large eyes of blue or green, long hair colored like the clouds around or like the night sky above and below. It was as though the elphs of Helvendah were one vast family.

Seeing these smiling families float passed him, Evan noticed only he and Kaven sitting here. Alone.

He looked at his host. The king was looking out at the passing clouds, subtly smiling and gently waving to all who called his name. *Does this* king *not have family?*

Only a daughter, he said…

Where is she? Where's her mother?

Monstrous thumps of a thousand drums suddenly pumped through the clouds, disrupting Evan's thoughts. On beat, the mist of the coliseum shifted from clear day-white to hurricane-black. Delineation between the clouds and the sky was indistinguishable. Chatter in the arena hushed, until the entire city became a silent part of the night. Above, the straight line of eight moons surrounded by a glittery celebration of stars were the only things in sight.

The invisible drums beat again. Louder. As they banged, the clouds briefly relit, this time blue.

Boom, they beat again, the clouds turned red before fading to black.

Bang, they thumped, green. *Bang*, purple, *boom*, yellow, *bang*, a color Evan had never seen before.

Boom, bang, boom, they thunderously thumped, faster

and faster, louder and louder. The colors of the clouds flashed and shifted in an instant, like a speeding, spinning rainbow.

From the dark sky beneath, more clouds rose. Upon them, elphs stood before large drums that appeared to have risen from the mist itself. As they struck their instruments, their booming music echoed through the coliseum. Evan could feel the vibration roll across his bony chest. He could feel his heart join in with the drums.

As their powerful music banged, Evan's mind wandered. He imagined life back on the dying ground. From there, he thought, this would sound like a terrible storm approaching. *But back there, there's no one left to hear it. There's no one left to run for cover.* At this moment, these deafening claps were the only sound on this entire earth. Except for...*except for the ants.*

Drummers beat toward a rapid conclusion; the clouds changing their shades before thoughts could identify a color. Evan looked across at the elphs, uniform with wide-eyes and proud smiles, their hue violently shifting by the second. *Blue*, they appeared as martians. *Gold*, they appeared as gods. *Green*, they appeared as goblyns. All the while, their smiles stuck. *Bang, boom, boom*, with a rapid succession louder than a firework crescendo, the drummers raised their hands to the sky and the music ceased. The cloud coliseum erupted in lightning-speed applause.

As the storm settled, each of Evan's senses that led to his empty stomach exclaimed in delight. On the table between him and Kaven was a feast fit for a dozen families. He looked around, and on every table was a miraculous mound of food.

On a plate made of ice sat a circle of open oysters lying on their shells of diamond. On another, thinly sliced and liberally seasoned red meats that looked like lamb and ham. There were all sorts of breads with all sorts of spreads, from green pastes that smelled of avocado, to brown ones with the scent of sage. There were twisted carrots that would have traveled for many yards if unfurled, luminescent beets, and basketball-sized tomatoes Evan couldn't even figure out how to begin to eat.

Stacked high as a centerpiece was a model of the entire city of Helvendah sculpted from various cheeses. Kaven reached over and snipped a piece off of what would have been his castle, plopping it in his mouth. Kaven closed his eyes, smiled, and slumped back in ecstasy.

Evan wanted to join, but thought it highly peculiar to pick at such a sophisticated feast with his fingers.

"Ah, use this," Kaven said, as he slid a strange set of utensils in the boy's direction. "You just slip it over your fingers."

It was a little gold clamp that went over his thumb and pointer finger. On the cap that covered the thumb, a miniature spoon and fork hybrid. *A spork.* Over the forefinger, a slight knife for dissecting the meal. *Only the elphs could make eating with your fingers feel so fancy.*

He daggered at the tower of cheese, approximately where his chamber stood, and tossed the bit in his mouth. Evan closed his eyes, smiled, and slumped back in ecstasy.

"Who made all of this?"

"That's a great question, Evan, but I couldn't tell you offhand," the king said. "For it could have been any of these elphs. Following the celebration, when all the elphs return to their homes, waiting there will be their assignments for the next Day of Suns. One day you might be the kingdom's chef, the next you'll be learning the ways of the warrior with Tellus. We do this to assure our elphs a full education. To give them the tools to be the best elphs they can be.

"Of course, we also do this to avoid boredom.

Monotony can lead to the downfall of an individual." Kaven mused. "And the downfall of an individual in a community as close-knit as ours could be the downfall of our community."

Evan loved this idea. To live in a place where everyone learned to do everything. Every man was a renaissance man. If anything ever went wrong in the city, anyone and everyone could contribute. *And to think, every one of these elegant elphs was also a silent soldier.* Considering they lived for eternity, Evan figured this varied lifestyle was likely the only way to avoid monotony.

As the boy ate, he turned his gaze from the overflowing dining table to examine the festivities. Whenever his eyes would return, more food appeared. He devoured the sliced lamb, then arising in its place, a bowl of steaming red soup that left the smell of lobster lingering in the air. Evan looked over and saw the king rising a bowl to his face to drink. *Even sipping straight from the bowl looks sophisticated when Kaven does it.*

Evan scooped the bowl and did the same. A slither of the warm bisque slid down his chin. He wiped his chin with his white sleeve. The red stain made the boy's wrist appear sliced beneath the fine garb. Before he could worry about the smudge, a pie composed of mushrooms, cheese, tomatoes, and bacon distracted him, begging to be eaten.

Evan picked at the pie. *Tastes like heaven.* Another thought corrected him, *Tastes like Helvendah.* A final thought added, *Tastes like Oblazio's.*

The boy looked around at all the food and coughed.

"Something wrong, Evan?" Kaven asked.

"No, no." *It's not that strange...he was, or is?...an elph.*

Evan felt his stomach expand beneath his white robe, certain this food wasn't composed of white dust.

While most elphs ate, others performed. There were beautiful songs by beautiful singers but to Evan, none matched the voice and sight of Delya. He wondered where she was. He looked, expecting to see her somewhere with her tense father by her side, but Evan became distracted.

Rising from below the clouds, red dots expanded as they approached. Evan could feel their warmth as they zipped forward.

Fire, he thought.

The fireballs flew between the clouds, whizzing through the air as if dancing to the unseen instruments. Evan's heart sank and looked around nervously. But the population was calm and unstirred by the blazing presence. *This is all part of the show*, he thought.

He recalled what Kaven said about the flames, *"...if we show fear, we have forfeited to the Great Fire. It is the fire that should be intimidated by us."*

Even still, the boy was unnerved by the fire. Looking at the flaming spheres, he counted. *Eight. Of course.* Evan wasn't sure whether he was being paranoid, but the fireballs seemed as though they were encircling their table, inching closer and closer. Without their heat, they still would have made him sweat.

Evan felt the cloud beneath him shift. He clutched to the ivory table, the only thing in sight that appeared to be solid. Their cloud was moving. Evan looked around and every elphen eye was targeted in his direction.

"Are you ready?" Kaven whispered with a relaxed smile.

Ready for what? Their cloud slipped to the center of the coliseum where it stopped, hanging just above the others so the city could see. The table full of food receded into the floor, and in an instant, a podium rose.

Oh, no. Do I have to speak?

Kaven stood and approached the lectern.

Thank God.

"Mighty men and women of Helvendah...the mightiest beings this Earth has ever seen..."

Though Kaven barely projected, the whole coliseum appeared to hear him with ease as they softly applauded his every word.

"My kings, my queens, my family..."

Kaven smiled, and several elphs stood on their feet, getting a better view.

"I welcome you here tonight to congratulate you on a successful Day of Suns. As always, it was one full of great accomplishment. Every day we set out to hone our skills and every day we do just that. We become better at what we do. And we do it all, don't we Helvendah?"

The king flashed a smile and the people cheered. Every move he made, every word he said, the elphs seemed to adore.

"From our pioneering practices in the sciences to our stalwart studying of the ancient laws of magic. To most impressively, the culmination of all of our learning to create the finest art in the lands—we study, we sing, we debate, we dance, we ponder, and we play. We do it all as only elphs can do..."

"But above all else, it's what we do the *most* that defines us. And that which we do the most is, my family, is love..." the elphs gently clapped in agreement. "We love deeply," Kaven said with a nod.

"This is a tradition that runs through our blood, straight back to the First Elph. Our One True King, not just my father, but the Father of Helvendah."

As the city cheered, Evan noticed the encircling fireballs seemed to vibrate too.

"We all know of his triumphs, building this mighty kingdom, all while maintaining peace throughout the Heartland and beyond. We all know of his dreams.... And while our kingdom remains strong, we're not blind to the reality that we have been, *and could be*, stronger. We know that the peace no longer reigns.

"Though the goblyns have long faltered, remnants of their terror remain. We've all lost loved ones..."

The crowd went silent.

"Helvendah…" Kaven paused, his serious stare circulating the coliseum. The elphs remained still, pointed ears perched on his next words. "We will lose no more."

The people stood on their feet.

The king held his chin high, stoic, and statuesque.

"Recall that morning amidst our deepest troubles, when life on the Heartland was looking hopeless, when we were reminded of our origins. When we were reminded that we elphs were crafted by the Eight themselves. And though we may not see them, they have never left us. That morning they blessed us with a gift that would forever change our fate. The Sacred Tomes gave us hope once more. They told us the truth and advised us on how to rise above the Fire stronger than ever…

"At times, the wondrous text spells out specifics that lead us on a straightened path. At others, their words are cryptic, and we must rely on our sharp and ever-learning minds to find the way. The Tomes gave us clues on how to regain our might and assure we never fall again.

"They told the truth. A truth we all knew…

"They told us the Lamp is, and will always be, the source of all power.

"And so, as many of you searched the planets, I continued to scour the Tomes for keys until finally, I found what I was looking for.

"The Tomes spoke of a foreigner who would lead us to the Lamp…

"And so, many of you then searched the countless earths, scouring the lands for this foreigner. Though we have failed before…finally…he is here."

The people roared, sound waves shuttering the cloud upon which Evan sat. He looked up at his king. His soft-spoken friend transformed into a powerful orator before his people. Evan knew it would only take a few words from him and the entire mass would move. The cheers chilled the flesh on his skin. Despite the throne being split eight-ways, there was no doubting who the real ruler was.

"You may wonder, *'How am I certain of this?'*" Kaven gestured toward Evan. "This amazing boy has come to us!"

The coliseum exclaimed louder...

"Inexplicably, he traveled across unthinkable space without an evident vessel, he survived the decaying Heartland, and most impressively, he walked out of Oblazio's labyrinth unscathed."

The elphs let out a collective gasp.

"Only a true child of fate could survive such terrors." Kaven shifted his gaze toward the boy and smiled. "Only a chosen one!"

Chosen one? Evan forced a smile back at the king. The boy wasn't sure he was fond of this title. Blood rushed from his face down to his chest, leaving him looking like an ashen elph without the glow. His heart uncomfortably glubbed at double-pace. *Chosen one?*

"As if we needed any further convincing, this morning, something remarkable occurred. I assume some of you were awoken by a little roar of sorts?" The crowd giggled.

"Legends have always said that the great sea dragon Zarkontoz resides in our Water Rise. I have always been a skeptic, but after today, I assure you...it is true."

Whispers slipped from cloud to cloud.

"This boy stood before the ferocious face of the beast and remained completely unfazed and unafraid of its evident might. Angrily, the Zarkontoz roared and retreated."

That's not precisely what happened...

"Legends also tell us that these great dragons only appear to protect the most important treasure of all..." Kaven spoke slower, softer, setting the tone for the coliseum. They all sat and stared silently.

"…A fairy…one of the Eight themselves…"

There wasn't an audible motion among the crowd.

One could almost hear a cloud move.

"I am by no means suggesting that this boy is a fairy. Never. I am however, assuring you that they are present. And they would only be so close to us right now, only for one reason…

"My fellow elphs, my beloved family of Helvendah, I introduce to you one that I hope becomes one of our family, the one you've all been patiently waiting for—Evan, The Leader Toward Light!"

The elphs erupted. Sparks shot and sizzled from the floating fireballs.

Kaven waved his hands gesturing toward and introducing Evan. *Leader Toward, oh, no.* Kaven joined in the clapping. He nodded his head, and waved the boy forth.

"Hope you don't mind that minor addition to your name," he whispered. "You can do this."

Evan exhaled and stood. The elphs got louder. As he approached the podium, Kaven spoke. "Prepare to be amazed."

The king stepped aside and the Leader Toward Light took the stand. *Prepare to be amazed? I don't even know what to say.* He peered down at the people staring at him. They cheered, Evan's ears ringing, and he hadn't even said a word yet. He hadn't accomplished anything, and he knew this, yet the applause that rained down from their clouds drowned out his worries.

Sure, it was unearned, but the power of the applause forced his cheeks upward. The boy looked at the elph's twinkling smiles, and Evan returned his, considerably less polished.

"Hello," he said softly. The crowd went still minus a few murmurs. "I, uh…I want to thank you all for being so gracious."

From the crowd came exclamations of shock. Their silence switched to a collection of conversations. Evan quickly turned his head to see the source of commotion. There was nothing, and then he heard a whisper escape from the mass mumbling that helped him understand the stir. *"He's speaking elphen!"*

Evan nearly forgot. This could be easier to impress them than he thought.

"You've all been so warm and helped me feel right at home."

That's a lie.

Yes, they've been warm, but you don't even remember what home feels like.

Shhhush! I don't know what to say.

The audience focused solely on Evan. A silence lingered, waiting on his next word.

Just say something!

"I'm sure most of you are more familiar as to what I'm supposed to be doing here now…"

Wrong thing to say. You sound nervous, don't sound so nervous.

Keep it brief, get to the point.

What's the point? Ah!

"But that's okay…I will do everything in my power to help you find the Lamp."

What power?

I think you're buying into their hype.

Nevertheless, the elphs loved his choice of words as they stood and cheered in support.

"I want to help you restore the Heartland…restore your Earth to its former glory."

The ovation continued. He looked toward the king, smiling and nodding in support. Evan decided to channel his inner-king. He'd puff up his proverbial chest and provide the people some hope.

"But not only restore your Earth to its former glory," Evan spoke louder, more confidently. He felt invincible behind the podium with a city screaming in support.

"But to bring more glory than ever before."

The cheers from the coliseum put the thunderous drum line to shame. The elphs erupted louder than they had during Kaven's speech. Even their king was brought to his feet. Kaven's blinding smile remained hidden, replaced by a proud grin that was all lips. He walked toward Evan and placed his arm around his shoulder.

"They love you," he whispered.

They love me?

Kaven raised his hand toward his people, waving and nodding to each of them. Evan followed the king's lead. He raised his hands and the elphs cheered hysterically.

They love me.

♡

Evan left the cloud feeling higher than Helvendah. Following the speeches, they circulated the crowd with Evan meeting many of those whom he'd hid from all day. He didn't lie when he said they were warm and gracious.

The men were genial, saying things like, *"We can't wait to work with you,"* or *"Doesn't he look a little bit like old Rakknastine? Hey Arti, don't you remember Rakknastine?"* The women were lovely, each one an eligible contestant for Miss Helvendah. But the already crowned winner in his heart was missing. He didn't see Delya anywhere. *Maybe she's singing the city to sleep again.*

Approaching the tower, Evan could hear a voice projecting from the rooftops. While rich and beautiful, it wasn't hers, for tonight, the voice belonged to a man.

Elphs stumbled into their towers, ready for sleep. Evan, who'd been tired from the time the first sun set, was enthused to join them. The duo entered the House of Duendelyn, elevated up to the top floor, but Kaven didn't direct the visitor to his room.

"That went even better than expected! I know

you're tired, Evan, but there's something I *must* show you."

Evan inwardly groaned. *Can it wait 'til morning?*

"What is it?" he asked.

"My life's work," Kaven said. "You've been able to see the other kings and queen's special gifts, but not mine. Calling what I'm about to show you *'special to me'* wouldn't even begin to capture its essence. This is *me*, Evan. Every ounce of my being, all the grindings of my mind go here." Kaven pointed ahead.

"Here?" he asked. They were staring at a blank marble wall.

Kaven chuckled. "Yes, here." He raised his hand outward and slid it down through the air. The solid marble wall followed his lead, slithering into the floor as if it were composed of slush.

They stepped into the round room and the wall reassembled. Floating above their heads, illuminating the small room, was a chandelier featuring glowing purple lights. Encircling the room were eight standing rectangles covered in white cloth.

This room feels familiar. Like it could've been at... Kaven must have sensed his fear.

"Don't be afraid," he said. "Nothing here is meant to harm. What I'm about to show you, very few eyes have ever seen. This is my pride and my passion, so I'm very protective. But I trust you, Evan. And I think what's here may be able to help you."

The boy gazed around, growing increasingly curious. "What are they?"

The king raised his arms, "I present to you, my mirrors."

He tossed his arms to his side, and off flew the sheets, falling to the floor.

Surrounding the room were eight standing mirrors, each intricately and impressively designed. Some were carved of gold, others silver, or pearl, or colorful luminescent stones. Several were rectangular, others oval.

Most featured the expected silver-tinted glass, but a few were colors Evan didn't think a mirror could be. He approached them, admiring their artistry. From one angle, his reflection was blue, looking like a meek sea creature. From another angle, he was red, like a mischievous demon.

"The final gift the fairies were said to have given my father was the most important of all. One that could give elphs the finest attribute of the Eight, one that, quite possbily, could lead to us equaling their might—the gift to create.

"My father was a brilliant creator. With help from his brother, they designed many wonders the typical man could never dream of. Among their finest work, they created portals that allowed for swift and safe travel from planet to planet.

"In theory, anyone can create, but it takes rigorous work and a focused mind to invent something that matches, or even exceeds the original vision we hold in our brains. Evan, I never like to boast, but I honor truth above all. And honestly," Kaven said with a laugh, "I consider myself the finest creator the Kingdom of Helvendah has ever seen.

"So, around you are my mirrors. But they are no ordinary mirrors. For lack of a better term, they are *magic* mirrors. Some of them are still works in progress. Some of them represent the elphen skills, this one for example," Kaven walked toward the triangular one, standing like a pyramid, "if its onlooker settles their mind and opens it to all possibilities, they can see their future self."

I don't think I wanna see that, Evan thought.

"This one is just as powerful," pointing at the next, also with three sides, this one pointed down. "If its looker settles their mind and accepts reality, they can see their true self, beyond their flesh and bones."

Though the idea intrigued him, Evan certainly didn't wish to see that either.

"This one," said Kaven, walking toward a small handheld mirror that sat on a desk and picked it up, "is my favorite. With this one, if I zero my mind in, I can see and hear any happening across the knowable universe. It certainly takes a lot of practice and knowledge of what you seek, but it's invaluable."

"This beauty," turning his focus to the largest mirror in the room, "I'm afraid I cannot fully take credit for."

This mirror, circular and film-thin, hung in free space without seeable support. Approaching from a side-angle, Evan almost missed it. But straight on, it was impossible to avoid. Unlike the other mirrors meant for one onlooker, this one appeared as though a dozen could stand before it and see their reflections in full.

"I modeled this one after that which my father and his brother created. I've tried to remedy the woes of the originals, but sadly, with minor success. Along with this little one," still holding the miniature mirror, "I was able to find you."

"Find me?" Evan said, his sudden disturbance instantly coming through. "I don't...I don't understand."

"I found you, Evan," Kaven said calmly, staring with his icy blue eyes. "Way back on your old Earth."

A murky black and white image of himself looking into a mirror, seeing a foreigner's reflection flickered in Evan's mind. Just as the picture faded from his mental view, the alien eyes illuminated. Their icy blue color numbed Evan. He stood, frozen and dumbfounded before the king.

The weighted words slipped from his mouth, "That was you?"

"It was," Kaven said with ease. "It was never my

intention to startle you, though I certainly imagine seeing another's reflection in the mirror would be unsettling. I had been discovering leads to where you were, getting closer and closer. I'd faltered, many times, but finally I saw you. At first, the connection wasn't strong enough. But that night, you were right before my eyes, I was ready to retrieve you then and there, but then you broke the mirror on your side, severing the connection."

Evan looked down at his hand. Remnants of five little wounds stared back at him. They were now five fully healed scars, looking like ages had passed.

"*Retrieve* me?" Evan asked. "Right out of my home?"

For the first time, Evan's quiet inner-mumblings about the king's intentions sounded.

"Evan, I meant no harm. But you are Helvendah's savior. You are our chosen one." The boy despised his choice of words. "Once you've helped us, I have every intention of sending you back."

Evan looked up at his round reflection in the traveling mirror. *A portal.* "Through this?"

"Yes," he answered. "But of course, there are the flaws which I spoke of. The pathways between the planets that my father created required a partner working on the other end. For Duendelyn and Oblazio this was not a problem, for only they used these portals. When I constructed this one, I tried to avoid such limitations, but to no avail.

"No one, not even an elph possesses the ability to teleport on command. So I had elphs scatter on various earths searching for you. Complicated matters indeed. If the elph that had been on your earth were still there, there'd be no problem. He'd be able to receive you. But I'm afraid he's already returned.

"But, as you find the Lamp, I will fix this," Kaven stepped closer to the boy, extending his handheld mirror. "In the meantime, if you want to see your family, you can use this." The mirror that could see any happening across the stars. "But I must warn you, it's not always pretty...you need to understand that your people's relationship with time is quite foreign to us. When days pass, distressing things happen to your bodies and minds that we elphs sympathize with."

"So, what are you saying?" Evan said sharply. "Lots of time has passed back home?"

The idea angered him. It felt like only a few long days here. Not much could have changed back at home.

"Oh, no, no. Not at all." said Kaven. "Of course, it is possible, but there's truly no way to tell. For we don't keep track of time around here. At least, not in the same way. It's pointless for us. For us, life is an everlasting shift between light and dark. For your people, no matter how many bright days there are, there's an everlasting dark one that looms over your head for the end. So fittingly, your people organize according to their set time. They create limits and standards based upon time of day and age of body," Kaven chuckled. "I quite truthfully couldn't tell you how old I was by your standards. So, in theory, your people try to maximize their production on earth, but from my observation, it really does nothing but limit them."

What do you know about my people? Evan clenched his jaw, grinding his teeth.

"I'm sorry, Evan, maybe I'm off track. My point is, here in Helvendah, time is irrelevant. I couldn't tell you how time moves here in reference to your earth, for it's simply not something we track. Back home, perhaps only a few mere seconds have passed."

"I want to see," Evan said.

"I warn you—"

"I don't care. I need to see," he said, extending his hand.

Kaven walked behind the boy, extending the mirror around his shoulder. Together, they stared at each other through the mirror. Evan's brown eyes that bordered on becoming black looked like a fire boiled beneath them. Kaven's iced blue-eyed stare looked like it could petrify a foe if they looked too long.

"How does it work?" Evan asked.

"Lots of practice. You must first visualize in your mind that which you want to see."

Home, Evan thought. The word was there, its meaning partially intact...but an accompanying image wouldn't appear.

Family, he thought. An image of countless elphs on white clouds sharing a meal floated through his mind.

Mom...Dad. He knew he had parents but they were out of reach. Outlines of their bodies entered his head but black clouds shrouded their faces. Evan tried to recall their voices but not even their words could slip through the gloom.

"I can't," Evan said. "I can't remember anything."

But this wasn't true. Staring at Kaven's blue eyes brought forth the image of a similar pair in his mind... *Maybe I need a reminder,* he thought. *Something to retrigger the memory...*

"It's probably all for the best anyway," said Kaven. "A time will come when you're ready to see."

Evan looked at the king's reflection in the mirror as he spoke, but something caught his attention behind their shoulders. It looked like a familiar red symbol was emblazoned on the wall.

Evan turned around. His eyes did not mistake him.

"A heart?"

Kaven laughed, "Oh, yes! As you taught me. Since I first saw the symbol I instantly grew quite fond of it. It certainly has special meaning to me. After all, our kingdom is the heart of the Heartland. I think it no coincidence that the one sent to save the land wore a heart's representation upon his chest."

*No coincidence...*Evan's face that typically appeared on

the verge of a scowl passed the verge.

"It's a beautiful and complex thing, the heart," Kaven said. "At times, it's the beating source of our emanating love. At others, it's a fiery avenger with a mind of its own. Of all our body's bones, flesh, and muscles, nothing is closer connected to who we truly are than our hearts..." The secret chamber went silent as though Kaven awaited a response. "Do you agree, Evan?"

I'm not really sure, he thought but failed to answer aloud. His eyes were distracted by a thin slit in the stonewall atop the heart.

"Is this a door?"

"Oh, yes," answered the king.

"To wh—"

"To my workshop," Kaven said. "Any respectable elph should have a proper, *private* workshop."

Evan looked at his cool eyes and held his stare.

"There's nothing in there of any real significance. Not yet anyway. There's plenty of works in progress, creations I one day plan to proudly showcase. But for now, nothing ready for another's eyes."

Kaven returned the frigid stare without strain.

There's something in there he doesn't want me to see.

Most men withholding a secret would show the slightest sign of discomfort.

Kaven showed nothing.

The king remained stone-faced and seemingly sincere. He held the face of an honest leader of the people.

Or one with countless years of practice.

♡

As the door of Evan's chamber sealed behind him, he stood alone for what felt like the first time all day.

Despite being the only person in the room, he couldn't shake the feeling of another's presence. His eyes scanned the area, only the gossamer drapery moved, swaying with the wind. Evan listened closely, but only the sound of the singer on the rooftops slid through the air.

The boy's gaze settled upon the mirror. Its presence now seemed strange and intrusive. He walked over to it. In the reflection, was only him. Every inch and stitch of his garb dazzled, from the diamond tipped-pin behind his ear to the sparkling ends of the robe that hung above his shoes. Evan looked exquisite, but he looked like an elph. *A dark elph.* More specifically, he thought, *I look like Kaven.*

He wondered if beyond the apparent image, the owner of the house were watching him.

Unpinning the crystal heart from his chest, he unfastened the cape. Evan slipped the cloak over the top of the frame covering the image of his costumed self and whatever possibly hid behind it.

On the floor lay opened white sheets, presumably his nightwear. Evan looked down at his robes. *What's the difference?* he thought, *Some sparkle?* He placed the heavy ruby heart in the pocket of his hoodie still hanging on the glass mannequin.

The spheres of light that hung overhead were still lit. *Let's give this a try.*

"Lights out," he said. They responded to his words, instantly diffusing their glow. He sprawled his body upon the ground, just as he was instructed to last night. The bed of air immediately detected his presence, slowly whisking him upward.

Air blasted beneath him, caressing him, relaxing his

muscles pleading for sleep. A coaxing lullaby whispered through the window.

Physically, he couldn't have been more comfortable, but sadly, his mind refused to settle. Lying in the bed, for the first time all day, he was able to hear his old friends chattering inside his brain. He had missed them.

I'm not feeling good about this.

What? Why?

Don't pretend to be blind. Sure, this place is beautiful. It's amazing by all visible accounts. You're treated like a god among kings—

And that's really the main problem. And you know this, Evan, an agreeing thought interjected.

I mean no offense, but why you, or rather, why me *a god? What have I done? What am I honestly going to accomplish?*

They don't even know. This is all crazy. We don't even know what we're looking for.

Sure, we do…the Lamp.

Yes, the Lamp…the same one that a once great elph searched for until it tore him apart.

But this is different, he wanted it for himself. Kaven, the elphs, they want to restore this world.

Riiight. Says who?

Yes, they do…to you.

We don't know these people well enough to assume.

Our guide told us, he told us that the elphs were the protectors of the Heartland.

And where is he now?

You know as well as I know…Glazzaliah said you're speaking in tongues. Yes, it's insane, but it's the only thing that makes sense. Everything here's insane.

That waterant trusted these people with your life.

And now he's splattered all over Kaven's cape.

I don't know…

You do know. You just don't wanna know.

Tossing atop his bed of air, sharing a heated mental conversation with the voices in his head, he quickly decided he hadn't missed them so much after all.

Alright, hush. I need some sleep.

The boy rolled over, eyes wide open.

Who are you kidding? You're not getting any sleep tonight.

Evan clenched his jaw, blew out a breath, and stepped down from the silent wind. Barefoot, he walked toward the balcony. The porch wrapped around the castle, connecting with the others. Some of the bridges dipped, others arched, all weaving together in an organized jumble.

Evan stepped out. A sudden breeze at his back was all the push he needed to explore. Onward he went, crossing several bridges. After only three crosses, he was certain he was already lost, yet uncertain whether he cared. Before him stood a twirling staircase that wrapped around the tip of a tower, leading to the top. *Why not?* He progressed, hoping to get a clear view of his whereabouts.

At the top of the flat roof, the singer stood across the way. The elph serenaded, unaware of the boy's presence.

One night late, Evan thought. The man possessed an incredible baritone voice, rich with experience, but elementary in the ears of Evan compared to Delya's.

Sitting on the roof, he leaned his arms back and stared at the sky. The stars glimmered liked hexed diamonds frozen in flight. The moons, the floating rocks in space that always enamored and invigorated Evan, tonight seemed bizarre.

Unnatural, he thought. Again, like last night, they were full. Again, like last night, they were lined up in a perfectly horizontal line, as though they were carefully placed on an invisible celestial shelf.

"Beautiful, aren't they?" asked a voice from behind Evan. Her voice sounded as though it were simultaneously polished and rasped. Evan lunged

forward in fear. Delya laughed.

She sat beside him, smiling and staring with her emerald eyes.

"Uh, very beautiful," Evan said, beginning to blush. He wasn't complimenting the moons and he knew she knew it. Her giggling smile changed to a satisfied one. She shifted her gaze from the boy to the sky.

"It's said that the Eight themselves crafted them specifically for the elphs."

"The eight fairies, that is?" asked Evan.

"Yes, the *Angels of the Lamp*. It's taught that the Eight crafted this entire world for us...the elphs, that is."

He shrugged and nodded. "Who knows?"

"I know," Delya said. "That it's all lies."

Evan chuckled. "What do you mean?"

"The elphs of Helvendah love to play pretend, masquerading not just as kings and queens but as gods mightier than the fairies in their tales."

Evan didn't know what to say. It was as though she heard his inner suspicions and actually had the courage to voice them.

The nervous boy tried to switch the subject. "So, why are you awake?"

The girl glowing with confidence smiled. "I should be asking you the same."

"Well," Evan said, "I'm only human. Our schedules are very different. I'm really tired, but I can't fall asleep."

"*Only* human?" she asked. "It's nice to hear some humility around this place. Especially from one we've so quickly put on a lofty pedestal. Especially from the one that's said to lead us to the Lamp..."

Her half-smile rose as if on the verge of spilling a secret. Her wide green eyes peered into his dark browns as if inspecting for treasure. Evan looked away.

"You are going to lead us to the Lamp, *right?*" said Delya, her brows raised in amused curiosity. "You are the one and only savior to this land, *right?*"

"No," Evan said, shaking his head in confusion and disapproval of the slipped-out word. "No, I mean, I don't know...it's what everyone seems to believe."

"Or *wants* to believe," Delya said.

"Myself included," he admitted. "I don't want to let you down." Evan clarified, but her smile had already escaped. "I don't want to let any of you down."

"I understand," she said. "There are plenty of people who want you to become just what they want you to be. And you're not the only one they're pressuring." Evan listened intently, eyes effortlessly set on the girl. "Me, everyone, really. My father wants me to be someone I'm not."

"And what's that?" he asked.

"Them..."

Them. Evan looked down at his royal white robe.

"I hear that...what is it that you are...Delya?"

Saying her name felt like a milestone passed, a weight lifted. The way her name glided off his tongue was a revelation. *Delya*, he thought. *Delya.* It sounded just as pleasant as it repeatedly, *Delya*...echoed *Delya*, through his mind. *Delya...*

"I don't know," she said frankly.

Evan smiled and nodded. He was surprised for he had expected self-certainty from her.

"It seems we are kindred," Evan said.

Delya laughed the purest laugh, a sound that left her glowing smile and grooved across Evan's shoulders before entering his ears and making him feel weightless. Her grinning eyes engaged his, pulling him into the little black holes at the center of the earth colored irises. If he got sucked into oblivion right here and now, if it were next to Delya, he wouldn't care. At this moment, high above the heart of the Heartland, her pure laugh was the only significant sound in the world.

"All of this leads back to your question," said Delya.

Oh, that's right. He retraced the conversation in his head, *Why are you awake?* She answered, "…I'm leaving."

"What?" He thought he'd heard her clearly. He didn't want that to be the case.

"I'm leaving Helvendah," she said. He had definitely heard her clearly. The carefree tone of the conversation vanished into the night.

"Why?" Evan asked. "How?" shaking his head. "You can't."

"I can," Delya said. "I shouldn't. But I most certainly can." Evan decided that was a poor choice of words. This was not someone fond of being told what they can and cannot do. "And I most certainly am."

Evan recalled the darkness, *endless darkness.* He remembered that madman and his maze, *and how he almost ate my face.* And of course he recollected the fire, *the flames…they went on forever.* He wished he could throw the looming fire from his memory. But it was everywhere. *It covered this earth. There was no earth. Just fire.*

He recanted the terrors of the dying land below, imploring her not to go.

"That's what I've heard," Delya said.

"And it's all true," Evan responded. "I've been there. And I'm lucky to be here now."

"I'm lucky that you're here now," Delya said. Evan resisted the urge to blush and look away, and instead remained locked on the girl's green eyes. "You've brought with you this buzz that I've never felt in the kingdom before…but I've got to see everything for myself."

Evan thought about the slight fraction of the world he remembered.

"This place is the greatest place I've ever been or seen, on this land or my old one."

"Really?" said Delya. "That's depressing."

Evan laughed. "I guess, I just mean that we should be grateful for what we've got. All these riches around us."

Delya leaned closer to the boy, still searching his eyes until hers widened. She nodded as though she found what she looked for.

"You are wise, Evan."

"Thank you," he answered, though he wasn't sure it was true. "As are you."

That he was certain of. This gorgeous elph with a voice that could bring down the heavens had the mind to debate its inhabitants once they hit the ground.

"Despite your wise warnings, *Leader Toward the Light*, was it?" she said with a giggle. "Next Day of Moons, I am leaving. And you are welcome to join me."

Evan re-imagined the dying, empty world below and suddenly, it enlivened with the sole presence of Delya.

We could do it. We could survive.

Shut up, Evan, a thought of reason interjected. *Don't be an idiot.*

"You know I can't. They need me here," Evan said. Delya raised an unconvinced eyebrow. He clarified, "Or, I mean, they think they do."

"That they foolishly do," Delya said. Evan's ego winced. "So, I suppose you're right. That said, my offer will still stand. You can meet me one day from now at the statue in the Garden of Kylen once you've changed your mind."

"*Once,* I've changed my mind?" Evan laughed. "You seem very certain that I will."

"Oh, Evan, it's not only the eight kings and queens that possess those special traits."

She leaned in closer to Evan's cheek. He froze like a blood-pumping statue. His mind was quite fond of images of the winsome girl close to his skin, but now as it happened in reality, her beauty was petrifying.

She whispered in his ear, "I *will* see you then." As her cool breath stroked his skin, her words slid down his ear, and before he could fully process them, he already believed her.

Her arms slid across his back, up toward his shoulders and she pressed her body closer to his. Evan's heart hammered as his mind worried that she could feel his heart beating wildly. There was a word for this gesture, *What is it? Ah…a hug.*

He returned the motion as he wrapped his arms around the elph. Though this was his first hug in recent memory, as they held each other tight, he could feel the lingering imprint of embraces past.

She whispered once more, "Consider that maybe my plan is best for both of us."

Delya released the hug. She looked into the boy's purple-dashed brown eyes, raising her side smirk. Evan's thoughts yelled for him to lean forward, kiss her perfectly full lips.

Wise thoughts advised otherwise… *You didn't even know how to hug the girl.*

Before he could make a decision, Delya back-peddled, still staring at the boy.

"Goodbye, Evan."

Only her voice could make those simple words sound profoundly sad yet mysteriously full of promise.

She turned and proceeded down the spiral steps, disappearing silently out of sight just as she had silently appeared.

Her words however, did nothing to quiet Evan's mind.

He wondered if she was serious about leaving. *And me leaving with her?* He was pretty sure she meant it, but he was never good as such things. Evan rose, jogging to the stairwell. He peered down but Delya was gone. He circled down the steps, and when he reached the bottom, didn't know where to go next.

Did I come this way, or was it that way? With all the coils and curves, with all the white on white, it all looked the same. Despite being alone and lost in the middle of the night, *at least I'm not on that hell below*, he thought.

Nope, only a hell high in the heavens.
Enough! Now, let's find our bed.

Thoughts bickered as he glanced over the side of a bridge, inspecting his whereabouts. Floating amid the castles' courtyards were the countless glass spheres. Evan wondered what they were for. *To look pretty, like everything else here.* Though they were pleasing to the eye, Evan had a feeling that wasn't it.

Staring at the hovering glass globes, Evan could see miniature reflections of Helvendah impressed upon each. But these mirror images weren't exact, for against the curve of the glass, the twisted and whirled towers of the kingdom looked straight and structurally sound; they looked almost like small city skylines seen from across a bridge and atop a hill. Those little inversed and altered images almost made Evan feel close to home...then in the reflection of the glass orb, he recognized a giant ivory cone directly behind him.

Evan turned, and there was a tall open window, its opaque shades fluttering toward him. Beside the window was the empty outline of a boy wearing dingy old clothes. The tired Evan entered.

"Lights out," he whispered and the lights did as he commanded. He dove upon his airy cushion and fell asleep, no closer to home or even an image of such a place.

*

Clouds brushed across his misty mind's eye. Evan tried to clear his eyes only to find no fingers to wipe with, no hands or arms to raise and no bodily source of his sight. His existence was vision alone, absent of any palpable connection to a brain. He was there, yet he wasn't. *Where am I?*

He simultaneously gazed at the space from below and above, focusing his vision on white clouds

Evan & the Land of Letin

accompanied by more clouds, shrouding even more clouds.

Deep in his mind, wherever it was, he began to comprehend the floating images before him.

At the center of the encircling valley of clouds, a beautiful and vibrant man rose. His chilling blue eyes scanned the surroundings. Around him, a vast crowd sitting on white mist. The man opened his mouth to speak, but Evan couldn't hear a word.

The speaker's face was stern, his eyebrows clenched, as he panned the audience with motioning arms. The people were undoubtedly his, for as he spoke, they mirrored his image. Their faces were serious, some saddened, others hardened and ready to strike.

The vision focused on the man's moving lips, trying desperately to interpret his words. For a brief moment, the king's gorgeous face turned vicious as his mouth opened in a roar that didn't need a sound to be loud. The speaker raised his hands, and as one, his people rose to their feet.

With the king's arm's spread wide, Evan noticed a glistening gem encrusted amid his chest. The tip of the ruby crest consisted of two-half circles curving toward the bottom meeting at a point. *A heart.*

In an instant the black sky above flashed red before quickly shifting to a white blaze.

He felt his body quivering and shaking, rocking back and forth though he wasn't within it.

♡

"Wake up, Evan," a voice said, as hands gently rocked his body. "Wake up."

Behind his sealed eyelids, he wished it were his father there to greet him. He wished he was back home, wherever that was, with all of his memories back and intact. He knew this was only a dream.

Evan opened his eyes. Kaven peered down upon him.

"You gave me quite the scare there. I thought it was best to let you sleep in this morning, but I was getting worried. The fourth sun is about to rise. We must get you fed and set out to work."

But Evan wasn't up for work. He didn't care which sun was rising; he would be set with sleeping all Day of Suns. But there'd be none of that with Kaven's big plans. Half-asleep, Evan was whisked and whirled while white linen constructed the day's clothes. When the textiles stopped their turning, Evan inspected himself. In his white leather hood, he looked identical to the eight elphs on the night he met them.

Down in the dining room, Kaven sat, enjoying a glowing grape. The king's white robe mirrored Evan's, from the length of their inseams to the width of their shoulders. Together, they looked like twin specters with an affinity for lavish berries. Though Evan's pennberry was just as plump and juicy as the day before, he could barely force down a bite.

Evan found his thoughts astir about his dream. *But it wasn't a dream…*it felt so real. *So tangible.* Yet not tangible at all for, *where was my body?* Evan found that his eyes had wandered and set upon the beautiful, effervescent face across the table…*it was him.*

"You're awfully quiet today, Evan. Is something on your mind?"

I'm often awfully quiet, it's you that does all the talking.

"Oh, no, no. Just a tad tired," Evan said, anxious to redirect the conversation. "What's on today's agenda?"

"Well today, Evan," the king said with his magnetic smile, "you fulfill your destiny."

Evan coughed. *I thought there was no rush.*

"And, uh…how is that?"

"Are you all finished eating?" Kaven asked. The boy nodded. "Very well, let's be on our way."

Evan & the Land of Letin

From the room-wide windows, they exited to a wrap-around porch. Floating aside the balcony were a pair of marble stepping-stones. Kaven stepped atop one, Evan the other, without second thought. The stones rose, and his legs shivered as he refused to look down. The rocks and their riders elevated, reaching the flipped-cone castle's sprawling flat top.

With the fourth sun rising at what appeared to be eye level, Evan couldn't fathom how high he stood. He was at the highest point of the highest tower in a city that sat in the sky. A thought suggested he could blow out the sun's flames. Another saw the little human sent flying with the slightest gust of wind, falling from the sky, as unseeable and unimportant as a speck of dust descending to the ground.

"This is Lady Milette, more affectionately known as 'The King Glider'. She only has the room for the two of us, but she's the fastest old bird on this planet. She once made the eight-bridge crossing in less than twelve…ah, I don't recall the specifics, but she holds the Final Earth record. I haven't taken her out in quite a bit, but I figured today would be perfect."

She's absolutely beautiful. With her picturesque pearl face and flowing white locks covering her frontal curves, she was the first woman-bird hybrid Evan had seen. Beneath her exceptionally longneck, her body belonged to a swan enormous enough to cross the heavens in a few flaps and cause tidal waves with a slight splash in spanless waters. Perched at the heart of her back was a white loveseat formed from her stone flesh. Kaven climbed aboard. Enamored by her elaborate detail, how each dash in her feathers was delicately carved, Evan slowly followed.

He settled in, and without hesitation the king exclaimed. "Rise!"

Kaven's hands danced, and the wings of the swan sprawled. In a few swift moments they were up, up, fiercely rising. Bursting through layers of clouds, puff misted their faces. Evan's heart rattled, and *higher*, its beat began to, *higher*, slow. He tried to inhale but with no success.

Can't. Evan clenched at his throat. *Breathe.*

"Can't," Evan squeaked out. "Breathe."

Kaven looked at his passenger, puzzled.

"What's wrong?" he asked, chuckling. The captain of the flight turned away. Upward they zipped, faster they flew, and quickly, Evan was turning blue. He threw his arms at Kaven for help. The king looked back, and after a moment, finally understood.

"I'm so sorry! Do forgive me, I keep forgetting you're not an elph," Kaven thrust his right hand toward the innards of his cloak. "We're not so easily affected by the elements."

From his robe, Kaven quickly pulled a glistening blue diamond and placed it upon the Glider's back. With a tap, the stone stood still and from it expanded a sky-colored film that enveloped the flying duo. Beneath the bubble Evan could breathe again, which he did so heartily with huffs and puffs.

"Thank," Evan said, panting, "you."

"You're very welcome," returned Kaven, peering over the side of the swan. "Now," he said with a smile, "grasp her feathers."

The slippery sleek swan had no feathers that could be grasped. Regardless, Evan tried, but it was too late. The King Glider plummeted, spiraling through the clouds as its pilot laughed. The unamused copilot, body pressed flat against the back of his seat, couldn't control his eyes as they rapidly fluctuated between popping out and aggressively sealed.

With all of his courage, Evan looked passed the bird's longneck. Ahead, nothing but a sea of red bubbled below him. They were heading directly toward the flames.

As Evan was certain he was meeting his fiery end,

Kaven pulled back with his forefingers and the Glider steadied above the flames, smoothly flying just above their licks.

Evan glanced at the hazy red horizon. The sea sizzled and roared. He swore it applauded its own majesty, rejoicing at the attention it received from the miniscule human. Sweat dripped beneath his hood as aspiring flames spit and circled in air, fighting for a better glimpse at the boy who suspiciously eyed them. Evan turned to Kaven to gauge his captain's comfort level so close to danger. The elph remained unmoved by the flames, as if he didn't even notice them.

Beyond the king's pearly profile, through the smoke-shivering air, Evan noticed several massive arches extending across the flaming sea and into the unseen. Miraculously, they stood unsupported. Inexplicably, they seemed to trail on forever. Kaven noticed the direction of Evan's attention.

"Those are my father's bridges—*'The Eight Bridges of Duendelyn'*, as they're called. They once connected all of the major lands of the Final Earth back to the Heartland."

"They went across the ocean?"

"That's right. Not all of the nations were blessed with the ability to fly. This made for far easier and safer travel for all. It was a collaborative effort between all of the people."

"Amazing."

Kaven nodded. "What's truly amazing is how long they've lasted. My father once envisioned a place where all the people, in all the lands, the mermen, the lyftmen, the trolls, the polefolk, all of them could coincide together in peace. Of course, this was long before the goblyns came to be…" Kaven momentarily closed his eyes and trailed off, as though suppressing agonized thoughts.

"Our Final Earth would have been one nation," he

continued. "My father liked to refer to his dream as '*The Land of Letin*,' at least to his family. Ironically, he valiantly died defending his vision at the hands of those he worked so hard to help. I suppose you could say his dream of Letin died right alongside him."

Kaven fell into silence. His eyes remained focused on the path ahead where land seemed to reside. With the King Glider drawing closer to a towering mountain, its peak appeared to curve outward over the fire, hovering above their heads like an all-encompassing canopy. The conical shadow that fell on the Glider and its riders forced a jittery wave down Evan's flesh. He grasped at his chest, suddenly feeling a rapid tapping above his heart.

What is that?

Evan felt something solid and small hanging beneath his robes. With an orchestration of the king's hands, the Glider was slowing down and Evan was distracted by fearful thoughts.

"Is this where we're going?" he asked.

"It is."

Against the black sky, nothing about the blacker mountain felt promising. The King Glider landed at the foot of the precipice. Kaven climbed out without hesitation. Evan was not so keen. He eyed the side of the giant mass. This was no ordinary mountain.

He figured it was once inhabited, for carved upon its stone sides was a corridor, spiraling all the way up to its peak. Along the honeycombed hallways were compartments that led within the mount itself. How this came to be was yet another wonder of this Final Earth. It was as though a monstrous snake once enwrapped the crag, and with a mighty squeeze, crushed its slopes and forever left its imprint. Evan didn't want to imagine the crawlers that possibly crept through the mountain's halls, but he did, and he wanted no part of them.

"This is Mount Asylia," Kaven said. "Home of the

goblyns."

Yeah, definitely no, Evan was sure. He didn't want to be here.

"Thankfully, they've been gone for countless days, leaving no signs of where or how they departed. It's as though they all suddenly disappeared into the air. I consider this yet another blessing from the fairies. However, I've been reading interesting things about this place. Magical things are happening here. Mysterious things, possibly dark, but no doubt magical. My research leads me to believe this place may lead us to the Lamp."

"Do you think it's inside?"

"Perhaps. The goblyns built cabins all throughout the mountain. I quite honestly find it difficult to believe that one of those ghastly creatures may have had it and not used it for evil." Kaven perused the former goblyn abode, turning back to Evan. "You will lead the way."

"I don't—"

"Nonsense," he said, helping Evan down from the Glider. "I believe in you. It's time you start believing in yourself."

The elph wrapped his arm around the boy's shoulder as they stepped forward. Evan couldn't fathom where to begin but the natural shape of the mountain seemed to dictate their course; the bottom would be easiest. Rising the steps etched from the stone, Evan's eyes couldn't settle.

Everywhere were carvings of peculiar symbols and sculptures of remarkable creatures. Not an inch of the mountain remained undecorated in its natural form. Even the gravel seemed littered with sparkling gems. But the oddest thing, Evan quickly realized, was how poorly cared for the art was. Every statue had a missing limb or a skull smashed in. The labyrinthine marks upon the walls had deep slashes through them and were stained every shade of deep red.

"What happened to all of this?" he asked, running his

fingers across a circular pattern on the stone.

"Before the goblyns, Mt. Asylia served as a spiritual sanctuary to the elphs. It's rumored that these cabins were carved out by the earliest elphs with the help of the Eight themselves.

"Look at this," he said, pointing into a massive hall. Its stalagmite tables and corresponding chairs rose right from stone. The stalactite chandeliers glistened as they hung from the high ceiling. "I wish I could take credit for this, but I can't. But I can tell you with certainty, no goblyn could comprehend such beauty. They ransacked and destroyed these halls when they claimed them as their own."

Evan walked on, his curious eyes leading the way. For once, Kaven steered the rear, as though the boy actually knew where he was going. Upon the reaching Mt. Asylia's first apartment, he peered his head into the darkness and quickly pulled it out. There was no chance he was blindly walking into a black room that once belonged to a goblyn. But of course, Kaven had a remedy, and pulled out a small glass ball, like those that floated around Helvendah. He tossed it in air, and upward it floated like a balloon, gently hovering above their heads.

"Ignite," Kaven whispered.

The globe filled with enough light to fill the dark cabin. At the center of the deserted space was a slate bed carved from the ground. Evan was instantly grateful for his bed on air. Under the direction of Kaven, the light traveled deeper into the room. The boy followed, slowly peering into the room's dustiest crests. *Nothing.*

Evan was certain that the world's mightiest power wasn't in this drab little room, so onward he marched toward the next. With the light encircling his head, he felt less afraid. Again, aside from the stone and surely agonizing bed, there was nothing. *This wouldn't be so hard*, Evan thought. If there was anything in these rooms he'd instantly see it, for being as they were, they were completely empty.

Onward Evan led, getting the hang of this, and into the next room—nothing. And to the next—nothing.

Four rooms in and, *oh, no.* This would be very hard. His dark brown eyes travelled up the similarly colored mountain. There were more rooms than he could ever count. *Are they all empty? Is this all a waste of time? How did this happen?* Either the goblyns had no possessions when the vanished or they impressively took all their belongings upon departure. Aside from ruined statues, scratches upon the stones, and the beds one might imagine only slept on in the underworld, there were zero goblyn remains. No shriveled corpses, *thankfully*, no forgotten trinkets nor abandoned clothes. *Definitely no Lamp.*

Nonetheless, Evan trekked on, feeling sillier and sorrier with each empty room. He glanced passed the peak, toward the clouds, when without warning, the weight of the sky came thrusting down upon him.

Evan fell to his knees, projecting a painful scream, echoing to the tip of Asylia. Kaven reached out to him and wrapped his arms around the boy.

Evan reached at the back of his neck, where it felt the entire Final Earth sat. He felt a thin string and instantly pulled it from his nape, over his scalp, and threw it onto the ground. It fell with a clank, as Evan let out an exasperated breath.

"What happened, Evan? Are you all right?"

"I'm fine, I just—" he noticed a grey medallion attached to a dingy string stuck into the dirt surface. *What is that?*

Evan leaned over to examine its details. The word *key* floated through his head, but that wasn't it. The shaft of the key-that-wasn't looked like two thinner shafts twisting together as one, spinning toward its head before splitting off, forming two long-fingered hands. The two miniature hands mirrored one another, meeting only at their fingertips, as they grasped what appeared to be a tiny grey marble. At the bottom of the charm, the curved scooping blade of the object gave this mystery a name.

"What is that?" Kaven asked with squinting eyes, peering closer.

"It's a, uh…a shovel."

"Meant for?"

"For digging," Evan said, reaching toward the charm.

"Don't touch it," warned Kaven.

It was too late. Evan scooped the little shovel from the ground. *Was this what was hurting me?* It seemed like a stupid thought, but Kaven seemed to think so. The boy felt strides better after removing it, but now with the little grey shovel in his hands, it felt nearly weightless. It was as though for the slightest moment, this miniature medallion had a mind of its own and it wanted to send a message…

"What do you mean, *digging*?" Kaven asked, extending his silvery palm toward Evan, awaiting the placement of the shovel.

Evan twirled its little twisted arms in his fingers, and with great hesitation, placed the necklace in Kaven's hand.

"You know…like in the ground."

The elph brought the charm close to his eyes, reviewing its intricacy. Its dull grey color looked lifeless next to his oceanic eyes.

Kaven laughed. "With this little thing?" Disinterested, he placed the shovel back in Evan's hands and walked on.

The boy looked down at the trinket like it was the most important thing he'd ever possessed. Protectively, he squeezed it until his knuckles turned red. Without much thought, he quickly decided this odd key-shaped shovel was indeed a key of sorts. Perhaps, the key to

Evan & the Land of Letin

finding answers.

An invisible hand danced in his mind as it gracefully scratched the words *Dig Deeper* right across the dark side of his forehead.

"Dig," Evan thought aloud. "I think we should dig."

Kaven laughed, shaking his head.

"Do you think we've searched all this time and never thought to dig?"

"Well, no—"

"We dig as far as we can," Kaven interjected.

"Dig deeper," Evan responded, an acerbic bite behind his words.

A smile grew across the king's face, seemingly amused by the boy's tone.

"There is no deeper," Kaven said. "There is only Death. Beneath our deepest layer there's only blackness. Oblivion."

*That couldn't be...*Evan thought.

"We've searched as far as we can, any deeper and there's no returning."

That's impossible, Evan thought. There were no specific lessons he remembered from the Earth Sciences course he took freshmen year, but Evan didn't need substantial details to know this. Planets were globular, therefore enclosed...*there couldn't be endless space within something.*

Of course there could be, a thought whispered.

The path around Mt. Asylia seemed endless. The empty rooms appeared to become emptier the further they progressed. Higher, closer to the black peak, closer to the starless sky, the less words the pair shared. With each passing room, despite the wind making figure-eights between their arms as they walked side-by-side, Evan felt a space rapidly expanding between the two. He knew Kaven felt it too.

Evan made a decision and didn't care to voice his plan of action. He progressed passed an empty room without searching. He heard Kaven chuckle and mutter under his breath. Then again, he passed another, without so much as turning his head.

Finally, the king froze and stared toward the fire. Evan knew he wasn't finding any immortal treasure in these caves, and realizing this, he felt more confident in his elphen hood than ever.

"We're leaving," Kaven said. The boy caught the coldness in his voice.

"Maybe we'll have more luck tomorrow," Evan responded, careful not to let his partner see the smile upon his face.

He wasn't sure why he found his current predicament humorous, but he did.

What is he thinking, taking me to some random mountain and expecting me to navigate our way to this Lamp? The whole operation suddenly seemed frivolous. Inwardly, he searched for a proper way to express his outlook, but he figured now was not the time. Looking at Kaven, stone faced, his blue eyes frozen over, he clearly didn't find their lack of success entertaining.

The stoic elph gestured toward the land and from it rose the Glider. Kaven stepped aboard without glancing backward. Evan hopped on the hovering swan, just as the king sent it flying.

Evan braced the backend of his seat, careful not to fall. Without a care, Kaven flashed forward, ignoring the flopping body beside him. When Evan secured his bottom to the pearly bench, nothing about their current whereabouts felt secure.

Flames slapped and slithered up every side of the swan. *Maybe I'm crazy*, he thought, *but it feels like he's slowing down.*

The Glider's wide wings retreated and tucked against its sides. Evan pulled his feet up as flares spat and sizzled upon the Glider's floor. The great flying machine now appeared like a toy boat upon blazing waves.

Evan had listened to the few thoughts concerned

about the king's intentions; not once did he become troubled. Moments ago, Kaven seemed lighthearted. But now, floating upon the Great Fire, the hard-faced elphen king was unmoved by their surroundings. Evan was afraid.

"Why are we slowing down?"

"What's that?" Kaven's smooth voice was monotone.

"Why are we slowing down?!" Evan yelled. He could barely hear himself over the crackling flames and his terrified thoughts.

"Blessed Eight!" exclaimed Kaven, his sapphire eyes reinvigorating. He quickly composed his hands and the Glider's wings unfurled. With an upward dash of his finger, they were again airborne, and the boy fully confounded.

"I'm sorry about that, Evan. Sometimes I get so lost in my own thoughts." *I know that feeling.* "And this fire never helps. Sometimes I look at it and I forget that I exist."

"I'm not sure I follow."

"Just look down at it. Go ahead, look."

Evan preferred not to, but he complied. The Great Fire spurred ripples around his flesh. He swore that monster was alive.

"Look at how vast it is, it seems to go on forever. When I think about all that the fire has taken, all that we've lost at its flames, I almost feel like I'll be the next to go right along with it. It feels like that unconquerable mountain. This is why we need the Lamp."

Without much thought, Evan voiced his thoughts.

"Have you ever wondered if maybe this whole *'Lamp'* thing doesn't actually exist? Like, maybe it's just something we've all been taught to, perhaps," he struggled to find the right words. "...Recognize a greater power beyond us?"

Kaven snickered and scoffed. "Never. The Divine Tomes say otherwise..."

"…That's fair. But maybe it's not actually a tangible thing, but rather…a life pulse within us. And all around us."

Evan hadn't expected to say these things. In fact, he hadn't known these things were in his head, but he liked them.

This time, Kaven did not snicker or scoff. Instead, he looked as though he let the human's thoughts intermingle with his.

"The idea interests me, but it's flawed. If the Lamp were within us, it'd be all we needed. We'd already be at peace."

"Maybe it's that we don't *realize* it's here, and if we did, we'd be a whole lot closer to," the thought shot from his heart up to his head where the word was found but couldn't fully be processed. *What a lofty concept.* "…peace."

"Who knew you were a little philosopher?" Kaven said with an amused smirk. "I like it…but I don't encourage it. I'd keep my novel ideas to myself if I were you. Some of the kings and queens won't be so fond of hearing their savior say they'll be no salvation."

"That's not what I'm saying at all," Evan tried to clarify. "In fact, the opposite. If we realize that it's already part of us, we'd be——"

"Enough!" yelled the king.

A flash of blinding red rose from the Great Fire, grazing the Glider's hull. Evan's arm shielded his face as he cowered in his seat. Without warning, the flames reached Helvendah heights, and in an instant returned down to sea level.

In a few majestic flaps, the King Glider returned to the flat top of Kaven's castle. To the right, the eighth sun shimmered as it fell behind the black clouds. To the left, the eight moons were rising like a pearl necklace showcased by unseen ethereal hands.

For the remainder of the flight, Evan let his thoughts

circulate and successfully suppressed most, but there was one rumination he had to let out. Standing atop the House of Duendelyn, he wished the whole kingdom could hear his confession.

"I will no longer share my *'novel'* ideas," Evan said. The king turned back toward him, his cold eyes chilling over the boy's black ones. "But it should be known that I am no one's savior."

"Believe me," returned Kaven, without the slightest trace of worry, "I've already started to see that."

Kaven turned, approaching the pair of twin winged-men carriages standing on the roof's perimeter. He walked briskly, several steps ahead of Evan.

The boy thought he heard Kaven speak softly to the statue. "…with the others."

With the others? Then he was certain he'd been heard him speaking to the statues.

"Return him to his room, Nabble," the king spoke to Evan without looking at him. "Then meet me in the foyer when you've changed."

♡

High above the streets of Helvendah, Evan saw a line of elphs trailing toward the Naliah like alabaster ants. Despite his proud moment of rebellion, he unenthusiastically dressed in his elph costume and felt wildly stupid. Tonight his bejeweled cape was in the shape of a heart.

I'm starting to hate this symbol. His feelings only deepened when he saw Kaven, his broad shoulders proudly featuring heart-shaped epaulets.

The evening festivities played out like a whitewashed repeat of last Day of Moons. There was the occasional out-of-place splash of color that left in a flash and left Evan yearning for more, for even the hues faded to black-and-white in his mind.

The food was too ornate, the music too bombastic, and the dialogue nonexistent. Though this night (*thankfully*) featured no speeches, the king remained stately and charismatic, all smiles and waves to all who looked on.

While last dinner, their cloud circulated the coliseum, tonight it remained floating high above the rest. Evan could feel their gemlike eyes pressing upon him, feeling the pressure, like heat attempting to force a pebble into a diamond.

Evan recalled the king's words on monotony, and looking around, knew it was nonsense. In a moment, Evan recalled so many of Kaven's words. They stormed through his head, flooding atop his own thoughts.

It's all lies.

He looked up at the eight moons and wanted to shoot seven of them down. *Hopefully one would land on Helvendah.*

His thoughts fell quiet and one word floated to the top of his muddled mind.

Delya.

It was decided.

Tonight, he was leaving.

The smell of burning owned the night. He wasn't sure how he'd missed it before. Maybe it was the initial elation of being rescued or the distracting beauty abound, but after only two days and too many suns, he could smell it everywhere. Floating high above the hell below couldn't save a soul—its scent was inescapable.

Blended amid the charred night, a four-piece chorus sang as one. Their sultry tone was not unlike the Great Fire, for between their four remarkable voices, there was never a break in sound. They gently quivered and proudly roared, as every listener eventually fell silent, withdrawing into their own blackness.

Evan traced their outlines from across the pearl tower. He couldn't see their eyes but he knew their eight assorted blues and greens could see his pupils from miles away. He slowly slid the curtain closed.

In the dark, Evan turned toward the mirror, barely recognizing his own shadowed face. Strangely, this was a feeling he was comfortable with. He stared at his black eyes as if they were endless, as though searching for the bottom of an abyss. He stared, knowing that beyond his black eyes, blue ones remained vigilant.

Evan smirked at the mirror and turned it away. Without rush or mental narration, he reclaimed his clothes from the hollow imposter. His red shoes were tightly tied, barred across the tongue; his dark blue jeans were neatly folded around his skinny ankles. He zipped up his black hoodie, complete with his old tin heart and lastly, he pulled the brim of the red cap just slightly over his thick brows.

To avoid the attention of any elphen insomniacs, he covered his civilian attire in his white leather cloak, pulling its hood over his head. Red hat still protruding, he stuck its brim out the door and turned it from side to side, assuring no passersby in the dark hallway. Evan pulled a deep breath in through his nose, air flowing toward his heart, before gently exhaling with closed eyes.

I should be more afraid than I am, Evan thought. *But I'm not.*

He exited his chamber and swiftly stepped down the hall.

Evan approached the winged statues standing at guard and serving as the elevators. He examined the marble wonders, and despite their blank states and featureless pearl eyes, Evan was unable to resist the sense that they looked back at him.

Evan whispered, "Can you take me to the garden?"

The statue lifted its chin and shifted its stare to his

partner across the way. Very slowly, as if expending much effort, the bird-man shook his head in disapproval.

Evan turned to leave, *Gotta find another way,* when a heavy hand clenched his shoulder. Startled, he turned back.

There, grasping his shoulder, were the large white hands with little claw nails of the other sculpture. With wide eyes, the boy looked up at the man's beaked and empty face as it slowly nodded. *Yes.*

Evan stepped aboard the carriage. The winged man wrapped his sculpted arms around it, and downward they plummeted. In a hazy flash, he saw every floor of the castle as one. A thought imagined how many elphs were fast asleep, another, how many elphs would be disappointed when they awoke.

They landed in the entrance hall and standing there was the rightful owner of the house. Evan wondered how this had happened…

From every story he heard, this original elph was loving, selfless. *A true peacemaker.* They quickly passed the liquid formation of the shielded hero and through an oddly already opened front door.

Flying through the ivory streets of the heavenly city, the more Evan mentally removed himself from Helvendah. Seeing Duendelyn, he suddenly realized these people, many his direct descendants, others his peers, were not like him at all. At the polished surface they certainly seemed like it, but with Evan's clear eyes, dark ones made deeper by walking the marble halls of Helvendah, he thought it was all a façade.

They came to my rescue so that I could come to theirs.

Maybe that's part of it. Maybe I'm supposed to hold up my end of the deal.

But there was no deal. From that faded, black and white night, Evan could still remember catching another's eyes in his reflection. Kaven planned to take the boy then and there from his very home. This was a kingdom without a king, rather eight. *But that's a lie, too.*

Evan witnessed the fire Kaven ignited in his people's eyes. He noted how the king slyly assigned himself as caregiver to the fallen boy. In superficially sharing his power with the other kings and queens, Kaven had more power than any of them knew.

Passing beneath the glass bubbles, seeing an inverted and straightened Helvendah, he couldn't help but wonder that if in any of these glossy replicas, life played out like it was planned. *Maybe Duendelyn's brought his dreams to life. Maybe I'm actually the hero they say I am.* Evan lowered his head as they neared the garden. Here, in reality, neither fantasy was true.

The carriage stopped and the winged-sculpture lowered Evan to the ground. It was as though this distinct line of greenery against the white was the statue's threshold.

The boy turned back toward the beast, and it lowered its marble beak. Evan thought as though the statue were wishing him luck. Evan nodded back.

"Thank you," he whispered. With a flap, the sculpture unfurled its wings and lifted himself in air, blending into the odd and extraordinary skyline.

For a final time, Evan tried to take in its many fascinating details. Oddly, he thought, the buildings resembled utensils, *an artist's twisted and warped utensils*, futilely sporking at the sky. There were more peculiarities than could be seen in eight lifetimes. Unlike the kingdom's residents, he didn't have that.

Evan turned away, entering the garden, hoping never to see Helvendah again but almost certain that he would. If not again before his eyes, a part of this place would surely play on in those visions of sleep in the indescribable, undesirable space that's both dream and nightmare.

He walked briskly with the wind at his back. Whirling in his ears, he imagined it whispering words of support.

The leaves rattled and waved like family wishing safe travels. His first trip through this spectacular forest, his eyes couldn't get enough of the green wonders around, this time, they remained focused on the path ahead, straight to the Water Rise. Nothing could distract him, except, *Who is….?*

Amid a small clearing, a girl stood, but not the one he came to meet. If not for her size, Evan may have mistaken the figure for a living elph. Instead, it was another memorial of sorts. Rather than flowing water, this one was comprised primarily of pale leaves. Her limbs were made of birch, with her left arm raised up and outward like a branch. Her twig fingers were spread wide, as if welcoming and waiting for a little bird to land in her palm. Around her head, tucked beneath her pointed ears blossomed a crown of purple lilies fit for Mother Earth herself.

But this was no mother, that was certain. Despite being an anonymous likeness, the girl's youthful exuberance bloomed through her petal-formed face. Her delicate features seemed so perfect, as though only the earth could've birthed her. This was a child. A child memorialized. *A child gone.* Her subtle rosebud smile carried her secrets. Evan knew she wasn't real, but when he looked up at her forget-me-not eyes, he felt a startling presence.

I know her, he thought. *But from where?*

Before another thought could answer, a white streak dashed across the sky. From the corner of his eye, it looked like a shooting star, or even a falling moon. Evan quickly counted. All eight were intact.

From deeper in the woods, Evan heard a splash.

Without a proper farewell to the floral princess, Evan ran toward the Water Rise.

There, floating behind eight fluttering lunar reflections, sat the flying object and the source of the sound.

"Are you insane?" Evan asked, in his best whisper-yell.

Delya giggled. "I knew you'd come."

"I-I-I…have no words…I'm in shock."

Her giggle evolved to a hearty laugh. "Isn't she stunning?"

That she is, but she, Evan knew, was not hers. Sitting at the helm of the great Lady Milette, more affectionately known as the King Glider, was not the king, but rather a smiling and sparkling Delya.

"Did you steal this?"

"Well, you see, Evan, *Leader Toward Light*," her jovial expression shifted to a royal, mocking one, impersonating the Glider's rightful owner. "*What is mine is yours, and what is yours is mine, for this is the elphen way!*" she concluded, raising her arms.

Evan couldn't help but briefly laugh. The seriousness of the situation quickly returned.

"So that's a yes. To both of my questions. You're unquestionably insane."

"I have no intention of returning. What difference does it make?" Delya said, leaning over the side of the swan. "Perhaps I'm mistaken, but it sounds as though someone fears Kaven of Akoya."

"Of what? No, not at all. I just think—"

Delya cut Evan off, "You should be." Her light demeanor darkened. "Let's not waste anymore time. Hop on."

Evan exhaled. *I'm actually doing this.* Without looking back at the welcoming wall of green, without thinking about the blackness below, he sprung his red PF Flyers over the King Glider's retreated wings.

His bottom slid on the sleek surface, his arm pressing against Delya's. Before Evan could apologize, she smiled. Whatever danger possibly laid ahead, Evan felt prepared. Perhaps her beauty blinded him or it was her dazzling cloak strung from diamonds, but *I don't think that's it.* Beneath the elegant exterior, he felt a hovering calmness within her, one he believed she could quickly convert to power. Evan felt comfort and hope, and hoped Delya felt the same.

She waved her hands, her fingers strumming on unseen strings. The swan unfurled its miraculous feathers, rapidly rising to the night sky. Glistening beads of water streaked across the bird's underbelly before falling back to Helvendah.

The young elph captained the Glider with command and confidence. A tilt of her hand, the mighty bird leaned accordingly, a tense fist, and it burst through the clean clouds and into the ashen world below. They passed the flowing Water Rise, the city's glow dimming quickly as they descended.

Maybe this won't be so hard with the Glider…and her.

"So, where precisely are we going?" Evan asked.

"I don't *precisely* know yet," she said. "You know, I still believe in life beyond the fire."

Evan looked out at the fiery horizon and swore he heard a light splash. *That can't be right.* He listened closer, closing his eyes. The swan's powerful flaps filled his ears, but an extra thrash echoed it. He opened his eyes. Its wings rose and fell with a great gust, but at his rear, Evan felt an extra thrust of wind. He peered over his shoulder.

"Delya, watch out!"

Evan wailed as a sharp claw gashed across his left eyelid. Delya veered the Glider to the right as the beast flew at their side. Evan clenched his eye, blood filling his palm. With his unscathed eye, he examined the attacker.

The black slits on its green eyes arrowed directly at the boy. Hissing, it flashed its bladelike teeth at Evan and dove for him. He ducked, barely missing another scratch from its paw's daggers. Its soft tail slid across his face as its leathery wings went vertical, turning the beast around for another charge.

A flying cat. The same flying monster from his first

moments on the Final Earth. Evan remembered it just barely missing him in the blackness, before flying up toward the white...*to Helvendah.*

It aggressively pursued, and Delya masterfully evaded. The right sleeve of Evan's robe was almost entirely dyed red. She urged the fastest bird in the universe to go faster, but with no success. The cat was quicker, as it slammed down upon a wing, digging against the pearl feathers. It scratched onward, and upward, clawing until finally, it grasped Evan's neck.

The boy gasped and the monster tightened his hold, piercing his flesh. The cat's contorted face growled, sending Evan's stomach achurn. Though it possessed the expected feline features (the moon-sliver eyes, the half-diamond nose, the revulsion in the face of a less distinguished beast), it also had qualities that were not quite human, but most certainly...*elphen.*

Delya crashed her fists against the beast's head. It didn't seem to feel it, not even turning to look at the girl. *It's over*, Evan's last thoughts whispered.

It's over and there's no life to flash before my eyes.

The cat focused even harder on Evan, looking fiercer and unsatisfied with the apparent pain, until his pupils widened. A pained shriek rung through the night, loud enough for every elph to hear. Evan heaved in relief as the claws released.

The cat swiped and clamped against the swan's neck, holding on fiercely, scraping against its skin. It squeezed and squealed, but quickly the swan snapped. Beneath an audible crack, Evan believed he heard a yelp of agony.

He peered back. Pulling the winged cat were two winged-men, the stone ones from the end of the corridor. Their mighty marble fists slammed against the inferior beast, scrambling in the blackness.

The King Glider was injured. The bird swirled downward, Delya unable to control its wings as it reached toward its broken neck, as though...*as though it feels pain.*

Before Evan could ponder the statue's senses any further, the swan upturned, sending Evan and Delya free falling to the land far below.

The only images that speedily slide-showed through his head were that of the grey winged-bengal with the elphen eyes. He peered for a last glimpse of Delya, but it was too late.

With a great thump, Evan slammed against the ground.

He expected that to be the last moment of his life.

But a single thought disturbed the nothing.

I'm alive.

A swarm of others joined in and rejoiced. *There's no pain. But how?*

He worked up the courage to open his eyes, fairly certain there'd be no bones poking through and all body parts were still intact. Wrapped around his core were an extra pair of arms, cradling his thin stomach. Evan felt movement below his spine. *I'm laying on someone.*

He squirmed, turning his head. An inch before his eyes was a pair of glowing jade ones. She smiled, completely unscathed. Amused by Evan's evident shock, Delya began to laugh. *How the...?*

"What?" she giggled, her arms still wrapped around Evan. "I *am* an elph."

A few yards away, the King Glider came crashing down. Evan's head sprung up. The bird's neck was now fully snapped, aggressively angled opposite the rest of its broken body. Lady Milette screamed in misery. He was now certain he saw red dripping down its formerly bloodless sides.

Evan jumped up, quickly walking toward the swan. The ladybird wailed as tears slowly filled beneath the boy's animal eyes.

"No!" Delya called out.

"Why is it crying?" Evan called back, his voice

quivering. "Why is *she* crying?"

"We can't worry about that now. We've got to get away, Evan. That monster will swoop down at any moment."

He wanted to run away, but he couldn't. This was a mere sculpture. *She shouldn't feel pain.* But she did. Beneath the layer of stone skin, Evan was now sure there was real skin. And beneath that skin, there was something not so different from him.

Though its marble face remained emotionless, beneath it, Evan could hear her slowly weep. Her whimpers became softer and softer until they became silent...

Lady Milette died.

Evan cried for the king's beautiful slave.

Like the sprawling cloud above, her motionless white body laid like a stain against the endless ash.

The pair walked beneath two toppled trees, its twisted branches interlocked overhead, forming an archway into the woods. Holding Evan's hand, Delya led the way. From her white knapsack she pulled out a small globe of light and placed it above their heads where it buoyed in air. It gently bobbed as though invisibly tethered to the two. Its subtle light greatly revealed the woods, showing more than was worth seeing. Everything was dead. Evan remembered this place well.

His PF's stamped upon the dry dirt as his thoughts swirled high, not yet grounded.

"What was that flying tiger?"

"I think that just about defines it," responded Delya. "Other than that, I have no idea."

"It came from Helvendah."

"And what did I tell you? That pristine kingdom has its fair share of secrets."

"I think it's safe to say I made the right choice."

Delya turned to Evan. "Never doubt it. They only looked to you for their own gain. Once you'd delivered, you'd be done for."

"And what if I didn't deliver?"

"Then they'd do what they did with the rest of them. Make you vanish and pretend as though you never existed."

"The rest of them?"

"Ah, Evan. You're too innocent," Delya stopped and turned to him, grasping both of his hands in hers. "You're not the first '*Chosen One*'. Likely, you're not the last. I just refuse to let you disappear."

The light dangled above their heads like glowing mistletoe. Delya inched within a breath of Evan's face, but the questions in his head shrouded her allure.

"What happened to the rest?"

The elph stepped back, crossing her arms, and peering over her shoulder. She sighed. "Sometimes, when I'm sitting alone on top of the tower, singing for the whole city, I can hear their shrieks turn to whispers in the wind."

"They're alive?"

"Of course," she said, with a hint of pride. "My people can often be twisted in their particular ways, but if there is one thing they're stern on, it's death. A true elph would never kill any creature.

"That said, some have been exiled for defacing life in dishonorable ways. We've been blessed with everlasting life. For us, the concept of death can be so foreign, so unimaginable, that when it creeps into the mind it can drive even the wisest elph mad. Knowing that some creatures don't live forever, it's...it's confusing. It's sad. Never could we be responsible for killing one whose death is already inevitable."

Evan was as silent as the decaying wood. He saw the king kill the ant and glide in the sky atop something he was fairly sure was alive. He was not so certain every elph believed as Delya did.

"But then, also, we have those who are like my father, who believe a tortured life is far worse punishment than death. They relish in administering pain."

"You and your father...complicated relationship?"

"To say the least, but no more complicated than my relationship with Helvendah as a whole." She weaved her thin fingers within Evan's similar ones and pulled forward. "Tell me about your home."

"I wish I could."

Delya giggled. "It couldn't be any worse than mine."

"That's not it. It's just when I got here, the weirdest thing happened. It's like the moment I woke up on your earth, everything about my life, my old life, erased like it never happened." He shook his head as Delya looked on. "Every now and then I get glimpses, but they instantly fade. I hardly remember who I was...or who I am."

"You're Evan," she said with a smile.

"I am Evan...but that means nothing."

Delya paused. "Maybe those memories wouldn't help, because who you are, what you are, is yet to be determined."

"Or it's already decided," Evan considered.

He turned to gaze at her glowing skin. Through his dark eyes, she was a half-shade short of perfection. He could spend days envisioning her eyes, her smile, creating elaborate fantasies built around her and they'd all come shattering down when faced with the actual elphen masterpiece.

She looked no older than Evan, no younger. In his mind's unripe utopia, she was probably born the same day as he, their very existence destined for this moment. But this couldn't be, *elphs live forever.*

"How old are you?" he asked.

"I have no idea," she said with her sweet snicker. "There's little reason for us to calculate such things. Once we've reached a certain point, we more or less remain the same until...well, forever."

"So in theory, you could be a thousand years old?"

"Whatever that means, sure...yes, in theory."

I wouldn't care if you were.

With fingers locked, dim and dazzling knuckles intertwined, the two traveled deeper into the forest. The blackness wasn't as black with Delya. Evan couldn't smell smoke clouds in the air or feel the ash fog rolling against his face, instead, he inhaled the girl's fruity fragrance and saw her light overtaking the night. In his mind, he saw the trees unwilt, fully revitalized and fertile once more. He could almost taste her scent. *Pennberries*, he thought, his tongue rolling against itself.

They walked for what Evan's mind labeled as hours, when Delya laughed, time appeared to accelerate. Evan's heart smiled as their day felt like passing seconds.

The girl decided they'd settle in a patch just large enough for them to recline. Evan didn't oppose. In their small clearing they were surrounded by fallen trees. Enclosed in their world, they sat facing each other at the center of the wooden circle, like the heart of a fire or the main sacrifice amid a shrine.

Delya tore a piece of cloth from her robe, pressing the fabric against Evan's scratched eye. She ran her fingers across his wounded neck, her touch alone was enough for him.

"Fire would be nice right now," Delya said.

"I was once told not to wish for fire," Evan remembered. "I was told it hears...and appears."

"You've been taught well," she said. "Most elphs pretend they don't fear, but I'm no fool. But now, ugh," she sighed, patting her sides. "My pack must have fallen. This adventure could prove more difficult without my amstones."

"Your amstones?"

"Yes, the gems of Helvendah. They're not just beautiful, they're highly useful. Each has its own characteristics, but with proper adjustments, you can find one for any need."

"Like the crystals Kaven used to create those force-fields?"

"Exactly, or the jewels used to create the blades on our shooting swords." She swung her arm like she once wielded such a weapon with ease.

Evan reached his hand into his pocket, pulling out a sparkling red rock.

"Like this?" he questioned.

Delya's face glimmered. "Where did you get this?"

"Kaven gave it to me."

"May I?" she asked, reaching out her hand

Evan placed his heart-shaped ruby in the elph's hand.

"From Kaven, huh?" Delya placed the heart on the ground between them. She ran her fingers across its sleek and faceted surface, and with a few calculated taps, the little heart went aflame. "I shouldn't be surprised."

The controlled fire flickered just below their eyes. Her green irises were now pierced with red. His dark browns, previously unseen in the black, were now twin suns in the dark night.

"Is it safe?" he asked.

She smirked, "You're with me."

Staring at Evan, she inched her way around the flame, settling closely at his side. She set her silver haired head atop his bony shoulder. Evan lifted his shoulder, gently bobbing her head back up. Delya looked up at him, concerned, until he extended his arm, sliding his hand around her back, squeezing her closer. Delya smiled.

"Yesterday, when I was with Kaven," he said, "he told me about his father."

"Yes. The One True Elph. The Only King."

"He spoke of how Duendelyn yearned for peace—"

"'The Land of Letin'," Delya interjected.

"You're familiar?"

"Of course. I still believe it exists."

"What do you mean, *exists*?" asked Evan. "Like in your heart, or something?"

Delya giggled against his chest. "While that's *probably* the most important, I mean as an actual place."

"I'm not sure I follow. You mean 'Letin' wasn't just a dream?"

"I can understand why Kaven didn't tell you everything. Of course it would hurt."

"I'm listening."

"Where to begin? Hmm...I suppose with the goblyns," she drew a deep breath and started. "When they appeared on the Heartland, we had no choice but to share it. The days passed without harm for quite sometime. We each steered clear of the other and there was some semblance of peace. But it was apparent that the goblyns were not satisfied and couldn't be contained. They repeatedly attempted to raid Helvendah. Needless to say, their efforts were thwarted, but the kings and queens wouldn't let their people live in fear. They ordered a strict restrain on elph and goblyn interaction. As history tells, such bans never quite go the way the ruling party plans. And as for the elphs, well, their worst fear came to be...

"This story, as so many of my favorites, centers around Helvendah's most adventurous and rebellious elph. She was the kingdom's most beautiful, most charming, and oh, of course, she just so happened to be a daughter of a king."

"You?"

She laughed. "While I'll gladly take those titles now, I could never in those days—not with her around. She, of course, refused to conform. Nonetheless, she was the pride of Helvendah. Each and every elph had a part in raising her, for she freely skipped around the city, always with the finest and freshest crown of flowers in her hair.

"As she got older, her gallivanting began to upset her father, for her curiosity took her far beyond the kingdom's confines. She'd go on daily escapades across the Heartland, full of hope and free of course. Her journey led her to a man that some believed to be a great goblyn, if there ever was such a thing...

"His name was Wardrake, of whom these woods are now named. Wardrake was a great traveler. He yearned for discovery, much like the elph princess. In hindsight, it seems inevitable that their paths would cross. It also seemed inevitable that they'd consider each other their greatest finding.

"Together, they were rumored to have found a land of unfathomable magic and natural abundance enough for the entire universe. The princess couldn't ignore such a land, a land that would belong only to the lovers. She left Helvendah, and though she never intended to return, she never had a chance. The goblyn couldn't suppress his inner-monster for long. He hideously ravaged and murdered the princess."

Evan was stunned to silence.

He didn't want the story to end like that.

Delya continued. "It's believed that her body still lays in her tower. Some imagine that she's still as beautiful as the day she was born. Others like to say that she's simply in a deep sleep, one she's chosen to take as a form of protection. That's all nice for stories, but the truth is, she's nothing but bones and a tormented memory."

"She's the one memorialized in the garden?" The one made of petals with a palpable presence.

"Yes..." whispered Delya, as though not to disturb the quiet fire. "Princess Kylen of Kaven."

♡

Evan looked down at Delya and gently brushed a silver wisp off her forehead. Staring at her sleeping face, *so serene*, he smiled. He imagined her a fallen angel or a shooting star in bodily form that had landed right on his lap. In Evan's eyes, the elph was every cliché revitalized and born anew. He closed his eyes and held her closer. She was lightweight enough to return to the clouds.

The orange glow pulsed against his eyelids as he tried to sleep. A crinkle in the leaves above forced his eyes back open and the arrival of blood thumping through his temples. He instinctively squeezed Delya tighter in protection. His next thought told him to wake her up for protection but...*It's nothing, it will pass.*

But it didn't. The rustling grew louder until it sounded as if it were lowering upon them.

"Delya," he whispered, his nervous eyes bulging. "Delya!"

The beauty slept on, undisturbed, her smirk-smile intact. Across the fire, against the fallen tree, a snake slithered against the bark. It squirmed, slowly swirling against the wood.

It's not so bad, he thought. *It's not hissing. It's not even...oh my*, Evan realized. *It's not a snake.*

A thick green vine, flourished with small leaves slid against the bark, seemingly, somehow spelling. Slowly, the vine twisted and scrawled, looping until finally, Evan recognized the letters.

G-N-I, its leafy green signature wrote from right-to-left. *R*, it scratched, a comforting cursive-print hybrid that reminded him of home. *O*, a lovely circle, and finally it finished, *L*, a leaf pointing out from the letter's top.

Evan read the word from the opposite direction it was written, as his brain was programmed to do.

"Loring," the word came out of his mouth.

Loring, he said the word again in his head, certain that it was a name. *Loring*, he thought.

"Loring?" it came out again.

Yes, a thought answered.

You.

The L began to recede, curling into the O as the R-I-N-G straightened and rapidly slid upward, back to land.

No, he thought. Evan had to follow. But, *no*, he looked down at Delya. He couldn't leave her. He heard his name slipping away against the dead leaves and disappearing into the dark.

I have to.

He delicately cradled her sleeping face, framing the masterpiece gently with his hands, giving it a final moment of adoration. *But no, I'll be back, and she'll be fine.* Of course she would be. This was the girl who had caught him from the sky leaving both of them without a bruise. Evan leaned over and kissed Delya's forehead.

He took off his elphen robe, hastily folding it and gently lowering her head against the makeshift pillow. He threw his arms up and quickly pulled himself from their own divine ditch and sprinted toward the sound of rustling leaves.

A breeze brushed against his face as he passed the black trees.

This probably isn't a good idea.

It's the worst idea, he said, nudging a branch.

Onward he ran, faintly seeing the endless vine wriggling ahead. The creeping plant could've been long gone by now, Evan noted. It was as though it waited for him. The swift rustling began to sound more like a slow dragging until, in a small opening where the white cloud brightened the dead land, the vine stopped.

Evan inched toward it, huffing mightily. He bent and examined the idle plant. This is how plants were supposed to be, its growing movements unnoticeable to the watchful eye. But this vine was sentient a moment ago, spelling that name...his name, consciously luring him forward.

He lowered his hand to the sleeping vine. It awoke, slapping its tendrils tightly around his thin wrist and thrusting onward.

Evan bucked against the ground. He pulled back with all his might, trying to unlatch himself with his free hand. He kicked against the crooked trees, trying to hook and gain leverage. With each attempt, the vine pulled faster, his body pounding violently against the ground.

"Delya!" he shouted. "Delya!" Surely she'd hear.

Evan slipped passed a final row of trees and down a brutal decline. His limp skin and bones fell to the bottom of the steep clearing. As he thumped down, Evan realized where he was.

Right back where I started, though it felt as if years had passed. Maybe it could've only been a few days, but so much had changed. Now, there was no guiding voice to direct him away from the looming tower, and even if there were, it'd be useless. The vine dragged him straight to the leaf-covered gate of the Witch in the Woods before releasing him. The vine receded into the rest of the foliage that blanketed the structure.

Evan stood. *Am I supposed to go in? Can I turn away?* It would certainly take little for the building's stalks to snatch him back up. His eyes attempted to climb to the top of the tower before getting dizzy. From the ground, its wide top seemed to graze Helvendah.

In fact, Evan thought, *the tower seems almost elphen.* He imagined stripping away the needled ivy and there was a tower straight from the city above. Its slim base grew larger as it rose, much like that of the house he was staying. Beneath the green was probably a smooth white marble. His mind filled with questions. He had to know.

Evan slithered his hand between a few thin branches, brushing leaves aside. He gasped. His heart stunned still as a cloud of breath circulated before his gaped mouth.

At the tip of Evan's finger, a fully thumping, fully recognizable organ that Evan knew to be a heart. Its petiole veins stemmed toward its ventricles composed of curled leaves, which sat beneath its green blade atriums. Its bract aorta pulled in air as the heart of foliage visibly beat.

Before Evan could pull his hand away, a set of white eyes slid open, and a mouth of jagged thorn teeth screeched. Its yell was pained, and drawn out. Starting low, it became higher, louder, and quicker, firing from its mouth rapidly like an alarm.

The creature of leaves grabbed Evan's arms, lifting him from the ground, relentlessly yelping in Evan's face. He turned from the sound, and from every angle around the tower, swinging high and crawling low, more of the monkey-like beings joined, all synchronized in their screams.

They drew closer, each fiercer than the next. Their number grew by the second, far more than Evan could count. One alone, with its branch arms fiercely grasping his arms could snap him instantly.

"Delya!" Evan yelled with all his might. The beast thrust its stem fingers against his face. He felt the side of his lip slit open but could hardly feel the accompanying pain. In this moment, his cuts were miniscule. His whole being was about to be shredded as they converged upon him. Instead of watching his own demise, he closed his eyes, forfeiting to what was.

As he surrendered, a soundless flash brushed against his closed eyelids.

…And the beasts fell silent…

Evan reluctantly opened his eyes. The demons stared upward. He followed their collective gazes. The light was gone, but its meaning not lost on the leafed creatures. Evan's direct foe snarled in anger, slinging the boy to his side. Together, with Evan's body dangling, they began to climb.

He didn't dare to look down, in fear of the fall and the trail of countless branched beasts behind him. He looked up, Helvendah not so distant, not yet sure which place he'd rather be. As they reached the top, a porch jutted from the tower's side. The beast tossed Evan atop the landing and let him go.

They scaled the side, waiting just below the porch, setting this perimeter as their point of no return. Evan stood, looking ahead. An open archway led into the tower. Though he couldn't imagine a being on the inside worse than the dozens on the outside, this had to be the case. The wooden beasts forfeited with the simplest and slightest flash. Evan looked back.

The monkeys looked more like men in this moment, their wide-eyes full of concern as one among them pointed their twig-fingers toward the door.

Evan walked on, fearful whispers circulating. He inhaled, ignoring the voices, casting away the charred scent in the air. The drumbeats of his heart thumped louder than his doubts, and their sound, their powerful sound, offered hope.

The floors were pure polished marble. The walls, like the exterior, were blanketed in green with sparks of flowers spread full in their prime. Vines draped overhead, stalks laid against the floor, all leading directly to the center of the room.

There, lying atop a floral tomb, was the witch.

Evan inched closer. She couldn't be dead, but she was so silent and still. Where her snow-white garb ended and her skin began was undetectable. He stepped forward. Atop her heart she held a purple bouquet, flowers of every size and shape, all similar shades. The posy appeared to have grown from and woven itself with the fabric of her dress, giving it a subtle purple glow.

Evan looked at the side of her sleeping face. This

was no witch. *Witches are old and...ugly.* Her face was soft, impeccable. Her black hair, which fell long below her shoulders, was glistening silk. Stepping closer for a full view, Evan found her single flaw. The witch no longer possessed her left eye. Atop the empty socket was a black patch that resembled a large lifeless spider sprawled out. Much to Evan's comfort, upon closer review, it was a fully bloomed lily dyed the color of death.

As he stared, she opened her remaining eye. Evan thought he should be afraid.

But he wasn't.

"Loring," she said. "Sit." Her weary voice belonged to someone triple her age.

"I-I—"

"I've waited so long for your return."

Evan stood silent.

"I insist," she said sternly, wheezing as she spoke. "Sit."

Her dying voice still had enough command to direct an army. Evan reluctantly obliged, awkwardly leaning one side of his body against the divan.

The witch closed her eye, and sniffed, smelling the symphony of scents in her room.

"I feel its presence. Where have you hidden it?"

Without a thought, Evan pulled the medallion from under his shirt.

"So clever," she said, with a hint of life. "I've watched you from afar. The time is now near...that is why I've brought you home."

"I think you're mistaken."

"The king draws closer, and if he has his way, the world we know will perish. We must end it before it begins. Only you can do that. The Eight gifted you at your conception," she said, nodding toward the strange charm. "You are the Child of Grey."

Evan knew there was a misunderstanding, yet he still had so many questions.

"Please, take no offense, but who are you?"

The witch chuckled and coughed with an underlying crack that didn't sound healthy.

"I take no offense. It has been incalculable days, immeasurable distances. I know how these long travels can plague the mind. Your question, however, is it not the ultimate unanswerable question?"

"I've heard that you're..." *How do I put this gently?... You don't.* "A witch?"

Again she laughed, hacked and cracked, which only seemed to humor her more. Evan did not get the joke, looking over her splintering body with visible concern.

"I must say, I've heard far worse. I prefer to call myself a naturemancer. No witch. That lacks vision, sweetheart." She paused. "There's but one witch in these woods."

Evan didn't quite follow.

"You said you brought me here?"

"Yes. As I recall, I appeared in my former form as to not scare you away. While I've never felt more beautiful, most prefer my earlier image."

Pictures shuffled through Evan's mind; the graceful girl welcoming him in his own reflection, the flowery princess memorialized in her own garden, this sleeping beauty condemned as a witch. It all strung together like leaves on a vine.

"You're the princess," said Evan. "Princess Kylen of Kaven."

"Do not mention his name," she said, a bite in her voice. "Not out of fear, but out of honor. That coward mentally mentions his own name over trumpeting fanfare enough for all of us."

"I'm not sure I understand."

"Oh, sweet Loring, it will do you best to remember it all quite clearly. I imprudently sacrifice my eye and can see and do things Duendelyn couldn't dream of. My father cuts out his own heart and, ironically, destroys everything but the Heartland."

Evan stood silent and baffled.

"You still don't understand? Oh, my dear boy," she said, rolling her eye. "Very well. Look out that window."

Evan hardly noticed the window under the shrouds of green. He walked toward it and brushed the leaf curtains aside.

On the horizon, the endless blaze. *The Great Fire.*

Words from stories told in the kingdom above echoed inside. Words from stories deep in his memory rose from the dusty layers of memory and became legible again.

Evan stared at the fire's taunting tongues, feeling each of the endless red flares had its own eye that stared back. Finally, he knew who watched beyond the flame. He brushed the green curtain closed.

Before Kylen could tell, Evan spoke. "*He* is the Great Fire."

"There's no saying what he'll do. He's a man who's laid forth many plots, all of which have failed. Now, without a plan, he is most dangerous," Kylen paused. "When you're willing to lose your heart to gain power, fearing the loss of life, you've already lost it. He now has nothing to live for, nothing to lose. There's nothing stopping him from forcing his affliction upon us all.

"Now, if you would," asked Kylen, "pass me that stick there, against the wall."

Evan did as she asked, and when he turned back, the witch (*the elph*) was already standing.

"Just perfect," she said, grasping her cane. She slowly began to walk toward the porch. Evan noticed at the foot of her walking stick, a dozen jittery roots, crawling against the ground like tiptoeing fingers.

Gathered on the landing, all of her leafed and branched warriors waited on alert. They stared at her, equally aweing and awaiting her word. Several gazed at Evan, on the verge of a snarl.

"You've met the dailauves. That king may have the fire, but he'll never have an army so faithful as mine."

Kylen raised her arms and the platform followed, only several steps to the building's top. At the roof was an overgrown garden unto itself, complete with curling trees like those in the wood, but these were vibrant, full of life, literally flowing with dancing flowers that somehow flourished without an ounce of sunlight.

The naturemancer stepped forward, raising her hands, moving her working eye over the fleet of flowers. She twirled her hands and the trees rustled. She moved them side-to-side, the branches and vines converged upon each other. They twisted, tightened, flowers invisibly plucking from the ground and joining the creation. As though hearing a music all her own, Kylen orchestrated the greenery in an improvised masterstroke.

"Let's model this one after that *metal dragon* they all fear in the land above," Kylen said with a laugh.

Finally, its peculiar shape began to make sense. With its widespread wings composed of thin branches and thick leaves, a plush posy cockpit and the front floral propeller, the word popped into Evan's head. *Plane...*

"Airplane," he thought aloud. "It looks like an airplane."

"Hmm. We have no such machines here," said Kylen, playfully prodding Evan forward. "Now, hop aboard. It will take you anywhere you please."

"But I don't know where I'm going."

"None of us do!" Kylen exclaimed. "Sometimes we simply need to dive deep within ourselves, explore the blackest bits of our being that we've suppressed for far too long. It's there in the darkness, there in the infinite nothing, that we find our greatest answers. My dear Loring, you will find what they're all searching for, for you're not searching for it at all, and that is why you're so deserving."

Evan didn't quite remember his mother, but he

imagined this being something a mom would say. Then, as the beautiful witch with the black lily eye approached, she leaned over, petals grazing his face, and kissed Evan's forehead. Her lips landed upon the very spot that had been blessed by a mother a million times.

Evan froze, fighting his body's urge to fall, as his head flooded with images of his past. He remembered his mother in full. *Grace.*

"Go on, now!" she yelled.

Grace, Evan thought, climbing aboard the botanic aircraft.

"There's little time to waste."

Grace. The princess continued to speak, but all he heard and all he saw was *Grace.*

"And take this!" she yelled, throwing her walking stick up to him. "Consider it a piece of me to guide you all the way."

Evan tucked the cane at his side, its wriggling roots settled. Without warning, the plane rose, not taking off like an Earthly plane, but much more like a helicopter.

Where are we going?

"To Mount Asylia," Evan said decisively. *But wait.* "To Delya. There," he pointed toward the woods from which he came. The plane followed.

"Slowly," he said. The craft responded to his movements and words as though synced to his mind. "Lower, I need a better look."

The lively wood hovered above its cold counterparts. Evan peered through the slits in the branches' endless braid, only to see more blackness. There was no sign of life, *no sign of…*

"Delya!" he called out. "Turn around, we've gone too far. Slower! And lower!"

The plane moved with the dexterity of a paper play-toy, turning front to back as though attached to a stick. It attempted to descend but brushed against the dead bark.

"There!" he called out. There was a speck of

glistening red in the otherwise conquering black. Excited, Evan yelled. "How do I get down?"

The agreeable aircraft answered, shooting a vine from the cockpit down to the ground. Without listening to his fretful thoughts, he grabbed the sturdy stalk and inched his way to the land.

He swerved, running toward the red light. Closer, *almost there*, closer…

No.

The light extinguished. Evan hopped into the ditch where they'd settled.

No.

He looked around frantically. "Delya!"

The abandoned forest echoed his cry.

"Delya…" he whispered. The leaves scraped against the parched and deserted ground. He felt nauseous.

He peered at the darkness above and wondered where she'd gone. Not a thought was spared as to her safety. She could take on anything. He wasn't even concerned about his wellbeing anymore. He just wanted her…

Her glowing hand to hold that made his feel just as vibrant. Her pure green eyes that made his common brown ones feel unlimited. He wanted her, *Delya*, the only person in this new life that reminded him there was life beyond his own dark and deserted dome.

Delya was gone.

Once more, Evan was alone on the dying land. Above him, Kylen's aircraft had caught up.

He perused the campground a final time. The only thing left for his eyes to fall upon, the crystal heart, or rather, *the symbol of a heart*. Evan lifted the heavy stone, holding it in his right hand, weary of what magic it possessed beneath the surface. And who might be helming that power miles away.

From behind the heart's second curve, a speck appeared. Crawling toward the center was an ant. Evan leaned closer, noticing its gentle blue glow. *A waterant.*

Despite his sadness, the little insect lifted a smile upon his face.

Evan wasn't one for divine signs or assigning sacred labels upon random, unrelated items, but against his character, he knew this ant was delivered straight from Delya. Surely the elphen princess was on his mind. She couldn't have known of his affinity for ants, but telling himself this crawling speck was sent from the girl who abandoned him would make this journey easier.

I abandoned her, he told himself. She could do no wrong.

"Hey little one," Evan whispered. The waterant froze. He swore it raised its microscopic head. He remembered, that if what the elphs said was true, *That's a major 'if',* he was speaking the waterant's language.

"Can you understand me?"

He looked at the ant, certain that it looked back.

Silence.

I guess not.

Still, Evan tried to remain hopeful.

"I hope you don't mind joining me," he said, tucking the heart and its little passenger inside his hoodie's pocket.

"Let's make the best of what's left of this place."

Evan climbed from the ditch where the hanging vine awaited.

"Higher," Evan said.

The timber wings lifted themselves in the thick of the ceaseless smoke, as far above the fire without fear of hitting Helvendah. Evan looked down at the flames and instead of feeling as though they looked back, he knew very well that they did.

He tried to comprehend it all, but it all seemed

impossible. This much he knew—Kaven was practicing some dark, unthinkable magic. Methods that if Evan's stories aligned, were founded by Oblazio.

He sacrificed his left eye, I believe. Yes, for his brother in pain. And in that moment of guilt and despair, Oblazio called upon any being who'd listen. *And someone accepted his sacrifice.* And rewarded the young brother with the power he craved.

By trading off his bodily might, he gained it elsewhere. Evan imagined the desperation needed to slice off a piece of one's own flesh. *Yet alone their heart…*

One can't live without a heart, it's just a fable.

Unless the power called upon has the power to keep you living…

Somewhere in the process, Evan imagined a ritual that bound the sacrificed flesh with an external force, in hopes of perhaps, controlling that force.

He gazed at the Great Fire below and felt sorry for the poor man who thought they could control fire…*The man who thought he could control his heart.*

But he had it all… Of course it seemed that way, even to the elphs among him. He was their vibrant leader, their most respected innovator. He lived in an infallible city in the sky. He held the promise of eternal life. *Was that not enough?*

Yet, *he had nothing…* Evan recalled no visible lover. No one to spend those unending days with. No family, except of course, for the castaway princess now labeled a wicked witch.

Before Evan could feel too somber for the lonely king, the sprawling fire reminded him of all the life lost at the hands of it. Surely cities as grand as Helvendah with people as impressive as the elphs, burned to ash, sprinkled and lost among the red sea. Evan pictured majestic creatures that could now only live in his mind. He remembered the little ants…

Evan peeked at the heart in his pocket.

Still there, so still.

He admired those waterants. So small, so insignificant, but so dedicated to fighting the fire against insurmountable odds. Evan too, was committed to the cause.

But what's a lone waterant? a thought asked.

Dead, another responded.

Splashed at the hands of the fire before facing it head on. *No wonder Kaven despised them.*

Finally, Evan knew what he long suspected. The king never intended to find the Lamp in hopes of restoring the land. He was just like those who craved power that came before him.

Something in the way the flames moved, their slick slithers, their tantalizing licks, hazily illuminated a small but similar flame, deep in Evan's mind...a memory so painful that he was glad this dark world buried it away.

This same reflection told him he had a place in this fire's story much bigger than simply playing the king's pawn. He didn't know his role quite yet, nor was he sure he was ready to, but one thing he knew for certain...

I'm going to be the most relentless little ant this fire's ever seen.

♡

The plane peculiarly lowered itself straight down to the ground like a spider on a string.

"Couldn't you have brought me to the top?"

The landed aircraft didn't budge.

Evan grabbed his walking stick and lifted himself from the plane, planting his Flyers upon the gravel.

Behind him, the aircraft collapsed on itself, branches curling, timber twisting, until each bit of the botanic plane was but a pile of compost. From the brown and green heap, petals of purple and blades of blue instantly emerged. Flowers of every color brightened the black ground looking like a fallen and flattened rainbow.

Evan shook his head, in awe of Kylen's magic, hopeful that her powerful presence guided him. He turned, evaluating the monstrous mountain. The dark mass looked bleaker than any shadow it could cast. Its peak, tangible with a closed eye and an extended pointer finger, was actually closer to untouchable. Evan remembered the ever-winding path, its countless compartments and urged his mind to forget them. He shuffled one red shoe ahead the other, and then repeated, inching up the incline.

His thoughts thrust forth doubts, *So far to go, and for what? There's nothing there.* He tried to force positivity upon them, *Thankfully there's this path*, too grand to be sculpted by man, too sculpted to be otherwise. This walk-able route was far optimal to scaling Asylia, which Evan had less faith he'd be able to do. Even still, his shoulders wilted, as though suddenly carrying a great weight. Clenching at his chest, he grabbed his necklace and removed it.

There in his hand, the key-sized shovel with its entangled arms embracing a grey marble, weighed at least eighty times more than his eyes told him it should weigh. It sunk his arm as though it were a light dumbbell. He stepped onward, each step, the charm becoming heavier.

Evan's free arm helped the other pull the weight upon his right shoulder. He wished for godly muscles or elphen strength that wasn't coming. The young man's thin tissues and tendons weren't enough to pillow the weight from sitting upon his clavicle, which he wasn't sure would hold.

His shoulder burned, abdomen seared, while his twig bow legs and their arrow pointed knees pressed onward, up and around the mountain.

Give up.

Drop that stupid necklace.

The pain progressed toward numbness, but the thoughts wouldn't quiet.

There's nothing up here.

Why are you still carrying this thing?

Evan had no response. He tried to ignore them and focus his attention outward.

There, he found the answer.

There was the fire.

There was the reason to fight on.

You can't do it.

You're nothing.

Give up!

Evan peered at the flames far on the horizon, and suddenly, it was as though the dark light revealed its many accomplices living right in his very head. No thoughts verbalized what he felt, for they hadn't had the power to. These constant assailants, these self-slashing thoughts didn't belong to Evan.

His heart felt weightless and in turn, he felt as though he could carry the world.

Without hearing the adverse whispers that quivered and quickly became desperate barks and bitter screams once they'd been spotted, Evan reached the peak.

With a vociferous cry, he threw the heavy medallion, feeling like a conquering Olympian. The little charm flew but a few short feet, just steps away from his PF's. His cagey chest rose and fell like it possessed a dragon. Evan felt powerful in a way he never thought possible.

Scanning the Great Fire from high above, Evan felt greater.

He wasn't sure how, for that didn't matter now, but he decided he would make his thoughts work for him, not the opposition.

One thought, brave enough to step from the shadows, spoke up.

That pendant. Get it. It's special to you.

Evan patted his hat-covered head and remembered, ever so briefly, receiving the special gift. *But from who?*

He turned, and in the glow of that glossy cloud, the black metal glittered. Evan kneeled, smiling. The tiny shovel-shaped charm stood upright, its nail-sized blade stuck in the ground, ready to dig the mountain one grain of dirt at a time.

As Evan pulled at the charm, the weight he anticipated, the weight it had just possessed, was suddenly gone. With a pluck of his fingers, it slid from the stony ground as simply as a sword from a scabbard.

Evan stood. *Now wha—?*

Before he could complete a thought, the mountain began to grumble and shudder, sending him back to his knees.

The tip of Mt. Asylia began to dwindle away, falling into itself. Evan tried to remain still, for there was nowhere to move. The ground around him fell. He clenched at the stone ground beneath his shoes and hoped this piece wasn't the next to fall. He closed his eyes and waited to drop. The sound of the crag grinding was unbearable to his ears. He furrowed, holding his charm so tight, feeling the mist of dirt engulf him. His thoughts didn't bother telling him it was over, for they'd already given up.

Then…there was near silence, save the sound of a single pebble falling, skipping against the stone.

Evan opened his eyes.

Before his lonesome slab were stone steps, spiraling downward into the mountain.

The darkness below made the night seem light. This dying land suddenly seemed vibrant in comparison. It made the black centers of Evan's nearly black eyes seem perceptible.

Evan stood, gazing in amazement. The opening was a perfect circle, its uncountable steps, the worthy lifework of endless generations sculpted in seconds.

He recalled asking why the elphs hadn't dug into the land.

"Beneath our deepest layer there's only blackness...Death."

Evan didn't believe it.

With his weightless shovel in one hand and Kylen's literal walking stick in the other, his thoughts were accordingly quiet. Evan descended the spiral steps, down the giant ant hole.

Deeper, deeper into the darkness.

Above and below, nothing but blackness.

Possible missteps hold promise of death. Deep awareness of this? Yes. But his mind is quiet. He does not fear death. In this nothing, this infinite nothing, how much could it differ?

He steps down, down, down, unable to see or feel his legs. His hand strokes the black walls for guidance, and soon even his fingers don't feel.

Where his flesh seals and the innards of this earth begin are indeterminable. Insignificant.

In this dark, as dark as death, everything is the same. A faint drip in the distance. The tap of his determined steps.

In this black, as black as oblivion, ground becomes wall, wall becomes ceiling, and ceiling becomes ground.

He steps down, down, up, without questioning.

The faint drip sounds louder, splattering on the face he'd forgotten. For a moment, he is ocean.

A glowing speck above nearly blinds his newly useful eyes.

Up, up, up, the speck gushes with life.

He reaches for it, pulling. Collapsing the blackness.

The water embraces him, thrusting him upward and into the light.

MOVEMENT 4
Evan & the Garden of the Lamp

∞

Evan's defenseless body plunged forward, against the crashing waves. Smacking against his body, the boy remembered his skin and bones and how feeble they were compared to the water. His red cap ripped off, swirling through the blue. He was afraid, and rightfully so, for unlike the Rise in Helvendah, here, there was no way for Evan to breathe.

He noticed a lavender hue to the water, perhaps his perception due to his increasing lack of oxygen. The tide whirled him, sending him up, closer to the surface. The purple world shimmered.

Finally, with a splash, he emerged.

Eyes closed, Evan floated as his mouth gaped for air. He inhaled deeply, a menagerie of scents parading through his nose. There were floral fragrances that reminded him of the forest intermixed with scents that were so fresh, so new, no association could be made. He opened his eyes, his mouth continuing to gape, this time in awe.

Evan's eyes skipped passed the mountains of crystal, ignoring the flowers and fruit that bore colors undiscovered, and focused straight on the center of the sky.

Beyond a glittering haze that streaked the air dangled a perfect purple orb. Evan approximated it to be the size of a small moon with the might of eight suns. He underestimated its power, yet knew it by its fabled name...

The Lamp.

∞

Swimming to land, Evan spotted his red cap and snatched it, happily returning it to his wet head. Out of the lake, he removed his soaked black hoodie and sprawled it out on the plush grass, right next to Kylen's now-resting stick. His fingers ran across his shovel amulet, unable to remove his gaze from the wonder in the sky, unable to grasp how there was a sky to begin with.

The horizon was a soft blue, free of black cloud blankets and fiery frontiers, just as he knew it should be. But he was within the Final Earth now, which meant there could be no true horizon. Beyond the Lamp, far across the sky, *There must be more land.*

Perhaps it was an illusion of the stories he was told, but simply sitting in its presence, allowing the purple rays to graze his skin felt invigorating. Between the darkness, the water, and now the light, Evan felt born anew.

His thoughts were carefree and peaceful when he

heard a shuffling in the grass. He turned...and there stood a silver-haired girl, clad in white.

"Delya?"

She turned, her emerald eyes, unmistakable. She dove, disappearing into the water without a splatter.

Evan rose, running to the lake. His heart battered as he noticed the water receding, down the hole from which he came.

"Delya!" he called out.

There was no sparkling sign of the elphen princess, as the water twisted around, tumbling down, out of sight and into the blackness.

Evan jumped into the damp pit, his shoes smacking against the muddy ground. He ran toward the hole, and as he got closer, *No*, the opening became smaller, *No!* and smaller, until it was gone, vanished as though it was never there.

"Delya!"

Evan fell to his knees, his hands scraping at the wet dirt. Desperately, he shoved the pendant against the mud, asking for a miracle.

All the joy, all the peace that he felt as he rose from that water was gone with the sunken lake.

Maybe you were just seeing things.

"I was not seeing things," he said aloud.

Delya was gone before, but hope left the possibility that she was somewhere safe. Now, this couldn't be the case. *I saw her go into the water*, now fully flooded down the hole, *that hole which closed, probably*...he wouldn't let his thoughts travel much further.

Evan cried. For a moment she was here in this paradise, and in that moment she turned away. *Why did she turn away?* With her went his desire to see the beauty still here.

He looked up at the Lamp, as though expecting this indifferent source of light to save the girl. Legend said this light was the most powerful force in the universe. As he stared at it, it looked back unmoved.

Evan wanted to yell, curse the land around him, until a great growling shadow flew across the sky. Terror ceased his tears.

What was that?

Evan's eyes followed its loud, grumbling sound, its source shrouded behind the trees. The monstrous snarl became louder, louder, as though tearing the trees apart, until it emerged. Evan glanced wide-eyed at its scowling red face and ran.

He stumbled out of the mud pit, sprinting at high speeds he didn't know he was capable of.

Unlike the black land above, *Or is it below? No time for that!* Evan could fly without fear of crashing into a tree. He glanced back, the flying creature's fierce red eyes set on him. He believed to have open space around him until he slipped, stumbling off the side of a hill, grasping the earth with a clenched fist avoiding a fall.

Evan thought, perhaps, this was a slight hill, like most hills he'd encountered. But it was not; below him was a mighty drop and a surefire death. The open fields he imagined to be among continued on hundreds of feet below.

The gnarling red beast zipped overhead, raising its right wing to circle around. Digging his feet against the hillside, Evan pulled himself up. He turned, peering at the horizon toward the loud monster.

It moved rather stiffly for a bird, *Or is it a dragon?* As it looped around, Evan noticed a back-fin glistening in the lamplight. Its head, *Is that its head?* was translucent, while its mouth, the source of the horrible staccato snarls, seemed to have a set of projecting teeth that spun rapidly with the capacity to slice.

Something about the winged-monster seemed familiar. It flew far from Evan, before turning once more. It dove straight back in his direction, lowering itself closer to the ground. Evan examined the creature's thin legs. Its claws almost resembled wheels.

On the flattop above, the flying beast landed with a series of crashing jangles and a resounding sizzle.

Evan stood, waiting, before approaching the metal monster.

A plane...

The devilish face was merely painted. On the side of the fuselage, elegantly scribed in white were the words, '*High Hopes*'.

Beneath its top-sitting wings, the door to the cockpit unlatched and slid open.

∞

From out of the plane stepped two metal-pegged legs. These rusted red limbs led directly to a wide-round torso with pole-like arms below a ball-shaped head. Its eyes blinked like a shutter on a camera as its metal sheriff-styled mustache wriggled.

Before Evan could mentally label the peculiar robot as such, from behind him hopped another. This one was boxier, shinier, and stood about a half-foot taller than his four-foot friend. Instead of hair, its rectangular face featured a widespread smile that looked recently waxed.

Evan backpedalled as the two peculiar automations clinked forward. Though slightly anxious about who or what moved them, these little guys were far too funny looking to be taken seriously. But something about them looked frustratingly familiar.

Upon their left-side chest, Evan noticed a emblem. In swirling white fonts, the two featured similarly shaped '*P*'s, not so different from each others, *not so different from...*

Evan took off his hat. '*P*'...*for...*

He couldn't think of anything relevant that began with the letter.

The red metal men appeared to realize the shared symbol, pointing from their hearts to Evan's hat.

Evan & the Land of Letin

With curious, squinting eyes, the boy tried to talk to them.

"Who are you?" he spoke slowly, clearly, as if speaking to a computer.

With a jangling waddle, the androids rotated. Painted in white atop the back of the shorter automation was the name 'MICHAEL JACK', above the number '20'. On the taller, sleeker model: 'COLE', '35'.

This meant nothing to Evan.

Casually, the mustached machine wobbled its way toward him, its visible ball-joint clink-tinking all the way. Michael Jack slipped his fingers into Evan's warm hand. Something about the cold tin felt alive. With a gentle tug, the little robot led Evan toward the plane.

"Where are you taking me?"

Michael Jack beamed his blank, lens-like eyes up at Evan. He was almost certain he'd seen this face before. The word *'home'* floated through his head as another told him his hopes were too high.

Cole threw his heavy rod arm around Evan's shoulder. Evan noticed two twin yokes and a pair of empty pilot seats. The notion of flight at the hands of two mute androids seemed unsettling, but he'd survived flying unpiloted in an aircraft of wood and flowers.

Number 35 stepped ahead, standing between the seats, and directed Evan toward the copilot command. He sat, as Michael Jack slid the door shut, and Cole stepped forward, pulling a small black knob and starting the engine.

Evan examined the dozen plus circular barometers he couldn't comprehend. He did notice, much to his pleasure, the fuel gauges were fixed on 'F'.

Oddly, for a brief moment, Evan felt like he'd been here before.

Nonsense. Of course not. *When was the last time you hung out with little tin-men?*

Michael Jack tested the yokes, sending them both

back and forth, as Evan clicked on his seatbelt. He felt like they were taking him home, *or somewhere closer to it…at least somewhere with answers.*

Then it was all gone.

From behind Evan, a pair of hands pulled a black covering over his face. Before the darkness, Evan noticed green fingers.

∞

Evan attempted to squirm, but it was useless. He reached for his seatbelt but his captor's clammy hands had already miraculously tied-up his arms, and quickly, also his feet, in what felt like a web of sorts.

He didn't bother screaming or speaking, for no words came from the other side of the black. His thoughts mostly berated him for parading into a plane with a pair of unknown drones. The loudest thought, however, one that he orchestrated from deep within, told the others it would all be fine. He believed this.

The plane wobbled and straightened, wobbled and straightened. Evan lost track of bumps in the flight after twenty-eight. He tried to keep his mind occupied instead of throwing forth worst-case scenarios.

We're probably going to crash into a mountain.

Or get tortured by Mr. Green Hands.

Evan ignored them, trying to focus on that purple light. At the center of the black sky in his mind, it was still there, bright as before. He couldn't verbalize why, nor was he sure he wanted to, but he felt unshakable in its presence, certain that all would be well.

Evan felt the plane descending, and swiftly, after a thump and a series of bumps against the ground, they were there. Wherever *"there"* was.

The engine shut down and Evan heard the door slide open. A cool wind caressed his bare arms.

"You will walk," the green hands spoke, his voice as slimy as his touch.

The tight netting around his feet released. The kidnapper clenched Evan's arm, raising and leading the way off the plane. He stepped upon what felt to be lush grass as the rigid grip pulled him forward.

As they moved, a swarm of voices grew nearer. Some whispers, some awes, but mostly roars; vicious ones that Evan couldn't decide whether they were victorious or vanquished. He stumbled as the surface upon which he stepped shifted. His PF's scratched and shuffled against what felt to be dirt.

In an instant, the voices fell quiet. Evan heard solo steps ahead slowly striding toward him.

"Their savior has arrived, General."

"Rather small, no?" a voice pestered from the crowd.

Cackles spread, each one a different note of nefarious.

"Silence!" the general's voice commanded.

The only thing more impressive than his fierce sound was how quickly the crowd complied.

"Have you no idea what this means?...There will be no more games," he spoke slowly. "There will be no more peacetime!"

Silence cut through the crowd.

"This land built on the promise of peace can no longer be that. Do you not remember what they did to the land above? Make no mistake, they will try to do it again. But we will not, we cannot let them!

"There is no where left to escape to. A war is coming!"

The crowd cried with rage as though they were already clad in armor.

"There doesn't need to be a war," a gruff voice sliced through the screams, returning them to silence.

The speaker's bulky steps stamped forward. Evan could practically hear their eyes piercing him.

"You said it yourself, this place isn't made for a war.

Look around! Does anyone see a city of elphs behind him? Those prophecies couldn't tell who will win your games, let alone who will lead the elphs to everlasting life."

A spatter of laughs trickled in the crowd.

"I'll believe a prophecy when all Eight appear before my very eyes and utter the truth. 'Til then, he is treated like the ones that've come before him...ones we all loved and respected."

Evan heard their curious whispers, their dispersed 'huh's and 'who's. He too was confused. *What?*

"Not one of you knows who this is?" the gruff voice laughed, bordering on a bark. "I swear sometimes you're a buncha mindless grunkshinns."

The black was pulled from Evan's face. He winced in the light.

The gruff voice called out. "Evan of Grace!"

The crowd gasped as the boy mirrored their surprised green faces.

Evan didn't need a bestiary to determine these creatures. Their wide, black-sclera and red-iris eyes, their ears resembling three-pointed leaves. Their skin was blanketed in blemishes, and their teeth, if they were so fortunate to still have them, where sharpened and poking from their mouths. *Goblyns.*

Only their garb seemed curious. Some wore faded denim jeans, others old leather jackets. There were even a few in full suits, one complete with a polka-dot bow tie. Strangest however, were those in caps similar to Evan's, wearing high-single-striped socks, carrying long wooden clubs.

Evan peered around him. He was standing on a brown dirt diamond, anchored by four white squares. *Baseball.* Evan was baffled.

"Listen champ, I know it's a lot to take in."

Evan peered at the grizzly speaker, his defender. From him, this was the ultimate understatement. The

Evan & the Land of Letin

lone non-goblyn made his green companions look amiable.

His broad, beastly shoulders towered above the rest. His skin was unseeable beneath his black fur. His face, so unfortunate, was splotched with spurts of white fur and deep-slicing scars. Evan thought he looked like a dog, complete with claws and a black nose, but partially human as well. He possessed brown eyes and a sincere smile that seemed to know Evan.

"Let's take you to your room," the mongrel said.

"My room?"

"You've got more right to it than any of us."

He stepped toward the crowd, the goblyns parting without hesitation. Evan followed.

"I'm sorry," he said, stepping forward. "But what is your name?"

"It hurts me to hear you apologize," the dog said. "I am Rokklius, and it's me who should be saying sorry."

"I don't understand, you just saved my life."

"From them?" turning back to the goblyns, all of whom now followed the dog and the boy. "They wouldn't hurt a soul. I made a promise to protect you and I failed. I'm lucky to have this opportunity again. This time, failure isn't an option."

"I'm sorry," Evan said. "I'm just very confused."

"Please!" Rokklius barked. "No more apologies...I fully expect you to be confused. But there are ways to fix that. It'll all make sense shortly."

"You failed to mention how painful these remedies are," a voice said. Evan recognized the commanding voice from before.

The goblyn stepped in stride next to Evan, closer than he preferred.

"I am Lieutenant General Vashard," his red eyes seemed to sneer as they looked down at the boy. "We will begin training tomorrow."

"Evan's not gonna play a part in this war," Rokklius

snapped.

"No part in this war?" Vashard snickered. "Aside from starting it, you mean?"

Rokklius snarled but did not speak.

Evan tried not to stare at the goblyn but each of his features deserved a second glance. Most noticeable was his Lamp-colored Mohawk with its braided tail trailing down his back. His white t-shirt had torn sleeves, while his ripped arms were covered in brands and tattoos that almost seemed animated. *That ink definitely just moved.* His three-point ears were pierced at every angle, and beneath his left-eye, a final tattoo—the number '8' tilted on its side—an infinite lemniscate.

"Like I was saying, tomorrow we begin training. If you're anything like those who've come before you, I expect great things," he looked Evan dead in his black eyes, his red rings blazing with veracity. "You owe us."

The general stepped ahead, a full infantry trailing behind. Each foot soldier fouler than the last, sending vicious growls followed by maniacal laughs Evan's way.

"Pay them no mind," said Rokklius. "Vashard is a great warrior, but he's got a lot to learn himself. There's no doubt he means well, but his methods are...uncertain. Here we are," Rokklius pointed ahead. "New Asylia."

Unlike the old, this Asylia was no a mountain, but a forest. And unlike the other forest, this one was alive. The goblyns seemed to disappear as they entered, blending in with the greenery. Atop the trees, sphere shaped compartments that looked to have grown naturally from the bark itself. Bridges made of branches linked the treetops to each other, endless links, like a sprawling web. *Like Helvendah.*

But also, nothing like Helvendah. Everything here was grown from the ground. There was so much green, but just as much red, blue, and every color that flowers and fruits could produce. Noticeably, Evan recognized an absence of white. *No blinding, mind-wiping white.* After life in Helvendah, this was refreshing.

Evan's ears tingled at the profusion of sound; the belly-quaking laughs from a group guzzling from theirs mugs, titters and whispers of children running on the planks above, birds swooping, chirping, joining in on the goblyn revelry. Evan's nose flared, trying to taste the scents; meats sizzled and smoked on a barbeque rack while incense floated from the open portholes in the trees above. His dark eyes roamed, latching on to a particularly peculiar tree house.

This one stood-out, for unlike the others, uniformly round, was square. Rokklius stepped on the spiral stairway leading up to this cube-on-a-stick.

"This one is yours. My cabin is just next door."

Evan followed, and froze as they reached the door. He tried to muster a comprehendible thought as his chest rose and fell rapidly. He could see his own reflection in the lustrous red paint.

He looked to Rokklius, and the dog gently nodded.

"I'll be here waiting, just outside the door when you're ready."

Without tapping on the brass knocker, Evan opened the red door.

∞

With a clink, the door sealed behind him. His heart strummed, determined to pop from his chest. He knew this room.

On the right wall, shelves stacked to the ceiling with what appeared to be thin sheets of cardboard of every color. His mind quickly reminded him what was slipped in each of those thin cases. *Music.*

To his left, another fully shelved wall. This one crammed with books. Evan walked nearer, running his hands across the spines of every color and condition. He leaned in, smelling their paper, their tangs of vanilla and musk, their supply of endless knowledge. Evan looked up.

On the top shelf, only leather-spined books. Evan looked away. He wasn't ready.

But he had no choice. On the far wall where his eyes fell were dozens of pictures. Each one was individually framed with mismatched fallen sticks, connected forming a patchwork masterpiece of memories.

Evan stepped forward, biting his lip, trying to force back the tears that were already slipping over his eyelids.

There were pictures of people he'd never known, but his eyes scanned to those he did. And as Evan did so, their names, their voices, their laughs, and their lives all returned, playing out in his head.

There was all eight of his aunts and uncles…*Aunt Rita, Uncle Liam, and, uh,* he cried with a bit of laughter, *Uncle Alec.*

Evan's cry shifted back to bleak.

His brother, *Caden,* a smooth smirk on his face. Evan knew, right after that picture was taken, Caden was off to read or rant about Rivendell. He missed those conversations he didn't even know he cared about.

His sister, *Clementyne,* a beaming smile ready to campaign. *Oh,* how he missed her. If there was anyone he wished he could talk to right then, it was her. It was Clementyne who would remind him that he had the strength to get through any situation.

There was his dad. Evan fell to the floor, unable to suppress the agonized sound. He missed him so much. Evan wished he had said thank you for all his father had done. He wished he'd said sorry for not saying thank you enough and not saying…*I love you.* He wished he told him he loved him a million more times, for he did, far more than he ever said.

And his mom, *Grace.* Evan held his forehead, wishing she were there to bless it. He pictured how she might feel now, at this moment, and impossibly, Evan knew she was in even more pain than he was. He clenched his fists, vowing, promising himself he'd find a way to see her again.

Evan peered up at the pictures once more.

Grammpa and Grams.

Their fiery death flickered in his mind.

This time, the image did not fade.

He pulled the red cap over his brows and wept until his eyes ran dry.

∞

At his grandmother's desk, the dented tin-heart and his diamond-cut one laid side-by-side, he examined the picture of a fragile, beautiful boy. *Evan Transce.*

He compared his dim reflection in the glass to the one beyond it. Sure, his hair was longer now, and quite a bit of it had grown on his face, but they more or less looked the same. He stared at the brown eyes that bordered on becoming black beneath his thick eyebrows. He'd completely forgotten that dash of purple atop his left eye.

He ran his fingers over the red tear tracks rolling down his cheek. That boy beneath the glass, smile spread, bare teeth beaming, looked incapable of crying.

Despite traveling through a dead forest, rising to a heavenly city of elphs where he was labeled a savior, he still felt like Evan. He'd ran from the label, he had thought he found some form of love and he quickly lost it. He'd climbed a mountain with the weight of the world and then traveled through darkness said to be Death. But he was still here. *Still Evan.*

His memories were mostly back, the people, some places from his past. He had hoped these recollections would provide him with answers with who he was. He was still so far from sure. He was still Evan.

There was a soft tapping at the door.

"Come in," he called, wiping away tear residue. He looked at himself. It was impossible to hide.

Rokklius slowly strolled in, his long claws clanking against the wood planks.

"May I sit?"

Evan nodded. The big dog lowered its hind legs on the wicker chair in the room's corner.

"How are you feelin'?" Rokklius asked.

"Drained...sad...confused."

"Understandably so. Let me do my best to help you sort this out."

Rokklius stood, scanning the wall for the right picture and plucking it off the wall.

He lowered a picture of Liam and Rita with their rescued dog standing sternly between their legs.

"Who are they?" he asked.

"My grandparents. Rita and Liam Powers, they—"

"And how 'bout this guy?" pointing his long black nail at the dog.

"Oh, that's Rocky. My grandparents rescued him. His previous owners used him as a..." half-way through speaking, Evan had the wildest idea. *No...no.*

"Used him as what?"

Evan looked up at Rokklius, and down at the picture of the dog. *Same colored coat, same long nails. No, no, no, stop it. Never.*

"Ah, nothing. He was a great dog."

Rokklius smiled, flashing his sharp canines. "Thank you."

Evan's right eyebrow raised as he slowly shook his head in denial.

Rokklius nodded and laughed, his sound somewhere between a pant and wheeze.

"Rocky was a more believable pet name than Rokklius."

Evan joined the laugh, still mostly in denial. "How? I don't understand."

"I'll explain what I know," Rocky said, lowering back in the chair. "Long ago, a relative way back on your grandma's side, whose picture is up there on that wall, was a great adventurer and world-famous scientist. After decades of searching and experimenting, he discovered a path from your earth to ours. Instead of sharing this find with the rest of the world, he feared the worst, and simply passed on his secret to his family, generation to generation.

"For a while, the family travels consisted mostly of fun, you know, camping, hiking, that sorta thing. It was their vacation. There was never any trouble. Over time, your family befriended the goblyn people, your grandparents especially. They brought artifacts from your world here, and with the help of our different magic and sciences, we reimagined and reinvented many of these things.

"Not long after the war broke out, the Great Fire spread across the land and sea. Hundreds of people across our planet were dying everyday. Your grandparents, the greatest people I've ever known, refused to just sit around and let this happen.

"Your grandpa offered forth his plane and expertise as a means of defense and to hopefully save some lives. With the help of Dystyne, who's gonna be so excited to meet you, they brought together Liam's ideas, most important of which was that plane.

"With the help of the necrobots, those little metal men you met, they'd fly above the fire, saving any and every life they could. Those fools in Helvendah thought the plane was a dragon. But as you know," he turned away from Evan, "one day, the fire finally caught them."

"You mean Kaven caught them."

"You know more than I expected," he sighed, his stare averting Evan's eyes. "The fire's beyond his control."

"I don't believe it." the boy said. "He's got everyone

thinking he's got no power, from his kingdom to the fire, and that's why he has it all."

Rocky raised a brow. "You're very familiar with him?"

Evan paused, picturing Kaven's hand lifting him from the rubble...the light at the end of his dark journey.

"On the surface...he was good to me. He saved me from Oblazio." He gathered his thoughts, and announced with disgust, "I slept in the house of my grandparents' killer."

"Your grandparents live on. Through you, Evan. It's clear that you've got their unbeatable spirit. And not only that, but they live on through me, and all of the goblyns out there. These people adored your grandparents."

Evan sat stern, silent, pondering.

"They live on through your family. Across many stars, they're still there...through that door, your grandparents used to travel to and from our land and yours."

"But one must be let through," Evan continued. "There must be someone there to invite you on the other side."

"That's right. Very impressive."

"Kaven attempted to inform me. It all seems like nonsense," Evan wasn't satisfied. "How did they get back home? When the fire got them."

"That's been the question on the minds of a lotta folks since their death. It remains the ultimate mystery. Your grandpa was a great inventor himself, many wonder if he hadn't created another pathway between the worlds."

"How did you get back here?" Evan asked.

"I hopped on Cyphur as he was let through."

"Cyphur?"

"Yes. That silver cat your sister brought home? That you accurately called *monster*? We share the same gift. They like to call us 'Therinelphs' or 'Masters of our Bodies.' We can take almost any form, as long as we've seen the intended body."

At this point, nothing could surprise Evan. But this was unsettling. *Cyphur was in my home. And that makes him...*

Cyphur was the monstrous winged-feline that he saw upon arrival to the Heartland and attacked him upon his departure from Helvendah.

"The kings and queens sent all of us with the skill across the worlds, searching for the Lamp, then finally shifting our focus to the one written about in the Divine Tomes. When I learned about Kaven's secrets, I could no longer respect his orders or those from any of his allies. I worked with the goblyns, your grandparents, and vowed to protect you."

"I...thank you."

"Now I vow to figure out how to get you home. For now, your grandparents' second home is the next best thing."

Evan nodded in agreement.

Rokklius rose, looking out the window.

"The night fog is coming. You could probably use some rest. Maybe you'd like to pop on a record to ease yourself to sleep."

Rocky winked at Evan. The faithful dog knew him well.

"I'll be right outside this door, if needed. Good night, champ."

Rokklius clicked his way over to and out of the red door. Evan felt he could rest easy with Rocky on watch.

The dog's suggestion was heavenly. Evan turned to the record-lined wall. There were hundreds, maybe thousands of titles, none that struck a chord. He was far too tired to think on this. Full of hope, he pulled at random.

The Planets, Opus 32 – Gustav Holst...this should work. He chose the side that started with "Jupiter, the Bringer of Jollity" which seemed an obvious choice over the opposite side starting with "Mars, Bringer of War."

Slipping the vinyl from its cover, he clicked the power switch, hearing the hum of unseen speakers. *I'm not sure I remember how to do this.* He lowered the black circle, aligning the center hole with the metal spindle. He let it go, wobbling into place. It seemed secure. But still no music.

He grabbed the needle, gently lifting and dropping it on the record's black outskirts. The disc began to rotate, *Searching for its groove.* The sound of dazzling strings soared through the air. Evan closed his eyes, smiling. He'd forgotten the unspeakable power of music and couldn't wait to rediscover it.

He recalled the last time he'd seen a record spin and heard its endless miracles. Looking over at that scratched tin heart, he remembered that special girl who made it and shared its lovely name. With closed eyes, he shook his head, realizing how blind he was to her wonder.

He removed his damp grey t-shirt, now several shades darker, and threw it on the chair. Grabbing the shovel dangling over his heart, he pulled the necklace over his head.

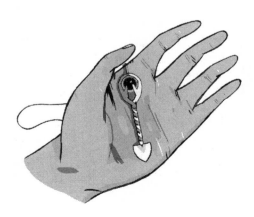

How strange, Evan thought. Its black coated exterior must have chipped away. The interlocking arms were now a lustering silver and gold, and its marble, *fascinating,* was now various shades of purple. The swirling streaks almost made the small ball look fluid.

He clicked the light switch off, lowering himself to the bed with the pendant still in hand. Placing it on the pillow-side nightstand, he peered out the window.

A dark grey mist filled the outdoor air, and shining vibrant at the sky's center was the Lamp. Its light cast a gentle lavender glow over the room that made Evan feel like he was already home.

His eyelids became heavier. He fought back, suddenly resistant to sleep, still enjoying the symphony shimmering in his ears, still yearning to stare at the royal globe above. But of course, it was impossible. The boy was beyond exhausted.

His lashes flickered and sealed, and with final whispering thought of the day, he noticed how remarkably similar the glow on his necklace's orb was to the Lamp ablaze in air.

In his own world of black, the purple light was both in the sky and in his mind. He sunk deeper into darkness, and there, for but a fleeting moment, he saw with clarity a purple heart afire in every human, elph, and goblyn. There, in the infinite nothing, was infinite light.

✺

"That's it? It's not over, is it?"

"Of course it's not, love. Just as all water is one water, and all fire is one fire, all stories are one story. This tale is far from finished, but that's enough for now."

"Pleaseee. Just one more chapter."

"I think this is the best place to—"

"Please."

...

"If you're looking for a happy—"

"Please. Just one more chapter?"

...

"Fine, love. Just one more chapter."

∞

Clouds brushed across his misty mind's eye. Evan tried to clear his eyes only to find no fingers to wipe with, no hands or arms to raise and no bodily source of his sight. His existence was vision alone, absent of any palpable connection to a brain. He was there, yet he wasn't. *Where am I?*

He simultaneously gazed at the space from below and above, focusing his vision on white clouds accompanied by more clouds, shrouding even more clouds.

Deep in his mind, wherever it was, he began to comprehend the floating images before him.

At the center of the encircling valley of clouds, a beautiful and vibrant man rose. His chilling blue eyes scanned the surroundings. Around him, a vast crowd sitting on white mist. The man opened his mouth to speak.

"My brothers and sisters of Helvendah. On this Day of Moons, a great tragedy has occurred.

"The one the Divine Tomes told would lead us to the Lamp left us in the night, and with him, he took one of our own.

"Princess Delya of Cyphur worked as our kingdom's eyes on a very important mission. She held close contact with the boy, agreeing to lure him to the ground in hopes of leading to a discovery. Out in the blackness, however, the beast living within that scuman couldn't be suppressed around her beauty. He defiled the princess, and left her for dead.

"My people, I promise you, her death will not be in vain. She was able to relay the critical information on to us before she went.

"The prophecy was right. That boy did lead us to the

Evan & the Land of Letin

Lamp…but at a great price."

He raised his hands, conducting the clouds toward him. With a few swift motions, a plain, pawn-like pillar of clouds sculpted away to reveal a portrayal of the beautiful princess. *Delya.*

"We will honor this great hero. Her memory will burn bright in our hearts as we take what's ours. As we take the Lamp!"

Kaven's gorgeous face shifted to a vicious one, crying out as he spoke. He raised both his arms, and as one, his people rose to their feet.

With the king's arms spread wide, Evan noticed a glistening gem encrusted amid his chest. The tip of the ruby crest consisted of two-half circles curving toward the bottom meeting at a point. *A heart.*

"Never again will the elphs of Helvendah fall. Never again will we fear death! Together, now we rise!"

In an instant the black sky above flashed red before quickly shifting to a white blaze.

Evan felt his body quivering and shaking, rocking back and forth though he wasn't within it.

Opening his eyes, the entire room was trembling. Evan hopped from his bed as he nearly fell to the floor. The books crashed down, the silent record player fell with a crack.

Evan shielded his ears, the blaring sound of bombing below, as though there was a battle beneath his feet. He heard squeals, cries coming through the window.

Sliding from the desk, the hearts fell to the floor. Gliding from the nightstand, his shovel joined the debris.

Evan stumbled his way toward the window. Staring at the Lamp, the sound grew louder, louder, as if it were impossible to get closer when it stopped.

A moment of silence.
A bird caws.
Goblyns shriek.

Rising above the green and grey horizon, a glistening city of white. *Helvendah.*

It slowly rose to the sky, careful to show every onlooker its incomparable might. It moved closer to the Lamp, and closer, until it positioned itself in air, blocking the light from Evan's view.

With an audible sizzle, the kingdom's bottom cloud began to extend, slowly but fully encompassing the purple glow with its white.

Evan wondered how long before the black clouds spread across the sky too, and the fire came raining down.

He fell to the surface, back to the wall, clenching his head.

On the now still floor, amid the broken-spine first editions and the snapped vinyl, one item still quivered. Evan peered over, shielding his eyes.

From his necklace, the purple marble began to grow, in shine and size, until it was bigger than Evan. He peered through the cracks in his fingers at the light. It seemed to have somewhat solidified, forming a lavender, bubble-like film. Steadily, it began to melt away.

Standing in the center of the room, wiping the remaining film off his grey bespoke suit, was a man. He bore a rich grey beard that shielded the bottom half of his face and wide tortoise-shell glasses that hid the top portion. Where his tie should be, a peculiar pendant hung that almost resembled a wooden spider.

Evan rose, not sure whether to prepare to fight or jump out the window.

"Who are you?" Evan asked.

"You'd think by now you would've learned that you're never really going to get the answer you're looking for with that question."

Evan wasn't up for meandering. "What is your name!?" he demanded.

With a chuckle, I told him. "Call me Loring."

Acknowledgments

There is no Evan, there is no Letin, without any of you. **Thank you**.

Ryan Evans. I sit here putting the final touches on this book and I think back to when I started it. Not only have you been here since the beginning, you *were* the beginning.

Sequoia Matthews. From the very first day I met you, you've inspired me to be my best me. You give me the will to wake each morning and the power to write each night.

Mom. Most mothers would have booted their boy a while back when he said he was dropping out of school to write about elphs and goblyns. You did not. You've stayed with and supported me, truly being the greatest mom this world has ever seen.

Dad. Your endless love is how I aim to love. Thank you. Your one-of-a-kind vision of the universe reminds me to always find a fresh perspective.

I miss you and love you more than I'm capable of expressing.

Judith Kristen West. Your strength and positivity lifts all those blessed enough to cross your path. I thank the Universe daily for letting me come into your life.

You were the editor Evan needed, and the spiritual champion I'm not sure I'm worthy of. You've made this book the beautiful thing it is. I could thank you ten times a day until the world goes black and I'd still never fully express my gratitude to you.

Tallulah Fontaine. Few can claim their favorite illustrator did the pictures for their first book. But somehow, inexplicably, I'm among that lucky few.

I set out hoping to have someone *like* you to the pictures...ya know, a sorta second-rate Tallulah that I'd probably just ask to emulate your style. Instead, I got the real, unbelievably gifted thing. You understood Evan from the go, and brought life to him and Letin in a way that makes me wanna cry while laughing giddily…like a true psycho. Thank you for making art so good it turns me into a true psycho. Thank you.

Grams. **Pop-Pop**. The few years I was able to spend at 828 were some of the most beautiful and magical years of my life. One day I'll build a home and family from joy and love the way you did and then, and only then, can I say I've done your legacy justice.

Chris. The "jam sessions" that gave life to Letin started as the elaborate games of action figures on rivaling space stations set on shelves above an old TV and a red-brick mantle above the fireplace…

There are no memories in my head and heart that are more important than our games.

Tori. I never sit down and set out to write a 4-part fantasy epic without you *showing* me it was possible. Your work ethic, your silent hunger, stirs a fire in my blood that makes me so proud to call myself your brother. Your love and guidance is everything to me. Your love and guidance has made me.

Nathan. Your intelligence and perspective on fantasy novels, fantasy football, and fantasy (turned to reality) relationships makes me a better human. I'm blessed to be able to call you my brother.

Tim Parisi. Your guidance keeps me rooted. Your food keeps the elphs of Helvendah brilliantly-fed.

Alie Smith.

Cheryl & Kevin Kramer.

David Grzybowski.

David Park.

Rosali Falcone. Evan's little green guide. I know there's probably 30 too many occurrences of "the boy" for your liking. But otherwise, know with certainty, your influence and input on this book was *so* crucial. You're forever VIP in the Land of Letin.

Aunt Mary Lou. **Uncle Mike**. **Aunt Donna**. **Aunt Ginny**. **Uncle Bo**. **Uncle Chris**. **Aunt Barbara**. **Aunt Rosemary**. **Uncle Bob**. **Uncle Pete**. **Aunt Lee Ann**. I'm the luckiest person in the world to be a part of this family. I love and appreciate you more than these pages allow.

Lyndsi & John.
Jamie & Brandy.

My Caracciolo's. I get absolutely nowhere on this green earth or that purple-tinted one several galaxies over without this crazy blood flowing through my veins. I love and thank you.

My Many Mothers & Children at St. Cecilia's Little Angels.

Bobby & the Browns.

John & the McGoverns.

Andrew & the Schmotzers.

Mr. & Mrs. Evans.

The Strauss's.

Jesus. **Yeezus**. **Yoda**. **Buddha**.

The Purple God. **The Electric Lady**.

The Holy CHVRCH of Mayberry, Doherty, & Cook.

MJ. **MJ**.

Van. **Paul**. **Art**. **Bruce**.

Johnny & the Moondogs.

Alyssa Joy.

Romalyn Cease.

Mrs. Shumaker. There's no Letin without that Pig Packet. There's no Letin without that assignment on the 2002 Winter Olympics. You were the first person to tell me I was a "writer." THANK YOU.

Mrs. Diveney. Multiple Intelligence Time was the most important time I ever spent in school. Ever. You let a fourth grader put on a play with all of his classmates, and for that, I was capable of writing this book.

Mrs. Hrivnack. You *always* believed…I don't sit down to write a book without those words circulating my head. *"It's what you do, when you don't have to do it…"*

Mrs. Forrest. Your courage to let kids dream (and actually do!) made SPC the most influential place for me on this Earth.

Mrs. Amicone. I didn't get the chance to use "littler" in this one. Maybe next time.

Sister Mary.

John Decker. **Matt Parisi**. **Michael Wicke**. **Shane Camardo**. You were my champions before I had anything to champion. I don't get to have the best illustrator in the world on this book without you backing me.

The Cast & Crew of '04's "The Wizard of Oz".

The Cast & Crew of '08's "Dinner at the MacGuffins".

Ms. & Mrs. O'Reilly. You both told me I should write. I owe you both everything for that advice.

19 Adele. **22 Taylor**.

SPC Class of '05. **West Class of '09**.

The Styles Brothers.

The Pyle Sisters.

Hardcore FF.

George & A Galaxy Far, Far Away. **Lyman & Dorothy**. **Jo & Harry**. **Junot & Oscar**. **Patrick & Kvothe**. **Mr. Nolan & Mr. Wayne**. **F. Scott & James Gats**.

JRR & CS.

Lindsey Ferguson.

The Folks At B&N Cherry Hill.

JOIN THE GOBLYN REVOLUTION!

Share a picture of you with your copy of "Evan & the Land of Letin" using #AHeartAfire for a chance to win a free copy of every book Jared T.L.C. publishes…until…forever…

@GOBLYNSCRATCH + WWW.JAREDTLC.COM

ABOUT THE AUTHOR

Jared lives in a little attic with slanted ceilings in the South of New Jersey with his Queen Koi and their two beautiful, canine sons, Theodore & Goomba. His actual last name is not T.L.C., but rather, Caracciolo (*Cah-Rah-Chee-Oh-La* ‾ _(ツ)_/ ‾?), and since he can barely pronounce that, he's opted out of using it so you don't have to struggle through it either. *A Heart Afire* is the first of the 100 or so books that Jared plans to write in this lifetime. He's currently working on several new projects that he can't wait to share with you <3

On Deck...

SAMMI SPECKTOR &
THE HORROR FIELD

Then Continue Evan's Journey With...

EVAN & THE LAND OF LETIN

A People In Two

Made in the USA
Middletown, DE
06 June 2016